A
ROUGH
WAY
TO GO

A ROUGH WAY TO GO

SAM GARONZIK

GRAND
CENTRAL

New York   Boston

Copyright © 2024 by Samuel Garonzik

Cover design by Sarah Congdon
Cover images from Stocksy
Cover copyright © 2024 by Hachette Book Group, Inc.

Grand Central Publishing
Hachette Book Group
1290 Avenue of the Americas, New York, NY 10104
grandcentralpublishing.com
twitter.com/grandcentralpub

First edition: May 2024

Grand Central Publishing is a division of Hachette Book Group, Inc. The Grand Central Publishing name and logo is a trademark of Hachette Book Group, Inc.

The publisher is not responsible for websites (or their content) that are not owned by the publisher.

The Hachette Speakers Bureau provides a wide range of authors for speaking events. To find out more, go to hachettespeakersbureau.com or email HachetteSpeakers@hbgusa.com.

Grand Central Publishing books may be purchased in bulk for business, educational, or promotional use. For information, please contact your local bookseller or the Hachette Book Group Special Markets Department at special.markets@hbgusa.com.

Print interior design by Taylor Navis

Library of Congress Cataloging-in-Publication Data
Names: Garonzik, Sam, author.
Title: A rough way to go / Sam Garonzik.
Description: First edition. | New York : Grand Central Publishing, 2024.
Identifiers: LCCN 2023041040 | ISBN 9781538743362 (hardcover) | ISBN 9781538743386 (ebook)
Subjects: LCGFT: Detective and mystery fiction. | Novels.
Classification: LCC PS3607.A7657 R68 2024 | DDC 813/.6--dc23/eng/20230914
LC record available at https://lccn.loc.gov/2023041040

ISBNs: 9781538743362 (hardcover), 9781538743386 (ebook)

Printed in the United States of America

LSC-C

Printing 1, 2024

For my family

"A man who doesn't spend time with his family can never be a real man."

—Mario Puzo, *The Godfather*

A
ROUGH
WAY
TO GO

1

I DON'T TALK about this much and I wouldn't want it to get around, but a few years ago I pretended to have jury duty so I could avoid my wife and child. We were still living in the city back then and Luke was only a few months old. Lauren was on the last of her maternity leave and I didn't have a job. I was sitting around the house a lot, and I didn't feel very useful. There were small, menial tasks I could perform, and I did them while my wife gave me instructions. She gave me a lot of instructions.

But then I opened the mail one afternoon and found a jury summons. I could hardly believe what I held in my hands, but there it was—a chance to get out of the house! I had to give Lauren the news. I wasn't trying to run out on her or anything—admittedly, the timing wasn't great—but in a few short weeks, I would need to get down to that courthouse. The letter had plainly said "Final notice." If I skipped it again, that would be breaking the law of this county.

"I'm sorry," I added.

She didn't say anything. But there was nothing she could do about it.

The next weeks seemed to move a lot faster—I couldn't focus on much else—so when the morning arrived, I was ready.

I lit out from the apartment, not long after sunrise. Even just getting on the subway, I felt an energy that was missing in my living room, that spark you can feel when you have an actual destination and a legitimate reason to go there. The train picked up speed, and we screamed down the tracks.

I hopped off at city hall and waited in line outside the courthouse with everyone else, and when they let us in, we all walked inside and sat down in a big room. They explained the basics in a no-nonsense delivery: we might get called we might not, *but this was our civic duty to perform,* no cell phones, and take all the bathroom breaks you want. Sounded good, so far. The guy giving the instructions was this older Black man with gray hair and a mustache. He was a funny guy. He said he needed a strong cup of coffee—he'd been up most of the night, driving back from Dewey Beach, where he'd spent his weekend working on a little house that he owned. That sounded pretty good, too. Having your own place that you could work on yourself—I wondered if he was building or fixing it up?—and it was down by the beach. He probably couldn't surf at his age, but he could fish. He could walk on the sand or swim in the sea. And the man was a civil servant. No business cycles in jury service, I guess, no boom and bust. Who knew how long it had taken him to do this, and sure, he still had to schlep into work Monday morning, but driving back from his own place at the beach where he could put in the hours whenever it suited him? That didn't sound bad at all.

At some point, my name got called and I went down to one of the courtrooms. The guard brought us in and then the judge explained the drill. We might get selected for jury duty, but before we could start into that business, he warned us that the trial would take about a month, and he needed to know if any of us had a good excuse to get out of this? A lot of hands started to go up. People looked at their calendars. I didn't, of course. But all around me people were checking their phones and raising their hands.

"My daughter's wedding."

"A big client meeting in London."

"They're coming in from the West Coast and it's such a big deal."

"*My mother's very sick. And we've always been close. She's everything to me.*"

"*The play opens in New Orleans. I've dreamed about it all my life.*"

But not me. I didn't say anything. My pad was clean.

Some folks just explained that they couldn't bear judging another human soul, these prisoners of conscience. The judge looked them over for a little bit, but in the end, he still crossed their names off his sheet. He was not an unreasonable man. After a while he read out a list of candidates, and when he called my name, I was very pleased.

Then just when I thought it couldn't get any better, they gave us a lunch break. I went to one of the places in Chinatown with the pigs and the ducks hanging in the windows. I ordered fried pork dumplings and dipped them in soy sauce with my chopsticks, downing a Diet Coke while I ate them, and they were huge, juicy, and crisp. It was after 2:00 p.m. by the time we settled back in our seats. The judge started to explain stuff about the case, just some basics. We'd be trying a murder—a man had been killed. My day kept getting better and better! I couldn't wait to hear more of the facts, then figure out if he'd done it or not, and convince the rest of the jury what I had discovered.

Later, when we all stood around in the hall outside the courtroom, I tried to chat with my fellow citizens, gripping and grinning. I couldn't remember the last time I'd done this, and it felt great to be around other people. In an instant, the afternoon was over. I took my sweet time getting home, practically skipping back to the apartment, but not forgetting, of course, to slump in through the door and collapse on the couch, exhausted and sore.

The next day got off to a casual start—we didn't even show up to the courtroom until 2:00 p.m. The judge asked us all what we did for a living. We had a teacher, a waiter, a security guard, and a few finance guys, but they didn't work at my old firm, and I didn't recognize any of them, so that wouldn't be a problem. There was a nurse with a great smile and green eyes who seemed funny and interesting. Then they came around to me.

"I'm unemployed," I said, and studied my belt buckle. When I picked my head up, the nurse's smile had vanished, along with everyone else's, and those greens eyes were now sad and concerned.

"But we just had a baby," I said, rebounding. "So, I'm pretty busy right now!"

The smile came back. It was good cheer all around, mostly.

And I'm a reasonable guy. No prior convictions. Very open-minded. This thing could go either way—just show me the evidence and I'll make a decision—and forty bucks a day works for me, too. I kept my answers short but polite and tried my winning, closemouthed smile. The lawyers nodded and scribbled their notes.

On the third day we started at 9:00 a.m. sharp, and it felt like things were getting more serious, but I didn't care. I would soon serve on a murder trial. The other people in the jury box seemed like a decent group, and I looked forward to working with them as part of a team. Then the judge explained that the following jurors had been selected. My chest swelled with pride.

"Oscar Martinez. Sharon Alboretti. And Thomas Not-you-either. Please stay. The rest of you are free to leave. Thank you for your jury service."

Wait a minute, I thought. What the hell is going on? That's *it*? You're *dismissing* me? And you're only taking *those* three jerkoffs? The rest of us can just *leave*? But when would I ever see these characters again? Miss Green Eyes and her nice smile. Mr. Creepy Defense Attorney and his stupid suits. Mr. Murderer sitting *right there* in front of us! What about me? Now, I just go and get lost? I have the rest of the day open! I'm supposed to just go back to my apartment and sit around with my wife and newborn son?

I went home to Lauren that night and confessed everything.

I was really very sorry. Much to my shame, I had been selected for jury duty—a murder case—and it could last a few months. To not show up would be unthinkable, a gross violation.

Lauren burst into tears. She was good and well pissed. Back in those days, she did this a lot, and whenever I tried to help her out or comfort her, I just made everything worse, so I needed to get out of the house. Maternity leave was a dark time in that apartment. My wife had developed a certain coldness toward me.

"You're such an asshole!" screamed Lauren. She had lost her patience with me. "How dumb do you have to be to get picked, actually picked, for *jury duty*? What's wrong with you?"

I didn't know what to say. I had tried my best to appear irresponsible and prejudiced—I had even worn what I usually wear around the house every day—and still, a high court of this land had picked me to decide another man's fate. I wasn't happy about it either.

That night I did what I could to smooth things over. I changed Luke when he needed it and fed him every couple hours, and when he had emptied the bottle, I held him tall against my chest and rubbed a palm up and down his ribs, sticking with it, until he roared out a good one. We paced half circles around his room and I bounced him gently, our little dance, until I heard his snoring on my shoulder. I wrote down eight ounces and number one or two in the sacred book, as necessary. Then I washed the bottles and nipples in the sink and left a clean set out for my partner on the early shift. That stuff didn't bother me. I just couldn't stay in that apartment anymore.

The next morning, I rose at a reasonable hour and headed down to the courthouse. I decided that I should hang around the court to get the rhythms of the place and get some basics down so I wouldn't fold under questioning. I just went back to the room where they dismissed me and sat outside for a while. When people started filtering in for the trial, I followed them inside.

I hadn't always behaved this way. Not long ago I was a much different type of guy, a *What are the next steps we're doing here?* kind of person. Serious.

Responsible. Completion-oriented. A decent citizen. I was a good soldier, obsessed with my work. But losing my job blew that all to pieces, and I hadn't been able to put them back. I was a little lost. I had spent many years as a good producer in a real seat at a great firm in a tough industry, but when I got laid off, I was out looking for a while, and I just could not find a job. It was rough. And it might have affected me—I know that it did—maybe more than I realized. It felt terrible. I don't like talking about this much and I don't think most people want to hear about it, either, and I can't blame them.

The judge reminded everyone that under no circumstances could we discuss any details of the case with anyone, not our friends, family, even our wives. I had been looking for this my whole life. Legal protection! I could return home after a long day doing God knows what and explain to my wife that I couldn't really talk about it, much as I would like to, but the law was very clear on this point. Although the way it played out, she never really interrogated me about the trial. She barely even brought it up. She did have a lot on her mind. So when I walked in the door at night, she had plenty of other stuff for me to focus on—but it wasn't that bad. Somehow, my free time turned out to be the hard part. The whole thing never started off that great from the outset, but then it got a little depressing and everything wound up sort of creepy by the end.

In the beginning, I like to think I was somewhat productive. I made it to the gym every morning. Then I would go sit in the assembly room with my laptop—they had good Wi-Fi in there—and I would spend time on LinkedIn or on cover letters, emailing people or keeping up with the world and politics and the markets and social issues and reading a lot without interruption. When the spirit moved me, I sent articles to old friends that I thought might interest them. Sometimes, my wife would ask me to bring home takeout, a little Chinese.

Since I was down there, I started following the murder trial they had denied me. I would go back to the courtroom and listen to them argue the case once or twice a week. Some parts were slow, but I found a lot of it interesting. During breaks in the hallways, teams of lawyers would walk together or huddle in discussion, and I'd watch them and wonder about their lives and careers.

But then I began to notice a lot of the same people sitting around me in the gallery every day. I figured that most of the regulars had good reasons to be there, but some of them were concerning. I wondered if they didn't have real obligations for coming, if maybe they were just the sort of people who hung around courtrooms because they found it more interesting than whatever else they could have been doing instead. The idea disturbed me.

Sometimes the walls began to creep closer as a terror would build in my chest, and I couldn't shake the thought that I had run out of answers or options. A courtroom is not a good place to panic, so I'd sneak away from the gallery and slip outside for some air. I'd go out and wander the streets. The people walking past seemed to move very quickly.

It was a dangerous game I had chosen to play, and I knew it. I worried about bumping into someone who might recognize me—even just a chance encounter with a casual friend of Lauren's could lead to hard questions, and if my story unraveled, the fallout would cause a great deal of damage. I was becoming unglued.

One night I came home from the courthouse and my wife started talking about going back to work. I was tired and a little distracted, but when she said some stuff about working remotely one or two days a week at corporate housing, I started to listen more closely. Then I heard something surprising. She said she wanted to move out of the city. A few hours away, close to the beach. She started explaining why—the schools, the space, some other stuff—but I had stopped listening. She tried to convince me for a bit, but I'd heard enough.

"It's okay," I said interrupting. "I feel like this could be really good for you, good for all of us. And it seems like this matters a lot to you, and that's what's important. Because I want to support you. C'mere. It's all an adventure."

I hugged her close.

I held her in my arms, and I was already thinking about the water, the sunsets, the open roads—anywhere else than a godforsaken tiny apartment in this cruel city where at any moment I might run into people from my former but now all sorts of fucked-up, shot-to-hell existence. My darkness was over. The days when I couldn't even get selected for jury duty, or convince a therapist to call me back, when I was lurking around courtrooms just to get out of the goddamn house, were done.

I hugged her again. She kissed me.

"Oh, thank you, Pete! Thank you! I love you," she told me. "Now we need to start looking at places. We have a lot to do. It all seems like a ton, but don't worry, I've already started. But I could use a little help here. When do you think the trial will be over?"

I kissed her and hugged her some more.

"I don't know," I told her. "But I hope not much longer. And I want to help. Because you deserve this. I love you."

2

THINGS HAVE BEEN better out here.

I'm not saying the transition was easy. There were a few incidents—I can get into them later, now's not the time. But I still think I've made some sort of progress in this place, and I'm glad we live around here.

This is a nice town. Not quite as fancy as some of the more famous beach spots in this part of the world, although, like everywhere else, you see bigger and bigger houses getting built and some real estate transacts at disturbing prices. And yes, we swell to bursting with summer crowds from the Fourth of July through August, and you can see in certain kinds of behavior hints of great wealth mixed with an unapologetic desire to spend it, but this place still doesn't have the same vibe or the social intensity of those sandy villages that became playgrounds for the Wall Street set a long time ago, although many inhabitants fear a similar fate will befall us, probably soon, if it hasn't already. *Enjoy it while it lasts,* warn many locals. This place still has its beaches and salt shacks, decent schools, the public park, a good diner, a few bars and restaurants, every type of gym or fitness studio known to man, a Little League field and a hospital within driving distance, as well as one regional bank, various law, real estate, architecture, design, and insurance firms, plus constant construction to stoke the local economy.

A small contingent of finance types commute or work from home. When they aren't working, people here tend to occupy themselves with their passions, like exercise and sports or booze or their children, and often a keen interest in their friends' and neighbors' personal lives and careers. This is a comfortable town. But sometimes, it can feel like not an enormous amount happens around here.

So, in this town, when a body washes up on the beach, it's the sort of thing people talk about—it's a big deal. We don't have a lot going on, so last week, when somebody rolled onto the shore with an incoming tide, it was the type of thing people wanted to discuss. People notice that kind of stuff around here.

They say a fisherman found him. Saturday morning, just after dawn, a surf caster was reeling in his lines when he spotted something in the water a couple hundred yards down the beach. Whatever was bobbing out there was big and dark enough to be driftwood or maybe some giant creature breaching, but when the guy walked closer, he saw a body getting rag-dolled in the waves. The fisherman ran out into the ocean, hoping he could still save him, but the victim had been in the water for days. But give that guy some credit—he dragged him in through the white water, got him ashore, caught his breath, and phoned it in. It's late September, off-season, so if he hadn't seen him, who knows when they would have found him, this time of year?

The newspapers Monday said the body of an unidentified man had washed up on the beach. Nobody around the gym, at the library, or even the moms at school pickup knew who he was. The moms know an awful lot about many subjects that I find helpful in my current role as a stay-at-home dad, but on this one, they didn't have much. Everyone's been asking questions, like *Who the hell was he?* and *What the hell happened to him?* I can't think of anything that's caused this kind of stir since we've lived out here.

People have theories. They're saying he was surfing. They found him in a wet suit, with a snapped leash tied to his ankle but no board attached. So they're saying he was surfing alone and that something went wrong—maybe he knocked himself out somehow. Maybe his board popped up and hit him in the head or he wiped out and plowed into the sand. Or broke his neck on the bottom. He could have breathed in some seawater. Imagine you go over the falls, the top of the wave snatches you as it rears up and rolls over, throwing you forward and slamming you down, driving you under, spinning and tumbling, getting tossed in the wash. When you reach the surface, you're disoriented—you don't see the other one coming or maybe your lungs just need air—but you take a deep gasp of something salty down the wrong pipe. That awful burning and coughing—that's a rough way to go.

But then today, I'm down here at this empty stretch of beach on a gray Thursday morning, watching Luke and his little friend Jake play with their trucks in the sand. I was just looking at my phone, going through the papers, when I see a headline in the local rag. They have the guy's name. They figured it out. I can hardly believe what they're saying, but there it is. I read the whole article twice and then glance up at the boys to make sure they haven't started to hitchhike.

"You want to hear something messed-up?" I yell over to Frank. He's bouncing on one foot and shaking his head to his shoulder, trying to get salt water out of his ears. He doesn't respond.

"Remember that guy who washed up last Saturday?" I ask him.

Frank's the kind of person who can sometimes leave you wondering whether or not he heard what you said.

"That was pretty messed-up," he says, finally.

"Yeah. The paper just released his name. I know the guy," I tell him.

I knew who he was. I'd recognized Robert Townsend the first day I saw him on the water, sitting on his board, and watching the horizon for the next approaching set. The ocean had been nearly deserted on a clear November morning with semidecent waves. That was almost a year ago now. If you work in this business—pardon me, *worked* in this business—you know who certain people are, even if you haven't met them. He was a fair-haired boy. A rising star. He didn't run one of the behemoths, but he was well recognized as the heir apparent at a midsize firm in the city. I figured there were worse people I could try to get to know.

So, that first day on the water, it was just the two of us out there, and I let myself drift over. We had a nice conversation.

What's up? I had asked him.

Hey, he had said. And he'd nodded.

That was the end of the chat. That was our first conversation. But that's how it started.

"Jesus," Frank says walking over. "He was a friend of yours? That's brutal. Who was he?"

"A guy named Robert Townsend," I tell him. "But that's not the messed-up part."

I'm not sure I'd have called him a friend. I'm not sure what I'd call him.

"What do you mean?" he says.

"I saw him. Right here. A week ago, that Thursday."

"Out on the water?"

"No man. Right here. He was sitting in his car. Watching the water. Just like me. I was down here, too, with the little guy."

"And when did he go missing?"

"Thursday."

"You saw him before he went in the water?"

"No, that's the thing," I tell him. "It was lousy. I saw him just sort of sitting there in his car and I walked over to say what's up. And we talked. We both said it wasn't worth it. *It's not doable, that's a bummer* kind of thing. Then we sat around for a minute or two. And then I took off."

"So, he went in after you left?"

"No. No. They found his car over by Hammy's."

"Huh," he says.

"That's what I'm saying."

"What time did you see him?"

"Around four or four thirty."

"Huh," he says again.

I could see him doing the same arithmetic as me. If Hamilton Beach sits about ten miles down the coast from this stretch of sand, at this time of year, with no traffic, back roads or the highway, that would take what, maybe twenty to thirty minutes?

"Why would he drive all the way out there just before dark to go in on some dog shit day?" I ask him. "Onshore wind. Starting to rain. Doesn't make any sense."

Frank rubs his neck and considers this for a sec.

"Was he any good?" he asks.

"Good athlete," I tell him. "But not really. Just getting into it."

Since we're being honest, I could add that he was probably a little better than I am, but I don't.

"Was he from the city?" Frank asks.

"Yeah. He's got a place out here. Big finance guy."

"He's out from the city, and he's just starting—he just caught the bug," says Frank. "Those guys go out in all kinds of stuff."

As a card-carrying member of the "guys out from the city who have a lot of time to make up" crowd, I should know that he makes a fair point.

"I was talking to him right here," I mutter instead, looking at the spot where his car sat parked that day. "It just doesn't make sense. Doesn't add up."

He looks out at the ocean for a little bit. We both do.

"How'd you know the guy, again?" he asks.

"He was a friend of mine," I tell him.

Frank thinks it over for a minute as I watch the boys dig a hole in the sand with a stick they found someplace. I wonder how long it will take to get them in the car.

"Yeah, that's messed-up," he says.

3

After that first day I didn't see Townsend again on the water until a couple weeks later. It was a decent morning with three-to-four-foot swells and light, side shore wind. Just the two of us, again. I had gotten out there before him and caught a few nice ones by the time he showed up, and I felt pretty good. He sat out behind the sandbar for a little bit, then jumped on the first wave of an all right–looking set and I took off on the second. When I paddled back out past the break, I pulled up a half dozen yards over from him, and even though this was booties and gloves season, and he wore a hooded wet suit tucked over most of his face, I recognized him. He turned to me, sporting a grin. I didn't force anything.

"What's up?" he asked and nodded.

"What's up?" I said and nodded back.

Everything was going fine.

"You live around here?" I asked. I already knew the answer, of course, but it seemed as good a moment as any to make my move, and that was the first club I could find in the bag. I figured he'd be a good guy to know. Maybe a game changer, even.

"I'm in the city," he said. "Just out on the weekends."

And he was still smiling. In my time out on the water, I would say hello to a few of the more approachable-looking regulars, but I'd never met anyone before that I'd consider a friend, although I'd heard about that sort of thing and believed it could happen.

"How about you?" he asked.

"I'm out here year-round now. I used to live in the city."

"Sounds like you got the right idea."

"Yeah, we've been here a little over a year."

"What do you do?" he asked.

I kept my chin up, but I already felt myself sinking.

"I worked in finance for a while and now I'm between jobs," I said. "But I look after my son."

He stopped smiling. Then he glanced out at the water. When he turned to look back at me, he was forcing a smile that didn't look right. I'd seen this before. Not often this bad, though—this one was brutal.

Cocktail parties are the worst. But really any kind of social gathering gets dangerous, even just running into someone on the street. When you're unemployed, anywhere people come together and feel the urge to speak, things can go wrong in the worst sort of way and often do. At any moment someone could ask what you do for a living, and then you'll have to tell them. But it gets worse. They make you watch. You have to *watch* the light drain out of their eyes as they fumble for their next words. Sometimes they look away.

But what was I supposed to do—lie to him? I wanted to get to know the guy, and I'd have to come clean eventually.

"I used to work on the sell-side," I added.

This only seemed to make him more uncomfortable. He nodded and kept smiling at me, but he was already somewhere else, and I'd sent him there by just answering one, simple question.

When I got let go, I wasn't fired. I was actually a good producer—one of the better ones on the desk. I was well liked and tried to mentor younger people. I didn't steal anything or yell racist comments or assault any women. And one day I got laid off. That was it. I'm sure everyone says this, but even though they were downsizing all these groups, I was shocked when the call came.

It sort of reminds me of paddling out on some huge, scary day. You think you have it timed right, but then this set comes bearing down on you, like 2008, and you dig and make it over that first bastard even if you can't help but notice, looking around you, that a few of your buddies are gone. You hear the roar of collision over your shoulder and hope they're okay, but you just paddle harder, and now there's another one right in front of you—some European disaster—but you dodge that one, too, you're still in the game. Then there's another clusterfuck. Another round of layoffs comes along, but you're still paddling, and then your old boss is gone, and you make it over another, but Jesus, how big a set is this? Until one wave comes. Somehow it always seems to come out of nowhere, but really it just follows all the rest. And that's it. You get drilled. And that's not fun, but that's business, it's part of the sport, no one asked you to play, they don't put a gun to your head, and if you can't take getting roughed up a little or making an ass of yourself, there's an easy solution—just stay on the beach. Of course, if you sit there long enough watching everyone else out on the water, you might miss getting drilled.

I didn't mention any of this to Townsend. He didn't bring it up, either.

"Gotcha," he said.

Then he looked out toward the ocean, hoping to find an incoming set. But there wasn't one. And I could have used it.

"I'm Pete, by the way," I told him after a good-size silence.

"Robert."

He tried forcing a smile. But then again, he turned back to study the water, scanning for the next wave.

"How about you?" I asked him. "What do you do?"

What else was I going to say?

"I'm in finance," he told me.

But he didn't look away from the horizon. He didn't look my way again. And I knew, of course, at that moment, he would have begged me, paid any kind of ransom, if I could just shut the fuck up and not ask him another question or confide any horrifying secrets about the life I had squandered. So, I didn't. We didn't speak for the rest of the session.

I did see him again out on the water another time—this would have been early summer. It didn't go well at all.

4

Most nights my son doesn't fall asleep unless I stay there with him in his room. Maybe I've indulged him too much and created a bad habit, I don't know. But the truth is I like it. It's something I can take care of, a problem I can fix. And if he calls out later at some ungodly hour, if he screams long enough, I'll go in there and hold him, even though some books say that's not what you're supposed to do.

So, tonight, I'm lying here on the couch next to Luke's crib, waiting for him to doze off. I hear a voice, somewhere in the darkness, whispering strange stories to me. He likes to chat with his dad in these moments, but I have to ignore him, or else he'll stay up all night. I keep staring at my phone, looking for every article I can find on this Townsend business, but none of them seem to discuss how he drowned. Is Luke *growling* back there? He claws at the air through the bars of his cage, and I need to stifle a laugh. But now Lauren's texts start coming in.

Don't forget music class tomorrow.

I take Luke to music class every Wednesday afternoon at 5:00 p.m., but my wife insists on reminding me about it every week. I only missed one time. But it was memorable, and she'd been fairly pissed.

Got it, I write back.

Does he have his blankey? He needs it otherwise he'll wake up in the night, she answers.

How much did he eat? she asks now. I'm not sure how to respond to this.

When my wife comes home, she never rolls in naked, she comes strapped, armed to the teeth with questions. *Why is he crying?* He just started. *Why is he crying?* I don't know. *Did you feed him?* I did. *Has he slept?* He has. *Has he been like this all day?* I don't think so. *Do you want me to take him for a sec?* I do. *But wait. I have to send this text, can you hold him for another minute? Stay there one second.* I can. *Where's his animal?* I don't know. *Where's his blanket?* I'm not sure. *When did he have it last?* I can't remember. *Pete. Pete, please. I need you to help me here. This is important.*

In fact, we often don't speak. She prefers to text me, even if we're in the same house. Sometimes, she will come home, creep through the door, sneak into our room, and hide there so that Luke won't discover her presence and demand to stay up with her for another few hours, but she still feels comfortable sending me texts filled with instructions from our bedroom. This habit doesn't bring out the best in me.

But tonight, after a while, when I hear that sweet, rhythmic breathing drift up from Luke's crib, I tiptoe out of his room, close the door with great care. My work here is done.

The lights are off inside our bedroom, the TV muted, and Lauren's already under the covers, but I don't think she's asleep. I still can't stop thinking about the guy who washed up on the beach.

"I had a pretty weird day," I say, and she gives me a deep *Just so you know I'm exhausted* sigh in response.

Lauren works a long week in an intense job. She's out the door well before 6:00 a.m. most mornings for an hour-and-a-half commute each way, and then she has Luke and me on her hands. I can understand why she's tired all the time.

"Did you see the paper this morning?" I ask her.

On my current program I can go long stretches—sometimes several days—without having a real conversation with another adult. So yeah, I know she's exhausted when she comes home, but I still wish that I could talk to her a little bit.

"Did Luke go down all right?" she says.

Of course, when we *do* chat, we don't tend to discuss a wide range of topics. It's pretty much Luke and logistics. We don't talk about current events or movies or books or strange notions we hadn't considered, none of that stuff. We schedule. We coordinate. We run over lists. Ever since we moved here, the last two and a half years, that's been about it.

"He was fine," I tell her. "No problem."

"Uhhh, I'm tired," she says.

I know that I'm a lucky man in a lot of ways—very lucky, even privileged—but what can I say? Sometimes it gets tough.

"You want to hear something really messed-up?" I ask her.

I just sort of sit in silence for a while on the edge of the bed, getting the feeling she doesn't want to hear much of anything from me.

"Do you know a guy named Robert Townsend?" I ask anyway.

"The one at GDR?" she mumbles eventually.

"Yeah. What's his deal?"

"I don't really know him," she says, and adds after a sigh, "I've heard he's sort of a jerk."

She reaches for her eye mask, but I ignore this.

"How do you mean?"

"He always seems a little too in love with himself," she grumbles.

"Right."

"I think he has a place around here actually."

He *did*. He *had* a place.

"Have you heard about the guy who washed up from the water last

Saturday? That was him. That was Townsend. They just released his name."

"Jesus Christ, Pete."

"Yeah, it's pretty ugly."

"That's awful. I think he was married. God."

She's looking over at me now. I hadn't really thought about his family.

"I've been trying to wrap my head around it. The whole thing doesn't make any sense."

"What thing?" she asks.

"What the papers are saying. That he drowned in an accident. It's pretty hard for me to believe."

"Pete, can I just ask you something? Don't get angry. Can you please be careful when you're going out there and doing all this stuff? I really need you in one piece."

"But that's what I'm saying. That's the thing. This guy, he didn't just have some weird accident. None of this adds up."

"All right, but can you just be careful and don't go too crazy? Hey. Can you not roll your eyes at me?"

"I was just trying to tell you something. What the papers are saying. Something's off. There's a lot more to this story."

"What do you mean?"

"I don't know. I'm not sure. It's just really weird."

"I'm sorry but it's been a long day and I'm just a little exhausted here, Pete."

"Like something sketchy."

"What did the police say?"

"Well, they're the ones who called it an accident. Why are you looking at me like that? What's so funny?"

"I didn't say anything. I just really need to get some sleep."

She's looking at me like I'm ranting about another one of my conspiracy theories. Like how they say there's no inflation, except college and health care and real estate, but yeah, there's no goddamn inflation—that's what I'm supposed to believe?

But now she puts on her eye mask and it looks like she means it.

"I'm saying, I don't know what happened. But I don't believe he went for a surf. Look, it's more than that, the whole thing—it just doesn't smell right, you know?"

"It doesn't smell right?" she says. She doesn't sound too impressed.

I pinch the bridge of my nose. Let's slow down here, a minute. The thing about Lauren is she's always been quick and smart and funny as hell, and she doesn't suffer fools, and these are just a few of the reasons I married her. That's all great. But she doesn't know a damn thing about surfing, that much I can tell you. If she could try listening to me for one second—even just as a novel experiment—maybe I could explain some of this better. And by the way, I'm not rambling about celebrity gossip or some terrible injustice from the latest big game, we're talking about a guy who's no longer with us—the guy wasn't a stranger—and whatever happened to him didn't happen that far from where I take Luke however many days of the week. So, I get that you're busy and spent, but am I just supposed to laugh this off and forget it?

"Are you all right?" she asks. "What's the matter?"

"I'm good. What's going on with you?"

"Nothing."

Lauren has a way of saying "nothing" sometimes that means a lot of different things, but none of them good or easy to fix. She shakes her head and lies back down on her pillow with a sigh.

"It just doesn't make any sense," I tell her for some reason.

"Can we talk about this tomorrow? I really need to get some sleep."

And not long after that, she conks out for the night. I wish I could say this sort of scene is unusual in my household, but it's more like a routine we've developed in the years since we moved out here. I also can't put the blame for this all on her, as much as I'd like to. And it's not just talking or spending time together—we have a few other areas that we could improve on.

Like those nights when my wife comes home late from her day at the office or one of those weekly mothers' groups she attends. Times when our little rascal's down and I'm already in bed. I watch her walk into our room, her heels clicking on the floor, and she'll take off an earring or two, groaning about her day. She'll sit at the end of the bed, still in her work suit, and let her hair down. My wife's a beautiful woman. So yeah, sometimes I take a shot on goal—go for a shoulder, a neck, an ear, even. *Pete. Please. Please, Pete. I'm exhausted. Please. Can you not? Really, can you just not, please?* Sure, sure. I hear you. So, I try something else, take another stab, show a little persistence, keeping it playful—you can't give up right away. Don't women want to feel adored? To be wanted? *Pete,* she says. *That's enough. I'm exhausted. Pete, please. I need some sleep. Please stop?* All right, all right, I know how it goes. Sorry, I'll leave you alone.

Was this routine ever cute? Was she always just sort of putting up with me? I'm not sure anymore.

Look, I know that she's a busy woman with a lot of shit to do. And that a lot of my shtick can get tiresome, and she just wishes that I could grow up, start acting like an adult because I'm a father now and she needs help. I try to remember that, too.

Then there are other nights. Sometimes we'll lie in bed, watching the latest binge-worthy show. Most of the time we're too tired, but it's one of our favorite things to do together, so we try to squeeze it in when we can. If a couple can't enjoy this kind of stuff with each other, that probably means they're in serious trouble. Once in a while, when we finish an episode, as the credits start rolling, she puts her head on my shoulder, maybe a hand on my belly and on occasion, who knows? Sometimes her fingers get a little more active. I might even pause the previews for the next episode. But, some nights, the two of us will start fooling around and we're taking our time and all that, but then it's just not happening. Sometimes it feels like nothing works the way it used to anymore. And so, I sit up as if I heard the little man and tell her *hang on a sec, I'll check on him, it's my turn, geez bad timing.* Then I'll creep into his room and lie down on the couch, listening to him snoring peacefully. I think about a lot of different things, lying there on that couch in the dark, and I wish a lot of these things were different. By the time I get back to bed, she's always asleep.

That's my move. If it only happened one time, I could call it something else, but at this point—it's a move.

Look, I know my wife's not stupid, all right? What do you want me to say? Huh? What the fuck am I supposed to tell her?

I never said it was all her fault.

And it wasn't always like this. There was a time when I wouldn't have believed this stuff could happen to us. We used to have a lot of fun together. We used to laugh a lot. We were coconspirators, accomplices. I wish we could feel that way again. I don't want to sound corny or anything. But back then, sometimes when we were together it felt like we knew something important that everyone else on the planet had missed out on, because they worried too much about a bunch of small stuff that doesn't matter. But those days seem like a long time ago now. I don't know. It's all very Springsteen, one of the early, sad songs.

But some stuff you remember. Some stuff you know. Back when I met my wife, for that first month, we were never apart for more than twelve hours. I always liked to keep things casual. But after three dates and one night with Lauren, I found myself calling in sick to work the next day so we could sneak off to spend a long weekend together, and by the trip back on Sunday, I knew that whatever I had going with this woman could be a lot of things, but none of them casual.

That's some of the stuff I remember. Some of the stuff I know. Or maybe I just used to.

But I hope, in some ways at least, I still do.

5

I GAVE IT a real shot. I really tried. Early in the game, when we first moved out here from the city, I put in the work. Since my wife was the breadwinner, that left me to take care of the home front, and I logged some long hours standing around outside preschool, with all the nice moms, day after day. The moms were all very friendly—for the most part, they ignored me—and I tried not to bother them. And for a few months, I managed to do this without any issues. But then one day, things changed.

I was carrying Luke to the car when I noticed Gemma, one of the nicest women in the group, walking toward us. I tried not to panic.

"A few of us are going to the park after this," she said. "Do you and Luke want to come?"

I thought it was pretty considerate of her to include us. It seemed like I couldn't say no.

So, Luke and I followed the pack to a good-size park, filled with luscious green lawns and trees turning the color of fall. We sat in a semicircle on the grass and watched the little tykes play together, stumbling around and stealing toys from each other, learning to share and apologize afterward. Some of the grown-ups were chatting, and at first, I didn't really participate—I just sat there trying to seem pleasant and nonthreatening.

Everything was going fine. But when the conversation turned to exercise, I felt like I should jump in—I let myself get too comfortable.

"Exercise is important," I told everyone.

"We go to this amazing cardio class," said Gemma.

"Cardio's really important," I added.

"Do you want to come with us sometime?" asked Anna.

I wanted no part of it.

"Would I be the only guy in the class?" I wondered aloud. There were many other ways I could have responded, but that's what I asked.

"Why would that matter?" Gemma frowned. I noticed that the women were all looking at me. They didn't look *angry*, but they all seemed to think that Gemma had asked a very reasonable question, and they were interested in how I would answer.

"Oh no, it doesn't!" I said cheerfully. A few of the moms nodded. The circle of eyes softened.

And in this way the issue was decided. Like an idiot—a damn simpleton and total amateur—I said that it didn't matter at all and agreed to go. We soon set a date, and a few days later, after drop-off, I followed a line of cars out of the lot and ended up inside a tiny fitness studio, brightly lit with wooden floors and wall-to-wall mirrors.

When we started jogging in place and doing jumping jacks as they cranked up the techno music, I knew I'd been screwed. I was the only guy in there. The workout wasn't easy, and I'm not a small man, so it doesn't take much for me to get pretty sweaty and smelly. I didn't stare like a pervert or fart or make any dick jokes, and I didn't talk over anyone or try to explain stuff or start lifting heavy things. I just felt like an asshole.

The instructor was a male model of some sort. This insanely ripped Italian guy with a barbed wire tat on his arm. He kept pacing the room, demonstrating the exercises, which were all very basic calisthenics, and saying things like *bene, bene* and *sì, sì* at all the smiling women, who loved every minute. *Grazie,* he kept saying! One time, and this really pisses me off, he comes over to me during the push-ups and starts correcting my form. I'm doing real push-ups, by the way, while most of the moms are banging them out on their knees, and he doesn't say shit to them about putting in work under a bench press, but he wants me to flare my elbows more—a good method to screw up your shoulders, just for the record. I kept my arms tight to my sides and my eyes on the floor. *Grazie,* he said.

And the whole time, all the moms were never anything but supportive and kind—they encouraged me! It got pretty bad.

I didn't need to see any more. I had tried to play nice. Tried to act like part of the team. And this had led me to an all-female dance cardio class flopping around like a fucking fool. I figured that soon I'd become *that guy,* the token dude who listens to their problems and gets invited to brunches or maybe—fingers crossed—a bachelorette party. I just couldn't take it. I wanted to be the best father I could, but I never signed up for *this.* And who would?

I was so angry I wanted to pick a fight. I wanted to gamble and risk more money than I ever had. I felt like doing something incredibly dangerous or tracking down an animal and killing it. At the end of that class, when the instructor clasped his hands together as if in prayer, bowing and thanking each one of us like he'd just won an Oscar, I wanted to howl. That night, I lay in the dark on the couch beside my son's crib trying to help him sleep, and stayed up watching videos on my phone—a guy snapping his tibia wiping out on a fifty-foot wave, or Marvin Hagler trading punches with Tommy "The Hitman" Hearns in their middleweight classic, that kind of stuff.

But that night, I made a decision. At pickup, I would be nothing but friendly to the moms, but the next time they brought up exercise class, I told them I'd pulled a hamstring.

Pretty soon they quit asking. There were no hard feelings. They still invite me to things outside of school—the playdates, the extracurriculars, so long as I bring Luke. I think this kind of stuff's important for him, they make it happen and I haven't forgotten that. No, I'm grateful to them and feel like we share a sort of bond, the kind that can come from serving with others under great pressure, or lending out wet wipes and sunscreen.

But I also believe in the plain simple fact that when a man comes to a point where he feels like something in his life has gone missing, then the guy better realize that he won't find whatever it is he thinks he's lost by snooping around for it in any of the moms at his kid's preschool. I'm pretty firm in this view.

Still, I knew I needed some sort of outlet. And after that day at the exercise class, I went looking for it.

The next morning, Luke and I went to a boxing gym and walked around for a few minutes. Later, I spoke to a guy at one of these jiujitsu schools I'd heard about on some podcast. I toyed with the idea of picking up a sport where I could really hurt myself or someone else—the thought of this intrigued me. But then one day I checked out this other kind of gym some people couldn't stop talking about. It had always sounded like a stupid cult to me because the fanatics never called it *a gym*, they insisted on calling it *a box*. These places look different from most gyms—they have no treadmills, Nautilus machines, ellipticals, or mirrors. My town's box is an industrial warehouse space with black horse mats covering the floor, a few squat racks, and pull-up bars bolted into the cement, and dozens of barbells and plates sit in the corners. The room has a single fan and sometimes smells a little funny.

That first day, I walked through the door, Luke rolling with me in the stroller. I saw that they had a separate children's playroom, with two munchkins bouncing around inside. An attractive woman at the front desk watched them. She looked like she came from a tribe of warriors that had killed and eaten most of the men in their lands and fucked the rest of them to death.

She told me that a session started in a few minutes. She even offered to watch Luke.

"How much do I owe you?" I asked her.

"Don't worry about it," she said.

I wasn't familiar with this sort of gym.

"Good luck," she added, winking at Luke.

I changed in the lone bathroom with a truck stop shower that didn't seem to get much use and led Luke to the rumpus room. He settled in without complaint. If either of the fight clubs had offered me free childcare on my visits, maybe I could have made a decent scrapper, but they didn't, so we will never know.

About a dozen regulars filed in. Men and women, some normal humans, a few who looked like you could use them for anvils, but they all wore different T-shirts or shorts advertising the gym's name. Several stood bare-chested or in sports bras. That seemed odd to me, but when class started, I didn't care. I was preoccupied. I'm not a Navy SEAL, and I've downed a lot of cheeseburgers since my marathon days, but still, I've tried not to let myself go. And five minutes into this, I really thought I would die. I don't mean just getting sick everywhere. Sure, I thought I might shit myself or cry, but I worried something more tragic, perhaps medical, could happen—the makings of a cautionary tale or change in policy. I kept dropping into gears I didn't know I had. It was rough. This was not an elliptical machine or jogging with a stroller and some sit-ups. I'm not kidding, at all. This was next-level stuff.

They made us do this insane mix of sprints, calisthenics, and picking up heavy things. Worse, it's all a race. So even if I had wanted to pace myself, after I watched a tiny Asian woman less than half my size lift twice the weight on her barbell, then sprint circles around me, I went to this strange place. I wanted to be on *her* team. But I just couldn't keep up. With anyone. I couldn't catch my breath. And when the buzzer sounded to end the madness, I lay on my back, staring at the ceiling, thinking about things. I didn't feel good at all. After a few minutes I collected myself enough to sit up and watch a couple of these animals sitting around chatting with each other. They all seemed like friends, part of a club, laughing together, their muscles swollen and obscene. I could hear them making plans to get drinks later or maybe barbecue that weekend, and then a few of them started making out with each other and I was too tired to look anywhere else. I still couldn't catch my breath.

The morning after, I had a hard time lifting my son out of his crib, and I was in a great deal of pain for several days. But they had free goddamn *childcare*. I didn't know if this stuff was good for people—sometimes it felt unnecessary, even sadistic—and I could hardly believe in our candy-ass, lawsuit-crazed society that a place like this could exist. But I wanted a lot more.

I've even tried to get my wife to go with me. Lots of couples come here together, and she likes exercise more than I do. She had never showed any interest before, but not long after we had Luke, she became obsessed with every workout class or diet in the United States. SoulCycle, Pilates, SLT, The Bar Method, Exhale—she does all of them but mine. She says the women get too muscular at my places and it makes them unattractive. I'm not so sure about that. But I do know that mine has free childcare and hers do not. Because I asked her. And then I checked.

6

OUR FIRST DATE was a disaster. You give a person a chance, and if they can't play nice, then usually that's the last you see of them and that's what I thought for most of this one. I couldn't even blame someone else because I had initiated everything. This was not a setup.

A few months after we moved out here, I saw him standing by himself with a stroller on one of his sporadic visits to pickup. I hadn't seen many dads there before, so I walked over to introduce myself. We didn't talk for long, and it was pretty basic stuff. When he showed up to school a few more times, we had some quick chats, and then one day we traded numbers. Arrangements were made, and a few weeks later, Frank and I went to the playground together with our boys. And he was just brutal.

He didn't *say* anything. Frank just sat there next to me on the bench, sighing and staring into space. I tried a few openers, but they went nowhere, so after a while I quit trying. He checked the box scores on his phone and chewed his gum. The guy was a wet blanket. Finally, at some point, he felt moved to speak.

"This blows," he said.

All right, let me explain something, here. I'm not a perfect man by any stretch, and I can do my share of whining, but when you're around other people and you have a job to do, you get on with it, no pissing and moaning. But *this blows*? I don't need that shit, okay? Now you may be here to huff and roll your eyes, but I'm not. So don't do it around my kid. I love my son. This stuff matters. Sure, sometimes the days get long, a few nights are worse, and it might get boring or even a little lonely—okay, okay, I'll admit it, I get lonely, all right? I'm lonely all the time! But that's not the kid. Don't you get that? What are you, *stupid*? The rough part is the role itself, the title, the self-worth stuff, the isolation—but that's where you come in, dipshit. That's why I asked for your number. Listen, if we both need to do this— unless you want to change diapers all by your lonesome—then you need some company, which means it's either me or the moms, and you don't seem like the yoga or book club type. I asked you here to hang out, man, talk about sports and movies and women, *Jesus*, do I need to draw you a picture?

I cracked my neck and clenched my teeth.

"What are you gonna do?" I said without much conviction.

He didn't respond. So, we sat there in silence, and this went on for a good deal of time. Just one more example of the adult male's innate ability to forge new friendships. Throughout history, women of all ages have shared smoke signals, emails, lunch dates, and secrets the *instant* they meet each other. But somehow, every guy I know still hangs out with a half dozen dudes from high school or college, or maybe the job, or that he met in his twenties in the city, and then, after a certain age, that's kind of about it, unless they think they can make money off each other. We just suck at this. And if we do exchange numbers, follow up, and sit next to another fully grown man watching our kids play on the jungle gym, two *boys* by the way, *genius*, what happens? You find some all-star with a full head of messy, cool hair, whose jeans fit him well, who probably gets laid a lot—all the moms at pickup kept looking over and smiling at him, and I did, too, I guess— but then what's the only thing this sweet bro can think to say? *This blows*?

I was close to calling it a day. I wanted to get out of there.

But then a funny thing happened. He'd been looking over toward the parking lot for a while—I'm not sure what he was hoping to see. He took his time, he kept on watching, and then, without turning around, at his convenience, he said something to me.

"Do you surf?" he asked.

I watched my son chase imaginary villains and thought about the question.

Do I surf? I did. Or I used to. Not very well. And not for a while. I still owned a board. And I did used to love it. But you lose some stuff when you get older and start to reproduce. I shrugged.

"A little bit," I said.

I glanced over at him, and now he was looking out at the boys on the playground with that same blank, thousand-yard stare he'd had since we got here.

But he started nodding his head.

"How about you?" I asked.

And for the first time, this dude sitting next to me on the playground bench turned his head slowly toward me and smiled. He grinned like he'd figured something out. Like he knew something I didn't. Like he might tell me.

And it was the kind of thing I'd want to know.

Frank knew a place I'd never heard of. Not reachable from any of the main public beaches with paved parking lots. We drove down this potholed dirt road surrounded by open fields of overgrown reeds that looked as though it belonged to some long-abandoned farm. At the end of the road there was a gap between the dunes, a short goat path leading through to a secluded beach. And over this slight rise in the sand, you could walk up to this hidden gem of a surf spot. Not the typical shoreline you see on this coast, with the waves crashing directly into the beach, a shore break, or shore *pound*, as some call it. Although people surf those conditions sometimes, the waves offer not only short rides but also dangerous mistakes. If you try to take off on the wrong shore break set, with that ankle-deep water, you can do some real damage to your board or more vital possessions—like your shoulder, your back, or your neck. But here, at this half-mile stretch along the coast, you had this point where the waves broke between fifty to a hundred yards offshore over several feet of water even at low tide. In other words, a gentle little surf spot perfect for longboards and clowns at my level. And unlike some of the more famous and popular breaks in this part of the world, which can draw several hundred hopefuls to the lineups, jockeying with each other for position, always looking over their shoulder for the opportunistic poacher, here we often surfed alone. I never knew they even had places like this around here.

Frank calls this spot the River, and I'm not sure why, but now that's what I call it, too.

We came up with a routine. On days with any decent surf, one guy would stay on the beach to watch the boys while the other went in the water. After an hour, we'd trade places. Our partnership was simple, but it worked. It was one of those little things that when you have kids becomes a very, very big deal. No babysitters required, no having to ask your wife for permission or a favor. We found a synergy, that thing investment bankers promise in every presentation that no business ever, in fact, achieves. Yet somehow, here we did.

Now, unlike Frank—who looks as if he belongs nowhere else on earth when he takes off on a wave, all grace and composure, drops in screaming, carving lines across the face—I'm not some fierce surfer. But even as an amateur, I was just grateful for the chance to paddle out. I didn't solve all the world's problems, but compared to watching a child's temper tantrum in my living room, I spent these magical, transcendent hours at this place. And it wasn't all surfing.

I read to the boys a lot.

At their age, those little animals often won't sit still, and maybe I can't either, sometimes, but I tried. I liked it. And why not? Getting to spend this time on the water always gave me this mischievous sense of sneaking off to do something fun and stupid—a kid's sport, sure, but we had found a way to play it while we were still on duty, not shirking anything. You're *out* there, not stuck inside, scrolling through your phone, counting minutes until the next meal. It felt like we were getting away with something. So, after a session, I would change out of the wet suit, not wanting to lie around like some gold-brickin' beach bum—these *were* mostly weekdays—and I'd make this time with the boys count. Anyone who's ever looked after kids knows that some days you're more involved than others. So, when I wasn't on the water, I read to them. We would tear through *The Little Engine That Could* and run with the bulls in *Ferdinand*, or just go crazy with *Where the Wild Things Are*. Sitting there on an empty beach, with my son in my lap, watching Uncle Frank on the water making it look easy, the boys and I went through all the old hits.

And for a little while down at the River, it was good. I thought I had things figured out. I still had the existential dread of any stay-at-home parent not making a living or curing injustice, but here, I could do this one joyous, frivolous thing. And I wasn't lonely. My copilot didn't talk a great deal and came off a little stoic at first, but he loosened up. It all worked. After these trips, I'd pull up just in time for school drop-off with salt in my hair and sand in my toes, pushing Luke through the parking lot with a smile and a hello for each one of the moms, feeling a lot cooler than I was or had any right to. I couldn't help it.

"Isn't it too cold to surf now?" a few moms sometimes asked.

"It's doable," I'd say, trying not to grin or hug them for asking me that. Because those days I was in on the joke, not just faking a laugh when I felt like the punch line. I didn't miss jogging behind a stroller. This was good.

But like a lot of good things, it just couldn't last. But when this one went wrong, in the end, what happened was pretty ugly. And when it went bad, I won't lie or deny it or blame anyone else. What happened, the whole thing, it was my fault. Like always. Who else's fault could it be?

7

I SHOW UP early at pickup the way I always do. No amount of time wasted sitting in this parking lot is too high a price if I can avoid that one day when I get here late enough that a worried school calls my wife. I'll sleep in a tent by the steps to skip that. I watch the SUVs turn into the lot and the more extroverted moms jump out and begin chatting with each other. One or two stay in their cars and finish a phone call or complete a text, half written on the drive here.

There's a father that I've never seen at pickup before waiting outside school today. He's standing by himself, looking at his cell phone, still dressed for the office. I could walk over and introduce myself—he might appreciate meeting another parent, and he does seem a little bored.

I stay in my car.

I've got no quarrel with the moms at school, but their husbands scare the hell out of me. I've met most of them, some more than once, and even though they all seem like very decent guys—a few really likeable, and so far we've had no incidents—I still try to avoid that crew if I can.

Most of this comes from thinking about what could happen if one of these couples has an argument. When you have little kids, the list of things to disagree about gets pretty long. And I pray I'm wrong about this, and hope to God I am, but I worry that even just once during the shouting, some underappreciated, sleep-deprived mother will ask her man, "Why can't you do more stuff with the kids? You'd enjoy it. What about that nice dad who comes to school pickup all the time? Why can't you be more like that?"

I think I know what the husband says next.

"Pete??? That guy!!!??? The one you made me talk to at the parents' night??? Him??? You want me to be more like that guy????? He's a loser!!!! You want to know why he's always spending so much time with his kid??? Let me help you out . . . The guy's unemployed!!! He's hopeless!!! Do you get that???? A few of my friends knew him from work, and they said HE SUCKS, HONEY!!! HE FUCKING SUCKS!!! He's not just whipped or beaten down by some real battle axe . . . The guy's a goddamn cautionary tale. It's easier to pick up the kids at school when you don't work. Pete??? Jesus, is that what you think a father looks like? Or a husband?? You want to be married to him?? THAT's the full-package deal??? He's the big door prize??? Come on—I see you laughing. Yes, yes, I know it's funny, come here, baby . . . See, it's so silly . . . It's okay, it's okay, I'm tired, too, it's not your fault, no, no, don't apologize . . . All right . . . I'm gonna go play some golf."

Some version of that. Anyway, besides Frank, I haven't gotten to know many of the other dads from school.

My phone starts to rattle inside the cupholder. Lauren only texts, so I have no idea who the caller could be. I try to ignore it, but the rumbling doesn't stop. It's someone persistent. When I give up and reach for my cell, turning it over, the name **drew** pops up on my screen.

Pretty decent of him to keep in touch with me since I went missing. He's always the one reaching out. I still have the infrequent text or chat with a few guys from the old days, but I admit to feeling flattered, even proud, that Drew, my old boss and mentor, still makes the effort to catch up with his wayward disciple. He hasn't abandoned me. Sometimes when I see his number come up, I hesitate to answer, but my reluctance is no fault of his. He's a good man—one of the best—and I owe him a lot, but sometimes, I just don't have much to report, and it embarrasses me.

Drew made a rare, dignified exit from the business about a year before the fateful morning when the tribal elders asked me to leave. This timeline of events wasn't coincidental. When he left the firm, I knew my life was in danger.

Drew and his wife retired to a pretty place up north in the country, with a nice view and a short drive to a few serious golf courses. He teaches a finance class once a week at a nearby college. I like to imagine him parked in a teachers' lounge trapped in some horrible conversation with long-winded colleagues, growing angrier and angrier, but knowing he can't walk away without offending everybody. The image fills me with glee.

"Gnarly waves, brah. Total drag. Heavy shit," he says in a fake stoner voice.

"What's up, Drew?" He loves to wind me up, an ancient tradition.

"I read about some drama in your neck of the woods last week—that's some scary stuff. Pretty sad. Young guy like that. Puts things in perspective."

"It is a little spooky. Gets you thinking."

"I bet it does. Anyways, I had to check in on my boy and make sure he's okay. Have you hurt yourself lately, bud?"

"I'm still in one piece, somehow. So far, I'm good."

"Do you only go out in small stuff on, like, a boogie board? With floaties and shit?"

"Don't worry about the floaties. That's my business."

"Damn straight, whatever turns you on. Just so long as you don't ding yourself up and I have to read about it in the papers."

"Hey, speaking of that—did you know this guy? The one they found. Townsend?"

"Yeah, I did. A little bit."

"What was he like?"

"That's sort of tricky."

"Why's that?"

"He was an acquired taste."

"World's worst asshole?"

"Correct. But that's between us, okay, bud? I'm talking out of school."

"Why was the guy so painful?"

"I guess there's two sides to everybody. The way they act professionally, doing business with them, and the way they act on a personal level when you're having dinner on a Saturday night."

"Okay."

"Both sides he was a dipshit. Total prick. We had some friends in common, which was unfortunate. I'm not sure how that happened. But anyway, we were at a few dinners together. Expert on every subject. The type that has a little success in one part of life, so he has the answer for everything on the planet, got it all figured out. He knows the right people, you don't. Every other guy at the table's not thinking about it the right way, so he'll explain it to you, like he's doing you a favor, gracing you with his presence. Gets old pretty quick."

"What about on the business side?"

"Worse."

"Why?"

"Couldn't trust him. He'd break a trade, impossible to deal with, he had tussles all over the Street, that kind of thing. Part of that was the place where he worked. GDR's a weird firm. But he was a drama queen."

"That's interesting."

"Not really. Actually, it isn't. But you were always a very weird kid. What are you up to over there?"

"Nothing," I tell him. "I was just curious." Part of me would like to hear more about what he meant by "weird firm."

"Are you working on one of your super-secret projects? My spider-sense is tingling."

"No, those days are behind me." Drew used to always call me out for my obsession with strange, off-the-run ventures, these doomed quests that tended to take up a lot of time and resources but would never make money or prove useful to anyone at all.

"Sure they are, buddy. Sure they are."

"How about you? You ever get bored?"

"Oh," he says slowly, thinking. "I have good days and bad."

"Do you miss it?"

"Nah. The place used to be a lot of fun, but it's just been a slow bleed, ever since the crisis, and now it's a much different game. Maybe that's not the worst thing in the world. Why? You're not thinking of trying to get back into it, are you?"

"I don't think so. But what makes you say that?"

"I mean, the business was fun while it lasted. But now? I just think you could find something more interesting. You're still a young guy. You could do a lot of different things." Drew has told me this before. The past few years, he brings it up every time we speak. I'm not sure how we got on it again. "But this watching the kid all day, the Mr. Mom stuff, sweet pea?"

I'm starting to wish we were still talking about Townsend. Or anything other than this, really.

"That shit's not too easy, by the way," I tell him.

"I didn't say it was, buddy. I know it isn't, believe me. But just remember that it doesn't last forever, do you see what I mean? In a few years, you're going to need something else. Something that fires you up. And you're lucky. You have options. You don't need to just go punch the clock some- where, you have plenty of money. Well, your wife does anyway, bud."

"Settle down. Easy." He's bringing out all the classics.

"Don't carry guilt with it, buddy. There's no reason to be insecure about that. It's totally cool. Your wife's a successful woman, something to be very proud of."

But now I see the first tiny monster being led out the school door, and as much as I would like to get into this, I can't let Luke stand around scared, wondering when his dad will show up.

"Look, this is really great stuff," I tell Drew. "This is a good use of time. But I've gotta hop here in a sec and grab Luke. But all BS aside. Thanks for calling, seriously. Good catching up."

I'm out of the car, walking past the moms, cell phone in hand, an upwardly mobile man of obvious importance, in heated discussion, carrying a sippy cup.

"You were always so sensitive." He laughs. "That's the problem with your generation. We tried this everybody-gets-a-trophy approach, and guys like you were the result. Take care of yourself, bud."

I hang up on him and scoop Luke into my arms, get a good snuggle on his neck, carry him to the car, and wave at the moms with their own tiny troopers. But I can still hear Drew laughing. The barking mad captain, more frightened of dry land than a maelstrom, still howling instructions at his terrified crew, deaf to their pleading, full speed ahead into uncharted waters, the course always headed forward straight toward the abyss. I miss that kind of thing. But I've lost that in my new life with the moms and the school pickups—it just doesn't exist. And sometimes I wish that I were the guy doing the right thing, reaching out to some wayward soul who everyone's worried about, just checking in on one of my boys, but ever since I went off into hiding, that's another one of those things that I've lost and I miss.

8

I FIND GANDLE after today's session at the box and explain that I need to talk to her about something pretty important. We sit on a metal bench where I catch my breath as the gym empties out, and soon it's just the two of us watching Luke hang from a pair of gymnastic rings, his feet scraping the floor. So I start to tell her about seeing Townsend that day down at the beach. And in truth, I'm more than a little excited—this could be a big deal.

"Slow down," she keeps saying.

The first couple of months after I joined the box, I mostly kept to myself and tried to stay out of people's way. I didn't jump in on any conversations, and nobody invited me to join them, either. Sometimes, Luke and I went by in the middle of the day when no classes were scheduled, the lulls known as open gym, when the main room was so empty that he would nap in the corner safely strapped in his stroller while I put in a less-frantic routine than the group session and tried not to wake him. We often had the place to ourselves. I liked open gym.

But one afternoon during these off-hours, Luke and I were there doing our thing when a woman came in and walked over to a squat rack on the other side of the room. She seemed like someone you don't want to piss off, so I kept my distance and gave her some space. But she was hard not to notice. She looked very difficult to injure. She came back the next day, and I began to see her around more and more, at a class or lifting by herself, until one thing led to another. I didn't start anything, but the woman couldn't help herself. She needed to get her hands on Luke, and you can't just go around grabbing other people's kids, so she came over and we got to talking. She told me her name was Beth, but everyone calls her Gandle.

And besides Frank, she may be the closest thing to a friend I've made since we moved here. I like to think she's a friend, anyway. But I've never actually spoken to her outside of this madhouse—our relationship consists only of the time we spend chatting after a workout. I'm not sure I'd even recognize her wearing normal clothes, since I've only seen her in sports bras and these booty shorts the women wear around here. I haven't seen her in uniform, either.

Gandle is a cop.

I had never known any cops before I met her, and something about this interests me—cops are sort of different. And Gandle isn't like any of my old friends, or the moms at school, and she's very different from my wife.

For one thing, she doesn't look like a lot of other women. Gandle is not much more than average height or weight, but she has wide shoulders and an upper back that slope into a wedge against her neck almost like a dolphin. Her legs are absurdly strong—her thighs are thick and roped in muscle—and her face is quite attractive. She tapes her wrists and fingers and covers her hands in chalk, but she still has blisters on her palms that seem to tear every day. I've known plenty of women who are great athletes, but I've never seen one before at any gym or beach or campus who looks like Gandle. No one even close.

But we talk a lot after these brutal sessions, and our chats have become a big part of my day. Or sometimes after the regulars file out, I'll let Luke run around the empty gym, and Gandle will teach him somersaults and tumbling, or lie on her back doing "airplane," pressing him up to the sky with her feet. So, if Luke seems happy to stick around after a session and I get to chat with an interesting woman who dresses the way she does, then I don't see a reason to hurry off anywhere else. She tends to leave first.

Gandle doesn't talk about herself much, but I've picked up on some stuff. She's had a rough ride. She transferred here from upstate New York a few years ago out of the only police team where deputies get a partner who lives in their house as part of the family—the K-9 unit. There's an ex-husband somewhere who doesn't sound like a nice guy, but no kids after much trying, and there will be no kids in the future and there is nothing else said on these topics. She misses that dog.

Today she sits motionless, listening to my story, arms folded, a hand covering her mouth—her expression isn't easy to read. I'm a little confused, here. I thought she would be pretty fired up to hear what I had to say. I mean, if this thing wasn't an accident and she runs with it, then this case could be a big one, the kind of thing that could make a career, maybe even get her bumped up from deputy to detective. And if she catches a heater like this, and bags a big elephant? People will notice.

But she stands up and paces the floor for a moment before glancing back at me. Whatever she's thinking, damned if I know.

"Maybe we should bring you in to talk with the sheriff," she says. "It's better if he hears this straight from you."

"That sounds great."

She's still looking at me curiously.

"What's the matter?" I ask.

"If you're going in there, then I need you to follow some ground rules."

"Okay."

Luke tries to lift a kettlebell twice his size, without success.

"Don't ask him about the case. In fact, don't say the word *case*, all right?

And don't ask him about the autopsy or any of this other stuff you keep bugging me about. That won't go over well."

One time, I asked her. One time, and she's giving me grief.

"Sure, of course," I say. "I wouldn't do that."

She bites into a blister and peels it away from her hand.

"And don't say anything about a heater," she tells me.

"I won't."

"Or bagging elephants. Or whatever. I don't know where you even get this crap."

"Just the facts, ma'am."

"See, that right there? That's the kind of thing I'm talking about."

"Got it. I hear you."

She's looking me over pretty well.

"And when you're in there with him?" she says. "Try not to seem *too* interested. Try not to come off so enthusiastic, you know what I mean? What's with you, by the way?"

"Nothing."

"Well, just remember what I said."

"Gandle. A guy like this? A guy like Townsend? This could be a huge deal if I'm right. Don't you get that?"

She rubs the side of her face and sighs.

"Yeah, I'm a little worried about this one," she says.

9

"TODAY SHOULD BE good," Frank said.

It was early one afternoon about a year ago and we were bouncing down the dirt road toward the ocean. His forecast seemed like high praise from a man who, until that day, had only ever said the surf was *doable, shitty, okay,* or *decent.* The boys sat in the backseat with their heads bobbling and didn't seem to notice. Frank explained that some hurricane in the Caribbean had sent us a groundswell, a long period, clean, but not so big that the River couldn't hold it without closing out, and I understood what some of that meant.

"You up for this?" Frank asked.

I didn't say anything. I hadn't decided yet.

"Just absorb the wave's energy," he said.

I shot him a look and he smiled. He wasn't trying to help—he was making stuff up, just being a prick.

"Don't look down," he said. "Look where you want to go."

The day was big. Well overhead. I might not have belonged out there, but I made it work. I survived the paddle out and sat there past the break, catching my breath. I kept my head on a swivel, trying to stay in the right position and not let some rogue tsunami sneak up and trap me inside, that terrible spot where I'd get pounded stupid by the next waves in the set landing right on top of my head. And I didn't want to drown in front of my son. I peered over a few cliffs and reared back in terror, but I took off on a couple peaks, making the drop, darting across the face faster than I ever have until they spat me out unscathed enough to paddle back outside the break and collect myself. I looked around the empty place, thinking, Did anyone just see that? Stupidest thing I ever did. But I'm alive. Let's do it again.

The wind dropped and the water kept getting glassier. The ocean looked like something I'd only seen online or in magazines, fancy places, the kind you can't help talking about even if you sound stoned trying to describe them. I came in after my turn on the water and walked my board up to the car. Frank sat in his truck with the boys. Everything felt good.

Neither of us saw a reason to rush out of there afterward. We had plenty to talk about after a day like that, and there were worse places to be than an empty beach, with a full cooler, watching the best swell of the year, while Luke filled his bucket with water and sand over and over again, telling us all about his plans on every trip. Even Frank wanted to chat more than usual—he'd dipped into the cooler without me. So, we sat there for a few hours and watched the ocean, drinking cold beer in cans, trading stories right up to sunset. We would have watched that, too, but we'd finished all the beer. And when we had emptied the cooler, we packed up, got the boys strapped into Frank's truck, and headed home from there. It had been a long day, and Frank was in no condition to get behind the wheel. So, like a lot of times back then, for a lot of the same reasons, I was driving.

I still think about the dark age. I don't think that I was trying to numb some sort of pain, or self-medicate, or look for a coping mechanism—that doesn't sound right. But maybe I thought, Here's something I can be good at. I'm willing to put in the time for a job with no interviews, no cutbacks or barriers to entry, no one to stop me from working, and I get to keep my own hours, be my own boss. There's still a sport I can play.

And for a little while, when we moved out here, after I started hanging out with Frank, that's what I did—I got back in the game. I can't remember when Frank started bringing his cooler with us. I just know I didn't complain. When you get a little momentum, things can accelerate.

So again, we got into a routine that became a ritual. Most of the time, we started down at the beach. After watching Luke for a long stretch and with the end of the day getting closer, I admit this part isn't very pretty, but a lot of the time I thought, Hey, I earned this, I *deserve* it. Sure, I wasn't working on an oil rig or putting out fires all afternoon, but I'd still been on duty, right? Didn't I work a shift? Sitting on the back of Frank's truck or standing in the sand—watching those two little rascals went much better with a beer in my hand. I told myself that I wasn't the first parent to sneak an attitude adjuster into their schedule. That's how it started.

Then things picked up speed. One day, we realized that after we got the kids down to sleep, when our wives came home from work, they could help us out. Because if they were around to watch the boys, that meant we could leave.

We went to Frank's shed a lot—it's a good-size shed behind his house. Inside, he always has a little project going, he shapes boards, he fixes stuff—the man builds things. And there was a point when the two of us spent a lot of time hanging out and getting loaded in that shed as Frank tinkered with some experiment that intrigued him. Some nights we couldn't even make it out after, and if we did, we slithered off to Lucky's Bar and Grill or, less often, the Old Bull Tavern. I tried to keep the Bull as a dinner spot with my son instead of stumbling in with Frank after a full day in the field.

But anyways, that was pretty much it. Frank's shed, the Bull, and a good bit of Lucky's. Some days, even if there was no surf, we'd still go to the River and just sit on the tailgate, with that cooler, watching the kids. Standing around a shed or the worst bar you can find, drinking beer and whiskey—I know that all of this must sound really impressive. But it wasn't. It got pretty dark. I'm not proud of this period. Maybe it started out innocent, but by the end it turned shameful, and I let it go on much longer than I should have. I regret most of it. I'm glad that it's over, I knew it would turn out wrong, something was bound to happen. And then, of course, something did.

We were just coming to the end of the dirt road, with the smell of the sea breeze still pouring in through the windows. I didn't want to be anywhere else. This song came on the radio, the one they play before kickoff at all the games, with that riff all the fans chant as they jump up and down, arm and arm in the stands. A great song for dropping the hammer. We listened to the intro, bouncing along the potholes, but then, right at the end of the road, just as the chords kicked in, I stepped on the pedal, spraying dust behind us, turning onto the blacktop. "Don't look down," Frank said, and he grinned, hanging his arm out the window, banging his hand on the door to the music. "Look where you want to go." I was really enjoying myself, and Frank looked happier than I'd ever seen him. Pedal down, we headed west, the fields flying by in the late September light, just off the ocean, an empty back road and a nice sunset. We had a lot of good energy. That intensity you look for in certain kinds of teams.

Frank saw the lights before I did.

"Cop," he said.

Glancing at the rearview, I saw he wasn't kidding. I pressed the brake and the speedometer started dropping, but it didn't look good. I signaled and pulled over. Frank put his beer in the center console and closed it. But that night, that was the least of my worries.

The cop took his time back there. I looked at myself in the rearview, a day's worth of salt water in my eyes, sun-red face and a stomach full of beer.

"Relax," Frank said. "We'll be all right. Just relax."

Chewing my lip, I didn't agree, and I couldn't relax. Like one of those workouts at the box, my heart rate was shooting off the screens and I tried to calm down, but I couldn't catch my breath. I started to sweat. Frank's face and his eyes—the way he looked wouldn't help anything, either.

The cop got out and walked toward us, an older guy. He stared at the boys in their car seats as he passed. I rolled down the window. He asked for my license and registration and I gave them to him. He didn't study them long—he kept looking up at the boys. Then he looked at me.

"Do you know how fast you were going?" he asked.

I didn't.

"I'm not a traffic cop," he said. "I followed you for a little bit back there. Do you know how fast you were going?"

I told him I wasn't sure.

"You were over sixty."

I didn't know what to say to that. Then he asked if I knew the speed limit. But he didn't wait for me to answer. He helped me out.

"That's a twenty-five."

I closed my eyes. Frank kept staring straight ahead.

"Where you boys coming from?"

We were just at the beach, I told him. He asked if these were my sons, and I explained the best I could.

"You had anything to drink? You have a few beers at the beach?"

I don't know how the book says you're supposed to answer that question when you get pulled over. We must have smelled like a brewery and looked quite a bit worse. Two red-faced idiots. I didn't want to lie to him—for some reason I thought it might piss him off. I stared up at him.

"No, I haven't," I said.

Which seemed to make him more pissed. He studied Frank, then glanced back at the boys, shaking his head. Then he looked back at me.

"Step out of the—"

But a voice called out. Somewhere behind me. I'd heard the voice before.

"*What about dis?*" Luke yelled with glee. Before anyone could answer, he threw a juice box on the floor. He leaned forward in his car seat, admiring his work, thinking through his next steps. "*Trash,*" he said.

The cop stood up straight and stared at Luke through the window. He stood there for a moment, watching my son who called out a few other observations that occurred to him. Frank didn't move. I don't know what he was looking at, but he never took his eyes off it.

The cop turned his head and looked down the road, as if he'd left something behind him back there. Then he turned in the other direction to see if it lay up ahead.

The road was empty.

He stood there for a while and then he sighed.

My insides were bouncing around in my stomach. Whatever makes you accelerate—once you pick up that speed, the stop's always sudden. And it never feels good.

The cop leaned his head back in my window.

"I think I'm going to do you a favor here," he said. "You live pretty close by, right? Why don't you get on home. Drive a little more carefully."

I let out a loud breath before I could stop myself. His idea sounded much better than anything I could have imagined. I nodded up at him. I felt empty. He handed my license and registration back to me and I took them. I kept trying not to smile. But then he had something else to say.

"I want you to listen to me for a minute now. I want you to know how something works."

I nodded again.

"Let's say someone was doing sixty in a twenty-five," he said. "Let's say they refuse a Breathalyzer, or they don't pass. And they have two kids who look under fourteen in the car with them. Just for instance."

He took his sunglasses off. He had blue eyes, and they were looking at me.

"That's not just a DWI. That's not a traffic violation, not a slap on the wrist. That's a felony, a criminal charge. You know what it's called?"

I didn't. I didn't know anything.

"It's called *Endangering the Welfare of a Child*. You won't just lose your license. Pay a fine. Do some time. Put it on every job application for the rest of your life. There's something else."

I looked up at him. He stared back.

"Yeah, that's right. You got it. They put you on the State Register for Child Abuse. Then Child Services gets involved. It's out of my hands. And they go from there."

Frank didn't say anything, either.

"So maybe you guys think about that. Maybe drive more careful."

I thanked him, and he didn't respond. He walked back to his cruiser. I waited there on the side of the road and after what seemed like a while, he pulled out and drove off. Luke waved at him as he passed us. But I sat there a little longer, doing what he said, and thought about what I'd heard.

We didn't say much on the drive home. I didn't turn the radio back on, so I had some more time to think. The boys were asleep when I pulled into my driveway and shut off the engine. I was done for the night. Frank would have to make it home himself, or he could sleep on the couch. He wasn't in great shape, but he'd driven a lot worse. I wanted to rush out of the truck, unclip my son, carry him inside, and gently lay him in his crib, but I didn't. We sat in the dark for a while, looking at my home. We could hear the crickets starting up with the ocean in the distance, and when the time came for me to unburden myself, I spoke to the windshield.

"Okay," I said. "That's about it for me. I'm done. No more. That's it."

When he didn't say anything, I shook my head and kept going.

"That was too close."

Frank rubbed his chin for a bit. I don't know what he was thinking, but I'd begun to care much less about that.

"This isn't working," I said, not worried about having the right words. "Whatever I'm doing here. It's not working. And if that didn't get my attention, then I don't want to know what it's gonna take. I'm done."

Frank sighed and didn't say anything for a while.

Then he looked at me and shrugged. "Don't beat yourself up. It happens. Stuff like this happens. Get some sleep."

I didn't respond—there was no reason to argue with him. I had a lot more to say but figured I'd save it. So again, we just sat there in the car, listening to the roar of the waves along the coast and then the quiet between them. After a while, Frank checked something on his phone and nodded. He looked up, out the window, toward the ocean, elbow resting on the door, his chin in his hand and said, "Tomorrow should be good."

10

THE POLICE STATION is a gray brick building with a flat roof. Except for the half dozen cruisers in the parking lot, it looks like a DMV. It doesn't seem busy. We don't see any undesirables or prostitutes lurking outside, thinking over recent missteps and next moves. No twitchy, violent offenders hand-cuffed and dragged indoors by their elbows, eyes hunting for more victims, or any long-haired, frightened hippie types getting perp walked inside. They do have a wheelchair ramp at the front entrance next to the stairs that helps with my stroller. I'm rolling in with backup.

Inside, the station is bright. At reception, a uniformed woman sits behind the open glass panel along a wide counter. It feels like I could be here to take out a deposit or fill a prescription. When I introduce myself and explain the reasons for our visit, she's friendly and doesn't seem bothered in the least by my small partner strapped in his seat. Maybe she sees this sort of thing all the time.

"Let me just check on this," she says, smiling at Luke.

I've never been in one of these places before. It's quiet. The halls are empty. A large Stars and Stripes hangs limply from a flag stand in the corner. Behind the reception desk, two patrolmen discuss a speeding stop and a "woman with real attitude, worse than that asshole in August." They stop talking and look over at me when one of them realizes I'm listening. I smile at them, but they don't return it. They start talking again in lower voices, and we pass the time like this until the receptionist comes back.

"You're going this way," she says. "Sheriff will be right with you."

The cops are looking at me again when she directs us into a little side room down the main corridor. There are a couple folding chairs spread out around a table. I leave Luke in his stroller and take one of the seats. We sit here for almost a half hour and my well-behaved backup starts asking some questions, a few of them reasonable. If he gets restless, he might make a scene. But we still have a good chunk of time before dinner and bedtime, at least.

When the door opens and the sheriff walks in, I realize I've made a terrible mistake. The man comes over to introduce himself, but we've met before, and our first date wasn't a good one. It's the cop who pulled me over last year. He shakes my hand, looks over at Luke for a sec with a half-smile that vanishes as soon as he looks back at me. He walks away to sit down behind the desk across from us. Leaning back in his chair, he folds his hands in his lap and doesn't say anything. I feel like an asshole. The sheriff sports a comb-over and an expression that suggests he would rather be somewhere else. Maybe bringing Luke was a mistake. I start to wonder if Gandle set this up as a prank, just to screw with me. The sheriff still hasn't said anything. Maybe he thinks I'm messing with *him*, that we came here as some absurd gesture of gratitude. *Thanks again for your help that day—yikes—I had a rough one! Look at this little guy, isn't he cute?*

But I need to stop feeling sorry for myself and get my feet under me a little bit.

"Well, thanks for making the time to meet with me," I tell him, feeling like I'm in a job interview.

"I appreciate you coming in," he says. "I was told you had some information about a recent incident?"

I figure I should get started.

"So, like everybody else, I read about a body washing up that Saturday morning and I wondered who the guy was. Then a few days later, when I saw it was Robert, the whole thing didn't make any sense. They say he went missing Thursday, but that's the weird part—I saw him that Thursday down at the ocean..."

The door opens behind me. Gandle walks into the room without saying hello. She leans against the wall across from the sheriff and folds her arms, but gives a quick smile to Luke, who looks happy to see her. She has a little notepad in her hand.

"Please go on," says the sheriff, without acknowledging his deputy.

"Well, I drove down to the beach that afternoon."

"Which beach?"

"It's a spot about two miles down from Daggett Road."

Gandle starts writing in her pad, and the sheriff is either getting all of this or will borrow her notes afterward, I guess.

"And what time was this?" he asks.

"It was about four thirty or five, and I was down there checking out the water, but it didn't look good."

"Four thirty or five," says the sheriff. The phrase doesn't come out as a question, but he doesn't sound too sure, either.

Thinking back to that day, what time *was* it? Not sunset. And it wasn't that late-afternoon light you get around here in autumn when the sky turns so pretty against the reeds and the leaves. It had been drizzling and windy; the sky was cloudy and shitty. I'd had Luke with me, after school.

"About five," I tell him.

"And you said something about the water?"

"Sure. Just that the conditions were terrible."

"Why's that?" he asks. For some reason, I feel like I'm meeting a girl's father for the first time.

"Well, with surfing, wind is a big factor. Because when it's really windy, especially as it blows onshore, it sort of flattens the waves out, and it makes the waves mushy and bumpy and—"

"People don't surf when it's windy?" he asks.

It occurs to me that he has lived by the ocean for a long time, and that in this part of the world, there are many people who will paddle out in all sorts of crap on their weekends, and that I am not the best guy to explain this.

"No, they do sometimes," I admit. "But it's a couple of things. You want the ocean sort of orderly. And when there's too much wind, it just churns it up like a washing machine and makes a big mess. It's not just the size of the waves."

I could tell him to picture a windswept bay with all those whitecaps moving in the water. Then imagine all that chop colliding with your average incoming swell from another direction—it makes for a lot of confusion. Whereas on a clear, glassy day, you can look out at the horizon and spot a wave coming, just a bump on the water line, and you watch it approaching, probably a decent bet there's one or two behind it, and then hopefully you get yourself in the right place.

The sheriff doesn't look swayed either way.

"Well, anyhow," I tell him. "I was down there and I saw Townsend in his car. I walked over and said hello and I asked him if he was going in the water and he said no. Didn't look doable."

Without much of a reaction, he asks, "And then?"

"Well. That was pretty much it. We didn't say much. I had my son with me and I had to get him back home, so we left."

"If you had your son with you, how were you going to go for a surf?"

"Well, I couldn't have gone. I wouldn't do that."

"Then why were you down there?"

"Sometimes I just drive down to the ocean to check it out."

He covers his mouth with his fist, taking a moment to process this. Then he scratches his chin.

"What do you do for a living?" he asks.

"I'm out of work right now. But I look after my son."

He doesn't respond. But he nods, as if something makes sense now—the first time I've seen him do this. I'm starting to think I could get a little annoyed here, in a minute.

"Anyway, I didn't stick around too long. I drove home with Luke. But the papers said afterward that they found Townsend's car up at Hamilton. That's a long drive, and this time of year, it gets dark pretty quick. So, it just doesn't make any sense to me that he would turn around from that beach and head up the highway to try again."

The sheriff takes this in for a moment and then glances over at Gandle, who has closed her notebook and seems pretty quiet today. The four of us sit around looking at each other.

"Okay," he says. "Is that it?"

"Well, I don't know," I ask him. "I mean, what's next?"

He considers this for a moment.

"We appreciate you coming in," he says.

"I mean, what are the next steps in the investigation? Given this new information."

Gandle shakes her head, staring down at the desk.

"Thank you for coming in," the sheriff says again.

Luke glances up at me.

"So, you're not going to do anything with this?" I ask. "That's it? Is that what you're saying?" Gandle doesn't make eye contact with me.

"Do you mind if I call you Pete?" the sheriff asks. "We may have some information that you don't. I'm afraid we can't discuss this type of matter with you any more than that. But we appreciate your help."

"Are you saying you think this was all just an accident?" I ask.

"What I think you need to remember is that a man has died here," he says. "This man had a family. Please try to remember that. And this is a very sensitive and very difficult time for that family. So that's something you might want to consider. I think that's what's important for you to know, right now."

"I've quit drinking," I tell him. Luke nods in agreement, and Gandle rubs her nose. The sheriff seems unfazed.

"Good," he says finally.

"I mean, if you're worried that my drinking has something to do with anything I've said. I don't drink anymore. I just want you to know that."

Gandle's face tells me that I'm doing worse than she could have imagined and won't do much better anytime soon. It occurs to me that I never mentioned that roadside encounter to her—it's not the kind of story you tell around the box, or one you bring up with cops.

"That's good to hear," says the sheriff. He looks over at Gandle for a second and then turns back to me.

"I hope that bringing my son wasn't a problem."

"Of course not," he says waving a hand at me. "I understand. We see that all the time."

"So then, what's next?" I ask. My partner next to me sucks his thumb and studies the players at the table. He can't help me, either. But at least he hasn't shit himself or fallen asleep.

"I'm worried you aren't listening to me now," the sheriff says, leaning forward in his chair. "There's been a terrible tragedy. No family should have to go through something like this. It's a very sensitive matter. I appreciate you coming down here, but I don't really have much more that I can say to you that would be appropriate. Can you appreciate that?"

I'm holding my tongue but wanting to scream—look, let's say Townsend thought I was a jerk and he wanted to ditch me because I suck since I'm out of work. I get that, I do. But you know Daggett Road? Great, good for you. Now how far is that to Hammy's? About ten miles, as the crow flies. But how long is that drive? Fifteen minutes. But at that time of day, it'd be more like half an hour, and he would know that. Yes, yes, he's out from the city, but he's not dumb. So you're saying that as soon as I turn off the end of that road, he peels out right behind me to drive half an hour in the rain over to Hammy's, and what, just hopes for the best? That somehow the clouds would part or the tides would change and the wind would suddenly shift? Why? So he can throw on a wet suit and sprint down to the water before sunset at six? And what if he just wanted to get wet? If he'd just said fuck it, I need the exercise—and look, it's a little embarrassing and I don't usually tell anyone else this, but I know how that goes. Sometimes I go for a paddle when the ocean's a wading pool, just to stay in shape for a sport I'm not really great at, and you betcha I look like a prick—and that's fine, Sheriff, whatever, but riddle me this. If Townsend's on my program, the Body by Pete, or if he wanted to paddle out only so he could say that he did, why not just go in down by where he saw me?

"Are you all right?" asks the sheriff. "You seem a little frustrated."

Well, when you try to help someone out and they treat you like a total piece of crap, how are you supposed to feel about it? Is this just your standard, bureaucrat apathy? Tax dollars well spent?

"Have you learned anything from the autopsy?" I ask him, instead.

Gandle's mouth drops open. The sheriff shakes his head, massages his palm with his thumb, flexes his fingers, as if he has a knot in his hand. And I figure if I'm down here I might as well keep firing away, since I've already made the trip.

"Is this case still open?" I ask him. Now Gandle's eyes glare like headlights, and she's flashing her brights. In her defense, I *did* tell her I wouldn't do anything like this.

"Well, so you know, this investigation is closed," says the sheriff. Gandle, aghast, looks over at him but just as quickly corrects herself, staring down at the floor. "And you should probably be happy about that," he adds.

"Why's that?" I ask him.

"Because you were the last person to see Robert Townsend alive. Nice talking to you, Pete. Thanks for coming in today."

He stands up and comes over to shake my hand, then makes his exit. Which leaves me sitting here with Gandle.

Now, I expect hell that hath no fury, and she has every right to be pissed, but on the other hand, this whole time, she stood there and didn't say a damn thing. And sure, I've been chewed out by all kinds of women in every corner of this nation, of different shapes and sizes, and I wasn't even dating most of them and I'll never get a chance to. But the truth is, it's a nasty business that doesn't get much easier. Gandle takes her time, moving slowly, like when she first steps into the gym, trading smiles and fist bumps with the regulars, all the monsters, glad to see her, scowling and ready to lift. She doesn't say anything to me. Doesn't even glance in my direction. But she can't help reaching out to rustle my son's hair as she walks out the door. When she leaves, I let out a long sigh, wondering how that could have gone any worse.

11

AFTER A FULL day of watching Luke, sometimes I need a little help. Today hasn't felt like a short one. We skip the box after the police station and make a trip to the local dump before the grocery store. Then we go home and sit around, looking at each other for a few hours, and I keep rehashing what I could have said differently with the sheriff and Gandle. But reliving it doesn't make the day go by any faster, and before long, I feel like getting out of the house.

Somewhere between sunset and last light we saddle up.

"Where are we going?" Luke asks as I clip him into his car seat.

"We're going to the Bull," I tell him, resting Monkey on his lap. He nods at this.

The Old Bull Tavern sits off the highway, a few miles outside of town. This time of year, we can find a few spots to park in around back, and we hold hands—*hold hands hold hands*—through the parking lot, like always. The inside smells of stale beer, fried batter, woodsmoke, grilled meat, and liquor, but now Luke sprints ahead, dodging traffic over to the empty pool table, and starts rubbing the cue ball along the felt. We sit at the bar, the way we always do.

I take him here a decent amount. We've all seen kids melt down in restaurants or airports, as parents and strangers beg them to settle down, and Luke's had his rough moments in the past. So, I think it's a good thing for him to learn how to behave himself around grown-ups, and he knows the rules. If he starts acting out or screaming or crying or throwing things, then he gets picked up and carried out the door, just like anyone else. But now he hardly ever throws a tantrum. People love to be around him. I'm very proud of Luke.

You should cherish a spot where you can feed the little guy and make an appearance out on the town. If I can chew up a couple hours while keeping out of my wife's hair and still watch him, who says that's not doing my job or helping her out? Plus, now that I'm not drinking anymore, I don't need to feel guilty about our routine. Even better, tonight I'm not just here to shoot the breeze and watch the minutes pass. I figure, if you need to find some information, you could do a lot worse than your local tavern.

Noel reaches from behind the bar to offer me a handshake and a good-size smile. They always have mac 'n' cheese for Luke, and there's a smoked mesquite chicken special tonight, so I order both with an apple juice and ginger ale. I'm not some animal—we bring our own sippy cup.

Noel is an almost supernaturally friendly Irishman built like a bouncer who knows a remarkable amount about the history, outcome, prospects, strategy, and controversy of every athletic contest past or future played by anyone at any level anywhere on any corner of the Earth. Sometimes we trade weight-loss or exercise advice and recommendations on self-help books. He's full of industry and optimism, and he knows a lot about many different subjects, since he reads a ton, works three jobs, and has a bunch of friends. In addition to tending bar, he caddies at a local golf course and takes care of an elderly woman. I've heard we can absorb things from other people, that we become who we hang out with, so, since we moved out here, I've tried to spend as much time around him as I can. Noel is a good man.

But he's a little jammed up right now. He has customers, a few couples, some regulars around the bar watching football since they started playing on these sacrilegious Thursday nights. Luke's asking people about the juice they drink, and I spread some butter on a piece of corn bread and hand it to him. I feel very good. I remember the last time we were here.

A couple of weeks ago, I was at a music class with my son. One of the moms from school hosts around a dozen of us at her home every Wednesday afternoon—she takes care of the whole show. They say music class is good for toddler brain development and other important things. But either way, it's a nice event, and it's good of her to invite us.

I was sitting on the living room floor with the moms in a half circle around an energetic guy who played guitar and rattled tambourines for us as the kids stumbled around the carpet, rocking out. Halfway through the class, Luke started a fight—not his first—and I broke it up. Luke needed a few minutes of time-out and one very public lecture on sharing, and when he returned from his neutral corner, he hugged the other boy and said that he was sorry. I hope the moms were pleased. Their opinions about this sort of thing matter to me a great deal.

The woman who hosts us is kind of interesting. She's very busy, but she still always seems like she's in a good mood—she's never been anything but kind to me, anyway. Plus, she has a good sense of humor. She's very bright and she went to a great school. She's also very pretty. And she has a good body, too. I would devour this woman, just inhale her, she could do anything she wants to me, I'd let her degrade me, whatever's she into, I want her to ruin my life. So basically, she's like most of the moms at our school.

So I just sat there, as usual, trying not to make eye contact with anyone, trying to stay focused on my son, who is also quite wonderful, in his own way. We need to get invited back. Then, just when my thoughts started to get weird, I felt my phone vibrate with a text from Lauren.

Where r u? she asked.

music class, I wrote back.

Fun!

So much fun, I agreed.

Send me pics! Fyi my phone is dying

OK.

I've thought a lot about my wife's cell phone battery over the years, but I don't have much interesting to report. Sometimes, I wonder if the text message is the worst thing that ever happened to marriage. This device that transfers every thought, worry, or question instantly into your spouse's brain, all the time, anywhere on Earth, without interruption. Texts are dangerous.

I took some pictures of my son, which got some smiles around the campfire, and I grinned at a harmless object on the floor. But I had a long way to go. On paper at least, Wednesday nights should be an opportunity for me. Because Wednesday is not Monday. Monday, when my wife goes to her Moms' Group meeting, which always runs late as they sit around, cackle, and probably drink wine from a fire hose. The same Moms' Group that I'm never invited to and, if asked, wouldn't ever attend. Wednesday is also not Thursday, which features her night class, the latest, pointless course she's decided to study. I can't even remember what she's taking. Now, sure, you might say that you need to respect continuing education and her industrious spirit and that's great, but it still leaves me home, watching Luke by myself, one more night out of the week.

Nights like this in a more civilized society would give me a chance to get back to the house at a reasonable hour, hand him off to my beloved, and enjoy my remaining years. I could drop him with Lauren and squeeze in a little surf before sunset. But half the time, she's traveling. She's always on some road show to bucket list cities like Baltimore and Boston for knife fights with the big mutual funds and insurance companies, or else she's in New York, a town where people just want to relax and not talk about finance. My wife comes home tired, and I don't blame her.

Did he nap? Has he slept? she asked. I didn't respond.

he NEEDS to sleep, she added.

Yes, I wrote back.

Sitting there on the floor, glancing up at my son, I checked the surf report on my phone, and not for the first time. It was still doable. The timing of sunset, the tides, the size of the three-foot swell at eight-second intervals, the direction and speed of the wind, the ocean and air temperature, the cloud cover—none of them had changed in the last twenty minutes. I don't need perfect. Just doable. I don't go in idiot conditions, as the cops and newspapers would have us believe my friend Townsend paddled into the other day. But I understand the itch. I know the feeling of everyday life in all its epic cruelty, conspiring to fuck up the simplest one-hour surf session and the brief feeling of peace it can bring. That panic of checking your watch, thinking of your calendar, negotiating with your own standards, because if today doesn't happen, you may not get another chance anytime soon. I know the feeling well. And maybe, though I don't believe it, maybe Townsend felt this same dreadful itch that fateful Thursday, a longing he couldn't smother. Maybe his wife kept texting. And maybe it killed him.

I looked up from my surf report to watch my son lose himself to the joys of dance, but still, I couldn't rest easy. We were miles from shore. Not long after, another text rolled in.

What time will u be home? she asked.

Now, this wasn't my first music class. I've danced this tune before. So I knew that if I texted my true hopes, she would only laugh at my dream to get on the water. Something would come up, she'd run late, send me on some painful chore. She'd wreck a train to stop me from surfing. It's gotten bad enough that I have wondered if she checks the forecast herself just to sabotage my plans. I'm not kidding. Whenever it's an epic day, the kind you wait for, and the water's packed with happy paddlers, somehow my wife isn't around to help out. In perfect conditions, my wife vanishes—and she never takes Luke, you can bet on it. If I didn't have Frank, I'd never get in the ocean. So, when she asked me what time I'd be home, I put some real thought into my response before I sent it.

About 530-545, I wrote.

OK, she said.

If I told her 5:15 p.m., fifteen minutes after music class ended, I'd screw myself, because she'd send me on an errand. But if I showed up at 5:45 p.m. for the handoff, I could be at the River a little after 6:00 p.m. and have about an hour until it gets dark and the scary fish come out. But I wasn't in the clear. I still had to wait her out. I tried to reach Frank—we could bring the boys, split it up, each get thirty minutes in, but I didn't get any response. He works on occasion. I knew I was on my own.

Where are u? she texted at 5:15 p.m. The class had finished, but some kids were still playing around, and the host hadn't kicked us out. She's a saint.

Still here, I wrote. I started sweating, not profusely. It was early still.

Can you pick something up for me?

Sure.

Can you get swim diapers?

Yes. I could. That's CVS. That's not a problem, open twenty-four hours. I know this well. I was still above water—you can pick up swim diapers any time of night.

he also needs that organic chickn and avocados has to be organic both for lunch tomorrow.

OK, I wrote. You're hurting me, I could have said, but I didn't.

And small screwdriver for batteries on fire truck. batteries out. need batteries.

OK.

What time r u getting home? she asked.

When my wife says organic that can mean only one place. I'm not sure if she knows this market is in a different mall from CVS or if she cares. Of course, she must know. Sometimes I think she likes sending me to two malls in opposite directions during rush hour. But I still had some daylight. Maybe I could drop him off, guarantee that I would get all the items on her list tonight, no problem, just after a quick surf?

also we're out of milk. WHOLE organic, she added.

Chernobyl. All is lost. Game over. He needs milk before bed.

He really NEEDS his milk before bed, she texted.

But if I left in a great hurry, maybe I could get him home by 6:15 or 6:30? I'd get maybe thirty minutes on the water. I don't know why she needed to add organic. I don't know how many cartons of *whole* organic milk I've bought the last few years, but it's a lot. Then again, the number of times I've returned home carrying my son and a fresh batch of pain-in-my-balls-to-get milk after being told we're out and he REALLY NEEDS it, only to find an unfinished carton sitting in the fridge. That's not a small number, either. I complained about this to her once. It didn't go over well.

I tried getting my son to leave. That didn't go over well, either. I tried again, but he started wailing and then he wouldn't stop. A few of them shot me understanding glances and all nonsense aside, no fooling around, no stupid fantasies, I appreciated this. But I wasn't going anywhere soon, that much I knew.

Half an hour later, I'd said my goodbyes and told our gracious host how nice it was for her to have us every week, and then apologized for staying so long.

"No problem," she said. "It's so much fun when Luke's around! Both of you."

I thanked her again. I strapped Luke into his car seat and, sitting there in the driveway, I saw a new text.

Where r u? he needs to eat

He will eat, I wrote.

Where r u?

Still at music

Don't stay too long after class it's not fair. She's very nice to host. I'm running late. not sure how long. U need to thank her for hosting.

OK, I wrote back.

My phone is dying, she said.

I thought about that hour around sunset, when the wind drops, the waves get cleaner, and the surf casters are starting up for the night. When you carry your stuff up the sand back to the car, with that smell of wax mixed with salt, and by the time you rinse off, get changed, pack up, stand there for a moment hearing the ocean, you look around and now it's dark out, but you can still see.

My son wailed from the backseat. When he's buckled into his seat in the car he likes to keep moving. Sitting still gets hard on him; he needs forward progress. It's not his fault. None of it's his fault. I texted my wife.

We'll pick up the stuff and get dinner on the road.

Good idea, she wrote back sometime later.

And so that's what we did. After we ran the errands, we came here and ate at the bar. I had a good chat with Noel while Luke worked the crowd, asking people questions or giving out instructions, charming man, woman, and child around him the way the little guy always does. A typical Wednesday, in other words.

Sometime later the texts started up again.

Where r u?

What time will you be home?

Send me pics

My phone is dying FYI.

———

But tonight has a different feel to it. So when the trickle of customers seems to stop and Noel stands, hands in pockets, peering over his taps, I get his attention.

"Have you heard about the guy who washed up on Saturday morning?" I ask him.

"Scary that. Fucking hell," he says and then winces, looking over at Luke. "Sorry, pal."

I wave it off. That's part of the sport; just put it on my tab with the others. Dad needs to get out in the world.

"Very scary," I agree. "Have you heard much about what happened?"

"Just that he drowned," Noel says with a shrug. I wait for him to expand, as he often will, but he doesn't.

"I meant, did you hear anything about how?" I ask.

"They're saying he either knocked himself out or that he broke his neck somehow."

"Broke his neck?"

"That's what I heard," he says. Someone catches his eye and asks for a pint. I wonder if they had done an autopsy, but maybe they can't always tell if certain injuries were pre- or postmortem?

"But a lot of people around here have been talking about it, right?" I ask him.

"More up at the course," he says. "Mental up there."

"Why? Was he a member at the place?"

"Sure," he says. "Longtime. Longtime."

My old boss used to say you could learn a lot about someone from how they play golf. Some guys claim to be six handicaps, but they can't break a hundred. Some throw clubs. And then you have your cheaters.

Noel tops off a lager, eyes scanning the room, and adds, "That's where they're doing the reception for him after the service. Expecting a massive turnout."

It would be, I guess, for a guy like that.

"Did you know him at all?" I ask.

"No," he explains. Sometimes, Noel sends me YouTube videos—motivational speeches. We watch rugby tournaments here at odd hours and he'll explain strategy to me. He seems colder than usual tonight.

"Ever caddy for him?" I ask. One of his regulars calls over for a Guinness.

"No," he says. "Never had the honor." Noel will share a drink and trade jokes with us most evenings but wears no trace of a smile now as he pulls a tap, the black stuff pouring down into the tilted glass like crude oil released from a pipe.

"Why do you say that?" I ask.

Noel dries his hands on a rag. "The man was a bit of a prick," he says.

"How so?"

"A few stories, here and there."

"What kind of stories?"

"I'd rather not say."

"A few hidden balls? The pocket wedge? Not counting a few strokes here and there?"

He hesitates but doesn't say no, and I wait him out.

"All right, a few years back," he says, "I knew a fella in from Cork, working over here, caddying at the club for the summer. Spends his nights getting pissed and pulling American girls. Anyways, the lad carried two bags for him on a Saturday. It's July. But your man's playing shite—spends most of his round in the woods. And the lad's on safari chasing after his balls. When they finish eighteen, fucking eejit tips him a fiver."

The standard freight for eighteen holes runs about a hundred bucks up there.

"The lad said to him, 'Well, stick with the game. You'll get the hang of it.'"

I'm sure that's just what Townsend wanted to hear.

"You gotta like that, right?" I ask. But Noel's not smiling.

"Fucker went and got him fired, though, didn't he?" he says.

"Shit."

It's funny how when people talk about a guy like Townsend, they'll tell you all about his résumé, where he works, and what an all-star he is. That's all anyone cares about. Meanwhile the guy would stiff caddies and then get them laid off.

"And the club—they went along with Townsend on that?" I ask.

Noel polishes a glass with a towel.

"Anyways," he says. "Terrible, what happened to the fella. Tragic."

I can't tell if he means Townsend or the caddy.

Sometime later, I need to get Luke home, and when we settle up for the evening, I make sure to leave a generous gratuity. We shake hands again and he makes silly faces at my son. Coming here wasn't a bad use of time. Noel may have started out cautious and light on specifics, but his story told me everything I needed to hear.

No way that guy's death was an accident. No fucking way.

12

THE OBITUARIES CAME out today.

I read them this morning along with everyone else. The *Times*, Bloomberg, even the local papers carried them. They focused on his career, his background, his wife, his charities. They all concluded he was a terrific guy. None of them mention any suspicious circumstances surrounding his death. None of them talk about those times on the water when he snubbed me.

Tonight, my wife gets home on the later side, and I'm glad to see her. I can't stop thinking about this mess and I need a sounding board, I want to flush it out. I let Luke stay up a little past his bedtime so Lauren could get a chance to see him, and he's not complaining. He's running wild by the time she walks through door, ready for action. She gets a good half hour in with him before she needs to carry him down to bed. I'm almost jealous of her when he rests his cheek against her shoulder. It's a nice feeling, and little boys don't let you have it too often. I follow them down a few minutes later and catch her tiptoeing out of his room. She looks exhausted. She works long hours, and this final effort of the day wipes her out.

I'm not sure why but I ask if she wants to stay up and watch a movie with me. We haven't done that in a while.

"Shhhhhh," she says.

"Sorry," I whisper.

"I'm spent," she says. "I'm exhausted."

"Do you want anything to eat?"

She shakes her head in response, and I follow her into our bedroom. Where I can keep bothering her.

"Did you read any of the obituaries today?" I ask.

"What do you mean?"

"Townsend's?"

"No. What did I miss?" She sits down on the bed and starts taking off her clothes.

"They're saying he was a business visionary and a charitable leader. A Christlike figure. Everyone agrees he was a great American."

"Okay," she says and rubs her forehead in pain. "Here we go."

I ignore her. I've done this before, and I'll do it again.

"I know for a fact the guy was the world's worst asshole."

She sighs and seems puzzled by this simple statement of fact.

"I thought you said you didn't know him," she says, frowning. Lauren's always second-guessing me, trying to piss me off. It never ends.

"He was sketchy," I tell her. "Not a good guy. Why you looking at me like that?"

"I didn't say anything."

Lauren doesn't like it when I criticize these masters of the universe. She's always so *impressed* with people. Always asking me pointless questions. Did I hear so and so got promoted? Or if I knew that somebody was the head of something? And by the way, that's a really big deal? Lauren's kind of a social climber.

"Do you know what a bunch of lottery winners these guys are?" I ask. "Do you know what a joke this business is? They get one goddam call right and then some idiot pension fund chucks them a billion dollars to let them charge the most egregious fees in history—what's the matter?"

"I just don't think I can hear this speech again tonight."

My wife's a little bit of a starfucker.

"Yeah, but these guys are worse than the rest of them. I hear that firm is shady as hell. Illegal shit. Did you know that?"

"Yeah. I've heard about them. They have a reputation. But I'm really tired tonight and the poor guy's dead, Pete, he had a family. Whatever sins he committed, he's been punished for them. What more do you want?"

I think of something that should have come up earlier and change tacks.

"Hey. Do you have people at your firm who do business with GDR? The fund of funds guys must, right?"

"I'm sure we do. But it would be people on the private equity team."

"Yeah, that's what I meant. Anyway. Could I talk to one of them?"

"Sure. What for?"

"I wanted to ask about Townsend. Why are you making that face?"

She shrugs at me.

"I told you nothing about this story makes sense."

"Okay," she says.

"I don't believe that guy drowned. It might have been a suicide, maybe—"

"Jesus, Pete!" She looks horrified.

"Or maybe not. I don't know. But it wasn't an accident. Where are you going?"

"I heard you. I heard you. I just can't do this again tonight."

She says that to me every night.

"So, can I talk to your PE guys?" I ask.

"Are you serious?"

"Yeah. Why not?"

"So, you can ask them if someone committed suicide?"

"What's your problem?"

"Do you really want me to say this?"

"Go ahead. What's the matter? You think I'll get mad?"

"Oh no. Of course not."

Is she laughing at me?

"Why don't you want me to talk with—"

"Because I work with these guys," she snaps. "Do you get that?"

I'm looking at her now, trying to tell her something. But she's seen this stare before and she doesn't seem impressed.

"It's *embarrassing!*" she adds.

"That's great. Thanks."

"Don't you have anything better to do?"

Damn, she's really going there tonight. I can feel my eye start to twitch, but I can't let her see *that*, so I look the other away. I need to catch my breath.

"I'm sorry," she says. "I didn't mean that."

Which is bullshit, of course. She meant every word. She wanted that off her chest.

"What for?" I ask. "You don't need to be sorry."

I'm glad we're having this chat. I really am. This is the kind of stuff I need to know.

"Listen," she says. "Please don't get angry..."

"Who's angry?"

She sits down on the bed and holds her face in her hands. She says, "I just think if you could talk to someone. You know, about what happened to you? Then you could work through some of it...please let me finish. You could work through it better. Because this whole *every finance guy is a crook, where's my government bailout thing?* You never used to talk this way."

She thinks because I spend my days in a hooded sweatshirt changing diapers that I'm dumb as a bucket of shit. She's just like everyone else. It doesn't matter what I say about Townsend, she could care less. I could tell her they found him wrapped in plastic. When you're out of a job, no one listens to you, even if you have command of the facts. Your opinion doesn't matter. You may as well not even exist to them. That includes your wife. Especially your wife.

"Just because a guy makes a ton of money doesn't mean he's a hero," I grumble. "And he wasn't some sort of saint. That much I know."

She looks more sad than frustrated now.

"When you get like this, it doesn't do you any favors, that's all," she says. "You're just so angry all the time. And then you get so obsessed with some of these *conspiracy theories.*"

The sketchiest prick on Wall Street drives out for a surf on the worst day of the year and now he's no longer with us. What rotten luck. But if I find any of this crap suspicious, that makes me some sort of tinfoil hat communist?

"When you get like this," she says, "you just don't make any sense."

"Just because I got let go doesn't mean I have shit for brains. I'm not stupid. I'm not a fucking idiot. All right?"

She looks up at me.

"I didn't say that, Pete. I really didn't. And I really can't do this again tonight."

With that she climbs under the covers and puts on her eye mask. Which means that we're done.

So I sneak out of the bedroom and step outside to walk this off. This is one of the only things I miss about the city. If you lose your head some night in your apartment you can walk out your door and wander into the streets, look in a few restaurant and bar windows, hear the traffic, feel the energy of a neighborhood, pass some other humans, but you're still anonymous on every block. These hikes feel a little different out here. The country gets pretty quiet at night. My sighs and my footsteps along the blacktop make the only sounds, so I must look like what I am—some guy walking up and down an empty road in the dark.

Lauren doesn't understand. She's just so worried about what people think that she can't see past anything else. She's not interested in whether or not I'm right or wrong, she just doesn't want to feel embarrassed. It's the only thing she really cares about. She doesn't get it.

The nights are getting colder, and this feels like it could be a long one— I should have brought a jacket.

Look, nobody wants to make an ass out of themselves, here. But I'll tell you something else she doesn't understand, and it wasn't easy for me to learn this either, and it's important. If you've ever struck out to end a game in front of a big crowd, then you know it's not much fun. But that's nothing, and I mean *nothing*, close to the toughest part of this sport, the thing most people don't like to talk about. The awful truth that one day—and you don't know when, but it always comes, and when it does, that's it, all over, you're done—one day, you won't see any more pitches. One day, you'll have nothing left to swing at. No fastballs, no hanging curves, no full counts, high heat, outside or in, nothing, none of that—one day, it's over. And after that you won't need to worry about looking like a fool in front of all the hecklers anymore, 'cause believe me, those stands will be deserted.

That's why I'm asking, *please*, Lord, I'm begging here, please just give me one more pitch—we don't need catchers or an ump, it doesn't even have to be a strike, I'll take anything, just put it somewhere over the plate, but please, I need one last at-bat.

And if you serve one up? I promise you, right now. I swear. I'm telling you—bet house, car, and dog on this.

I'll jack that thing. I'll crush that shit. I'm going fucking yard.

13

I'M NOT REALLY sure why I wanted to do this. A whole team of psychiatrists probably couldn't figure that out. If the cops drag me handcuffed down to the station and interrogate me for weeks until I confess all my previous sins, I still couldn't tell them why I'm here at Townsend's funeral. Maybe it was just a good excuse to get a sitter. It *did* give me a chance to wear a suit at drop-off this morning, where some moms whistled and threw me catcalls. I pointed at them and pumped my fist. And in case it ever happens again I'm trying to think of another move that will be even cooler. But I do feel a little bit weird about showing up today. Maybe I just wanted to get a look at some of these faces around me. But I keep worrying that if the wrong person sees me here, they will jump up from their seats and call me out as some kind of fraud.

A large crowd gathers for the service, as expected. The mass of mourners fills the church until the pews overflow and leave the walls covered with a standing audience. I give up my seat to a late-arriving couple. When you don't really belong somewhere, I figure the least you can do is ensure you stay out of people's way, keep quiet, and not take up too much space. This has worked for me in the past, anyway.

There are worse ways to learn more about someone than going to their memorial service, even if the method is a little grim. I wondered why they didn't hold the ceremony in the city, but early into the priest's words, he mentions that the Townsends were far from recent arrivals to the area, which I didn't know. It seems the family has lived out here, or owned houses, for many generations. The priest acknowledges the father, Alexander Townsend, with reverence as a force in the community. He talks about watching Robert grow up alongside his older brother, Carson.

The eulogy today will not be delivered by a college friend or old roommate of Townsend, but by Mark Resner, the president and founder of GDR, instead. Something about the speech feels formal, like a lecture on Townsend's résumé, a life well lived with many victories but not a description of a person, a real human being. He doesn't bring the funny stories. But he does speak in glowing terms about the recently widowed Brooke, who sounds like a saint. Trim and fit for his age, Resner doesn't have a single hair on his head, but he wears it well, he *owns* the look. It seems to fit the hard angles of his face and jawline, along with his pale blue eyes, devoid of pity or understanding. He has the appearance of both a king and his most trusted hangman. The reading glasses he donned for his speech make him seem no less formidable when he pauses on occasion to look up from his notes and glare down at the audience.

After the ceremony, the priest invites us to a local country club for a brief reception, and I follow most of the audience filing out to make the trip. So many people drove out from the city that the caravan to the next event is a long one. I park in the gravel lot behind a putting green, walking past the regal fairways, and soon I'm ushered alongside the other mourners toward the large clubhouse on the hill. The building doesn't look too imposing or fancy, but the outside has a simple elegance to it. There's nothing too grand in the dining area, which has been cleared away for the several hundred in attendance. They have a buffet in the center of the main room that the guests mostly ignore. But a small bar at the far wall gets a good amount of use from a big huddle of people, many of them men, around my age, none of whom seem unemployed. Barbour jacket kind of crowd. Some of them look like they have better things to do.

"Hey, Pete?" whispers a voice behind me.

I turn around to see someone I used to work with a long time ago. Crawford ignores the handshake I offer and comes in to embrace me, the moment getting the better of him.

"Hey, man!" he whispers in my ear.

"Craw, good to see you. Sorry about the circumstances."

"Been a while," he says. "How're things?"

"Fine, you know. This is brutal."

Senior managers around the firm would sometimes call Mike Crawford a good athlete. Some people called him rangy. We never worked in the same group, but I met Craw when we were both embryos fresh out of school, trying to find a desk that would keep us around. He was raw in those days, but even then, you could see how well he navigated the traders or salespeople who tended to terrorize the rest of us. He was versatile. I noticed throughout his career that he had this ability to switch from product to product, with a knack for leaving some dysfunctional group busy killing off its veterans in time to jump aboard a growing team on the lookout for strong players willing to learn a new game. And sure, sometimes all the usual annoying pundits liked to grumble that he never became an expert or even fluent in certain products, because his résumé was so promiscuous. But he made up for it with a good deal of hustle and a total lack of interest in what his critics had to say. Guys like Craw tend to know a lot of people. I should have guessed he might be here.

"How's the old crew?" he asks. "How're the boys? You speaking to any of them? How's Drew? You still in touch? I heard he moved out to the country to become a writer or something. What's up with that? That true?" Craw speaks softly, though it seems difficult for him. He's not a natural mourner. He doesn't like to sit still.

"Drew's teaching," I tell him.

"Jesus. They let him around kids? That's scary shit."

"I don't know. I think he's pretty into it. I could see him being good at that stuff."

"Well, he's a good man. He's a real dude. And you were always his boy. You two geeks, thick as thieves. By the way—that was fucked-up what happened to you at the old shop, I was surprised to hear it—what the hell was all that about?"

"I don't know what to tell you."

"What a shit show."

"Yeah, but what can you do?" And what else can you really say? You don't rag on your old firm or complain about the injustice in how they treated you, list names more deserving of a bullet, rip on the guys running the shop now, a group so defective and mediocre, they could only wind up in management. In fact, they can't find the bathroom compared to the ancient masters who built the place and you grew up underneath, as if the business could soon file for bankruptcy and sink into the ocean ever since you had to hand over your employee ID. That's not what you do.

"What are you up to these days?" he asks.

"Very little. Are you still at...?"

"Yeah, still around," he says. Craw was always a survivor. "But the place isn't the same. It really kind of sucks. Not like the old days. Speaking of, how did you know Townsend?"

"Out here mostly," I say, moving quickly. "How about you?"

"My wife's old buddies with Brooke."

For some reason, I remember in our first years together at the firm that Mike Crawford earned a reputation as a man with a great many conquests, including a few coworkers. Over beers one night, I pulled him aside and offered him some advice that was probably presumptuous of me to give. I told him about how he had such an obvious future ahead of him. Run wild outside the building, but why not skip any internal temptations and the risk of getting fired, or sued, or ruining your reputation? He listened, undistracted, looking me in the eyes. *It's a big city out there, go nuts,* I probably added. He nodded in agreement. *Appreciate you,* he said to me. Years later, I discovered from reliable sources that he soon went on a streak of passionate encounters with a score of beautiful colleagues across all ages, races, job descriptions, and rank with no complaints or negative ramifications to his career. Craw, of course, never brought up this subject with me. I didn't, either. Someone told me he met a lot of women at the firm's gym, which was something else I didn't know you could do.

"Shit, this thing's fucking awful," he says.

"Hey, Craw, speaking of that. What have people been, you know, saying about this?"

"About what?"

"About Townsend."

"What do you mean?"

"I mean about what happened. Like, how did he drown? Have you heard anything?"

"Well, he was out here Thursday before last. He went surfing and I guess something went bad. They think he might have knocked himself out. Pretty scary."

"But what are people *saying*?"

"I don't know. I don't have much else for you."

"Has anyone been asking about—"

"Shit. Hold up. There's my wife. I gotta go deal with some shit. Good seeing you, man."

"Good seeing you," I tell him. "Good catching up."

"Don't *good catching up* me, motherfucker," he whispers. "I ain't got time for your ass!"

Craw pushes past me toward his wife as I bring my napkin up to my face, trying not to giggle at a memorial service. I'm glad I came here. This was a decent idea.

But a few feet to my left, a man is staring at me. He seems about my age, still a bit of a schoolboy complexion, hair parted neatly to the side, ready for his yearbook photo. He seems unimpressed by whatever he's looking at, though it might just be his resting face. Unable to think of a better option, I step over and extend my hand.

"Peter," I tell him, and he responds with a firm shake. I can see some puffiness, a bloodshot irritation in his eyes. He's been crying.

"Brian," he says. "How do you know Crawford?"

"We worked at the same place. Same analyst class. Good to catch up, hadn't seen him in a while. He's a good guy."

I look over for Craw and find him standing next to his wife, inspecting his shoes, uncomfortable and chastened.

"He's fun," says Brian hatefully.

"He's a good man."

"Where are you working now?"

"Well, I'm out of work right now."

"Oh," he says. I get that a lot.

"Yeah."

"What are you looking to do next?"

Talk about something else. Change the conversation.

"How did you know Robert?" I ask him.

"Friend of the family," he says. "*Longtime* friend of the family." A painful smile forms on his face, and he considers the tumbler in his hand, tilts the glass back and forth, churning a finger of brown liquor inside it. He studies the drink, remembering something. Jutting his chin toward a thin man standing alone against the far wall, he adds, "Carson and I were in diapers together. I've known the Townsends a long time. Long time."

Carson, the older brother, leans his back into the wall, head hanging low. He didn't speak at the funeral, either.

"I'm sorry," I tell him. "This is rough."

"Yes, it is."

"How's he doing?"

"What do you mean?" he says, eyeing me strangely.

"How's Carson taking it?"

He seems to think about it for a moment and then looks over at me as if to say, *Take a wild guess.* It wasn't a great question. It never is, but you still ask it, in these moments.

"As expected," I answer myself.

"As expected," he agrees, inspecting his drink again. "But even still. It's hard to see him like this."

"I don't think I've ever met Carson."

He seems puzzled by the comment.

"How'd you say you knew Robert?" he asks.

I sometimes wonder if, at some point in your life, if you spend too long looking for a job, then the feeling kind of scars you and never goes away. Socially. You get asked to name your best relationships, and what you used to make a year within five minutes of meeting someone enough times, it stays with you. One more interview.

"We met from surfing."

"Really? Where was that? Out here?"

"Yeah, I live out here."

"Are you *from* here?" he asks with contempt.

"No. No, I'm not."

"Right."

I don't like the way he's looking at me.

"Well, nice meeting you," I tell him.

"Yes, of course. Peter, right? A pleasure."

Oh sure, a laugh a minute. We shake hands and he wanders off, both of us probably thrilled to be rid of each other.

The gaunt figure who leans against the back wall with his arms folded, frowning at the floor, looks several years older than his brother. He's still standing by himself, watching the scene. He looks about as friendly as a cactus. Whereas I can see Brooke at the other side of the room, surrounded by a circle of well-wishers. She hugs the couples who approach to offer their respects. I think on it a minute and decide I may as well walk over and take a shot.

"Carson?" I ask. His head jerks up at me, and his eyes are a little startled. "Peter Greene."

He looks me over like a coyote before accepting my handshake.

"I'm very sorry for your loss."

"Have we met before?"

The idea seems to disturb him quite a bit.

"I don't think so."

"You don't think so?" he says. Even if he did just lose his brother, this guy has an edge to him.

"No. I'm pretty sure we haven't."

I'm starting to figure out why he was standing by himself for so long.

"Well, it was a nice service," I tell him.

He snorts at this and peers down at the carpet.

"I'm sorry," I say.

He ignores me. I can picture Craw watching this somewhere and mocking my progress.

"The whole thing's hard to believe," I tell him. "It doesn't add up."

Carson turns to look me over for a second, the first time he's really acknowledged my presence. But he doesn't feel compelled to speak.

"It just doesn't make any sense," I say to fill the silence.

He stares at me skeptically.

"Remind me," he says. "How did you know my brother?"

I'm not sure what it is about me that makes it impossible for every person at this damn service to believe I could have been friends with Robert Townsend.

"From surfing. We used to surf together out here." I notice that several faces in the crowd appear to be studying our conversation. They also seem to find my answers unconvincing.

"What was your name again?" he asks.

I tell him for the second time and, as if to justify my credentials, feel the need to add, "It's strange, but I saw Robert, actually, the day he went missing."

"You what?" spits Carson, wide-eyed and baffled.

"I saw him down at the beach."

Carson's mouth is hanging open.

A familiar voice calls over my shoulder, "Excuse me, I'm sorry to interrupt."

It's only my good pal Brian, who arrives just in time to screw up everything. Carson ignores him, still frozen in place.

"Brooke was looking for you," Brian tells him, adding, "Is everything all right?"

Carson seems to come around and snap out of his daydream.

"Yes," he says and turns to me. "Nice meeting you. Thank you for coming. It's Peter Greene, yes? Well, good speaking to you."

We shake hands respectfully, and he turns to go. Brian follows him, but after a few steps, he stops and looks back at me. He looks at me like I'm a pimple not yet ready to pop, one that squeezing too early will hurt like a bitch or worse, leave a scar.

"Do you mind?" he asks.

"Excuse me?"

"What did you say to him?"

"We were just talking."

"Was that really necessary?"

"What's your problem?"

"Don't make a scene. Nice meeting you. A pleasure."

"Yeah, good meeting you. Solid. So, what's the problem?"

"Let's not make a scene," he says again.

Oh, this vicious little bastard, I think, smiling back and gritting my teeth.

When he walks away, part of me wants to follow him, or just grab him by his collar and ask what he meant. *Do you mind?* These WASP scumbags with their secret codes and *Don't make a scene!* They act like I came here and asked if I could become a member.

My mouth is dry. I need a sip of water.

Scanning the room, I don't see anyone else who looks worth bothering. No sign of Craw, either. So, I gather myself enough to slump away from the wall. I head toward the entrance, needing to find a place to regroup, hopefully somewhere with a bathroom.

Escaping down the main hall, I see a door marked "Men's Locker Room." It seems as good a spot as any. Inside, the walls are covered with photos of tournament winners holding trophies. I pass the shower, then make my way over to the toilets. The urinal is one of those old head-to-ceiling jobs, a wall of porcelain with a bucket of ice filling the drain.

I take an irregular piss, little spurts of burnt orange spraying the frozen cubes, sending them steaming. I'm too wound up, excited. I wash my hands in a sink flanked by a good selection of complimentary items. Shaving cream, razors, deodorant, ibuprofen. It crosses my mind to steal a handful of each.

But I'm not sure if I should linger back here too much longer or take another pass at the buffet. I wanted to keep a low profile at this thing, but now Brian's bristling—maybe that punk's even started whispering about me to his buddies. I stare into the mirror long enough that I feel the need to look over my shoulder. I even peek under the stalls, checking for feet, but the bathroom's empty.

"Hello?" I call out, my voice bouncing off the low ceiling. There's no response.

I creep from the toilet area into the old locker room. This space isn't much bigger than a good-size den, with rows of stacked mahogany and wire cabinets with members' name plates stamped across them circling a few wooden benches. A lone felt table sits in the middle of the room. There's a glass ashtray, unused in this era, placed in the center of it, filled with a stack of score cards and pencils. Beside the ashtray rests a little white book. *Club Directory.* I chew my lip for a moment. The smell of Clubman and Vitalis, hair gel and tonic seeps through the rafters.

"Hello?" I yell again. "Hey, buddy, is that you?"

The room is silent. Glancing around and up at the ceiling, I don't even see a smoke detector, and nothing that looks like a camera, just a sign on the opposite wall marked "Exit." So I snatch that little white book from the table, stuffing it into my pocket like a British spy returning a cigarette case to his dinner jacket, and skip out the back door, down a ramp lined with Astroturf protecting the wooden floor from spikes until I'm outside the clubhouse, the grass under my loafers smooth as a putting green, a casual stroll, no need to look over my shoulder for any followers. I can see the parking lot, even my car in the distance. No chance to say a last goodbye to Craw, but he'll get over it. I keep walking, smelling the freshly cut grass mixed with the salt, the sand, and the sea breeze, walking and smiling to myself.

You never know when a little book like this could come in handy.

———

Luke was never a bad sleeper, but some nights he still makes a ruckus. Tonight, after the service, I'm not asleep—in fact, I haven't even gone to bed yet—when I hear his wailing rip through the house. Most nights, I try to let him cry it out for as long as I can stand it, but tonight doesn't sound like he's calling for Mommy or Daddy so much as shrieking in terror. I slip into his room and see him in his little bed, sitting up on his knees, howling his lungs out.

I hug him close, whispering, "It's okay, it's okay," and feel him sob on my shoulder. But the screaming has stopped.

"Did you have a bad dream? Huh? Did you have a bad dream?"

He sniffles into my ear.

"I'm scared," he says.

Still holding him against my chest, I carry him over to the wall and reach up to the highest bookshelf. I grope in the dark, fingers tracing past the thin hardcovers until I feel what I'm looking for. We have just the thing for this sort of job. The best home protection product a family could find. Everyone should keep one of these somewhere in their house—you have to defend yourself. But you need the right ingredients if you're going to make this stuff. First, you take your average spray bottle and then you go and fill it with tap water and then, well, that's pretty much it. Of course, you can't let him see you mix this magical potion that will protect him forever, and you should probably store it in a safe place. But now you have some monster spray you can use for the prevention or removal of any scary creatures.

"Should we use the monster spray, buddy?" I whisper. "Monster spray?"

I can sway and rock him gently, still hugging him with one arm while I open the closet and spritz inside. *Pow! Pow!* Slowly, slowly, I drop to one knee where I shoot underhand, spraying mist at any of those bastards hiding under the bed. *Get some!*

But tonight, he doesn't stop crying.

"What's wrong?"

"I'm scared," he says.

"It's okay. There're no scary monsters. C'mon, let's go to bed."

"There's a man outside," he whispers.

"What?"

"A man," he says.

I dart over to the window and stare outside into the night, eyes scanning and scanning at nothing but dark. I can feel my heart against his chest.

"No," I tell him after a while. "No, there isn't."

But I'm still looking.

"I'm scared," he says.

"There's nobody out there."

We're not rocking and swaying now. I've never heard him say anything like that before.

"Will you stay with me?" he asks.

I keep looking out the window.

"There's no one out there," I tell him again.

I stand there holding him and watching for some time. But still nothing. At some point I whisper, "C'mon, let's go back to bed." I'm able to pry his arms loose from my neck and get him back down under his blanket. I settle in on the couch and lie there, listening to him next to me. He doesn't fall back asleep for a while, and it's a long time before I do.

14

ONE DAY, BACK when we were still living in the city, something strange happened in our apartment building. I was talking to this woman in the elevator. She started telling me how her cleaning lady had to move back to her home country for some reason, so now her place was a mess and she needed to find a new service. I went outside for a walk, carrying my son in a Baby-Björn strapped across my chest.

I knocked on her door later that afternoon. She was an older woman, a widow who lived alone, and she had a big apartment with good views of the city, a nicer place than mine. I was polite, but I got right to the point. I told her that in my current station in life, I pretty much watched my kid all day, and that I was around the building a good bit. I also mentioned that I owned a Pack 'n Play. And then I added that if she was interested, I could clean her apartment.

We looked at each other for a little bit. Then she told me that her old cleaning lady came twice a week, and I said that I understood. She asked if I did bathrooms and laundry. I did. She said I hadn't told her how much I was looking to get paid. I asked what her last cleaning lady got. She told me, and that sounded fair. Then I told her that I didn't mean to barge in on her like this, that I wasn't trying to press her or anything, not trying to sell her a used car with another buyer on the line, so she should take however much time she likes, and if interested, she knows where to find us, we're around. And I assured her that if she said no, we'd depart as friends. She didn't need much time. She said *I am interested. What days work for you?*

A few weeks later I was in my therapist's office trying to explain it.

"It felt really good. Her shower was a mess, plenty of hair in the drain. She's an older woman and all, but I got in there and scooped it out and put a little Drano down it. I do the tub, the shower curtains, the toilet bowl, that tricky space behind it, the sinks, the mirrors, the countertops, dust every flat surface I can reach, and then I vacuum the carpets and mop the floors. When I do her laundry, I fold better than I ever have in my life. It's a weakness of mine, but I want to do a good job. The little man spends both his naps in the Pack 'n Play, and I feed him and change him upstairs whenever he wakes up. I play some of my audiobooks for us on my phone. Sometimes he's not happy and he lets me know it, but we make it work. Something about it just feels *good*, getting it all done myself, doing two things at once—I don't even need to shell out for a babysitter. It isn't just the money. I'm not exactly coining it, but I just like to feel useful. I don't own a tool belt—I'm not too handy, and this thing, it's not much, but it's the best I've got going. I don't know if I'm guilty of something I can't quite explain, like I'm borrowing or being a tourist. I'm not sure. But it feels pretty good."

The therapist leaned forward and looked at me.

"Would you say you have an entrepreneurial nature?" she asked.

"I don't know," I said. "I don't think so. Maybe I don't."

"I think you should start a business," she said, her eyes brightening.

"What kind of business?"

"You could start a men's cleaning business. You could go around with other men. Men very much like yourself. And you could clean women's houses. Women would like that. The business would do very well."

"I don't think I want to do that."

"It would do very well," she said. "Women would really like that."

"I don't think *I* would really like that."

"It would make a lot of money. You should really look into it."

"I'm not going to look into it. I'm not going to start that business. That's about all I can tell you."

"You're too worried about what other people think," she said.

The next day, I told the woman in my building that I had to stop because of a schedule problem. I thanked her, she wished me luck, and we shook hands. Then I asked if it were possible that she not mention this to many other people, especially not anyone who lived in the building. People like my wife, for instance. I remember saying that, more than once. She closed her eyes and nodded and told me she understood.

I thanked her again.

15

THIS AFTERNOON, FEELING nauseous and bloated after another one of these stupid workouts, I'm lying on my aching back, sprawled on the floor, recuperating from this crap. Most of the time, during these quiet moments of recovery, Gandle stares out across the cosmos as her breath settles, sometimes unwrapping tape from her fingers, ignoring most of my questions or lectures, taking this well-earned moment for herself. But today she's looking at me. Since that day I blew up down at the station, Gandle's been acting a little weird.

"Have you been lifting a lot of weights or something?" she asks.

I'm not really ready for a close-up right now.

The rest of the class has wandered off to convalesce and reflect on things somewhere else. It's just us sitting on the floor in an empty gym. Pools of dusted chalk blot the black floor mats around us like milk stains. I don't think this stuff's great for you. I think something's wrong with my back. I don't feel good at all.

"Leave me alone," I tell her.

"No, you look huge. You're looking big, Pete."

I close my eyes. One thing I learned from school is that sometimes, if you just turn around and ignore a bully, they won't bother you anymore.

"You know what I was just thinking?" she asks.

Then again, sometimes they keep bothering you. Sometimes they slap you upside the back of your head, which doesn't feel good, either.

"That you should be nicer to me?" I tell her, resting my hands on my forehead.

"I was thinking about your case."

I sit up a little too quickly, and for my efforts, I feel light-headed for a second or two, like that first cigarette after the 10K. She's never said that before. *Your case.*

"What about it?"

I want to ask her if they've reopened it. I can never catch my breath after these things.

"How much do you deadlift these days?" she asks.

"I have no idea." Which isn't quite true.

I've been doing this nonsense for almost two years now and I might look a little thicker in some places, but I do not look *huge* in the way that word gets tossed around places like this, where people rip their shirts off when they get caught up in the moment. My belly certainly hasn't gone anywhere. It might have something to do with my diet of eating nothing but shit. You can't take a guy like me and put him on the cover of a men's magazine, promising *Get Ripped at Any Age.* And sure, like most born-again gym rats, I have those dreams of the day my wife stares wide-eyed and horny at my remodeled torso until she stands up and cheers and shouts for my dick, but if I've made any progress toward this goal, she doesn't seem to have noticed. But I do know how much I can deadlift these days, that I'll admit.

"But you've been lifting a lot lately," Gandle says, again.

"How about you? You lifting a lot? No one could ever tell in those baggy clothes that you wear."

She's nodding at me, smiling.

"Yeah, but I'm just a teeny little girl. I need a big, strong guy like you to protect me. You could teach me things. Look at me, Pete."

For a brief moment, as ridiculous as this sounds, I wonder if she's flirting with me.

"Okay, you're right. You don't work out enough."

"Yeah, but I'm just an itty-bitty girl," she says. "But Townsend? He was a big, tall guy. He was a basketball player, six foot five. He kept in shape, but he still weighed two-twenty, two-forty easy, probably more. He was a big guy. But you knew that, right?"

Gandle's stretching now, legs spread out on the floor. She reaches over to touch her toe, chin not far from her knee.

"Yeah," I say. "Probably. So what?"

She has her elbows now on the floor in front of her. She's still looking at me.

"So, let's say his death wasn't an accident." Gandle sits up. "Then whoever killed him would have had to carry his body down to the ocean. Fifty yards, and he's walking or running in sand. That's a lot of weight to carry. And it's dead weight. That doesn't sound easy. A big guy like Townsend, that's a big load, carrying him over sand. Look at me, Pete."

"Doesn't sound like fun to me."

"A heavy load like that. You wouldn't drag him. You'd carry him on your shoulders, like we do with those sandbags."

"It gets the lungs going."

"Yes, it does. Except our heaviest sandbag over there? That's a hundred pounds. Think about those buddy carries we do."

A buddy carry is a throwback, one of those fun exercises from school day PE classes that become torturous as you get a little older. You kneel down to pick up another person, reaching one arm between their legs as they slump prone resting over your shoulders, then stand up with them. It's also known as a fireman's carry. And then they ask you nicely to run (or shuffle, in my case) around the gym or the parking lot the best you can with another person hanging off your back.

"Those aren't easy, either," she says. "What's the first thing they say when we do those buddy carries around the box?"

"Good luck with this shit?"

"Grab a partner your size. Buddy up. Someone your size."

"So?"

"So, I figure whoever killed him was probably a pretty big, strong guy. A big strong man. That's who we're looking for."

As painful and annoying as *this* buddy is being right now, she makes an interesting point. The idea hadn't occurred to me, I'll admit. She sits cross-legged, still, undistracted.

"That makes sense," I tell her. "That sounds right to me."

"Thank you. So, should we be looking for a big strong man like yourself?"

"What?"

"Where were you that night?"

"What do you mean?"

"I mean that day you were down at the beach. You see Townsend. Have a little chat with him. It's four thirty p.m. Where were you before the beach?"

It was a Thursday, a Thursday afternoon.

"Where else?" I ask. "At home. Nap time. Two p.m. kickoff. We would have just got back from the library. After Luke's nap, we drove around, just to get out of the house, and we went down to the beach."

"Where'd you go after you saw Townsend?"

Where did I go? It was a school night. The library doesn't stay open too late. The gym gets too crowded after 5:00 p.m. We were leaving the beach. How many more options do we really have to choose from?

"I can't remember."

"Did you eat at the Bull?"

"No."

And I don't think we did.

"Why not? You eat there all the time with him, right? Luke's a big hit at the bar."

"It was kind of crummy. It had just started raining. No spots in the lot on a Thursday. I'd have to park on the road. It's a long walk with a kid in the rain."

"So, where did you go?"

"We would have gone home. We went home."

"So, you have dinner at home, the three of you?"

"No."

"Why not?"

"Because my wife works, you know that, she works, and she goes to the gym after and then Thursdays, she has her thing."

Gandle knows what my wife does.

"Moms' Group?" she asks.

"Night class."

I could add that you'd understand if you ever had kids, but I don't. Some things you don't say.

"So. What time does she get home?"

"Around ten, ten thirty, eleven."

"So, she'd tell me she saw you when she got home by eleven?"

This doesn't feel like flirting.

"I'm asleep when she gets home. Wait, what are you asking me? What are you saying?"

"I'm saying from two p.m. to eleven p.m. the day Townsend goes missing, you don't have an alibi."

"What are you doing? Are you messing with me? I just told you, I was with Luke."

"Three-year-old alibis don't hold up very well. And then, of course, you were the last person to see Townsend alive."

Where's this coming from? I thought we were friends.

"We don't know that," I tell her.

"Who else? You know anyone else? Anyone we missed?"

"I ate at home with my son. What is this? What are you doing?"

"I'm just curious. Just doing some thinking. Like you, right? You're always thinking."

Is this payback for screwing up in front of the sheriff?

"Sure. Except I'm the guy who came to you and walked into a police station, saying something was wrong. Saying none of this made any sense."

"Yeah, that's a funny thing. Have you ever heard about how some criminals like to hang around their crime scenes afterward, check them out? Maybe so they can get a sense of the cops' progress—so they know when to feel that breath on the back of their neck?"

"No, I haven't."

"Or they're just looking for a thrill," she says. "They're a little bored. Maybe they're bragging."

"What the hell are you talking about?"

"I'm talking about a guy who spends most of his days alone—"

"I'm with my son."

"Alone," she says again. "A guy who doesn't have an alibi for a nine-hour window. This guy is about six foot three, and he lifts, he weighs—what are you, yikes, about two-thirty these days? And he isn't a random stranger—this guy knows the victim personally, just like he knows the beaches around here pretty well. I'm talking about the last guy to see the victim alive, except nobody else can corroborate that, and this same guy, he keeps asking the cops for more information about what happened—he even went snooping around the victim's funeral. That's what I'm talking about, Pete."

"This isn't funny."

"No, it isn't."

I've had enough. I just wanted to help out. I had information they needed to know, so I went to her, and now this?

"You think I should be a suspect?" I ask her.

"Do you think, given what I just said, that you should be?"

"If you're so fucking smart, why did you guys close the investigation?"

"How do you know the investigation's closed?"

"The sheriff told me."

"So, you know it's closed. Because a cop told you?"

"Don't look at me like that."

"What are you, a rich kid?"

Gandle's never said anything like that to me before. Not even Frank has.

"What the hell is that supposed to mean?" I ask, glancing over my shoulder. No one's within earshot.

"A lot of people aren't crazy about cops. Like the kind of people we usually deal with. They never grew up thinking that if they had a problem, they could call the police and they would come help them. But not you, right? You trust the cops. And that tells me something."

This doesn't make any sense.

"The sheriff said the case was closed," I tell her.

"Because cops never lie, right? They always tell the truth? And they always tell the truth to suspects?"

"This isn't funny."

"Neither's asking me about an autopsy."

"Stop it."

"You wanted to know about physical evidence. I'm just asking you some questions."

"Give it a rest."

"Where'd you go that night?"

"That's enough."

"Do you want to speak to an attorney?"

"I don't need this shit."

"Was he heavy that night?"

"Hey, fuck you."

Her face darkens. I'm grinding my teeth, and I said that with more menace in my voice than I should have. She glares at me for crossing the line, and I'm trying not to glare back. And now she breaks into a wide smile and giggles.

"Oh, I'm just fucking with you, Pete. Look at you. Oh, poor baby. It's okay. Wow, feel those arms, damn, have you been lifting? Wow, you're so strong. So big, Pete. So big and strong."

"Real funny," I say, pulling away from her. "Jesus."

"You're sweating. Do you know that? You're really sweating. It's cute. I like that, Pete. You'll fold under questioning. It's cute, though."

"Hilarious."

"Oh my god, I really needed that. You're blushing, Pete. It's sexy. That was really nice. That was good. Oh, I can't wait to do that again."

16

I CAN'T REMEMBER when I stopped answering my home phone, but it's been a while and I don't think this routine of mine will become one of Lauren's favorites. What's the best news I've gotten from a landline call the past couple years? It seems like last-chance warranty, onetime offer scams, and not much else.

"It's for you," she says tonight. In fairness, it had been ringing for a long time. She adds with a bewildered expression, and a *my god, what have you done* tone in her voice, "Carson Townsend."

I'm off the couch pretty fast. No need to keep him holding.

"Peter?" he says. "It's Carson Townsend. We met at the service."

"Sure, of course, how are you?"

"I need to ask you for a favor."

"What can I do for you?"

"We didn't get a chance to finish our conversation yesterday. And I have a few questions I'd like to ask you, if that's all right?"

"I'd be happy to. Fire away."

"Would you be able to meet in person?" he asks.

That sounds pretty good to me.

"No problem," I tell him. "Let me just check my calendar. See how my week looks. Can you hold on for just a sec?"

Even though she's almost turned away, I still catch Lauren rolling her eyes—it's not the first time I've seen her do this when she hears me say stuff like that. So, I guess that makes us even, since this routine of hers isn't on my list of favorites, either.

"Remind me," Carson asks. "Where did you say you worked?"

I tell him where I *used* to work, for almost twenty years, that I'm retired now, but don't mention if it was my decision. And I have to turn my back to Lauren so that I can't see how she responds, so we don't have a problem.

"I know some people at that shop," he says. When he mentions a few names, he may as well have told me he knows some guys who *run* the firm.

"They were a little above my pay grade." He doesn't laugh. If you're a heavy, a real somebody, that's not what you do, I guess.

"When you first started there, it's been a while, I can hardly remember, who was running investment banking?"

That was a long time ago. "Foltz," I tell him. "But again, I wouldn't really have—"

He cuts me off. "We did a decent amount of business with them back then. And by the time you left, who had his seat? Who was running banking?"

"Dutton. Dutton was the head guy. But again, we sort of worked on different floors. I don't know if you ever knew Drew—"

"How about Dwight Hoffman? On the equity side. Or Scott Cassetterra, who ran the group?"

I don't know them, and I'm a little confused.

"No. But, Cassetterra—wasn't he a Bear Stearns guy? Do you mean Steve Cassatterra? I think he was at Bear and Drexel before that."

"That's right," he says.

Now that we've cleared all that up, we move on. Somehow, I figure out a couple times that work, and we set a date.

"Looking forward to it," he assures me before hanging up.

Downstairs, in the kitchen, I find an unrepentant Luke has covered most of the floor with his dinner and broken a plate in the bargain. He's bawling, wailing loudly, blaming others, and he won't respond to any of my attempts to calm him. Lauren, for her part, has given up. She holds her face in her hands and sobs softly from exhaustion. But when Luke throws his sippy cup and sprays milk across the table, she screams loud enough to wake the devil and pounds the table. "That's enough! That's enough! I just can't take it!"

I've been here before, and there's only one thing to do.

I take a sponge and paper towels from the sink, crouch down beside Luke's chair, and start picking up the mess. He thrashes and yells at me not to clean it up, earning himself a time-out, a sentence that I will have to impose—it doesn't seem like Lauren's up for that duty tonight—so I get to play the heavy. But down on the floor, on my hands and knees, scrubbing the damage, my mind is already somewhere else. I'm thinking about this meeting, and not just because I'll get away from this madhouse for a couple hours. Carson seems a little prickly, but he's also a somebody, a real guy. And it occurs to me that when he asked all those questions about my old firm, he'd done a pretty good job of figuring out if I was lying to him.

17

CARSON TOWNSEND HAS the kind of home that can make you think through what you're all about. For some people, it's not enough to put a number and their last name at the front of their driveway. They need to give it a title. With a house this big on so much property, maybe they figured they had to name it something.

They decided on Goose Hollow.

A long, gravel driveway lined with cedar trees winds up to the house. I park outside the garage next to the only car there, a Jeep Wagoneer that has seen plenty of summers. The house is an old, faded-shingle place that looks like a manor. It sits on about a dozen acres of what was probably once farmland. Orange leaves are scattered across the green lawn. I wonder how long they've owned the place. It feels ancient.

A slight, gray-blond woman answers the door. Mrs. Townsend wears sneakers with khakis and a sweatshirt.

"Hello?" she says, with a friendly if confused look on her face. "Can I help you?"

"Well, maybe. I'm Peter Greene, and I came by to meet with Carson, if I'm in the right place?"

"Hi, Peter. Kathy." We shake hands. "I hadn't heard we were expecting visitors today. Someone was nice enough not to tell me." She grins, rolling her eyes.

"Oh, sorry about that."

"Don't be silly! Come in. Come in." She ushers me inside her home, smiling. The front hall has the feel of a winter ranch house. "It's nice of you to come all the way out here to see him."

"Nice to meet you. I'm sorry about the circumstances."

Every inch of this place, the whole structure, even the inhabitants, whispers understated wealth. Shabby chic. A lot of the houses in this area were built by people so wealthy they refuse to ever inhabit them, as if their presence could ruin the property. But this place feels well used, lived in. This is a home. They keep it very clean, but you can see signs of wear, dampness, a crack or two in the paint, mold on the shingles. Living in a house so close to the water, you get to smell the salt in the air and see the light off the ocean. But stuff rusts out here.

"We're going this way," she says, leading me down the hallway. "I'm going to put you two in here."

She leads me into a room that feels like a study. It has a fireplace with charred logs resting on the andirons and ash covering the floor. The walls are full of books, and a tall stack of newspapers sits by a desk topped with notepads and paper.

Carson walks in after a few minutes, and we shake hands. He looks like some sort of old English rock star who has long since retired, joined a country club, embraced the new uniform, and stayed off the carbs. He wears a collared shirt with khakis. He's thin, almost scrawny, but his clothes fit him well. He has a handsome face with some mileage and wrinkles—he can't be younger than fifty—but his hair is magnificent. He wears his dark mane long, hanging straight, thick, luscious, floppy, and well below the ear.

He sits across from me in the more comfortable chair, leans back, and laces his fingers in front of him. It doesn't look like he's pleased that I'm here.

"Thank you for meeting with me," he says. "Did Kathy get you anything?"

"I'm fine. Thanks."

We sit looking at each other for what feels like a while.

"What line of work are you in?" I ask him.

"I run a family office."

He means *his* family office, of course. Meaning the guy made so much money he has enough to manage on his own—he doesn't need to make a living investing anybody else's cash.

"Do you work out here full-time?"

"I do," he says. There are worse people to know than the local Warren Buffett.

"What sorts of investing are you focused on?"

"You mentioned that you saw my brother the day he went missing."

He didn't invite me over to talk shop, I guess.

I cut to the chase and try to take him through that Thursday, but he doesn't let me finish a sentence without peppering me with questions. You're certain it was him? How can you be sure? What did the two of you discuss? What about his appearance? Was he acting strangely, or under duress? Did you notice if he might have been drinking? Taking medication? How sure are you on timing? Do you drink or take any prescriptions yourself? He interrogates me about distance and logistics, and when I tell him why the surf was so terrible, he asks me to explain it to him again, along with my qualifications in ocean sports and knowledge of the region. He crouches forward in his chair and points his finger at me when it suits him. It feels like a deposition. More than once, I can only tell him, *I'm not sure, I don't know* with a sigh, feeling spent.

"It doesn't make any sense," I add finally.

He looks down at the floor, taking it all in. He doesn't say anything for a while.

"Who else knows about this?" he asks.

"Well, I told the police, if that's what you mean. I went down to the station and met with the sheriff, but he didn't seem too interested. Now I've told you. And that's it."

"Keep it that way," he says. I also may have told my story to Frank and Noel and Lauren and a few of the moms at school. But I look back at him with a determined expression on my face.

"Is there anything else?" he asks. "Is that it?"

I might add that, if anything, the cops seemed more interested in me as a suspect. That I'm still not sure if Gandle was interrogating me in the gym or screwing with my head to prove a point.

"I guess I'm saying that I don't believe your brother drowned."

"He didn't."

"How do you know that? Was there an autopsy?"

He closes his eyes for a moment, wincing, and takes his time before answering.

"I want to make something absolutely clear right now," he says. "If we discuss certain matters, then you coming here today, this entire conversation, goes no further than the two of us. It stays in this room. I'm deadly serious about this, understood?"

"Of course."

He studies me skeptically.

"My name can never be mentioned, not to anyone. Agreed? Not even the police."

"Agreed."

"Because if you ignore this warning, there will be consequences. Grave consequences. And I'll tell you right now... You will have a very, very serious problem with me."

"Agreed," I tell him again, unsure of what else to say. He hesitates for a moment.

"They performed an autopsy," he explains. "And I've seen the results. My brother didn't drown, Mr. Greene. No water was found in his lungs."

At some awful point in the final moments of his struggle, a drowning man can't keep holding his breath. When the body becomes desperate enough for air, it's eventually forced to inhale, but rather than finding oxygen, it draws salt water into the lungs instead.

I've been hitting the books.

"Did the coroner find that suspicious?" I ask him.

"No, he didn't, as a matter-of-fact."

"Laryngospasm?" I ask. He shoots me a glance, perhaps surprised by the question. In some cases, a victim inhaling salt water will trigger an adverse reaction as the water passes their larynx. The vocal cords may instinctively seize up and contract to prevent water entering farther, but this measure closes off the windpipe, causing the victim to suffocate so that an autopsy won't find water in their lungs. These cases are sometimes called a dry drowning.

"No," he says shaking his head sadly. "His neck was broken. He fractured his CI and C2, the top two cervical vertebrae in the neck. Damaging the spinal cord can cause immediate paralysis, in which case he would have been immobilized in the water, and then likely drowned." Before I can ask, he continues. "But *severing* the cord can block the brain's signals to the rest of the body, causing a stoppage in breathing and…" He pauses his recital of the notes he has clearly memorized and looks at his hands. "Instant death." Neither of us speaks for some time, and the back of my neck starts to ache.

Townsend's injury isn't unheard of among people messing around in the ocean. Every year, some unlucky people get paralyzed just bodysurfing the wrong wave.

"The pathologist," he says. "He described the fracture as a 'clean break,' commonly associated with blunt force trauma. Violent impact. In a fall, for instance. This kind of neck injury is sometimes known by another name. Have you heard this term before?"

"No."

"A hangman's break," he says.

We sit in the quiet together for a bit. The thought occurs to me that, despite his strange vows of secrecy, he's waited to tell this story. He wants someone to hear what he knows.

"What else?" I ask.

"Some minor abrasions," he explains. "Cuts and scrapes that likely occurred during his body's time in the water. He did have one large contusion on the side of his head, a deep bruising at the temple. But it wasn't possible to determine if the injury was sustained pre- or postmortem."

The board maybe, I wonder. Or he could have hit the bottom, going over the falls. I'm thinking through the scenarios when I notice that Carson looks to have aged ten years in the last hour.

"So, what do you think happened?" I ask him.

"I don't know."

"But you're going to find out."

"Yes. Yes, I will."

I rub my neck, looking around the room for a moment. For some reason—I can't explain where it comes from—I ask him, "Do you want some help?"

"Help?"

"Yeah."

"What kind?"

"Another set of eyes."

"Do you have someone in mind?"

I open my hands.

"That's not why I reached out to you," he says.

"Maybe not. But here I am."

"Yes, but I don't think so, if I understand what you're asking."

"Why not? I got a sitter."

"I'm afraid I just can't do that."

"Do you have anyone else looking at this for you?"

"I'm not sure why that's relevant."

"Maybe I can turn up something you haven't."

"What kind of experience do you have?" he asks.

"I'm a quick learner," I tell him. "I'll figure it out."

"What's in this for you?" he asks.

"We're talking about your brother here, aren't we?"

"I know who we're talking about," he snaps. "What's in it for you?"

I take a moment now. There are things that only an asshole will ask you, but that doesn't make the question unimportant, and it doesn't mean you owe him a response, but you better think through an answer, even if you just keep it to yourself. So, I take a moment with this one.

"It matters, doesn't it?" I ask, looking back at him. And I could add that right now I need to do something that matters. Or that lately my phone isn't ringing off the hook with chances to work on something that does. But I keep it simple and say, "It matters to me."

"Are you looking for money?" he asks.

These kinds of guys, they can't help themselves. It's the only language they speak.

"Nobody said anything about money. You called me. Remember?"

"Maybe that was a mistake," he says, going chippy and suspicious all of a sudden. That's the problem with billionaires. They always think everyone's out to rip them off.

"So, now what? Just let this go?" I ask him. "Let bygones be bygones?"

He stares at me for a moment, as if puzzled, and says, "Has it ever occurred to you that what you're trying to do is very dangerous?"

"I just want to find out what happened to your brother."

"No. You're trying find out who murdered my brother."

"Yes."

"I'll put it another way. What would happen if whoever did this found out that you were looking for them? They may not be the kind of people you'd want to know that sort of thing."

I could see how that might make me feel a little uneasy.

"What if they find you first?" he asks.

That doesn't sound good, either.

"What sort of people are we talking about?"

"I think you're missing my point," he says.

"Which people?" It sounds like he has someone in mind.

"I'm going to remind you one more time to keep this meeting to yourself. I hope you can understand why this isn't a trivial request."

"Wait. You must have some idea who's responsible. Can you think of anyone who might have wanted to harm him?"

"I'm not looking for a partner," he says.

"I'm not looking to muddy the waters."

"Thank you for coming to see me."

At this point, my only chance is to persuade him that I'm not going to quit. If you don't have a clue what you're doing, you may as well convince people that you'll never give up. This can work. And it drives people nuts.

"What about just hedging your bets?" I ask. "Giving yourself a backup in case you don't find anything?"

"No," he says simply. I guess this approach can also get you chucked out the door.

"Wait," I tell him. "You're worried about being discreet? I live out here. I know the people. What do you think draws more attention? If some flat-foot private eye knocks on your door, that doesn't happen every day to most people, they're going to remember that. What about a journalist?"

His face fills with disgust at the word. "There you go. A reporter's whole purpose in life is to get attention. But someone like me?"

"Someone like you?" he says, and I'm not sure if his tone is meant to be insulting or not.

"I'm pretty off the radar these days. I'm not trying to make the headlines. Do I seem like a name dropper?"

There's the hint of a smile that he quickly snuffs out.

"Let me ask you something," I say. I'm remembering Carson standing alone in that crowded room at the service. "Robert had a lot of friends, right? And they'll call and tell you how sorry they are for your loss. Well, how many of them are knocking on your door saying they think he was murdered and that they want to help you find out who did it?"

He doesn't answer, but I can tell by his face that my guess isn't far off.

"And when you tried to explain to them how none of it makes any sense?" I ask. "How did that go?"

Carson seems to have gotten smaller in his chair. It's exhausting when you care about something but no one ever wants to buy what you're selling.

"This meeting," he says. "And our discussion never took place."

"Your name never comes out of my mouth."

He rubs his temples for a minute.

"What do you know about GDR?" he asks.

"A little bit. Not a lot."

GDR. Jesus. GDR. Earlier he kept saying "these people" and "they." GDR. I should have guessed. When he doesn't offer anything else, we sit in silence for a few hard seconds, but in the end, I can't stop myself from saying, "Why do you ask?"

Which seems to break him out of his spell. He has never looked angrier than when he scowls at me for some time as if to say—*Why do you think?*

A voice calls over my shoulder.

"How are you two getting along in here?" asks Kathy, shuffling into the room. "Is everything all right?"

Carson ignores her. His hateful eyes stay fixed on me as he sits there, fuming.

"We're great," I tell her.

"Are you sure?" she asks, looking at her husband, who still doesn't respond. He's rattled.

"Yup, just catching up," I assure her.

"Oh, that's nice," she says, smiling at me now.

"Mr. Greene was just leaving," Carson explains without looking away from me. It doesn't sound like a suggestion.

"I'm sorry about that," she says. "I was just checking in. I didn't mean to interrupt."

"No, not at all," I tell her.

"Are you sure?" she asks.

Carson has a look on his face that says he's quite certain he wants me to leave. Maybe he's shell-shocked that I managed to squeeze so much information out of him. In which case, that makes two of us.

"Oh yeah," I tell her. "I should be going. I have to get back to pick up my son." This isn't strictly true, but I should get out of this house before Carson causes a scene.

Carson stands up and we shake hands. He grips my palm in a death clutch, as if he's strangling a small animal, and then he stalks out of the room without saying goodbye.

"Would you like anything for the road?" Kathy asks. When I decline, she offers to walk me out. It seems like she's in a pretty good mood for someone who just had a death in their family.

We make our way through the great hall to the front door and she follows me outside, then closes the door behind her. "Are you sure everything's all right?" she asks out on the lawn in a collaborative voice.

"Oh, of course." Her face is warm but concerned.

"It really is very nice of you to come out all this way to see him. We don't get many visitors. I know that he appreciates it."

There's something maternal about her tone. As if she's babying him. Is this how some marriages wind up after so many years? Somehow, I can't see mine reaching a similar place.

"I'm very sorry about Robert," I tell her. "How has he taken it?"

"Carson?" she asks, stepping out with me to the driveway. "Well, with Carson you never know, of course. He'll be all right. I take good care of him."

She really does. And I really should get home. I have a decent drive.

"Nice meeting you," I tell her again, opening my car door to climb inside.

"It was awfully nice of you to visit."

Buckling myself in the driver's seat, I try to process what just happened. GDR! Jesus Christ. GDR. That look on Carson's face.

My phone vibrates with an incoming text. New messages from Lauren.

Where r u?

What time will you be home?

I can see Kathy standing on the doorstep watching and waving goodbye to me. She's still smiling, at least.

18

I DIDN'T GET the shakes and I didn't get the sweats. I didn't throw up all day long the way some guys do when they go on the wagon or lapse into a twisted delirium filled with visions I couldn't interpret. My face didn't turn into a pale mask of death. I did go through a thought-provoking number of Diet Cokes, and I still do, I guess. There was a hellish anxiety and insomnia, but I had some experience with these symptoms before I quit drinking, so here, again, the picture becomes muddied. But I can remember a few of those nights after the sheriff pulled me over, lying awake in the darkness next to Luke's crib, watching reruns of the worst mistakes in my life, even the sober ones, some of the scenes awful enough to make me shudder and moan, even cry out, sometimes so loud I worried it would wake the little guy. And if I had, it would have been just one more thing to feel shitty about.

But I didn't miss it all that much. Sure, sometimes you find yourself thinking about some pint filled with luscious lager, golden like summer and glowing bright as the sun, beads of sweat running down the glass like droplets sliding off some glistening nubile as she steps out of the ocean, bronzed and perfect and dripping with salt water. That kind of stuff stays with you awhile—it doesn't go away very fast.

It wasn't that tough, though, really. And it got a lot easier as time went on. The occasional dumb craving felt like a small burden when stacked next to the long list of horrors I didn't have to put up with anymore. I didn't miss the mornings—I'll tell you that much. Those dreadful days after. Waking up to Luke's wailing with a throbbing head and my mouth stuffed with cotton. Lauren shooting me those angry, knowing looks around the house, and always the guilt, the feeling of sneaking around, that I'd done something shameful that I needed to hide. It didn't do a ton for my marriage. There was even a point after too many nights of coming home, smelling foul and creeping into bed at the wrong hour, when Lauren accused me of cheating on her. I hadn't, but those conversations weren't fun. There really wasn't very much about the dark ages that I missed.

Sometimes it felt like the hardest part was just filling the hours.

Last summer, when no waves had come for weeks and we didn't have enough else to do, Frank and I went to the beach anyway and sat around, watching the boys play in the sand. It had been a rough stretch. It was July and the sun was out and it was very hot and the kids didn't have school.

"I was thinking about getting a new board," I told him.

Frank studied a divot in the sand he was making with his feet. Time passed.

"Just trying to figure out what makes sense," I went on.

"Right," he said.

"Yeah. I was looking at some used ones the other day."

"Okay."

This didn't have to be so difficult.

"Maybe something with more float. Might makes things easier. What do you think?"

"It depends," he said and let the matter rest.

Some people could get a little sick of prying this stuff out of Frank, the way he guarded these precious pearls as if they were sordid secrets from some shameful family history.

I looked at my watch and wished I hadn't. The sun wasn't helping anything.

Frank had a tennis ball with him, and he rolled it back and forth between his hands, thinking things over. At some point, inspiration hit.

"Let's get something going," he said. "You see that log over there?"

I looked at the driftwood drying in the sun, a good way down the beach.

"Twenty bucks," he said. "I bet you I can throw this past the log from here."

Luke glanced over his shoulder at us and furrowed his brow.

"Sure," I said. "That works."

Frank heaved the ball, and we watched it arc through the cloudless sky, then bounce and roll to a stop a couple yards before the log.

"You fucking whore," Frank muttered. He was talking to me.

Frank yelled for the boys to go and fetch the ball. Neither of them did, and after a few minutes, I stood up and went to retrieve it.

When I came back, we sat there on the beach watching the boys and the ocean. For a while, we didn't accomplish much beyond that, nothing you'd be sorry to skip.

"So, Pete," Frank asked. "Guy like you? Night like this? What are you up to?"

"Very little."

"You want to go to Lucky's?"

"Not really."

It didn't bother me that Frank kept asking, but my answer never changed. Lucky's wasn't one of the things about booze that I longed for, after I quit.

"You're still high on life," he said.

"Yup."

"You know Manny was asking about you the other night?"

"Jesus," I said, blinking. "How's that guy doing?" I shuddered thinking about the massive bouncer, a dreadlocked Maori who guarded over the evil place.

"He misses you. He was asking why you don't come by anymore."

"I'm too scared of him. That's why."

"Oh c'mon. He's a teddy bear."

He wasn't. Late one wretched night at Lucky's, I stood in the parking lot and watched Manny beat a guy so badly it almost made me sick. It looked like a bear mauling a salmon.

"I think I'll skip this one," I told Frank.

He shook his head at me and watched the water for a bit.

"One more time," he said. "Twenty bucks I can throw it past the log. C'mon. Double or nothing."

That same night of the fight at Lucky's, I can remember sitting at the bar afterward, drinking myself stupid and wondering what had gone wrong in my life. A few hours later Manny lumbered over, still in high spirits, and we got to chatting. He asked me if I wanted to hear something funny, and it didn't seem like a good idea to turn him down. He told me that he came from a place called Waikato and was one of seven brothers. "Okay," I said, craning my neck back to peer up at him. "So, you come from a big family." He smiled, looking down at me and said, *Yeah, but I'm the smallest.*

The boys were breaking ground on a sandcastle. Dinnertime was still a long way off.

"Let's go," said Frank. "Two to one—I can do it on the fly."

I wondered if there was a more productive use of time.

"Fifty bucks I'll hit the fucking thing," he said.

There seemed like a lot of things I'd never get a chance to do.

Frank threw the ball up the beach.

At pickup today, I'm strapping Luke into his car seat, and I see Frank across the parking lot stalking over toward me. Maybe to give me some shit about missing yesterday's session. The problem with finding the perfect system for coparenting is you can't help but resent the guy you rely on so much if he can't make it. He's got something on his mind anyway. When he gets over to my car, I notice some moms looking over at us, including a few who don't usually pay a lot of attention to me.

"Hey, man," he says. "This guy came by looking for you."

"What?"

"Down at the River. This guy was asking about you."

"Who was?"

"Some dude," he says.

"What dude? Who was he?"

These days, besides my wife, most of the time it doesn't feel like many people are out there running around looking for me. I don't have a clue who this person could be.

"I don't know," says Frank, who doesn't seem to have a much better idea. "I was coming in off the water. And there's this guy sitting there in his car, at the end of the road. He rolls down his window and calls me over, like he needed directions or something."

"What did he want?"

"He asked if I was from around here, if I came down here a lot. Asked if I heard about that guy they found the other week. He says, were you the guy who saw him here that day—the one who talked to him before he went in the water? I said no, and he asks me if I knew the guy who did. And I said, *No. Sure don't.*"

Maybe the cops reopened the case? Or they could have sent in someone new to take another look or get a second opinion? Someone from a different jurisdiction, maybe?

"Why'd you say no?" I ask him.

Frank shrugs. "I didn't like the guy."

"Why not?"

"I didn't like the way he looked."

"What do you mean?"

"Kind of a hard-ass," he says. "When I told him no, he kept asking. He goes, *You sure you don't know? You don't look so sure.*"

"Was the guy a cop?"

"No."

"How do you know?"

"I told him to fuck off," Frank says, and he doesn't seem very sorry he did. "If the guy was a cop, he would have busted my balls about it."

"Why'd you tell him that?"

"I didn't like the way he looked."

These two must have really hit it off. This sounds like real chemistry.

"So then what happened?"

Frank screws up his face, as if reflecting on some hard truth, and after giving the matter a lot of thought, he decides to accept this injustice, since it can't be remedied.

"He just sort of sat there and smiled," he says. "He smiled. And he looked at me a little while, almost like he was gonna do something about it."

I can see Frank standing there at the end of the dirt road, just before the dunes, this guy still in his car, the two of them staring each other down. Some guy who happened to be parked right where I saw Townsend.

Frank rubs his neck and says with a sheepish grin, "But, I'm kinda glad he didn't."

He looks very pleased to let me know the mean-looking dude never backed him down. Which is exciting and I'm happy for him, but I'm a little less worried about whether Uncle Frank came out looking like a pussy. There's other stuff on my mind right this minute.

"What time was this?" I ask.

He thinks on it for a moment.

"Maybe around five?"

That's not what I wanted to hear.

"And then what happened?"

"After a while he took off. He smiled and gave me a little wave."

"Which direction? When he turned off at the other end of the road—which way was he headed? Do you remember?"

Frank shoots me a skeptical look. Most people wouldn't notice that sort of thing.

But I still think I know which way he went, anyway. I have a feeling, when he came to the end of that road, he hung a right. Steering away from town. Heading toward Hammy's beach, where they found Townsend's car. If he had been out there retracing Townsend's final steps, he'd want to make that drive himself, at the same time of day, so he could walk the route, trying to pick up a scent and get a feel for the scene. If he was out there cutting for sign, if he was the enthusiastic type, the kind who likes to roll up his shirtsleeves—

This has me thinking back now to when Gandle rattled me with all her questions that day in the box.

"You sure this guy wasn't a cop?" I ask him. "A private detective? Or a reporter, maybe?"

"No way," says Frank, smiling himself now.

Unless he was another kind of guy. A persistent sort, it seems. The kind who made Frank worry about pressing his luck. The only other person I've ever seen do that is Manny.

"What did he look like?" I ask. "I know, I know you didn't like him."

"Big. White guy. About our age."

"What kind of car?"

"Range Rover," Frank says, hatefully. "Black."

I wish I hadn't asked. *Be on the lookout for a black Range.* Around here that doesn't do me a lot of good. And how many cops drive around in Range Rovers? How many reporters? I don't know what I'm supposed to do with all of this, and Frank doesn't seem too sure, either. I'm trying not to look shaken up, but my act wouldn't fool anybody. I can feel the sweat running down my back, and my stomach's already going.

"Anyways," says Frank. "I thought I should tell you."

19

I HAVE COME to believe that if my wife makes it home and is watching my son, then I should leave and go somewhere else. I feel strongly about this. On the rare nights when she doesn't have a Moms' Group meeting or a night class, it's best if I'm not home. I've tried "relaxing" in my house while she watches him but haven't seen the best results. *Can you get him for a second? I need to use the bathroom.* Of course. *I need to shower, so I just need you for a minute.* Half hour gone. *Mommy needs to get a coffee in town. I need you to watch him. I haven't eaten all day.* An hour lost to Starbucks. *Here, I just need to send this email, can you hold him for a sec, I just can't.* Makes sense. *I have to call Vanessa. He went number two, can you change him?*

These requests seem odd because if I ever want to accomplish anything, I get it done with the little man right beside me. On most days, whenever I shit, shower, or shave, he watches these efforts like I'm a dangerous convict who needs constant surveillance by a thumb-sucking guard who makes sure I don't hide any contraband inside my mouth or my ass. When I take out the garbage, my personal assistant demands to come with me, but this doesn't make carrying the leaky trash bags go any faster. If I need my precious Diet Coke, or have to do any errands at all, I strap him into his car seat, and he gets a shoulder ride around the store. As for reading something that requires concentration, you learn the dark secret that small children can be distracting. But I manage. I don't call for help.

So, I think it's best that whenever she decides to spend some Mommy time with Luke, I soon leave the area. But I won't claim that I accomplish a tremendous amount during these hours, since I often don't make it much farther than the gym, the library, or the beach. And yes, when she watches him, she also finds time to send me texts, lists of instructions—things I need to get done before returning. I've thought about marriage and parenting prior to text messaging or even mobile phones. A dark and primitive period. All those poor children raised by parents with no help from these devices, the endless suffering they endured without the constant stimulus and messaging until, of course, all these kids grew up into violent savages. Generation upon generation lost. I think about this a lot.

I've always loved libraries and I'm not ashamed to say it. Here at the town library, Luke can play in the kids' area with the toy kitchen set and Daddy can do a little research, get out of the house, he can think. I don't care if everything's online these days, I like the atmosphere with no distractions. Usually, I sit downstairs at the children's table on a miniature chair, my son making plastic pancakes topped with letters. But I'm alone today, on the first floor with my laptop at an empty big boy's table, hitting the books.

Goldburg, Dower & Resner began life in 1985 during the middle innings of the first LBO boom. The three founding prospectors were alumni of Drexel Burnham, Bear Stearns, and Morgan Stanley. The basic premise of an LBO is for an investor to buy a company by putting up some of their own cash and borrowing the rest, often a large portion, in order to fund the purchase. The acquired company's cash flows are then used to make interest payments on the new debt. It's not dissimilar to the mortgage you might have on your house, only they're borrowing, using leverage, to purchase a business instead of a home. Hence the term *leveraged* buyout. But the tricky thing about borrowing a lot of money is that it usually makes people look either really smart or really stupid. You tend to wind up being very right or very wrong.

Since its founding, the folks at Goldburg, Dower & Resner—GDR— have looked pretty damn smart. I read some articles about the early days of the firm, when the field of competitors was smaller and they bought some cheap businesses that generate stable, predictable cash flows. They had some early wins with big scores on a cable TV operator, then a group of radio stations, and a billboard company.

But the more recent articles keep mentioning the *late* Goldburg and Dower—two of the three founding partners are no longer with us. Not long into my reading, I come across some sobering headlines.

ADAM GOLDBURG, 50,
BUYOUT FIRM FOUNDER, DIES

Adam P. Goldburg, an investment banker and philanthropist who was a founding partner of Goldburg, Dower & Resner, the leveraged-buyout firm, died Sunday at his home in Nantucket. He was 50.

Tom Foles, a spokesman for the family, said the cause was an unknown medical condition.

Mr. Goldburg played a crucial role behind the success of Goldburg, Dower & Resner, which he founded alongside the investment bankers Thomas K. Dower and Mark T. Resner, formerly of Morgan Stanley and Bear Stearns, in 1985.

Henry Kinderrsen, the renowned private equity investor and

Chairman of the Wharton Investment Committee, was quoted at the 2007 Endowment Alpha Conference as saying, "Adam Goldburg is one of the few competitors I admire in this industry because of his rare combination of fundamental research and risk-taking instincts. We've been fortunate to invest alongside GDR."

Mr. Goldburg structured the financing of many of the firm's highest profile takeovers. In 1985, Goldburg, Dower & Resner took over Patriot Advertising, an owner of outdoor billboards, which was later sold to Clear Channel in 1989. In 1987, the firm bought Oracle Cable, later purchased by Time Warner Cable.

After graduating from the Wharton School of the University of Pennsylvania undergraduate program in 1971, Mr. Goldburg started his career at the Manufacturers Hanover Corporation. In 1978, just as the leveraged buyout industry was beginning to flourish, he joined the high-yield bond department of Drexel Burnham.

Mr. Goldburg was an enthusiastic athlete. He played on the varsity squash team at the University of Pennsylvania, competed in triathlons in recent years, and was a member of Winged Foot Country Club and the Nantucket Golf Club.

He also contributed to many charitable causes, including his alma mater, the University of Pennsylvania. He was a trustee of the New York Public Library, Sloane Kettering Hospital, and Achieve Charter School...

An unknown medical condition at fifty. But none of the other articles or the obituary mention anything more specific than this. Maybe his heart got him? But fifty isn't that ancient, and this guy was healthy enough to still get out there and run all those triathlons. Fifty years old.

My palms are sweating and my mouth feels dry. This next headline doesn't look much better. From August 27, 2002.

THOMAS K. DOWER, BUYOUT FIRM FOUNDER, 45, DIES

Thomas K. Dower, an investment banker and philanthropist who was a founding partner of the private equity firm Goldburg, Dower & Resner, died Friday morning at his home in Jackson, Wyoming. He was 45.

Teton County sheriff's office said in a statement that it "suspects the death to be suicide due to a self-inflicted gunshot wound." An investigation is underway.

According to Teton County sheriff's deputy Travis Carver, the office received a 911 call at 11:15 a.m. Mountain time from Marisa Jones, a housekeeper, saying that Mr. Dower had been found "bleeding from his head and not breathing on the floor." Emergency personnel sent to the scene pronounced him dead at 11:41 a.m.

Tom Foles, a spokesman for the Dower family, said that Mr. Dower "had been battling severe depression privately for a number of years."

His wife, Susan Thompson Dower, said in a statement, "This week, I lost my husband, a great and charitable man." She added: "Words cannot express my shock at this tragedy. Although Tom had struggled with depression in the past, I still cannot believe my husband would take his own life."

Mr. Dower graduated from Brown University in 1978 and began working in Morgan Stanley's corporate finance department. He became one of the youngest partners in the firm's history and ran the leveraged finance division before leaving to found Goldburg, Dower & Resner in 1985.

Forty-five years old. Battling depression privately. That's the way to do it, of course. But it's supposed to have a better outcome. We all go through our dark times, but Jesus Christ. Imagine a guy starts his own business, an investment firm that prints money. He does well enough to have places in New York and Jackson Hole and who knows where else. He has a wife and family. He's out there, fly-fishing the Snake River, looking at sunsets over Grand Teton in August—and that's when you decide to check out?

I knew that the firm had a nasty reputation, but Jesus Christ, what a history. Talk about paying the price. You work that hard only to punch out at forty-five or fifty years old. But now add Robert Townsend, the up and comer, the heir apparent, to the list. Goldburg, Dower, and Townsend all gone by their fiftieth birthdays—that's some streak of bad luck they have going in that office. An unknown medical condition, a suicide, and now a "drowning." Plus, GDR isn't some General Electric or JP Morgan with half a million employees—not that many people even work there! And these were all top-level guys who could have run the whole place at some point, not a couple of working stiffs. It seems like their senior partners have a rough way of leaving the business.

"Where's the little guy?" a voice asks me.

It's just Felix, one of the regulars I see around the shelves once in a while. "He's back at home."

"What are you doing here, then?" he asks, sitting down at my desk.

"Getting some work done."

"What the hell are you talking about? You serious?"

I look around, hoping nobody heard that.

Felix and I met about a year ago, the last time I snuck some lunch into the library. The management frowns on food in the stacks, but I hadn't eaten all day, so I picked up an everything bagel with scallion cream cheese, salmon, and tomato. As I tucked into it, I noticed a man at another table, watching every bite I took. He looked like he worked at a video game store or fixed computers for a living, but he seemed as nervous as if he'd stolen some. I tried to chew more quietly but he only grew more interested until I lost my appetite and stopped eating.

"Are you going to finish that?" he asked me. When I thought about the question, it seemed like I'd regret whatever answer I could give him.

"No," I said. "Do you want the other half?"

He sat down with me and finished the rest of my lunch. He twitched and shifted in his seat, eyes darting around the room, checking for informants. I gave him my spare napkins, and he needed them.

"Are you a sports fan?" he asked. "I could see you as a sports guy."

"Sort of."

"You're not?" he snorted. The guy wore a black Spider-Man T-shirt, a fanny pack, and several chins, but now he studied me suspiciously. "What line of work are you in?"

I explained my situation, and this seemed to make him less uncomfortable. He told me his name was Felix, and I felt I had to ask.

"How about yourself? What do you do for a living?"

"I own a business," he said proudly.

"What kind of business?"

"Sports memorabilia store."

"Hmm."

"That's right."

"Where's the store?"

"Here in town. Do you know where the mall is?"

"Sure—you're over there in the mall?"

"I run it out of my house. I live behind the mall. I also do some trading."

"Stocks?"

"Some of that shit." He waved his hand, scowling. "But comics are where it's at."

"Hmm," I said again.

"That's right, my man. Do you know much about comic books? Best investment you can make. I'm not shitting you. This isn't some get-rich-quick crypto currency crap."

"I didn't think it was."

"It's not. Do you know the only asset class that has never had a down year, a down quarter, in the last fifty years? Even in the crisis?"

"Is it comic books?"

"That's right," he said.

"I never heard that. So, what are you up to here today?"

"My lunch break. They have a charging station for my phone. And the comics section's good. If all these"—he looked over his shoulder—"these fucking twats don't bother you."

He meant the librarians. He shook his head, disgusted. I wondered how they had wronged him but didn't want to get him started.

Sometimes he ignores me. And sometimes he swings by my table to pitch me business opportunities. He seems to know an awful lot about subprime mortgages, the time-share industry, Air Jordans, screenplays, US mint coins, and cannabis. We haven't matched up on anything yet, but I don't mind him asking—it keeps me in the flow. But I guess today he came over here to mess with me.

"How about you?" I ask, getting ahold of myself. "What do you got going on?"

"I think that asshole over there's looking at me."

"Take it easy." The place is almost empty. There's a guy sitting a few tables behind me over in periodicals, trying to read a newspaper. "Just keep your voice down."

Felix rubs his face.

"What do you know about uranium, Pete?"

"Not a lot."

"Well, you're going to want to fix that. I'm talking about the miners here, my man. It's a no-brainer. Very basic."

"I'm not that liquid. I'm not really whipping 'em around these days."

"Don't give me that Wall Street trader bro bullshit," he scoffs. "I've heard that stuff before, man." He looks over my shoulder again, concerned. "What the hell are you working on, then?"

So, I walk him through it as best I can. I've told this story a few times by now and might be getting better at it. I even wonder if Felix could help me out somehow. He might be an amateur crime enthusiast, who reads mysteries and studies police procedures when he's not too busy buying low and selling high. I've known a couple guys like Felix over the years, even if he's a more hostile version of the standard model, but part of me believes that our survival as a species could well depend on some strange scheme or passion that these degenerate alchemists might someday pursue. As long as the librarians and other skeptics stay out of the way.

When I finish giving him my update, he looks at me for a moment, and scratches his chin.

"Don't waste your time with this shit," he says.

"Thanks, man. I think I'm gonna need to sneak out of here in a minute."

No one likes to get second-guessed. I have the sudden urge for a family dinner at home and maybe some Greco-Roman grappling with Luke on the living room floor before bedtime. Lauren tends to watch disapprovingly, since he's just had his bath, until she sulks out of the room—she doesn't understand wrestling, the sport of kings and old roommates—but there's no time to explain.

"Hey!" shouts Felix, eyes clouding over and heated.

"What's wrong?" I ask him.

"Hey, man!" he screams peering over my shoulder, shouting. "What's your problem?" This doesn't sound good.

"It's okay. Take it easy."

"What the hell are you looking at?" he barks at the guy, ignoring me.

The man tries to study his sports section.

"Sorry," I tell the poor bystander.

But the guy's heard enough. He's standing up now. Like a good citizen, he folds the newspaper and returns it to the display where he found it. He doesn't seem in a rush, but he keeps moving. Probably off to rat us out to the powers that be, who will chuck Felix out the door and maybe me along with him.

"Scumbag," says Felix. "Mind your own business."

The guy wants no part of this. He doesn't stop to complain at the front desk, just heads out the front door without even a glance back at the hostile stranger he somehow offended.

I'm a little worked up and not sure what to do. Felix can make trouble sometimes, but nothing like this.

"Motherfucker," he growls. "Kept looking at us."

I turn again over my shoulder. The room is quiet now and all the tables are empty.

"What's the matter with you?" Felix asks me.

I don't answer him. Still going over whatever just happened, a thought occurs that doesn't make me feel any better about the whole thing.

What if the motherfucker kept looking over at *me*?

20

A SMALL CREW of weekday regulars packs the Sunrise Diner this morning. The booths and counter are segregated from white-collar to blue. A lawyer, an insurance salesman, and a real estate broker sit at their usual table behind me, discussing local politics and some recent construction. They have lived here their whole lives. Most of the bigger guys hunched over the counter, with goatees and work boots, drinking black coffee, take their breakfast to go and say very little. In an hour, a group of older gentlemen, now retired journalists, doctors, attorneys, a judge, and a novelist, will take their round table in the back. I like eavesdropping on them when I can. They will have each inhaled every newspaper known to man before sitting down for discussion. The judge, a tall, balding, gray-haired man with a white mustache, maintains order and dignity among the participants when required. Every group needs someone like the judge.

My old boss was the best guy I ever saw at this. And it wasn't just keeping the inmates in line and making sure things started on time. He was a reductionist. Drew could funnel complex topics through his distillery and brew up an explanation clear enough for the rest of us to digest. He also knew people. He knew what turned them on, what scared them, and when they were lying. He could boil people down, too.

I started out in the business as Drew's Sherpa. My job was to carry our leader's gear up the mountains in all types of weather, wearing a smile. The life of a Sherpa isn't for everyone. Most people know the first person who climbed Everest, that crazy Kiwi ex-beekeeper Sir Edmund Hillary. *Well, George, we knocked the bugger off!* But his buddy, Tenzing Norgay, never got the same press. But I was lucky. I've known plenty of good climbers forced to follow arrogant, idiot captains on doomed expeditions that leave them exposed on some rock face as the weather moves in, trapping them to a fate of pulmonary edema as their fearless leader whines, *look, no one could have seen the storm coming, so let's not point fingers*, and the Sherpas are stuck there listening to that crap and freezing their balls off, with those terrible headaches, until their lungs fill with fluid and they drown in their own blood.

I'll never forget this one meeting—the first time I ever heard this magical sales pitch about an exciting new opportunity for the firm. A structured product. Credit derivatives. The same stuff that blew up the world in 2008. But before all that, before the sky darkened, I was just another guy sitting in this conference room, listening to some smart young men presenting the latest thing.

I didn't understand any of it. Not one word. I'd never heard of most of the stuff. They might as well have been speaking a different language for how much I understood, and they were. CDS's. CDO's. A CDO of CDS's. A CDO squared. A tranche of CMBX. I looked around at the other salespeople. A lot of smiles and nodding heads and jotting notes in pitch books and little else. Which meant they didn't understand one damn thing, either. After the run-through, no one had anything to say besides Drew. I can't remember the answers; I could barely follow his questions.

I thought the guys upstairs told us that we're supposed to take risk down and get closer to home?

What's the collateral requirement?

What's the counterparty exposure?

Isn't this just a bet on correlation?

What default rate are you using and what's the recovery assumption?

What happens when the models don't work?

Yeah. You just said that. What if they don't?

What's the liquidity in this stuff? How can that be?

Who's buying this?

This doesn't feel like getting closer to home.

Drew listened to their responses, expressionless.

When the meeting ended and everyone left the room, Drew just sort of sat there for a little while, staring at the table. He shook his head and finally said, to no one in particular, "This will all end in tears."

He looked out the glass doors of the conference room. He saw everyone head back to their desks, back to their phones.

"This is gonna be a shit show," he said. "This is gonna be a disaster."

They used to say you could be right on direction, but less often timing, and usually not both. And Drew was a little early on this one, a couple years, even. But he was very right.

Drew still treats me like his Sherpa. If you start working for someone when you're twenty-three, they'll always see you as a kid no matter how much older and balder either of you get.

"What up, mothafucka!" he says, answering his phone. "Holler at ya boy!"

"What?"

"The kids in my class say it."

"Gotcha."

"I don't know. Maybe it sounds better coming from them."

"Well, stick with it."

"Let's never speak of this again. What's going on?"

"Just had a question for you. What do you know about GDR?"

"Uhhhhhhh." He groans, as if I just canceled snow day and told him he needs to get on the bus to school.

"In what way?"

"Brutal. Count your fingers. You're always getting screwed. It's a weird fucking place."

"How do you mean weird?"

"Impossible to deal with. Cultish. Insular. They have a weird culture that's hard to explain. You wouldn't want to work there, bud. Wouldn't want to invest with them, either."

"Do you know some guys over there?"

"Other than Townsend? Yeah, a few."

"How about his brother?"

"Whose?"

"Townsend's."

That was a dumb goddamn thing for me to do. I shouldn't have said that.

"Don't know him," he says. "Why? Did he have a brother there?"

I'm playing with fire here. Drew doesn't miss much. I need to squash this.

"Nah," I tell him. "No reason. Just heard he had one in the business. So, what are the guys at GDR like?"

"They're not worried about going to heaven. Put it that way."

"Right."

"Why? What's up?"

I knew he would ask. Drew's traded information his entire career, living by the code of give a little to get a little. He's done well by this.

"Well," I say. "Just hear me out on this one."

He chuckles and I picture him in the old days at his desk leaning back in his chair, arms folded, focused but half amused, listening to my latest idea. So, I stumble through my current pitch.

"Huh," he says, after I finish. "You know something, sweat pea? That actually wasn't as stupid and uninteresting as I thought it would be."

"Thanks, man."

"No sweat," he says and draws a long sigh, shifting gears. "What else you got?"

"Not much. What do you think?"

"I think you're heated on this thing because you figure it doesn't add up. Maybe it doesn't. And now you're trying to connect the dots. Okay, I get that. But a private equity firm killing somebody?" He clucks his teeth. "I don't see it."

"I'm just asking."

"Yes, you are, bud. Good for you. You still sound like Eeyore, by the way. But GDR? Whacking one of their own guys? I'm not having the shock of recognition here so far."

I can't mention Carson. That's suicidal. Drew's an old salesperson. You want to keep something a secret, don't tell a goddamn sales guy. That's pretty basic stuff.

"How about just as a hypothetical?" I ask.

"I hate hypotheticals."

"Who else would you look at for this thing?"

"You ever talk to his wife?"

"No."

"But you're so good with women. That's strange."

"Yeah, yeah. Maybe I should talk to her. But back to GDR, let me just ask you—"

"My butt itches," he says.

"Let's say it was GDR. Let's say I'm right, OK? Then why? *Why* would they be involved?"

This earns a deafening sigh.

"Give me a second, bud."

He sounds pained. But I can wait.

"Hypothetically," he sneers, then grows more serious. "He threatens them somehow. Backs them into a corner where they don't have any options. Which doesn't make much sense to me. But. Somehow. He'd have to scare the shit out of them."

"Which means?"

"I wouldn't want to go to prison. That would suck."

"Me, neither. It really would."

"Maybe one of their clients—if they pissed off the wrong guy. You know what, bud? The more I think about it…I'm not sure what you're up to here, but I'm not crazy about this thing."

"Wait. Go back to what you were saying about their clients."

"Let's just forget it, all right pal?"

Drew can lose patience. The guy can turn on a dime. He was the sort of guy who would happily sell people all the rope they needed to hang themselves, but if they took too long with their last words, he was also the kind who would run up behind them, force the noose around their neck, and kick them off the scaffold himself.

In the old days I could read him better, pick up on the warning signs. I remember this thing when he'd say *okay*. Sometimes he'd meet with someone, and once they had finished giving him an update, or he had delivered a verdict, he would look at them for a second and then say *okay*. And that was it. But some guys didn't get the message that the meeting was over, so they'd keep rambling because who doesn't want a little more face time with the boss? So you'd watch him sit there, getting angrier and angrier as some guy kept talking his way out of a job. It's funny how we work so hard all our lives and think we're so smart, but sometimes can't tell when we're digging our own graves. Hilarious.

"All I meant to say is I'm missing something," I tell him, not liking that I'm still walking on eggshells. Or wondering if he's an old friend or just my old boss. What kind of friend is someone if you're always worried about pissing them off? If you're a little scared of them?

"Do you remember what I used to tell you was the first rule of this stuff?" he asks.

When I worked for Drew, there were a lot of first rules about a lot of different stuff.

"I don't know," I admit. "I give up."

"Don't get carried out on a stretcher. Don't blow yourself up."

I let out a long sigh before I can stop myself.

"I'm not really sure why—"

"These are the wrong guys to fuck around with," he says. And maybe I'm out of practice, but I can't tell if that's a warning or a threat.

But I do know what he means when he pauses for a moment and then says, "Okay, bud."

21

AN AMBITIOUS MOM organizes swim classes on Wednesday afternoons at her house. Armed with a clean towel and goggles, I lean on the pool's fence with a handful of my comrades, watching the teachers wade in the shallow end with our kids. Luke wears a rash guard and holds a floatie tube, his legs *kick, kick, kick* lashing at the water. I take pictures and video of his progress. Some of the girls in his class seem like future Olympians, their tiny bodies skimming across the pool flat as boards, propelled by their fluttering feet. A few have even begun using their arms in the crawl. The teacher makes Luke roll onto his back to practice floating, which he does not like, and soon I'm thinking about how long it takes a body to sink to the bottom, to then turn and rise back to the surface, wondering if salt water affects the equation. I don't mention this to anyone else.

At the end of class I bundle Luke in his towel like the other kids, his lips almost blue. We thank our host for having us and say goodbye. In the driveway, one of the nicer moms mentions she needs a little assistance installing a new car seat, so I raise my hand, stepping forward. She happily watches Luke and her daughter while I get to work. But I haven't trained with this model or its components, and soon I'm crouched in her backseat sweating like an ape, trying to solve the seat belt equation, my hand jammed between the car's filthy cushions searching for a latch. She observes my efforts and begins making some suggestions, but then offers to give it another try on her own. A few minutes later she figures it out herself.

"Thanks anyway," she says, smiling warmly.

"No problem," I tell her, knowing that we will not speak to each other again for some time.

When I get Luke settled down and strapped into his seat, we head to the library. I have more work to do.

Downstairs, the children's section is empty except for Amy, the friendly librarian. Luke heads for the play area. We're regular customers, and Amy is nice enough to open a large container of LEGOs for us. Luke appreciates the gesture so much that he turns the box upside down, pouring the contents all over the floor. But she doesn't seem worried. I stand here restlessly for a few minutes, watching Luke run off some energy, but when he finally kneels on the carpet and begins assembling pieces, humming softly to himself, I sit down at a desk by the wall, *my* desk by the wall, and pull out my laptop.

I've put together a list of a few dozen GDR background articles, and I'm still grinding my way through them. Most are deal-related summaries of transactions, who did what to who. It's a lot of dry stuff with few surprises, but reading them lets me check their titles off the list. On occasion, I glance over at Luke. I plow through a few contentious stories about GDR-owned businesses that were overleveraged and forced into bankruptcy. GDR has been involved in a fair amount of litigation, and I start jotting down their adversaries. But then a story near the bottom of my list, with an innocuous headline from a magazine that I never even knew covered finance, draws my attention. I read this one carefully.

ACTIVIST INVESTOR

On the morning of September 17, 2015, Grady Walker answered a call he didn't recognize. Walker is the former CEO and founder of TrueServ, a franchisor of over 1,000 fast-food restaurants in the southeastern United States. The caller was Mark Resner, CIO of the investment firm Goldburg, Dower & Resner. Mr. Resner had an offer for Mr. Walker.

The story describes how GDR tried to purchase his business, but Walker declined. They tried to haggle with him on terms and tried upping their price, but it sounds like he just wasn't a seller. The company was in the middle of a turnaround—he didn't want to add debt onto a cyclical business and didn't want a private equity firm involved. But it sounds like GDR didn't take no for an answer. Instead, they went hostile. Extremely hostile, according to this article.

Mr. Walker alleges that GDR began to wage a campaign arguing for the sale of TrueServ in the best interest of shareholders, as well as trying to oust him from his role as CEO. The public fight was ugly and spirited, with GDR making accusations of incompetence, abrasive behavior, and even sexual misconduct.

Mr. Walker claims GDR employed an army of private investigators and detectives to follow and harass his family, friends, neighbors, and current and former employees. He claims the goal of this campaign was to intimidate him and, as he puts it, "dredge up dirt against me and my family."

"I never said that I was a saint," Mr. Walker adds. "Can I be intense or volatile at times? Sure. I don't deny that. But their accusations are without merit and a misrepresentation of my personal behavior." Mr. Walker claims that strange individuals were repeatedly questioning his friends and neighbors, asking for information about him and his family. He adds that unidentified individuals would also approach his family via social media, asking personal questions and allegedly sharing photos of Mr. Walker and other family members that could be seen as reputationally damaging. These accounts have mysteriously disappeared since he reported the incidents.

"How is this not criminal?" Mr. Walker asked. Representatives of GDR declined to comment.

But it seems that didn't matter. In the end, after a year's worth of public fighting, TrueServ's board voted to remove Walker as CEO and agreed to sell the business he founded to a group of investors led by GDR. Although Walker was kicked out, the article claims he netted $700 million in cash from the sale. It doesn't seem to have left him any less bitter.

"A windfall?" he asked. "What the hell does that even mean? That's the dumbest damn thing I've ever heard. That's absurd. To put your whole life into a business only to have it stolen by parasites? You call that a windfall?"

There's a picture of him near the end of the article. Walker's an older man with a full head of gray hair, neatly combed, parted on the side. Wearing jeans with a button-down, he leans on a fence, ignoring the snowcapped mountains in the distance behind him as he stares into the camera. He looks pretty pissed.

As he should. Just because Walker wound up an obscenely wealthy man doesn't make what happened to him right. It was extortion. And somehow GDR got away with this shit! There's no secret—the whole sordid story is right there in front of us—but where's the outrage? Where's the follow-up? No one seems to care. Nobody wants to do anything about this.

That's kind of a pattern. Do you notice how nothing ever really happens to these finance types? They never end up going to prison. They make a boatload of money, blow up the world, get bailed out by our government, who would never pay a single one of our mortgage payments, of course, and then these same guys just hand themselves a bigger bonus the next year. They do that, but they don't go to prison. They don't get convicted or indicted or even accused, let alone investigated. The media can call them titans or big shots, but these guys are somewhere between con artists and kidnappers, maybe even murderers, stealing whatever they can while it lasts. They just rip and run.

I try to imagine how I would feel, sitting at home one day, getting a phone call from Luke telling me a stranger approached him with a bunch of photos filled with unpleasant information about his father. I've never heard of anything like that. The private investigators, the surveillance, harassing someone's family—you have to wonder how any of that stuff is legal. Was the world of leveraged finance so dull that they needed to use such sinister methods? For hundreds of years, anyone in the game could always get their feelings hurt, lose their money or a job—but to go after a guy's family?

I glance toward him, but Luke's not over by the toys. I don't see him anywhere else, either. Picking my head up from the laptop now, I try to listen for a moment, but I don't hear him. Amy's not at her desk, either. The room's empty.

I was sitting between him and the door to the stairs. Could he have made it past me? Wouldn't I have noticed him walking by my desk? That's why I picked this table in the first place.

"Hey, Luke?" I call out. But still silence.

I'm standing up. There's a fire exit by Amy's desk that says "OPEN DOOR ALARM WILL SOUND" in bold letters. Should I try it? What if he made it outside somehow? I skip to check around the bookshelves when I hear a "Hello?" from Amy, just as I turn a corner and see them sitting on the floor inspecting a stack of books. Luke's sucking his thumb, staring off into space. He doesn't even notice me.

"Were you looking for us?" Amy asks, bright-eyed. But her smile begins to fade. "Sorry about that," she says.

"It's no problem," I tell her. "I'm just trying to keep an eye on him."

22

OVER THE YEARS, I've learned that you will sometimes meet these very special women who are so lovely and exquisite, so kind and decent and graceful, that they could only wind up married to a real shithead like Robert Townsend.

I was expecting an ice queen, but Brooke Townsend seems incredible. Although she clearly looks shattered, she still comes across more like an old friend from college, one you could meet for dinner, not see at a charity function. She wears blue jeans, a navy sweater, and she appears, for this region, disgracefully brunette. When I phoned her and asked if I could meet her to offer my condolences, she was nothing but polite, if a little distracted. The free world must have called since the news. As for me, I found her number in the *Club Directory*.

Today she welcomes me through her front door, and I notice this home feels very different from Carson's model. His place seems like some foreboding mansion on a secluded island, whereas Robert built a summerhouse. Even the weather cooperated. There's no Nor'easter today, there's barely a cloud in the sky. The well-decorated inside has floor-to-ceiling windows and beautiful tile floors. This is one of those "modern" upside-down houses, where a massive living room, open to a dining table and quite a kitchen—all the action rooms, really—sit upstairs. The kind of place where you could throw a decent party, if you felt like it, and you did that sort of stuff. We take a seat on the couches in her living room, which surround a large glass table and unlit fireplace. A nice light pours in through the high windows on either side of us, but there's still a coldness to the room. Then again, I should remember that my host just lost her husband.

Brooke's not alone, though. She has a friend sitting two cushions over who, not wanting to just leave Brooke abandoned in a big house after the funeral, has stayed with her for a week. I'm glad that she has. I talk with Nia for a couple minutes, and it turns out she's funny and interesting—she works at one of these new media companies, and her job sounds like just about the coolest way anyone could ever make a living on the planet. She also has a very nice laugh. And not for the first time since I walked into Brooke Townsend's home, I start thinking about how, in the years since I got lost and distracted, it seems like I missed something important but these people didn't—they went out and grabbed it. So I'm not sure how much we'll see each other in the future, but if these guys ever do want to hang out again after this, I'm around, I'm up for it, and I'm totally down.

"How about you?" Nia asks me. And I know this next part could get rough—I've got a little chink in the armor. "What do you do?"

"I worked in finance for a while. But now I take care of my son."

They both smile politely at this. They're trying, and I appreciate that, but I've seen this before. Now the light in their eyes begins to drain, and sure enough, Nia pulls out her phone, and starts scrolling through her feed. This happens. But what can you do?

"How did you know Robert?" Brooke asks me.

"Well, we met through business but mostly from surfing, I guess."

If I can keep my fibs small, that will help this conversation and go easier on my conscience. I don't feel great about lying to a widow who just invited me into her home.

"Were you out here last week?" I ask Brooke, careful not to say *when it happened.*

"No, I was at the office. I came out that Friday night," Brooke says, head in her hands.

"When did Robert come out?" I ask.

"He flew out Wednesday night." Brooke sighs, shaking her head. "To get in some surfing." I can't pull out my phone to take notes, but I would if I could.

"He told you he was coming out to get on the water?" I ask, maybe a bit too sharply.

"You know Robert," Brooke says, rolling her eyes and smiling. "He worked hard but he could always get away with taking days off. If the surf looked good, he would take the helicopter out the night before, work from here, get some time in the water, and be back in the office the next morning. He was obsessed." Nia nods her head in agreement, eyes still glued to the phone in her hand.

That sounds nice. Having a job where you can sneak out of the office because the snow or the water looks enticing, commuting via helicopter—boys will be boys. That all sounds pretty good. Except what she said doesn't make sense. Townsend looked at the same surf reports I do—there's plenty of websites to stare at longingly and see what you're missing. But that week? No forecast would have told him the conditions warranted taking a sick day. Not even close.

"I was stuck in the office all week," Brooke goes on. Maybe talking to someone feels therapeutic right now. "So I drove out late Friday night. I'd been trying to reach him all day. The last time we spoke was Thursday. He called me just before he went in the water, the way he always did. But when I got here so late on Friday, I went to bed, I was just so exhausted. I can't believe I did that. I didn't call the police until Saturday."

She seems determined to torture herself about this. Even though it couldn't have made a difference, she's still working herself over. I could tell her that, in some similar situation, I have no idea when my wife would have even started to worry, let alone called the authorities, but the time elapsed would be significant and noticeable. And the texts she would send me while I was missing—they wouldn't age well.

"These guys just don't get it," Nia whispers to herself, thumbing through some email.

I need to get my head back in the game.

"Have you spoken much with the guys from GDR?" I ask Brooke.

"Oh yes, they've been great. I'm actually having dinner with Mark tonight. I should probably get cleaned up before," Brooke says, laughing to herself. She must mean Mark Resner.

"I thought he gave a nice eulogy," I offer.

"I wish he hadn't mentioned the poker stories," Brooke says, her head in her hands.

"Oh, that's bullshit," mutters Nia to her phone, shaking her head disappointed. "That doesn't work."

"I'm sorry, what were you asking?" Brooke says to me, smiling. "You were saying something? I'm a little distracted."

I'm a little distracted myself, Brooke. I need to get it together.

"You were just talking about GDR," I tell her. "About Mark Resner."

"Yes. They've been incredible. Lifesavers." But she leaves it there, and before I can think of a follow-up, she asks, "Can I get you anything to drink? I think I'm going to need a cup of coffee."

"I'm fine," I tell her. As she stands up and heads for the fridge, I follow her over. Her kitchen is a mess. Dishes are stacked high in the sink. Trays of finger food and assorted plates line the counters and a garbage bin looks close to overflowing. An army of people have dropped by or sent care baskets and their condolences are piling up.

"Can I help with anything?" I ask.

"No, no," she says.

"I could take out the trash. Really, it's no problem. I need the exercise."

Brooke insists she's fine, but when she reaches for a shelf, back turned to me, Nia appears, nodding, flashing two thumbs-up, and mouthing *yes, yes* with enthusiasm. She even slides open a hidden drawer to another swelling trash and recycling can.

"You don't have to do that," Brooke says.

"Maybe you could just bring it outside," suggests Nia.

The three of us get to work, pouring cans and plastic bottles out in the sink and adding them to the clear bags I hold open. Nia directs me downstairs to their garage. I drop the recycling in a marked bin but loiter in the damp room for a moment, looking around. There are no cars parked inside, but they have two road bikes, several sets of golf clubs, both fly-fishing and surf casting rods, a wide range of Yeti coolers—this collection must cost about as much as my car. A tall stand-up paddle leans into a corner, and a board storage rack is mounted against the far wall, with three sets of arms jutting out like branches. A split-tailed-fish shortboard and a large stand-up paddleboard hang from the top and bottom arms. The middle arms of the rack are empty. I'm not sure what I'm looking for. Townsend had a leash on his ankle with a snapped rope, but they never found the board.

"That's a big help," Nia says, dropping another clinking bag next to mine. "I've been doing it all week." I realize she noticed me looking at the boards, but she seems sympathetic. "It's hard," she says. "C'mon." I take a last glance around the garage, still uncertain of what I'm hoping to find.

When I follow her back upstairs, we see Brooke sitting on the couch, studying the fireplace. We take our seats around her. Nothing is said for a few moments.

"Have you seen much of Carson?" I ask Brooke.

"Who?" she says. Which, in a way, is a real answer.

"Were Robert and his brother not close?" I ask. She rubs her face and looks embarrassed by my questions, but in fairness, she hasn't slept in a week.

"I don't know. Was he close with Carson? No, I guess he wasn't."

"I never heard him talk about him much," I offer.

"No, he didn't. But Robert did try, he really did try with Carson."

"I don't think I've ever even met Carson," adds Nia. She's looking at Brooke.

"Those things are really hard," says Brooke. "It was complicated. Sometimes there's only so much you can do."

Wall Street attracts some competitive characters. Ambition is more of a prerequisite for success in the industry than brains or anything else. Some people can't do anything, *anything* on Earth, without keeping score. They can't help themselves. So, think about two overachieving brothers, in constant competition, always one-upping the other or needing to scream *mine's bigger.* Not difficult to imagine forty years of those conversations could cause more than a little friction. Harder to think that it wouldn't.

"What time's your dinner?" Nia asks.

"I think it's seven," says Brooke, and I sense it may be time for me to go somewhere else.

I say my goodbyes and thank Brooke more than once for having me. When I stand up to leave, Nia offers me an unexpected hug. She's a good hugger and she smells very nice, but I don't feel better about coming here, and now I think it really is time for me to leave.

Outside, sitting in my car, I look back up at the house and think how a dream home like this one—beautiful, enormous, well-kept—could get lonely. Summer's over now, and that house must feel empty. I'm glad I didn't bring Luke.

But before I forget my reasons for coming, I jot down some notes from our conversation. I use this little app on my phone.

Robert he came out Wednesday night for the surf.

He needed to get away from GDR?

Some action on the side?

When another option crosses my mind, I write it down, too—even if it's unlikely, you always have to do this, or you forget and you lose them. You need to write down the ideas that conflict with your story.

Brooke's lying to me?

She comes out late Friday, doesn't see him and doesn't call anybody?

That does seem a bit odd. Unless they slept in separate beds? That might explain it, and also why she felt so embarrassed. Maybe the Townsends fell into that lonely habit, the dirty little secret no one tells you about marriage? I don't know, but it's time for me to be getting home.

I back out of my spot and I'm easing along the gravel driveway, passing the garage, when I see it. Not visible from the road, but behind the bushes, in the edging that lines the yard, lying on its rail in the mulch-covered ground, is a surfboard leaned against the side of the house, the soft top foam deck facing the sun. I stop the car and get out for a closer look.

The board is a nine-foot, light blue Odysea LOG. A product of the Catch Surf company. It's incredibly popular for beginners, experts with a sense of humor, or bigger guys looking for a higher wave count. Just to be sure, I creep over and turn it upside down to look at the bottom, blank white, without graphics. You see these things everywhere. But the day Townsend went missing, when I saw him down at the beach, this one was strapped to the roof of his car.

I'm sure of it. I'd seen him on it before.

So how the hell did this nice LOG make its way back here unless he drove it himself? And if Townsend drove this thing back here, in the opposite direction of Hamilton Beach, then you can shut the door on that theory about him deciding to squeeze in a session, unless you believe this is one of those boards that lets you see in the dark.

For some reason, as I start my car up again and turn off Brooke's street onto the main road, following it out to the highway, I can't stop looking in my rearview. Over and over, checking to see if a black Range Rover's behind me.

23

COMING IN HOT to pickup this afternoon. Nothing has gone right today.

Here's what happened. This morning the forecast said about three feet and clean, so I decided to take a little break from the nonsense and sneak in ninety minutes on the water, just to clear my head. It was a misty, gray weekday and I had the place to myself. I was out there a couple hours and didn't see one other person, not even a dog walker or a beachcomber. Then I come in, walk up the beach to my car, change out of my wet suit, take the Tide bottle shower, put on my clothes, feeling pretty good about everything, patting myself down for wallet and keys and then—I notice, somehow, I can't find my phone. It's not in my pants, not in the center console, and it didn't fall out in the back. I looked under every towel and wet wipe and soda can, between the seats, and nothing. Now, of course, this happens to me a decent amount and I always find it somewhere. But then, as I scrounge through all my crap, I look in my backpack, and my laptop's not in there. And I know I brought it this morning—I was in a hurry, but I'm sure of it—since I'd planned on getting some work done at the library after the surf, but now it's not there. They didn't touch the wallet or the keys in my pocket, but some fucker stole my laptop and my cell phone. And all around me, the whole place, the beach, the road, was empty, not a soul.

I freaked out a little bit. I threw a fit, tried to settle down, but I couldn't, so I just hopped in the car and hauled ass back home. And sure, the whole time I'm wondering if I'm just going nuts—but when the hell do I ever leave the house without my cell phone? And I swear I brought my laptop in the backpack so I could sneak some food into the library the way I always do. And what work can I do without a computer? Not much. So I tore my house apart for hours. I turned it upside down, cursing myself for all the clutter I've never gotten rid of. And you start to realize how helpless you are without this crap because I wanted to call the library to see if maybe I left the laptop there yesterday somehow, but I don't even have internet for the number to call on my landline. I don't have shit. So the panic keeps rising as I'm more and more convinced someone actually snuck into my car—I never lock it, I don't know why, probably because I'm a damn idiot—and now some fucker breaks into my car and steals my stuff but leaves my wallet and cash alone and I don't like the timing of this at all. But then it gets worse. In the midst of this shit, I notice I've lost track of time and now I'm late to pick up Luke from school.

I spit gravel peeling out of my driveway and start tearing down these roads as fast as my nerves can handle. So now my tires are screeching through the turns as I tell myself *slow, slow, settle down*, the worst thing I could do is get pulled over or get in an accident, so just slow down, relax, easy, easy—as I'm pinning the pedal against the floor. If I could just call, maybe I could stop what's coming, call the school, call Lauren even, but I can't, I'm trapped with no moves. All I can do is count the minutes and miles—doing the math, my eyes darting between the road and the clock and the rearview—scanning for a black Range Rover or anyone else behind me. There's nothing. Maybe they already got what they needed? If someone were tailing me, it would be pretty damn obvious, chasing me around town at this kind of speed. And if I'm late enough, that's a whole new pot of problems for me.

I jam the brakes a few hundred yards in front of Luke's school and try to ease into the parking lot like a decent human being. I've no trouble finding a spot. Even the slowest mom fled the scene a long time ago. Luke and a young teacher sit together on the front steps, waiting on me. I mop the sweat off my forehead with a beach towel and step out of the car, praying I've made it in time, getting my apologies ready.

"Hey guys! I'm so, so sorry about this. It's my fault."

"Oh, it's no problem."

"No, no. Hey, buddy. Hey. Sorry I'm late."

"Are you all right?" she asks as Luke ignores me.

I can feel the beads already pouring off my face again.

"Sure. Sure. You ready, buddy?" I ask him.

"I hope you don't mind," she says, and I know what's coming, I'm ready for the bullet. "I called your wife," she says.

"Okay, great," I tell her. "Thanks. Thanks a lot. Sorry about that."

"I left a voice mail," she says.

Well then, that's the end of it. I'm finished. It is what it is.

"And then she tried me back and I missed her," she says. This is getting better and better. "But then I called and I reached her and we spoke."

"Thanks. I'm sorry about this," I tell her again. Luke seems pleased.

"Of course. But the thing is. I think now, maybe, she's a little bit, *worried.*"

"Yep."

"I'm sorry, I didn't know if I should um, call *her.* Or *you!*" she says with a shrug, smiling and swaying her head from side to side between the two choices. This woman and I say hello to each other twice a day, five days a week, whereas she has never met my wife in person, to my knowledge. But then today, of course, she calls her. She doesn't call me. Which is super helpful. Just what I need.

"Oh, it's no problem," I tell her. "Don't worry about it! You can try either one of us. But here, why don't I give you my cell number, not that I'm ever going to be late again, right? But just so you have it. In the future, you can always reach me. All right? For anything that comes up. You can always call me. Just call me. Okay?"

"Great!" she says brightly. "I tried you a few times, but it went to voice mail. Let me make sure I have the right number."

I need to get the fuck out of here.

"Okay, buddy," I tell Luke, clapping my hands together. "Time for us to go."

By the time I manage to clip him into the car seat and drive over to the box, they're already half an hour into the session. I get him situated in the playroom and don't even bother changing clothes, which is just as well, since I didn't come here to work out today. I sit on a bench, waiting for the class to end, and try not to stare at everyone throwing weights around, which gives me a chance to torture myself a little more. Maybe I just lost my stuff and I'm driving myself nuts? Looking for a cell phone or set of car keys or a stuffed animal takes up a big part of my life. But the laptop? And this happens how many days after I meet with Carson? Just think through the odds. Some goon came by the beach looking for me. Then that guy pissed off Felix at the library. And I'm supposed to believe it's all just a coincidence? No way.

After the session's over, Gandle sits on the floor by a kettlebell and medicine ball, catching her breath. The last time we hung out, she messed with me and it wasn't so great, but what the hell can I do? I need to tell *somebody*.

"Do you have a second?" I ask her.

"What's up?"

"It's been a rough day," I admit. I try to explain what happened earlier down at the beach as best as I can, grateful to have someone who might know what to do. She's very cool about it. She listens carefully. I need to remember she doesn't come here when she's off the clock to hear complaints about stolen property.

"Sorry to bother you with this. I don't know if I should have."

"No, no," she insists. "It's no problem. I'm glad that you did."

"It's got me a little rattled."

"Of course."

"Anyways, I'm not sure what else to say. What do you think?"

"Well, one thing I can do is check in with the local pawnshop. See if the laptop turns up."

"Do you find a lot of stuff there?"

She shrugs her shoulders up around her hawser of a neck. *I'm trying to help you out here, tough guy. What do you want me to say?*

"Thanks."

"No problem," she says, still studying me. She doesn't say anything else, so I kind of study her back until I lose the contest and then look away. There's a lot more I'd like to ask her, but I'm not sure if I should. I have to be careful here. I need help, but after the other day, I don't really know if she's on my team.

"Do you need me to come down and fill out any kind of paperwork or anything?" This isn't one of those questions that's been gnawing at me, but it feels a little quiet in here and I'm filling the space.

"No. That's okay. I'd rather you didn't," she says with the trace of a smirk. I guess she's keeping it off the books.

"Great. Thanks. This thing has kind of turned me upside down."

"No problem," she says. "It's unsettling."

"Right."

"Anytime anyone gets robbed. Someone breaks into their house. Or their car. It's invasive."

"Yeah, it is."

"A total stranger," she goes on, unnecessarily. She's folded her arms, and she isn't exactly rubbing my back. "Some stranger going through all your stuff."

"It's unsettling," I admit.

"Stealing your shit."

"Do you think this could have anything to do with what happened to Townsend?" I ask finally, since I can't take any more.

"No, I don't," she says, without needing to weigh the matter over too carefully.

"It's just kind of a coincidence."

This earns me another shrug. "I don't see it," she says.

Maybe I could give her something? So long as I don't mention anything about Carson. Or going to see Brooke Townsend at her place.

"Unless," she says, "there's something you're not telling me?"

"So...the other day I heard this guy came by the beach looking for me. And it spooked me a little bit."

"What guy?"

"I don't know. I heard he wasn't a cop. But I don't know. And then, you were screwing around with me the other day—so, I've got to ask. Is there any chance you'd tell me if you guys were looking into me as a suspect?"

She doesn't seem happy with the question.

"Let me be as straight with you as I can. I have no clue what you're talking about."

"Well, if he wasn't a cop and somebody stole my stuff this morning, it's just kind of a coincidence."

"Where's Luke?" she asks, looking over my shoulder.

"Do you see what I mean?"

"I need to get my hands on him."

"Hey, I'm not kidding. If there's someone out there looking for me, following me around—then what? What's that tell you? What am I supposed to do?"

"Take it easy, okay? Go home and get some sleep. I told you to let this thing go."

Later, back home, I get Luke fed and down for the night. I'm hoping for a few hours of relief, a chance to process what happened today. But not long after, I hear Lauren walk in the front door. Her footsteps sound angry, they keep growing louder, and they're headed right toward me.

"Hey," I start.

And get no response.

"I'm sorry about today," I try again.

I don't know what she's doing, but I guess she's decided that she doesn't need to stop doing it just to give me a response.

"Everything's fine. But it was a crazy day. It's kind of a long story."

She's going through the mail, flipping through a stack of envelopes, reading, turning them over, reading the other side, discarding them. This could take a while. She seems to be doing it pretty carefully.

"Are you all right?" I ask her.

"Hey," she says without looking up at me. I guess it's going to be one of these. So, I need to use caution here because, unless I can turn this around, this is happening.

"Look, I'm sorry I was late. But can I just explain?"

"Why are you such a fucking asshole?" she screams. And it's on. She's picking up speed. "What's the matter with you? Do you think this is funny? Because you're Mr. Laid-back? The whole *I don't give a shit* routine?"

I could interrupt her, I could stop the tantrum and gnashing teeth, but I want to hear this. I hate all that stored-away resentment. I want to know what she really thinks. Go on, Lauren, let it out.

"Do you know how bad this looks?" she says. "You think people don't talk about this kind of thing when they see him sitting there alone with Ms. Yanni? Do you get that?"

Oh, I think I get the picture. *How bad this looks.* In one sentence, she's summed up not just her darkest fears but her entire moral compass. Anything to keep from feeling embarrassed. She's all about social status and keeping up with her peers, and I've offended her perfectionist standards. Her all-or-nothing acid test. No nuance, just cut-and-dried. There are two types of people on planet Earth—investment banking partners and total pieces of shit.

This is what she always does. She always builds from the silent treatment to the screaming fit. But tonight, she's hitting me with both barrels of conditional love to make sure I get the message. Her eyes could scald me right now.

"And you never fucking called me!" she screams.

Shit. I guess I lost track of everything. I should have used the landline, but by the time I got back, it just slipped my mind, with Gandle messing with me and every other damn thing. That's not good—that one's on me. "Do you know how worried I was? Did you even know Ms. Yanni called me back after you left? How would you?"

"Someone stole my cell phone," I tell her.

"What?"

"I got robbed today."

"Are you serious?"

"Some scumbag stole my cell phone. And my laptop. I just had sort of a crazy day."

"Jesus."

"Yeah. Down at the beach. Someone stole them out of my car."

"Oh, Jesus."

"I should have called you from home. But I was already late and—"

"Are you sure they were stolen? *What?* Why are you looking at me like that?"

I don't really know how to answer any of this. I can't keep this up forever. I try forcing a smile, rubbing the back of my neck, but I need to get some sleep.

"It's just that, with Luke. You never know, right? He's always hiding things."

"Sure," I manage to say through gritted teeth. I know that sometimes

Luke picks things up and doesn't put them back when he's done with them. I've noticed this over the years. But at least Gandle came up with that shit about pawnshops.

"You've looked, right?" she asks and hovers over the couch. She worms a hand into the cushions. I could see myself getting a little pissed in a minute. "You looked?" she asks again when I don't respond.

"Yeah."

Does she think I'm just sitting around the house watching TV?

"Do you remember the last time you had it?" she asks.

I'm running out of moves, here.

"Pete?"

"What'd I just say?" I snap. And I'm going for it—my voice is loud and my eyes are angry.

When Lauren stares back at me, there are no tears, but I know I won't get another word out of her the rest of the night. She's done with me. Not much is going right this evening.

Things quiet down a little and I try to apologize, but she's not having it. And it is my fault—I could have handled this better. I need to just sit there, smiling, and take it. I don't know why I can't learn. Whenever I have a flare-up with my wife, I never come out of it healthy—I always walk away feeling dirty and mean.

Later that night, I peek into our bedroom, assessing the scene. She lies on her side, curled up in bed, facing away from the door. The duvet and sheets are pulled up over her head, and she probably has her eye mask on underneath, many layers of protection, whatever it takes, anything to spare her the sight of me. The lump under the covers is draped at an angle over the middle of the mattress. I don't think she's looking for company.

So, I steal a banket from the foot of our bed, creep into Luke's room, and settle onto the couch next to him. There's a pillow already there waiting for me.

I tuck myself in and study the ceiling for a little while. No answers have come to me yet when I hear a disturbance. Luke's fine, still snoring, but something's stirring, somewhere in the dark, sounds like it's below me. For a moment it stops and then starts again. I lean over the precipice and slowly lower myself down, resting my weight against the top of my head on the floor and peer under the couch to see my phone lying on the carpet, glowing peacefully. Now it vibrates again in the dark.

I have twelve new messages, it seems.

Nine of them are from LAUREN and, right at that moment, I can't bring myself to read any of these. I think I know the gist of what she wanted to tell me, but then three, check that *four*, messages from FRANK.

Tomorrow looks good? he asked me at 5:33 p.m.

What do u think?

Doable?

Hey

I could have sworn I brought my laptop this morning. The library's the only place it could be. Unless some fucker stole it. Or else it's somewhere around here, maybe.

?

Frank's still texting me, looking for answers.

Speak, he says.

I don't know what to think anymore.

Pussy

I need to get some sleep.

24

THE SHERIFF IS standing outside my front door, and he doesn't look pleased.

He had called me this afternoon and said that he'd like to speak with me, but that he would prefer we talk in person. So, I told him that he could come by around eight, that my wife had to work late, and that I would be guarding the home front, watching the little guy after I get him down to sleep. The sheriff said that he understood.

I watched his car pull into my driveway from my upstairs window. He sat in the dark inside his cruiser for a minute or two, looking at my house. When he got out, he walked over and examined my car, then one of my surfboards lying on the front lawn next to a very large, plastic toy car. My son likes to ride in it as I push him up and down the street. The sheriff ignored Luke's vehicle. Then he walked up and rang the doorbell. Twice. And although I have a lot of respect for his profession and would never wish harm on any officer of the law, I did tell him, when we spoke earlier, what time Luke goes to sleep.

I open the door for the sheriff, hoping that if I can make a decent impression, it will put him at ease.

"Thanks for stopping by. How are you?"

"Can we talk inside?" he says without returning my smile. His face is scarred by years of worry and not enough pleasantries.

"Sure, sure, come on in. Why don't we talk in the kitchen. I don't want to wake up my son. We've got thin walls in this place."

He follows me but seems to take his time, looking around my house, inspecting the contents, even though there isn't much to see.

"Can I get you something to drink?" I ask, trying to keep up my casual bit.

"I'll take a beer. My shift's over."

Opening the fridge, I can't quite remember the last time we had a visitor, off duty or otherwise. "Sorry. We don't have any beer. Do you want a soda—we have Diet Coke, water, or milk? My wife may have some wine if I can find it."

I realize after I say this that I'm not sorry about what I have on offer. I made a mistake, Sheriff, but I fixed it. Don't you see?

"Water's fine," he says.

I offer him my kitchen table, and he sits down, which seems to take a modest effort. He takes off his hat and rubs his head for a while. I realize that if I was looking for a safe place to feel comfortable and speak without fear of judgment, then this table—the scene of so many prior interrogations, all those *Pete, I feel like you're not even listening to me*—wasn't a good choice. He sits down in my chair, but there's no reason to let him know this—he's used to sitting where he likes. I take a seat across from him, resting my elbows on the table, and he keeps turning his head, studying the room. I think how we could have met anywhere—lots of places would have been fine—anything but inviting a cop into my house.

With a cop in your home, you start thinking about little mistakes. That ticket for a busted taillight you got and maybe didn't pay on time, or a taillight you fixed yourself. Your credit score, that stupid Gap card, your employment record. Thinking how you might stop doing your own taxes. Looking at women for too long, losing your train of thought, making them uncomfortable. Driving like a lunatic when you're loaded with little ones in the car or interviewing a dead guy's relatives. Those kinds of things.

"So, what's going on?" I ask him.

"Oh, I've just been hearing a few things lately."

His fingers drum the table as he stares at me, but he doesn't go into specifics.

"What kind of things?"

"Has there been any luck with your missing property?" he asks. He could have said stolen. I scratch my beard, considering the right response. All my options have their drawbacks.

"I found my cell phone," I tell him. "Thanks. I don't know about the laptop."

I found it camouflaged in the bookshelf, hidden between a row of hardbacks and the bottom shelf. God knows how it ended up there, but I have a tiny suspect in mind.

"Maybe it'll turn up," he says.

I was led to believe my incident would stay off the record, but now I wonder how much Gandle told him about our conversation. Probably everything, which wasn't nice of her.

"Yeah, hopefully," I tell him.

"Let me ask you something on a different topic. Did you go to Robert Townsend's funeral?"

"Robert was a friend of mine."

"That's not what I asked."

He looks pained.

"Yes. Yes. I went to the service."

The way he's talking to me, it sure feels like I'm a suspect of some kind.

"And then one of my deputies told me something strange." As if it could be one of hundreds. "You're worried that you could be some sort of a suspect?"

"I'd heard that there was a guy looking for me. Did she tell you that?"

"A suspect in what?"

I could have met the sheriff anywhere. Anywhere but my kitchen table. Here, at this place, where hopes come to die, where dreams are buried, like a wishing well that laughs when your coins hit the water.

"I wondered if it could be related to Robert Townsend's death," I tell him.

"Well," he says, hitching a thumb in his belt. He leans back in his chair and studies me like a disappointed relative. "I'm not sure why you need to believe this was something other than an accident, but you do, and that worries me."

"Well, this was a little bit of a strange accident. We can admit that at least, right?"

The sheriff rests his face on his hand, fingers covering his mouth. He looks as if he *does* find something odd about all this, and it's me.

"And what about the guy who came by the beach looking for me?" I ask him.

"Maybe he found your laptop."

"Did you look in to this at all? Did you investigate? Was there an autopsy? Have you spoken to people who knew him?"

"You're not making me feel a hell of a lot better."

"Have you talked to someone like Carson Townsend?"

Now, from the look on his face, I can see that I've made a terrible mistake, and this might not be a small one. I'm too long out of practice and acting like a rookie, getting defensive, running my mouth and leading with my chin. I'm glad Drew's not here to see this.

"Jesus Christ, are you serious?" And there's nothing droll in his voice now. "How the hell can you even ask me that? You think this is my first day in this seat? That family's been out here for years. A guy like that, with something like this? Of course I talked with him. I drove out myself and handled it. You think that was easy for me? You think that's a fun part of my job?"

Maybe I am a little careless sometimes. Carson gave me a simple warning. Keep his name out of this mess or there'll be bloodshed. I may still wiggle out of this one, but if I do, I won't make that mistake again.

Meanwhile the sherriff's mood is only growing worse. He's passed concerned.

"Wait a second," he says, eyes widening. "Don't even think about it."

"About what?"

"You're not thinking of going out there and talking to him?" he says, pointing his finger at me. "Jesus, what is wrong with you? A guy like that? If you start asking questions about this, do you have any clue what could happen? About his brother? Do you know what that could do? Please tell me you understand. Tell me you get that."

He looks scared. The sheriff's scared of Carson. And he should be—a guy like that, with his resources? Someone like Carson could prove that Sheriff Butterfingers botched the investigation.

"I understand," I assure him. "You just didn't seem to be taking me seriously."

"Don't test me on that one."

"I wouldn't do that."

"You know, the longer I talk to you, the more you give me the creeps." He's trying to provoke me now, trying to piss me off enough to say something stupid. "I get the feeling you're barely listening to me. I don't want to have to come over here again, you understand?"

"You won't."

He doesn't look too convinced. So, we just sit here, staring at each other for a little bit. But he grows calmer after a while, almost dejected. He exhales and shakes his head.

"Look, I'm going to tell you something you need to hear," he says, holding up an open hand. "Listen to me now. I've been doing this a long time and I've come across a certain kind of guy. I've seen a bunch of 'em. I've even known a few cops like this. Guys who aren't doing what they wanted. They're bored with the job or where they're headed—they think they're better than where they're at. You with me? They can't deal with it. So, they sit around, dogging it. Right? But then they get pissed. They can turn on a dime—it happens pretty fast. Matter-of-fact, there's only one part of the job they really do like. These guys like accidents. They like car wrecks, a brick through a window, seeing a big crash. They want to hear the sound of breaking glass. And if they can't find an accident, sometimes they make one."

He takes a good pull on his water and wipes his mouth with the back of his hand.

"Do you know anyone like that?" he asks looking at me.

If I feel a little threatened listening to something like that, I'm not sure that's a good thing. In fact, I'm sure that it isn't.

"That's not gonna be me."

He looks down at his watch and starts shaking his head. Then, as if in some sort of pain, he rubs the back of his neck with a sigh. There's no ring on his finger.

"I think it's time for me to get going," he says. "Feels like we're about done here. Thanks for having me over."

He stands to leave, and it doesn't look comfortable—maybe it's his back or a knee. The sheriff isn't that old, but he has come to the age when a lot of things start to hurt and you find fewer solutions to fix them. I walk him out, and he pauses in my doorway, looking around, then down the hall toward a bedroom. Finger paintings of various quality hang from the door.

"That's my son's room."

He nods and keeps staring down the hall. Then he turns to me, and when we shake hands, his eyes aren't filled with kindness, but I meet them.

"Nice talking with you," he says. "But think about what I said."

I stand in the doorway and watch him lumber back to his car, until he stops at the edge of the lawn and lingers for a moment to look at my surfboard. It's a longboard, a big one.

I could tell him right now. I could tell him how I saw Townsend's board at his house, the same one he had on his car that day down at the beach. And I might ask why the hell he would have driven home and out of his way to drop his board off, maybe switch it for another, and then race in the other direction back out to Hammy's. But I have a feeling that if I do, the sheriff will ask how I happen to know this, and I don't think he'll like the answer. I could tell him I was just passing by the house, except you can't see it from the road. He'd still talk to Brooke, either way. And if I told him that it was the same board, would he even believe me? What did Gandle say that day she was messing with me at the box about criminals who like to hang out at their crime scenes? Something about how they're bored and it gives them a thrill?

The sheriff glances back over his shoulder at me, pursing his lips. Then, at last, he turns and leaves.

25

DREW CAME THROUGH like he always does. The old firm represented Grady Walker in his takeover defense against GDR, and Drew called in a favor from a banker over there and found Walker's contact info. The next part was up to me.

I didn't want to just cold-call the guy, so I worked up a carefully worded email. I went through several drafts. I tried to convince him that I'm a freelance journalist of some sort (extremely freelance) who used to work in finance, and I am looking to learn more about what happened when he was pushed out of the firm that he founded. I told him how outraged I was by the few details the magazine article provided. For a moment, I considered mentioning that I'd hoped to speak with the author of that article, but last night I was disturbed to discover that the young journalist is no longer on planet Earth. A tragic turn of events. I wanted to ask if Walker had heard that the poor writer had passed away just six months ago, or that the unfortunate thirty-eight-year-old Mr. Levin had made his exit via a single-car accident, and from the pictures online, it looked like a very nasty crash? But in the final version, I deleted this question before I hit send.

It's a long shot and I know it, but what other choice do I have? The chances that he responds to my email are slim, and even if I can get him on the phone, the odds that he'd be willing to talk with me about GDR—let alone give me something helpful—are probably a lot smaller.

But he did sound pretty pissed in that article. Of course, he wound up with a boatload of money to take the sting out of the bite. And it had been a few years since the whole thing had happened.

Anyways, I sent the email and took Luke to the park with a big group of moms. We sat on the grass in a circle, and I felt like some sort of ape who had once wandered off from his home in the jungle and was now welcomed back to the tribe. I tried not to look at my phone.

Within an hour, just out of degenerate habit, I needed a little distraction and reached into my pocket. I saw it right there at the top of my inbox—a reply from Walker.

He got to the point.

Let's talk. What times work for you?

Walker seems like the kind of guy who can really hold a grudge.

Pacing back and forth in my kitchen, I can still watch Luke playing outside through the window. I need at least one glass sheet between me and my assistant, to keep his outbursts separate from this call.

From what I've read about him down there in the children's section, it sounds like Grady Walker was never designed for long hours at the library. This is a large American. The "loudest guy in the room" type. Walker is the sort of man who is always accidentally knocking into another person, then introducing himself, telling an offensive story, then slapping them on the back, hard enough to cause further injury. He's not someone I can see pushing a stroller.

"Mister Peter Greene," he says when he answers the phone, his drawl all confidence and melody.

"Thanks for taking my call."

"Oh, that's all right. Word around town is you're a decent guy, a little off the radar, but a decent guy." For a second, I wonder what he means by this or who he's talked to. "So, what can I do for you, sir?"

"I wanted to ask about what happened between you and GDR."

"It's out there. It's all public."

"I understand and I've read the articles. If you don't mind, I'd still like to hear your version."

"Short story is I got robbed by a bunch of thieving-ass sons of bitches."

"That's what it sounded like."

"I guess you're looking for the longer version?"

"I'm sure it's not your favorite thing to talk about, but if you don't mind."

"I don't give a fuck. There are parts of this crap I'm legally prevented from getting into—which is a barrel of laughs—but I don't give a shit who hears what *I* think of these motherfuckers. How much time you got?"

"I appreciate that," I tell him.

Walker now lives in Ketchum, Idaho. Sun Valley is the kind of setting where you could decompress, get away from all the madness and maybe pour yourself into some serious fly-fishing, mountain biking, or skiing. Some people who move to these sorts of places find a sense of peace and clarity for the next chapter in their lives. Grady Walker isn't one of them. This man sounds more like a general without an army.

"I had my first job in a Waffle House when I was twelve years old. Now, don't worry—I won't be long—good parts coming up. So I worked my way from scrubbing toilets to the grill and then to manager, and I saved a little and begged and borrowed a bit until I owned my first store. I ran it pretty well, and then I borrowed a little extra, and pretty soon I owned a couple more. And that worked pretty well. So, fifty years from when I started cleaning shitters, turns out I run a business with about eight hundred stores that employ around twenty thousand people. Our stock went up by forty times since we went public—I never sold a share. But then I get a call from Mark Resner, a first-class sonavabitch. He wants to buy this business I started, tells me how much he thinks it's worth. And the thing is, I never asked. I tell him thanks for calling. You know what he says? He tells me you're making a mistake. I laughed at him. He says if I want him to keep his media team out of it, we should keep talking. So, I said all right, let me help you out. Go fuck yourself."

My phone vibrates.

Do you think you can help out a little bit with something? Lauren texts me and manages to pose the question as if I've spent the past years missing in action, unwilling to do a single thing for her or my son.

"You still with me?" Walker asks.

"What happened next?"

We need ORGANIC whole milk and blueberries and

"Well, the next morning I was in Wachtell Lipton's office, lawyering up and trying to cover my ass. We brought in your banking guys that night to talk about defense. Did we wanna use a poison pill? What about a proxy fight? That sort of thing. Not how I wanted to spend my Saturday. So then we had a little more back and forth with my friends at GDR. We got into some name-calling. Pretty soon after that, the articles started coming about how I was running the place into the ground. Bunch of nonsense. The arbs got involved, trying to buy up as much of the stock as they could for a quick flip. The board shit their pants. I'm calling the real money guys, long-term shareholders, telling them to sit tight. But that's the usual bullshit. I was ready for that."

"Did you give any thought to going private?" I ask for some reason. "Topping their bid?"

"That's what your boys suggested. I barely had the capital, and I didn't want to lever up. Maybe it was a last option, but it wouldn't have mattered. That's not why I lost my ass."

Inside, Luke prepares an imaginary meal on the toy kitchen set. I know where this is going next.

"It started when one of my neighbors complained that some flatfoot came by his house asking questions about me. Turns out they had an army of private detectives digging up anything they could find. The first envelope showed up on my doorstep a few weeks later. Just pictures. Head shots, nothing racy. But I knew all the women. There was no message inside, just pictures. And now, it's been in the papers. This what you wanted to hear? What can I say? I've been married more than a few times."

I read the articles—the infidelity, the lawsuits settled out of court—but I hadn't imagined waking up one morning to find a gallery of a life's worth of indiscretions on my doorstep.

"Then magically, these kinds of stories start popping up in the press. All of a sudden, I'm a sexual predator—I was never running a company—just playing grab-ass my whole life."

"So, what'd you do?" I ask.

"I bowed up," he says. "What was I going to do, back down? I'm not proud of it, but I hired my own guy. A private consultant."

"Private security?" I ask.

"Something like that."

Neither of us says anything for a moment before he goes on.

"I had to see if I could find something on them—maybe they'd back off. I don't know if I ever would have even used it."

"Did you find anything?" I ask.

"In a couple months it was a moot point. My own board knew it was GDR leaking all this crap—I dated a couple women in the business, and they made it seem like I ran a casting couch—and that they were putting out stuff from the divorce papers, ex-girlfriends, all the rest. But the board didn't have the spine for it. They had a firm bid on the table and didn't want a proxy fight. A few months later, they chucked me out. Of course, by then, two of my daughters are getting approached by new friends on Facebook and whatever else. Complete strangers chatting them up, and pretty soon they ask if they want to know some stuff about their dad. See some pictures, maybe? These are some sick bastards."

His voice trails off, and I don't know how to respond.

My phone buzzes again, Lauren calling me—something terribly important and urgent, no doubt.

"You probably know most of this already," he says. "Why'd you reach out to me?"

"Have you seen the news that Robert Townsend died a few weeks ago?" I ask.

"Terrible to see 'em go young like that. When he had all those years ahead of him to rip people off. Tragic."

"I want to know what happened to him."

He considers this for some time.

"You don't figure it was an accident," he says.

"No, I don't," I tell him.

"What have you got?"

I give him what I *have* got. The ocean conditions the day he disappeared. My encounter with Townsend at the beach when he explained, clearly, that he wasn't going in the water. The total lack of interest from the police. Some creep looking for me. Then seeing that board back at Townsend's place. I give him everything except Carson, because as Grady Walker shows, there are certain people you'd rather not piss off. Wrapping up, I tell him that no, I don't figure his drowning was an accident, and I think this mysterious firm played a role in his death.

"Who'd you say you work for?" he asks.

"I'm not working for anyone."

"You're not working for anyone."

"No."

"Anybody working with *you* on this?"

"No."

"Nobody else?"

"That's right."

"Lonesome dove, huh?"

I listen to him breathing into the phone for a while when I don't respond.

"Well," he says. "Either way this goes, son, you let me know the next time you're out west. I owe you a steak, and the first round's on me. How can I help?"

"The investigation you did into GDR? Is it possible I could see some of the information your guys collected? That could be really helpful. Do you think you found anything that could tie them to this?"

"I don't have much for you on that. Sorry. But I'm under a legal contract that prohibits me from commenting or sharing any further information on that subject."

"I had to ask."

"I'd like to help. Believe me, I would. But some things are just out of my hands."

"No problem."

"I'd be putting myself and my family in real jeopardy."

"I understand."

"It's also unethical. So, I'm sorry to say it, but I just can't help you with that."

"Appreciate your time."

"212-377-5959," he says. "Ask for Anthony, 377-5959. Anthony. He'll be expecting your call. You talk to him. You two'll figure this shit out. And if you need any resources on this thing, legal or otherwise, *any* fucking resources, you can call me directly. That clear? I've got a little cash lying around these days if you catch my drift."

"Yes, yes. Understood. And thank you!"

"So. How 'bout it? You ready to put in a little work?"

"Yup. I'm on it. Thank you."

"Don't mention it. Like I said. Either way this goes, next time you're out west, let me know when you feel like a decent steak."

"Thanks again."

"Okay. Go get 'em."

26

A COUPLE MONTHS ago, I asked Frank if I could borrow his drill.

I brought Luke over to his place one night, walked onto the front porch, and carefully opened the screen door, which hung slightly crooked, with rusted screws jutting out from a loose hinge against the soft, rotted wood of the doorframe. Frank fixes what suits him and not much else. I didn't even knock, just blurted *Hello?* hardly waiting for Stacy to call me inside as I ushered my little accomplice in ahead of me, without breaking my stride. It was a nice way to operate—I liked our system. No reservation, no call ahead, no invitation necessary.

Luke sprinted into the den, hearing the television, but came to a sudden stop looking at Jake, sucking his thumb on the couch beside his exhausted mother. The room was stuffy and hot. Jake ignored us, eyes never leaving the screen. Stacy, in her nurse scrubs, sat up smiling to greet us. "Hello! Hello, Luke!" said the poor woman. "Would you like to watch some *PAW Patrol?* Does that sound good? Yes, it does! Yes, it does! Oh, hey, Pete."

Luke seemed very interested and I picked him up to plop him on the far corner of the couch. "Is Frank out in the shed?" I asked.

She folded her arms. "Yup," she said. "Good guess." She wasn't smiling anymore. It seemed like a good idea to leave.

"I better check on him," I mumbled and crept past her, through the room, down the hall, and out the back door into the night. Outside, I could breathe again, and feel the air move freely without resentment.

Frank's shed sits on his lawn a few dozen yards behind his house and isn't much more than a tiny barn. He built the thing himself. I opened the door and stepped inside.

"What's up?" Frank asked me.

"Not much. I just caught up with Stace for a little bit."

Frank cringed as though he had just lost a great deal of money on an unexpected outcome. His life had been full of bad bets, as well as long stories, and the longer arguments that tend to follow them.

"I'll bet that was really awesome," he said and turned back to his saw table.

A lone bulb hung from the ceiling. The room smelled of new wood, a drying wet suit, polish, resin, finish, and wax, and I could understand why he never wanted to leave the place. Or maybe he just needed to get away from the house and all the shouting. It seemed as good a time as any for me to ask.

"Can I borrow your drill?" I asked. "Tomorrow?"

"What for?"

"I want to put together a playhouse for Luke."

He scratched his cheek. "Huh," he said after a while.

"Do you want to see it?" I asked.

Frank wiped his hands with a rag and followed me to his driveway. A long cardboard box was strapped to my roof rack. He looked up at it for a while, and I don't know what he could tell from there, but he nodded and said, "Yeah. No problem. I can put it together."

"Thanks, but I was thinking maybe I could give it a shot?"

He sighed.

"Do you just want it to get done?" he said. "Or are you trying to learn something?"

I wanted to learn something, sure. But there were other reasons I needed this, even if I didn't feel like getting into them with Frank, although maybe he understood some of these things well. He rubbed his neck and contemplated, chewing on his lip. At last, when he finished conferring with himself, he shrugged.

"It's a two-man job, anyway—you might need a little help," he said letting me off the hook.

"Thanks," I told him, smiling. "Thanks, I mean, that would be great. What day works for you?"

He pulled out his phone to check his calendar and probably the surf report. Frank had a small racket keeping vacation homes in running shape. He took a lot of calls about shower mold, or a clogged drain, the boiler's on the fritz, a dead car battery—the job meant fixing a lot of problems. He worked odd hours and didn't like his customers, but said he needed more of them.

"It looks shitty tomorrow," he said, optimistically.

"Tomorrow's good for me."

"All right. That works."

The next day Frank arrived before noon. Summer was almost here and I had covered Luke in suntan lotion, and soon the scent of grass and wood mixed with Banana Boat filled the air. No clouds were out, but we still get a decent wind in through the yard this time of year, and we would need it. The three of us were in shorts and T-shirts. Frank wore boots (the good kind that I didn't have), while Luke and I worked in sneakers. Frank brought his toolbox. I own one myself, but it sat unopened on the grass. Mine held a few ancient screwdrivers, needle-nose pliers, a hammer, measuring tape, pushpins, and a box cutter, but these simple playthings made me sick, and so I kept the box closed to hide my shame.

Frank has a DeWalt. The electric drill driver is cordless and comes with a yellow frame, a black, ridged collar, and keyless chuck atop a variable speed trigger switch—that responds to the pull of a finger! And then beneath the base of the main pistol-grip handle a wide battery pack hangs attached like some high ammunition magazine on a military grade weapon, giving it a symmetry and balance in the hand, and I have no idea if there are other brands or models of the cordless drill driver, but I cannot imagine they could ever rival the DeWalt. *Where size meets power.* It's so true.

Before Frank arrived, I spread the contents of that big box out on the grass. This was an undertaking, and I knew it, since I had spent the prior night reading the instruction manual, a decent-size effort in itself. Now a timber yard sale lay stretched out on my back lawn, in different stages of formation, some shingled slabs (obviously the roof), a side block that matched the picture on the box, but mostly nondescript lumber. The box had weighed a ton. Frank flipped through the instructions and kept them by his side, along with a box of screws the manufacturer provided.

It was like some sort of puzzle. Frank soon explained the rules. He would stare at the pages of the instructions and call out a number.

"M-12! M-12! Two! There should be two," he cried, then muttered to himself softly. "S-3…S-3…S-3. Six of those."

Our team leaped into action. Luke and I scampered to the scattered wood, trying to find the pieces with correct dimensions, and then we'd inspect their sides singing a chorus of *M-12? M-12?* And find the corresponding number. Then we brought the timber to Frank. He eyed the pictures on the page and arranged the parts, comparing slopes and angles. Frank organized the tiny dime-bags of screws and would tickle through them, whispering things like *S-3, S-3* until he found the matching part. He inspected the screwhead, picking out the right tip from this tiny kit he'd brought, then cranked the chuck, which locked the bit into the drill. Pinching the screw between his fingertips, he ground the first few turns himself to set it in place. Then, kneeling there with the drill in his hand, he placed the tip inside the drive, squeezed the trigger, and eased the handle down until the shank slipped through the wood. I tried to notice everything he did. He made it look easy.

I needed to use that fucking DeWalt. Frank didn't argue. So, I got down on my knees, read out the number in the picture, even found the S-7 "5/8th wood screws" myself. Frank brought me a plank, I double-checked the digits, and then I hovered over it and held my breath. I revved the DeWalt like a motorcycle with my savage grip. It began to violate the screw and make this awful shrieking sound. My shaft was stuck! So I stopped and gathered myself for a moment. I tried it once more. But again, I heard the metal wailing. I couldn't find a purchase. I felt a hand on my shoulder.

"You're gonna strip it," Frank told me. "Did you change the bit?"

I had not.

"Here," he said and knelt down next to me. "Hold it like this, okay? Do you feel that? You like that? You like it? Yeah, you do. Now pull it out and put it in your mouth." He stared at me, eyes crazed, gritting his teeth. I asked him if he was finished.

"Sorry," he said. "Get the right tip. Don't squeeze so hard. Steady and drive it down."

Things got better. We worked together. There were heavy or awkward stages, needing two pairs of hands to hold things flush, but I helped and got some coaching. Some angles were easier than others. It felt like building a little house—we set a foundation, then the posts, girts, four solid walls, doors, handles, hinges, a plastic kitchen screwed into an open window, two clocks, trusses, beams, and then a brown-shingled gable roof with a good steep pitch to shed the rain. I stood on my toes, reaching to attach the rooster weather vane. A small crew member watched in awe, shouting instructions, growing more and more excited. After a while my thumbs, my thumbs! My fragile thumbs began to hurt. But I never wanted to stop.

Then somehow it was hours later and when I checked my phone, the news was not good.

Where r u? it began and

Where R u? and then

Just tried calling you?

Call back. Where r u??????

Is everything all right??

WHERE R U PETE??

We're home, I wrote and added, Sorry.

Why r u not picking up your phone? she asked.

We're working in the yard, I told her.

I'm coming home, she said.

I told Frank that we needed to hurry up. He seemed to understand.

When I heard Lauren's car pull in, my mouth went dry. Since I hadn't told her anything about the project, I couldn't ask permission, and I knew the surprise would provoke an extreme reaction that could go either way. She might thank the heavens for our creation...or she might not. This was no small project. And no big yard. So, if this went sideways, I was on my own—Frank couldn't help with that.

I heard a door slam inside, the echo of footsteps. They were moving very fast.

"Oh my god," Lauren said, storming out to the back porch. "What have you done? What is this? It's incredible! Oh my god. Hello! Hello! Yes! Yes! I see it! Did you help build this? Oh my god, I love this thing. Can you show Mommy what you built? Oh, it's so good!"

My small assistant took her by the hand, dragging her toward his kingdom, and she looked back at me and her face was beaming as she said, "Amazing, Pete. Amazing."

Luke gave her a tour of the construction site for a bit, but then she turned and rushed me. She hugged me close and whispered, "Oh, you sneaky bastard." Then she hung her arms around my neck. She kept looking in my eyes and didn't stop. And I'm a married man! It had been a long time since some strange woman had looked at me as if I, alone, held her whole attention because I had all the answers, smiling as if to say this would soon work out well for me—oh yes, it had been a good long time, and I had sorely missed it. She was gleaming.

I turned to check on Luke but saw Frank instead. He was staring at the playhouse. He was staring at the thing he'd spent his whole day building and he looked like he wanted to take an axe and chop it into kindling, and then when he had finished that, he'd come and do the same to us.

"It was all Frank," I said. "I don't know what the hell I'm doing."

He looked over at us and his face softened. I hadn't forgotten him! He would get the full credit he deserved, and then I'd play my sheepish humble self. Maybe he noticed some imperfection in the house I hadn't.

"Hey, Frank," Lauren said. "It looks great! Thank you so much. I love it."

"Hey," he said.

"Thank you," she said again. "Thank you so much for your help. It's perfect."

"Yup." He smiled. "There it is."

I wondered if that dark look was aimed at me. If I had crossed a line. I'd humped his leg all day long—even worse than Luke—and maybe Frank felt like he'd just seen something sacred defiled by an amateur. Maybe I came off like that deluded fan who sneaks into the winner's locker room and pretends to be on the team, hugging players, popping corks, spraying beers, and giving speeches in the celebration? I've done that kind of thing before.

"All right," Frank said. "I should get home."

"Come back soon!" cried Luke.

"Thanks again," I said. We waved goodbye, and he slipped into his truck. I heard his tires on the gravel drive. "Uncle Frank's a sweetheart," Lauren said to me, grinning. "But he's a chatterbox." I laughed as she leaned in and kissed my neck.

"He can be a little peculiar."

"Look how happy Luke is in there!" she said. "This thing—it's just the best! He can use it all the time! He'll have friends over! How did you come up with this? It's perfect!"

I hugged Lauren tight while we watched Luke man the battlements, and I felt very, very good. I thought about things like luck and the stuff that matters, and then I slipped my hand down her back and took a righteous grip of her naughty little ass. I grabbed that thing like she was an unsuspecting bridesmaid or royal sister passing down the aisle. "Hey," she said, but she winked and grinned up at me, and so I was smitten—but still dragged away and beaten by a mob of outraged, screaming guests.

Luke poked his head out of a drive-through window to take our orders but soon began to lecture. He needed us to know about the tools and building products, the raw materials, the assembly methods, and warned of labor trouble, but he offered remedies to fix them. It just kept getting better. I never wanted it to end. Why deny that? Why can't I brag about this one thing?

The two of us stood there together, watching him.

All right, I told myself. That's done. That works.

All right. What else? What else? What next?

27

I ALMOST MISSED the train. The sitter was late, and when she did show up, Luke had a meltdown before I could leave and then he took a raucous dump that I cleaned up because it didn't feel right to just drop that carnage in her lap and go sprinting out the door. It was a frantic exit. I have two meetings in the city today, and when you're unemployed, you can't be late, you just don't let that happen. My fingers smell of A&D ointment.

Some time, a change of trains, and a couple stations later, I step off the subway at Union Square and walk a few blocks until I find the address. It's a nondescript building stuck between a nationwide bank branch and a big-three pharmacy, which describes most places in the city, since just about every independent operator with character and charm was long ago destroyed by rising rents and the inevitable march of a bunch of different things. Inside, I take the elevator up to a midlevel floor and walk inside what feels like an accounting firm. A receptionist leads me to a back office and offers me a chair. Soon after she leaves, a guy walks in and sits down across from me behind a simple desk. He looks about my age.

I had expected a greaseball. Some chubby Peeping Tom wearing a fedora and short tie, pouring over nudie pics all day with a cheap cigar hanging from his mouth. But Walker's guy comes off like an ex-cop or a boxer who still hits the gym pretty hard. His nose looks as if it's been involved in some previous disagreements, and you get the sense that breaking it again wouldn't really bother him. He wears a suit that fits him well, no tie, and a spread collar shirt. He's dressed a lot better than I am.

"Just so we understand each other," he says. "I strongly advised my client against this sort of meeting, but he disagreed. So I'm doing what I'm told, but if I hear something I don't like, then it's over. And here's the thing to remember—this conversation never took place."

"Got it."

"You don't want to test me on that one. This never happened. Does it look like I'm kidding?"

It doesn't.

"No problem," I tell him.

"Good." He smiles and his eyes are nothing but sweet. "Now could you please empty your pockets for me?"

"What's that?"

"Take out your cell phone—empty your pockets—nothing personal."

"Are you serious?"

He stands in response, opens a drawer in his desk, and pulls out some gadget that looks like a walkie-talkie.

"Just relax," he says. "Relax. C'mon, turn off your cell—lay it on the table. It'll just take a sec. This will only make us closer."

"Are you trying to see if I'm wearing some kind of wire?"

He walks over and waves this magic wand up and down me, as if scanning for traces of radiation.

"Take it easy," he says. "All done. See? That wasn't so bad. Now, don't we both feel better? Wouldn't you rather do this than get the lawyers involved? Sit down. Sit down."

Walker never said anything about this kind of crap.

"It's part of the job," he says, opening another drawer. "Don't take it so personal." He pulls out a manila folder and plops it onto his desk.

Settling back in my chair, I try to figure out if I'm overreacting or backing down from some kind of test. But this guy is the best resource I've found since Townsend washed up on that beach.

"Let's talk about GDR," I tell him.

"Bad actors. Not people you'd want to do business with. They're always skating the line of legality, and in a few cases, they may push past it. The harder we dug, the worse stuff we found."

"Like what?"

"It's a long list. In 2012 they were sued by a rival private equity firm that bought a media company off them. They accused GDR of inflating their revenues to get a higher price."

"What was the outcome?"

"Settled out of court. Our understanding is they used their own investors' money to pay fees and damages in the case."

"They used client money to settle when they broke the law?" I ask, almost whistling.

"The year before, they terminated an employee named Ajit Probda, a principal and member of the investment committee. They fired him for cause and denied him severance or benefits. Mr. Probda was caring for his wife, who was suffering from leukemia."

"Is that true?"

"It all starts at the top."

"What do you have on Resner?"

"We're getting to him. In '02, GDR bought a business—a struggling electronics retailer. The purchase price was many multiples of the stock's trading levels prior to the deal being announced. The retailer was highly leveraged and filed for bankruptcy within six months."

"It happens."

"Except the retailer was seventy percent owned by Mark Resner in his personal account."

"Jesus. So, GDR bailed their CEO out of a bad trade in his PA? How the hell is that legal? What did his limited partners do?"

"Not much," he says. "The fund's other investments were highly profitable, and it delivered a decent return. We did some work on his investors. Many of them seem unsophisticated, even if they represent large institutions. We also think they have a lot of foreign money, maybe Asia, we think some Middle East and Russia. It was an area of focus for Walker during our work."

"Why?"

"Doesn't matter how smart GDR is or what kind of stuff they do. In the end, fundraising's the whole business. Without money coming in the door, not much else matters."

"These guys are in marketing, not the investment business. What's so funny?"

"That's what Walker said."

"What else?" I ask him. "What else did you find?"

"Resner sits on the board of his alma mater. In 2009, three other board members accused him of directing endowment investments improperly for his own benefit."

"What came out of that?"

"Resner's moved up to chair. The three whistleblowers resigned. Look, there's a pattern of behavior here. The guy's had seven children with four different wives. In every divorce, he tried to get full custody of the children and each time was denied. Six of the kids refuse to speak with him. Two of his exes alleged emotional and physical abuse."

An image of Resner speaking at the funeral pops into my head.

"What about Townsend?" I ask.

"To get along, let alone advance in that environment, you have to be at least a little ruthless. But he was less of a focus for us, when they went after Mr. Walker."

"Did you find anything on him?"

"His mentor at his old firm was a guy named Mitch Patchett. Townsend got him fired. Word is it was on a nickel-and-dime compliance issue, and Townsend took his seat. Patchett hired him, gave him his first job. Your guy's career was about exploiting relationships and then crushing people who did him favors."

There's that same pattern of behavior as Resner. But still no smoking gun.

"So what do you think happened to Townsend?"

"That's not my department," he says.

"I know. But you must have a view."

"I don't."

"I mean, you know this stuff cold. You must have an opinion."

"I know what it means."

"You're telling me this was all just a coincidence?"

"I'm telling you I don't need to have a view. Matter-of-fact, I don't want to have one. Doesn't help anything."

"Why not?"

"It's my job to look out for Grady and his family. What you're doing here, this thing, it's no good for him. What happened between him and GDR, it's in the past. He needs to move on. And now you come in and stir this up."

"Doesn't mean I'm wrong."

"The last time he tussled with these guys, how'd that work out for him?"

I drum my fingers on the table for a little while, thinking through a different angle.

"Okay. Okay," I start. "Off the record…"

"Don't try to get one over on me."

"I'm not. So, let's forget about GDR for a second."

He looks skeptical but not as hostile now, staring back at me.

"Say you have a guy washing up on the beach, in a wet suit. Leash on his ankle. His neck's broken and he's been in the water a few days. Let's say it wasn't an accident."

"Rings a bell," he says.

"All right, but let's say someone had asked you to pull something like this off?"

He rolls his eyes and chuckles at this. "That's not my department, either."

"Yeah, but humor me, off the record. Let's say it was. Someone asked you to do a job, make it look like an accident."

The way he's grinning reminds me of Luke protesting his innocence.

"You've thought through this already, haven't you?"

"We're gonna run out of time here," he says.

"C'mon. What do you think?"

He leans back and folds his hands in his lap. He looks like a guy taking a break after a full day on his feet.

"All right," he says. "I think killing someone's a lot easier to do if you don't care how it gets done. Broad daylight, witnesses—whatever it takes— just so long as they're gone. *But if you want to be a little more subtle, then it starts to get harder. Maybe you think it's better if somebody just disappears?* But the problem with a missing person is people tend to go looking for 'em. Now, getting rid of somebody and making it look like an accident? That's interesting. And to pull that off would take someone pretty good."

"Why?"

"Too many things can go wrong. First you need to get to the guy, you need a place to do it—and remember this is a decent-size guy, too. You'd want privacy for this sort of thing—nowhere public. But remember, if you get him at his house, you can't leave signs of breaking and entering. You need to know his schedule and figure out where he'd be. And when you do him, you can't leave signs of a struggle. The ocean helps get rid of that, but if he went kicking and screaming, they'd still find evidence on the body. Skin, DNA, hair under the fingernails—you'll just sort of have to trust me on that one."

"Okay, so what's that mean?"

"Means you have to jump him somehow and do it quick and clean. But then you're talking about moving a body. Now, you think about that. That's a good way to get caught. And you need to plant a car at the scene without leaving any traces of yourself in the vehicle. To have that many things go right for you—it all says the same thing."

"What's that?"

"Inside job."

"Why?"

"You'd need to know his schedule, exactly where he'd be and why. What's he doing there? It has to make sense. You need somebody close to him. Or somebody close who could hire a professional and help him out."

"And could afford one."

"That's right. Could afford one and know how to find them. And then you have the surfing thing."

"What do you mean?"

That schoolboy smile creeps over him again. "There's just something about it that's really cute. It fits him, you know? It would take so much to pull off—it's not some hit-and-run. But it adds up. It's plausible. It's cute. You plan something so well, but then..." He looks at me. "*You* come along and fuck everything up."

He grins wider as I'm trying to take this all in.

"All that assumes, of course, that this wasn't an accident," he says.

"What about motive?"

He lets out a deep sigh, scratches his head, and rubs his eyes. "Motive's always a pain in the ass."

"What's so funny?"

"Ahhh."

"C'mon. What is it?"

"Most of my day's background checks. Credit scores on bankers or franchise managers."

"Right. So?"

"Sometimes I miss my old job. This stuff is kind of fun. Know what I mean?"

28

BEING IN THE city gives me an excuse to catch up with Craw.

Whenever you meet a guy who has to commute home every day, I think they appreciate if you pick a place by the station. They have an easier time saying yes, at least. So I asked Craw to one of those spots on the balcony inside Grand Central underneath the great windows, where we sit overlooking the bedlam of the concourse below and the army of professionals hurrying across the marble tiles, eyes fixed on their phones, glancing up on occasion to avoid a head-on collision before they make it to their tracks.

There used to be a Mexican place downstairs in this train station, and they sold these margaritas that could do terrible damage. I remember meeting a client here for drinks after work, back when I was just starting out in the business. Sometimes, three instead of two can make a big difference. Anyway, when the customer left me to catch his train back to the suburbs, the summer sun was still out in the early evening sky, and I rose up from the bowels of that underground cantina like some horny mythical Kraken unleashed on the streets to call every woman in my phone, filling their voice mails with a lot of nonsense and lies and none of them picked up or called me ever again, and I woke up on my couch the next awful morning full of agony and shame, without prospects or pride. Craw says the kids at the office are much different now. They do a lot of group stuff together and want more meaning in their jobs and their lives.

"For a while," I tell him, "after I got whacked, we all talked a lot. But then, we kind of trailed off. Fohler's in Denver doing private wealth. Libby's at one of the small shops. Woody's down in Austin, he's gotten into real estate, parking garages. I heard it throws off a lot of cash. Who knows?"

"Who the hell knows," he agrees. "There's gotta be something else big out there. Gotta be something coming up." He stares out at the other tables, eyes wide, wondering about the next great adventure. The next new thing, where it's all happening, and can't miss.

"Hey, Craw, I wanted to ask you—"

"Something better than this shit," he says.

"You were close with Townsend, and…"

"Nah, not really."

"Well. Sure, you were. I was wondering…" But he shakes his head, inspecting a plate of french fries and grabbing a couple that suit him.

"No," he says. "I wasn't."

"What do you mean?"

"I didn't really know the guy that well," he says flatly.

"We caught up at his funeral."

"I was there with Anna. You still have to go to that kind of thing, though, right?"

Now I'm remembering something about how his wife was such good friends with Brooke. I guess he only went to the service as a supportive husband. Thinking back to that day, he was pretty chatty and didn't seem particularly overcome with grief. I never saw this coming from Craw, one of the finest networkers of a generation, who has a thousand relationships all over the place.

"You just never got a chance to know him?" I ask. He glances at me like he smells something not to his liking. He puts his glass on the table and wipes his lips with his sleeve.

"Where you going with this?" he says.

"Sorry. I don't get out much. Too much daddy day care. Not enough sleep."

I'd prefer to avoid telling him what I'm up to, if possible. Given some recent events, I'd rather this chat leaves a small wake. He doesn't look satisfied with my response, but he also doesn't look particularly worried about it, either.

"So, anyways," he says, reaching for his glass. "I know you were close with him, but I wasn't. He was a...big personality," he decides after a pause. That's a dignified phrase, but to describe someone who's just died that way suggests that Craw—who could charm the pants off almost anybody and often did—hated Townsend worse than poison. Maybe Craw even suffered some wrong by his hand.

"It's all right," I assure him. "It's all right. We're off the record here. The first time I met the guy he didn't give me the time of day." He didn't really ever, I could add, but I don't. Craw grins at this. "I know he could be a little bit of a dick," I explain.

"Hey, the man's no longer with us. But shit, he was *your* friend."

"He was a big personality," I agree. "You want another order of these?" But he waves me off and I lean back in my seat to regroup. So, Craw wasn't close to Townsend. I'm not calling for a check, though. I need more than this. Your wife's friends and their husbands will always know a hell of a lot more about you than you could ever feel comfortable with.

"Anna and Brooke are pretty close, right?"

He finishes his beer in response as I add, a little too quickly, "What did Anna think of him?"

"Do we have to do this?" he complains. I've offended some part of his code, speaking ill of the deceased and now bringing the wives in. He doesn't appreciate me testing the taboo.

"Did Anna ever mention anything?"

"Man, you're really going there? You really wanna get into this? Shit." He looks away, shaking his head.

"Off the record?"

"Off the record?" he asks in a dopey voice. I shouldn't keep saying that. I sound like a reporter. Craw hates journalists—he sees them as nothing but threats, just walking disasters that could cost him his job. Still, the way he answered my question tells me my instincts about something weren't far off.

It also occurs to me that before our encounter at the funeral, we hadn't spoken in about a decade, and now he can sense that nostalgia didn't drive me to email him from the wilderness asking for this reunion.

In the uncomfortable silence that follows, I only know that I can't speak first.

"Man, if I check out," he grumbles, "I hope you don't go around asking what women say 'bout me."

"It's not like that," I tell him. Craw loses his smile and looks at me.

"Anna hated the motherfucker. All right? Good enough?"

"Why?"

"He was a bad guy!" he spits.

"How? This is just between us."

"Real bad guy," he says again. "That's it. Okay? Treated Brooke like shit. I mean, more than your average knuckle-dragger. Real abusive, awful shit."

"Physically abusive?"

"No. No, man!" He glances around the bar. "What the fuck are we doing here? Why are you—? Look. I heard he was just really cold-blooded, not just screaming matches but really bad. Ruthless. I heard something weird about..." He trails off.

"About what?"

"About some sketchy shit. Lot of sketchy shit going on. Who knows? But Brooke was always very cool, and he treated her like a dog, so Anna always hated the sonofabitch. I mean, she doesn't even hate any of *my friends* that much."

"What kind of sketchy shit?" I ask, but he waves me off. He wants no part of this.

A thought occurs to me. Craw is still with the firm, but I am not. Looking at him now, it's unsettling how long it's taken me to understand something so crucial about Mike Crawford. He's not some lucky backslapper. He was never a hothead, either. It seems he learned a few things long before I did, like the importance of discretion, even though I was the one giving my little speeches. Maybe not everything's an accident.

"Sorry," I tell him. "Let's keep this between us. All right? Hey, I'm sorry I asked."

"Yeah, done. That's done, man. That shit works for me." He half chuckles, as if explaining the obvious to an amateur. Then, thinking on this, he feels the need to warn me. "And if this does get around, you and me have a problem. Cool?"

"Sure. Understood."

Craw learned not to get caught flapping his mouth about certain topics that can piss the wrong people off. Women, for instance. Whereas I must have slept through that class. But I'm running out of moves—I don't have a long list of sources that I can hit up after this meeting. And pretty soon Craw, the once incorrigible legend, who used to run giggling through this city's nighttime adventures like Luke at the playground, will need to get up and walk off, still a bounce in his stride, so he can catch the next northbound local up to the burbs—maybe grabbing a tallboy for the trip—to get home in time for a late dinner with Anna and tuck in his girls. By the way, legends like Craw always have daughters, you can bet on it. After their storybook runs come to an end, these dudes face a reckoning filled with long, sleepless nights spent worrying over their offspring, nature's karmic revenge against players since Henry VIII. So when he does glance up at the clock to leave? This chat is over. And then I've got a train to catch, too.

I could have handled this better. But he's not a summer intern anymore and he was never a slow one, so if I try to lead him somewhere, talking clever, he'll see right through me, and it will only earn me another *where you going with this?*

"What about him and GDR?" I ask. In the interest of chase cutting.

"This is getting better and better, man. Am I supposed to pay for this beer, too?"

"All right, all right."

"You're looking for dirt on GDR? Sketchiest shop on the Street, and you're asking me about them? And oh, by the way, the most litigious, most lawyered up, most vindictive motherfuckers out there?"

"Just between us girls."

"What are you doing, man?" he snaps. Now he imitates my voice in a whiny, unflattering tone. "*Off the record? Just between us?*" He's taunting me. "Why would a guy like you want to go digging up shit about this kind of place? Huh? You want to go around asking a lot of people about that shop? Talking about how a guy died? How you think that's gonna work?"

I'm starting to realize that if Craw looks scared, he's not worried about himself.

"I saw him, okay? I go to that beach however many days a week, however many months out of a year. I bring my kid there and we swim in the water. I live out there. So that Thursday afternoon we're down at that beach and I see Townsend and we talk, except here's the funny thing, Craw—the guy wasn't going in the water, okay? *Just between us, off the record.* He wasn't going in the fucking water, but now I'm supposed to sit around and not wonder what happened?"

He folds his arms and looks at me for a bit. After my pitch, we stare at each other long enough that I wonder if he's turning sympathetic, but soon he gets tired of this contest, and when he speaks, he sounds even more pissed.

"You know what I know," he says. "What everybody hears about those fucking guys. Bad dudes. Go figure. Your friend wasn't a good guy, all right? Why do you want to hear that from me? Sounds like you knew that already. How many other people you gonna ask?"

"Yeah. Sorry. I understand. Sorry. Forget it." After a moment, Craw looks down at his watch.

"Look. I gotta catch the 6:57," he says. "Thanks for the beer. Good seeing you. You're a weird motherfucker. Next time we do this, let's catch up on some other shit."

"That'd be great. Sorry about this."

I wave for the waiter and Craw stands to leave, putting a gym bag on his shoulder. The man still looks frustratingly young.

"Hey Craw," I say as we shake hands and I stare up at him sweetly. "All this stuff? Don't worry, this will only make us closer."

He snorts, shaking his head, a half-smile growing. But it fades as he looks around the bar. He stares down at me for a moment, hands on his hips.

"All right. Look." He sighs. "Between you and me? I heard your boy was trying to take off. I heard he was talking about leaving GDR."

29

OUTSIDE DROP-OFF THIS morning, Luke stands at my feet, leaning forward like a sprinter coming out of the blocks. I'm holding him by his backpack, suspended by the straps. It feels like waiting in line at the local nightclub, hoping to catch an approving eye from the clipboard-toting bouncer Ms. Yanni. Until finally—without even asking how many girls we got with us—she smiles and waves Luke inside where the joint is bumping, and he rushes in there like a bloodhound let off his leash.

Heading back to my car, a thought occurs to me. There are four Range Rovers in the parking lot. Three of them are black. It's not something I've noticed before, and I'm not sure if I should care or if this is just another sign that I'm well on my way to going crazy. I'm having this feeling more and more lately. I've always hated Range Rovers of any color, really.

It's no way to start my day, but I sit for a moment, watching the lot through my rearview. Taking inventory. Let's think—I know Hannah from Minnesota, she drives one and it's somehow always very clean. I've thought sometimes about how, if things had gone a different way, we could have had a nice life together in it. She's still here, walking slowly, but let's ignore her (if we can) this one morning. The next one up has a ski rack. That's the Fowlers' car, and I can see their nanny at the back of the queue—Lauren has told me the dad is kind of a big deal and wonders why I haven't met him. The white Range pulls out—the driver's a little bit of an ice queen. That leaves one unaccounted for, parked in the back corner, no beach tags or bumper stickers, windows tinted.

I decide to sit here and wait. The final few stragglers file out, but none of them seem to notice me idling dumb as a post. And no one comes to claim the last black Range. Which doesn't necessarily mean anything. The big lot still has a handful of cars, one pickup. It could belong to a teacher. It could be a lot of different things. Doesn't mean there's somebody in there following me. There's no way to cruise past it—the spot is flanked by a curb and grass, and there's no path alongside it naturally—so if there is a guy in there and the situation deteriorates, the front lawn of a preschool isn't the best place for a confrontation. But I can't take this much longer. I'm an American—I didn't grow up in East Germany under the Stasi. And so, before I can stop myself, I hop out of the car and stalk toward the Range Rover, nothing subtle in my approach. I get up so close, my breath fogs the windshield. I peer inside, and sure enough, it's empty.

I'm making a schmuck out of myself, and it's pissing me off. I feel about as cool as a turtleneck. I'll crack up if I keep at it like this—it's no way to live. You need to keep your mind on what you need to do. You focus, figure out what's important, don't let yourself get distracted. Otherwise...what? You're sitting in a damn parking lot jacking yourself off, counting SUVs.

Not long after leaving the school, of course, a few miles down the highway, I notice a black Range Rover two cars behind me. One thing leads to another and I find myself at the library, needing to sit with my back to the wall. But today the place seems very busy. The woman at the table across from me spends a few hours managing a backpack with enough provisions, zippers, and clasps to climb Everest. The front and back doors somehow turned into the local train. The flow of traffic never seems to stop, and I crane my neck to look at every entrant. Each footstep echoes slowly—when did everyone start walking with a cane?

So, by the time I pick up Luke in the afternoon and pull out onto the highway, he starts wailing about how he wanted to go to the playground and how we're going the wrong way. Somewhere behind me, there's a black SUV, model unknown, but I'm in no mood to find out. So, with no hint of a signal, I pull a hard left across a double yellow into the driveway of a restaurant and spin the wheel, U-turning, and run up on the grass. Without stopping, I'm nice enough to flick my blinker before I swerve left, back onto the highway, heading the other direction with cars on both sides honking and shouting curses at me. Luke stops wailing. *"Look out,"* he says.

I stop in a gas station and we pick up some ice cream. Maybe the threat of a violent crash has settled me down. I've almost stopped thinking about what a popular car that is, or trying to remember when it became so fashionable around here. To be honest, part of me is feeling a little slick, fast and loose like a real operator, already planning my next escape. I'm thinking of back roads with too many turnoffs, garages with several exits, or just picking up the beach driving permit, and taking the air in my tires down. How the hell can someone mysteriously follow me at a distance if they're stuck in the sand?

Later at the playground behind the high school, I'm glad to be off the road. It's nice back here. The trees are full and bright, the leaves jittery in the wind, and even if it's only just after four, the shadows are long, the light already getting low this time of year. I'm parked on a bench, watching Luke, when I hear something over my shoulder.

"How you doing?" a guy asks, standing behind me. He's a few inches taller than I am and built like a butcher. He looks pretty comfortable in his skin.

"Hope I didn't sneak up on you," he says smiling, like he's recognized an old friend he likes to tease.

"Nah," I tell him, since he scared the hell out of me. The guy opens the gate, steps into the playground, and comes over to sit down on the bench next to mine.

This has to be him.

"Nice spot," he says. *Who else could he be?*

"Yeah, it's all right." But how did he find us? I must have lost him. There's no way he could have stayed with us. I glance back at the parking lot but don't see his car.

"Good place to catch up," he says. If he's been following me for however many days, maybe he already knows that we come here, and just took a good guess where I'd be.

"Do I know you?" I ask him.

"Sure."

"I don't think so."

"Sure, you do."

"Yeah, sorry. It's still not coming to me."

"I'm the guy who's been looking for you."

I don't see another soul around here, besides the three of us. No one who would even hear me shouting.

"Oh yeah. Why's that?"

"Want to talk to you," he says.

"Well, what do you want?"

"What's the matter? You got somewhere else to be?"

"What do you want?"

"Lot of work to do?"

"All right, who the hell are you?"

"You saw a guy one day down at the beach, huh? Okay. Then you go to the cops and tell them about it. Fine. You're just a concerned citizen." He shoots me a friendly glance. "Or maybe you just need a way to pass the time?"

How could this happen? If GDR sent him, why would they know about me? How did I get on their radar? Did I slip up somewhere?

I don't answer him, but he doesn't seem too bothered.

"Okay. Whatever," he says. "Six of one, half a dozen of the other. No problem. But then you go to his funeral?"

"Are you some kind of cop?"

"Why'd you do that?"

"He was a friend of mine."

"Bullshit."

"I don't know what your problem is, but—"

"Don't lie to me."

"Look. I'm not sure what this is all about. I'm not sure who you are, either."

"So," he says, since he's the one asking all the questions. "You go to his funeral and snoop around and you talk to his brother. You're talking to some people, huh?"

"I got an idea. Maybe we got off on the wrong foot here. Maybe now's not a great time, but we figure out a better place to meet? Then you and I can talk about this over a beer or a coffee, that kind of thing?"

"Quit fucking around," he says. Now his smile has gone somewhere far away.

"I think this conversation's gonna be done here pretty soon."

"So you go to his funeral, you talk to his brother. But then you go by his house. And you talk to his wife."

"I don't know who you are, but—"

"I'm someone you really don't want to meet. And I know who you are. I know your name. Don't forget that. Ever. You got me, Pete?"

My breath is coming hard. This is the moment, the moment you learn you've gotten yourself into something worse than anything you could have imagined, and now it's really happening.

"Go on. Keep fucking around," he says.

"I think you got the wrong idea."

But this guy doesn't want to hear it. He leans in closer.

"How'd you like me to come by your house?" he asks. "Come knocking on your door. Think about it, huh? Sometime when you're not there. Maybe your wife's home, yeah? She answers and then she lets me inside, you see what I'm saying? Would you like that?" *Is he fucking serious?* What kind of guy says what I think he's trying to say? He keeps going. "And after we're done with that, while I'm in the neighborhood—you know what's next, right? Hey, speak of the devil," he asks, a puzzled look in his eyes. "Where's the little guy?"

I don't want to take my eyes off the sick bastard, but I have to glance over my shoulder. The playground's empty. *Where the hell could he be?* But I can hear the evil fucker, feel him moving, so I turn back and sure enough, he's standing up now, towering, hands in his pockets, just a few steps away. He stares concerned and innocent at me, but I have to look back to the playground— still nothing—until a tiny hand pokes out the top of the twisty tube slide he crawled up somehow. I glance back to find the guy. He hasn't come any closer—his feet are still planted. He's just watching me.

"Tough to keep track of him," he says, smiling as sweetly as any mom at pickup, like we're on the same team.

My kid? He's coming here and *threatening Luke?* We have to do this here? Where my kid comes to play after school? What kind of people are these? What kind of man would come find me and—

I need to stay calm. Think about what I need to do. But first, I need to breathe.

"Never know where he'll run off," he adds helpfully. The guy turns and steps out through the gate, onto the grass. I could follow him. Follow him to his car, get the license plate, maybe? But then I'd have to leave Luke. The guy stops walking.

"Don't," I tell him. Don't mention my son again. Don't say another word. But I bite my tongue, so instead of a warning, it probably sounds like a plea.

"So maybe, you quit fucking around and mind your own business. That'd be good. Otherwise. You heard what I said. Nice catching up with you, Pete."

He shrugs, and then turns on his heel and walks away, not in any great hurry. For a bunch of reasons, I'm wondering if he has a gun on him. But maybe that's just what he wants me to do? Probably. Or I could chase him down, right now—he's a half dozen yards away and that's the last thing he's expecting. And he wouldn't want to cause a scene, right?

But then, as if he can hear my internal debate, up ahead on the lawn, when he reaches the back of the school, he stops to study the brick wall in front of him like he's forgotten something. Maybe he has something else to tell me? But he never even looks over his shoulder. He stands at the corner of the building for what seems like a while, then puts his hand up and leans against the wall, reaches down, pulls out his dick, and starts painting the brick with a steady stream. He takes his time, and only once he's done, given it a shake, and zipped himself up, does he turn back around, and he's smiling again when he waves goodbye to me.

30

I DON'T KNOW what to do. But I need help.

I have to think, just slow down and think. I need Gandle. I need to talk to Gandle and tell her some bastard threatened my son. I'm calling her cell phone, again and again, but she's not picking up, so now I don't know what to do. I could call 911? Call 911 and say what, that I need to talk to Officer Gandle? They'd never put me through to her radio or dispatch, and then what do I do, just try to explain all of this to some random cop? I've left her a message. I'll try a text. That's all anybody uses anymore, right? Maybe even the cops.

Hey it's Pete.

Got a problem!

This is an emergency some goon from GDR just threatened Luke and I don't know what else to do. Sorry but need your help.

Need to talk to you please

Now I can't do much until I hear back. I just pace behind the school, pushing Luke in his stroller, just waiting around, as always. Just doing laps between the red brick of the schoolhouse and the monkey bars back here.

Where r you? she writes back after a few minutes.

Playground behind the high school

Luke OK?

Yes yes I'm scared shitless need to talk to you.

On my way, she says, and I let out a sigh of relief.

She's on her way. She's on her way, so I just need to calm down and get some air in my lungs and Luke's fine and I'm here and no one's going to hurt him and then when she gets here she'll know what to do and I'm calm so I'll explain what I can and the rest of it she'll figure out. She'll figure everything out because she's probably seen stuff like this before, maybe even all the time, so we'll talk it through. So, we're good.

But who the hell are these people? They threatened my kid! Jesus. What kind of firm does that? They send some shady bastard for a little chat with me. At my son's playground! I try looking into these scumbags and that's how they respond. They don't ignore me, no threats of litigation, don't go after my reputation, don't just tell me to back off—no, none of that. They just *go after my family*. That's how they react! That's Mafia, drug lord, terrorist shit. It's goddamn sick! What kind of people do this? They're hiding something bad enough they need to kill a guy and then they threaten *my* family?

It's fifteen, maybe twenty minutes later when Gandle's police cruiser pulls into the parking lot, pretty fast. She walks toward us over by the jungle gym. It doesn't seem like she's in any big hurry. She looks pretty casual.

"Are you all right?" she asks.

"Yeah, yeah. I'm good."

"That's right," she says. "And Luke?"

"He's okay. He's fine."

She nods at this.

"How about you? You're fine, right? You guys are both all right. Yep. You're safe. Luke's safe. You're fine, you're good—and that's what matters, all right? That's what I want to know. That's all I care about."

"We were just sitting here. And I started talking to this guy."

"But you're good. You're all right." She sounds confident. She shoves her hands into her pockets, rocking on her heels, and looks around the field, nodding like some wise old coach seeing some extra hustle in practice.

"Tell me what happened," she says.

I'm trying. I start again. But she keeps telling me to slow down! That's what she keeps saying to me! Slow down. As if I'm some emotional wreck? Like I'm hysterical. *Slow down, Pete. Slow down.*

I tell Gandle what happened. The whole damn thing. I keep having to start over because she keeps interrupting. She keeps asking, did he *say that?* He used *those* words? What did he *actually* say? And how do you even describe what someone looks like? He's a big guy. White dude. American. What the hell does that do?

She's not writing any of this down. I've seen her do that before, always in her little notepad, like the great detective. But she's not writing any of this down. She's just looking at me, furrowing her brow. Great. She puts a hand on my shoulder.

"Pete," she says, sort of rubbing my back.

"Do you think you can find him?"

"This whole thing, it's a lot. It's a lot."

"What is this?"

"It's okay. It's a lot. It's a lot."

She keeps saying that!

"What the hell does that mean?"

"You're putting a lot on yourself…"

That's not how a cop's supposed to talk. That's how my wife talks. How she starts some conversations, like the ones from the dark ages, the ones that end with her saying, *I wish you could see someone.*

"Do you think I'm making this up?" I ask her.

Luke cackles with glee. *Making dis up!*

"No. No. I didn't say that."

But I'm in no mood, so I'm packing up the stroller, I don't like where this is going.

"You think some random guy at the playground was just talking shop and I started seeing messages in the fucking sky?"

I shouldn't swear in front of Luke. Or at a cop. But the hell with this. Luke's already in his stroller, so I find his little Bear and hand it to him before he freaks out.

"I didn't say that, either." Gandle's voice is slow and calm. "I said. *This is a lot.*"

"It's a lot of bullshit."

I don't need this. Not from her. Like *I'm* the crazy asshole for protecting my son! Now she's giving me *you need help* eyes.

"Pete. I'll check it out. I will. I'm going to look into this, all right? But I need you to calm down. Can you do that for me? Let's calm down for a minute and then you can get him home."

When you get back to the house, you start asking questions. After you sit the little guy down in front of a half-broken train set, you give him a cheese stick, you open a snack pack and hand him the top, because he likes the top, and then plop down on the couch yourself. Now the interrogation can begin.

How the hell could they know? How the hell could GDR have found out I was looking into them? I know they have resources and an army of private investigators. But who would tell them?

The last person I met. Brooke. She told me she was having dinner later that night with Resner, and I could have come up just because my visit was top of mind. Or maybe something struck her as odd about our conversation, a few too many pointed questions—*are you sure that's what Robert said?*—and I spooked her. Then again, she might wonder why Robert never mentioned my name. She's not stupid. Maybe she knows a lot more than she was willing to share.

The sheriff or Gandle. Hard to believe some dumpster diver could have a line into the police, but then that's what journalists do—they cozy up to some guys at the station. And there's always one—the cops say there's always one leak in every precinct with an entrepreneurial streak, who gives out scoops too early to their reporter buddy, and when the story hits, it gums up an investigation. Every cop has a side hustle. Plenty of them looking for a weekend "private security" gig that pays a hundred bucks an hour. The sheriff or Gandle only had to mention that some weirdo was asking questions about Townsend's death to the wrong guy at the station. That's all it would take.

But the list of suspects has a few other names, too.

Drew. The thought of my mentor, the one guy I trusted in the whole wretched business, the idea that he could have betrayed me on this somehow? It would take a bitter and ungrateful Sherpa to believe such a thing. Still. Drew's a salesman. The guy loves to talk. Worse, he lives for the scoop, he wants the skinny, digs for the scuttlebutt like some bloodhound reporter. He's one of those guys who just needs to *know*. So, if he asks too many questions—sometimes he's not as subtle as he thinks—then stuff gets around. When I didn't tell him everything, that wasn't an accident.

Then, of course, there's Carson. My meeting with him could have gone better. Why did he warn me so much about keeping my mouth shut? What was it he said? *What would happen if whoever did this found out that you were looking for them? What if they found you first?*

It's well after dark and Luke has gone down when I see the headlights in the driveway. Even with the high beams scorching my eyes, I can still make out the roof of the cruiser as it parks in front of my house. Gandle doesn't turn the car *or* her brights off. She just sits there. I close my front door behind me and shut the screen door, gentle as a surgeon, stepping out to greet her. She rolls her window down and leans her arm on the door.

"How's Luke?"

"He's fine," I tell her. "He's asleep." Gandle shuts off her lights.

"Sorry," she whispers. She looks at the house and grimaces.

"It's all right, he can't hear us. He's out cold. He's fine."

"How about you?" she asks.

"Did you find anything out?"

"You doing all right?"

"I'm fine. Did you find anything?"

She sighs and keeps looking at me.

"So that's a no?"

"Nothing so far," she says.

"Well, that's just fucking great."

"You sure you're doing all right?"

"Stop asking me that!" I tell her. "How do you think I'm doing? Huh? Take a wild guess. Why you looking at me like that?"

She has this great bullshit detector, these great instincts, but doesn't use them to find this scumbag. Instead, they're always aimed right at me.

"Calm down, Pete," she says. "It's okay. You had a very long day. And I understand. And I'm trying to help you out. But I'm worried about you."

"Did you even check? Did you even look into this at all? Do you think I'm just making this up just for yucks? Did you bother?"

Her face registers nothing.

"I spent the whole day at the place," she says. "I talked to the principal at the high school, the athletic director, a coach, a few teachers, a custodian, spoke to some freshmen, sophomores, juniors, even a few seniors. Nothing."

"That's bullshit. That doesn't make any sense."

"No one saw anything, Pete."

"I don't believe that. Is there something you're not telling me? You're looking at me funny."

"No, there isn't. I did check, just like I told you I would. You asked and it's Luke and I checked."

"And nobody—not one person saw anything?"

Gandle looks at me awhile. Then she opens the front pocket of her shirt and takes out her tiny notebook. She opens it, glances up at me for a second, returns to her pad, clears her throat, and begins reading aloud.

"Clyde Johnson, janitor. Forty-six years old. Mr. Johnson said, 'I saw a guy. He was out there on the playground this afternoon. Watching a kid. He's a big guy, like over six foot, little heavy—he's a white guy. He was wearing a hoodie and jeans. Black or maybe blue, dark blue hoodie, I think. I've seen him here before. He just sat there. He looks kind of creepy. Not a lot of folks come to that playground, but he comes here a lot, goes there with a kid. I hope it's his kid, it must be. But he's always alone.'"

31

I DON'T WANT to stand next to her cruiser all night, so I ask Gandle inside the house to hash out the rest of it. Or as much as I can tell her without sinking myself. But this has gone too far, they're threatening my kid, so she needs to hear more about this if she's going to believe anything.

I try to start with something safe and easy. Do you know much about the place where Townsend worked? Not really? I give her a short version of their whole shady history. I don't get into Carson or Grady—it's too risky—and I don't think that they'll help, however this ends up for me. Then I try to go over the timeline, step by step, so she can see everything more clearly. I came down to the station to tell you and the sheriff what I saw, and you didn't seem to care or believe me. I told you I wanted to keep looking into what happened, you told me not to, and I should have listened. I went to the funeral. I told you about seeing that surfboard and then you fucked with me. The scary guy comes by the beach looking for me, I thought my car was broken into, and I was wrong about that, maybe, but I'm pretty sure I was being followed the past few weeks, and then today the scary dude comes after us at the playground.

She sits on my couch, listening, as I pace the room. She doesn't stop me to ask a lot of questions, and I wonder if she's taking me seriously.

Then again, she's here, she came inside without protest, wearing jeans and a T-shirt, and so however much of this is getting through to her, she's hearing it on her time off.

"Pete," she says. "I want to ask you something. Don't get angry."

I'm getting tired of hearing that.

"Sure," I tell her. "I won't. Go ahead."

"How would this firm—how would GDR send someone to intimidate you? I mean, how could that be?"

"They have resources. They do all sorts of stuff you wouldn't believe. I can send you the articles."

"No," she says softly. "I mean, why would you be on their radar? That doesn't make sense. Let's say they're involved in this somehow. Why would these guys be worried? How could they have even heard of you?"

If I'm not careful here I could checkmate myself pretty easily. It's not an unreasonable question, but an honest response could get me thrown through a window. And if I don't answer at all, she won't believe any part of my story.

"Well, what about my visit with you and the sheriff."

I agreed not to get mad, but right now, Gandle doesn't seem like she's playing by the same rules.

"What the fuck's that supposed to mean?" she asks, eyes narrowing. Some of the gentleness has gone out of her voice, too.

"Do you think you guys could have told anyone about that?"

"I think you've had a long day. I'm going to chalk this up to the pressure you're putting on yourself. But you need some sleep."

"No, no," I tell her. She must think I'm accusing her of trading information in some crooked scheme. "That's not what I meant. But what about the family? I mean, did you guys mention any of that, maybe give an update to Townsend's family?"

Gandle pries open her fist and stretches her fingers as her neck and shoulders begin to decompress, but she could still detonate if I say the wrong thing.

"The sheriff," she says. "That's something the sheriff might do. Maybe he followed up with Brooke, to confirm the sequence of events from that day. I don't know."

"Or maybe I mentioned to someone around town how I saw him. I've told the story a few times. I tell it to someone like Noel and it gets around. Sometimes I run my mouth."

"Yeah," she says. "You do."

"So, my name's out there. These guys are following this thing closely."

"So what?" she says. "So, you were a witness? Why would anyone call you thinking you were looking into them?"

They sent a guy down to the beach looking for me, and he keeps calling and he won't stop and now the guy's coming out and threatening me.

"Pete?"

I can't do this on my own anymore. I can't think of everything. I need help. Need her to buy in, and work with me, even if that means taking a little risk. Feels like I'm under the lights, here.

"Pete?" she says. "Is there something you're not telling me?"

I'm exhausted and starting to fold under questioning.

"Okay, let me ask you. If I tell you something, do you have to let the sheriff know?"

"Are you kidding? Jesus. You know what, it's getting pretty late. I could lie to you if I wanted to, but I don't have to. No. Hell no. There's no way I can guarantee you anything even close to that. Should we pinkie swear it's between you and me? What the hell is wrong with you? Do you ever listen to me? What did you do? Tell me right now. What did you do?"

So far, my bargaining has left me looking silly and weak.

"The other day," I spit out, "I went to see Brooke Townsend."

I have seen this woman put some brutal weight on her back and do some amazing stuff with it, but I've never heard her groan the way she does now. She puts her face in her hands. I have to ignore her and get through this. "I went by and I talked with her for a little bit. And she mentioned she was having dinner with Mark Resner that night. The guy who runs GDR? Right. So. Wait. Wait up. Sit down."

"Don't say another word," she whispers through gritted teeth. She reaches a hand down to her hip for a gun or a nightstick, but thank God she's just wearing jeans. This is all going very badly.

"If the sheriff finds out he's going to freak."

"No kidding!" she hisses. "You don't think I know that? Why do you always tell me shit I already know?"

"I'm sorry. I fucked up, all right? But Jesus Christ, do you know what I found there at her house? The same board Townsend had with him the day I saw him. You think he went home to drop it off and grab a different board, and then turned around? Right before sunset? That doesn't make any sense."

She mutters something to herself about *stupid wingnut*. She's staring daggers at me.

But I never get the chance to argue my case. A sound rumbles through the house that makes us both go quiet. We trade glances as the noise draws nearer. Hard footsteps in the front hall are heading straight toward us.

"Is everything all right?" Lauren asks.

For some reason, it feels like we've been interrupted doing something shameful and interesting. Even Gandle, for a brief moment, springs off the couch like some flustered teenager whose parents found her rounding the bases with some scoundrel. But she recovers and lands on her feet.

"Everything's fine," says Gandle.

"There's a police car in the driveway," Lauren points out, not unreasonably.

"That's me," says Gandle, smiling like a camp counselor.

"What's wrong?" Lauren asks.

"Nothing. No problem," Gandle assures her. "Stopping by. I was just in the neighborhood."

My wife looks at me for a moment, as if beginning to ask something, but decides better of it. She turns back to Gandle.

"I'm Lauren," she says, extending her hand.

"Beth. Nice meeting you."

"You sure everything's all right?" Lauren asks. Her mood keeps down-shifting from alarmed to confused and now she sounds almost ambivalent, as if she's telling Gandle she's parked in her spot.

"Of course," says Gandle. "Everything's fine."

"So, what's going on?" she asks.

I haven't come up with much so far, and it feels like I need to contribute, but Gandle pipes up again and says, "I was just about to take off, actually."

It doesn't look as if Lauren's going to beg her to stick around for a drink.

"Nice meeting you," says Lauren. But there are different ways people can say that kind of thing.

The two of them stand looking at each other for a moment. Like two gunslingers sizing up their opponent, they study each other using some mystical sense—damned if I know what they're thinking—but they seem to discuss a great deal, in some unspoken language, ancient and unknown to man. Gandle is the first to back down, bidding us a good night before seeing herself out. Then again, this is Lauren's house. Some bouts aren't easy to score, but I'm not sure judges would call that a win. It still leaves me here to face a fighter with a reputation to protect who wants to send a message to future challengers.

"What's going on?" asks Lauren.

"Nothing," I explain. "She's a friend from the gym."

"Why did the cops come?"

"It's all right. Everything's all right."

She closes her eyes—that's not what she wanted to hear.

"I can't do this tonight," she says. "I really can't."

"She was just stopping by."

I can't tell her about the guy at the playground. It'll just scare the hell out of her, and that won't do anybody any good.

"Why was there a cop here?" she asks. "Why'd she decide to stop by?"

I have to give her something. Which means I'm going to confessional a second time tonight.

"Okay," I tell her. "You know how I keep talking about all this stuff with Townsend? So, I followed up with the police on something, and I know Beth from the gym, so tonight, she was just following up on something with me."

I'm keeping this light on specifics.

"What are you talking about?" she says.

"Everything's all right."

"What are you saying?"

"I've been working on this Townsend thing."

"What does that even mean?"

"I'm trying to figure out what happened to him."

"You're being really weird. Are you fucking with me?"

"No. No. I don't know why you'd say that."

Her mood's shifting gears again. She looks pretty pissed.

"You know this thing that you do? I've wondered sometimes if you're trying to make me look stupid, Pete. It's not cool, at all. Do you think I'm stupid?"

"No. No, I don't. What thing?"

"When you lie to me. I can tell when you're lying."

"I'm not."

"I really hate it when you lie to me."

"I'm trying to tell you what I've been working on."

"So, you're working now?"

"What'd you say?"

"You heard me."

She's really coming at me tonight.

"I'm not lying," I tell her. "Right now, I just have this thing I need to do."

"So, you're doing *this*?" she says, and her voice is harsh and getting louder but the real bile is in her eyes. "Well, that's just great. You have this thing you're doing. Working with the police? Great. Where's all this going? What next? What do you want to do next? I mean, why are you doing this?"

"It's important."

"A lot of stuff's important," she says.

"What's that mean?"

"Have you even thought about trying to find a job? Don't look at me like that."

"What about Luke?"

"I'm not *talking* about Luke," she screams. "Are you listening to me?"

"Yes."

"I can't do this again. I can't go back to the way it was in the city. I'm not going through that again. I'm really trying, but you can't keep doing this— you can't go on like this."

"What are you saying?"

"I'm saying I'm not putting up with it, anymore."

"Okay."

"This is yours to screw up."

She's told me that before. It drives me insane. Something about the phrase doesn't sound like we're on the same team, that we've both made mistakes but together we'll figure it out.

"I wish you wouldn't—" I start.

"This is yours to screw up," she says again.

"What does that even—"

"It means I'm not going to be in *that kind of marriage.* Okay? I'm not going to *stay* in that kind of marriage. Do you see what I'm saying? Is that clear enough for you?"

The warning isn't very subtle. Final offer—take it or fuck off. As in straighten up or she's gone. This is yours to screw up, didn't you hear her?

"Okay," I tell her again.

"I'm done with it," she says.

It all happens pretty quick. We sit here together without speaking for a while, and I study my knees to avoid her glare. But I don't scurry off. I sit in the awkward quiet, my pulse slowing down enough to think through what I could say to her beyond *okay* and *yeah.*

I could tell her not to worry, again. Or that I don't like having my integrity questioned, and I might let her know it turns out I've got a little list of demands in my pocket as well, and maybe someday I'll corner her like she just did to me and hammer my point home without mercy until I finish off with some threats, very serious threats, that I don't take lightly, that aren't funny, either, if she's saying what I think she is. And the stuff about lying, as if marriage is all about radical honesty? Here I thought it was about relationships between men and women, most of them anyway, and so what, no fibbing or screwing with each other ever? Are you kidding me? I mean, is that what we're doing all day, searching for truth? And Jesus, what about what she does for a living? And then she brings up this shit, just like in the old days? I won't forget this.

Part of me wants to ask her, *Wait, so you're telling me that at any moment, you could go batshit, freak out about everything and then decide to take off with most of the money and all of the kid, so I better not disappoint you or you'll make me wish I was dead?* Well, what else is new? I'm a married man, honey. You don't think I know how it works?

But I don't say any of this to her, of course. No, I think I'm done for the night. If you're going to stick up for yourself, then you need to pick your moment carefully, and right here, this place, this isn't the spot. I'm in deep enough. No. When you're this far under, where I am right now, down at these depths, where the water gets darker, the pressure's building so loud, and you know you can't spend too much time this deep or things will start to go bad, you might already have been down for too long—and if it feels like you're starting to get a little confused here? Well, that's not a good sign. So, you need to figure out something pretty soon, and it'd better happen pretty fast.

32

THE MORNING ARRIVES on schedule and doesn't seem to care how much I slept. It doesn't bring any solutions, either, but I'm grateful when Luke wakes up and forces me to go through our daily routine—it's a distraction I need. I get him fed, dressed, and dropped off on time. And then, like a lot of parents after they wave their kids goodbye at the school steps, this nervous dose of reality creeps in as I think through the hours ahead, planning next steps. Many of them will get a second cup of coffee. I prefer Monster Energy.

They say you should start with the most annoying task on your to-do list. When Kathy picks up my call, at least she's in a good mood.

"Hello, Peter!" she says. "Of course, sure. I remember you. How are you?"

"I'm doing great. Is Carson there? Could I speak with him, please?"

"Let me check and see. Would you like me to call you back or...?"

"I can stay on the line."

"Oh," she says. "Well, if you can just hold the phone, please."

The wait for her to come back isn't easy. They own a big goddamned house, but it seems like she must be *crawling* through every room to find him.

"Peter?" she says finally.

"Yes."

"He'll be with you in just a minute. Thanks for holding."

There's something very strange about this woman. She may be a saint, but I don't have time at the moment to deal with her routine. Carson doesn't hustle coming to the phone.

"Yes?" he says.

"Carson? It's Peter Greene. I need to talk to you. Someone came by the playground yesterday where my son and I were. This guy came and sat down—"

"What is this?" he butts in.

"Listen to me. A guy. I don't know—I've never met him—but this guy came by and threatened my kid."

"What are you doing?" he snaps.

"I need to know who these guys are. What are we talking about here? I need to know just what kind of—"

"What is this?" he asks, incredulous.

"I know the last time we spoke that I—"

"You're calling me?"

Some creep threatened my kid, do you get that? But I can't lose my temper with him or I'll never learn anything.

"I should have listened—"

"Don't say anything else," he says. "Listen to me very carefully right now. Who else have you told about this?"

"I spoke to the police. I called from the playground."

"Did you mention my name?" he asks. "Did you say anything about me?"

"No. No. I did not."

"Don't lie to me."

"I never have, and I never would, but I still need to know more—"

"Don't," he growls. "Goodbye, Mr. Green."

The prick hangs up on me. He hangs up on me so I call him back, and now he doesn't pick up, and so I just let it ring. I dig up the *Club Directory* and try to find his cell or another number, but it's just his landline listed. I try him again.

"Hello?" she says.

"It's Peter," I tell her less politely.

"Oh, Peter," says Kathy. "I'm sorry about this."

"It's no problem," I say, composing myself with difficulty. "Could you get him for me?"

"I don't think now's a good time, if you know what I mean."

"No, I know, I know, I understand and I'm sorry, but—"

"Oh, don't be silly!" she says merrily. This woman is an idiot!

"Could I talk to him, please?"

"Oh no, it's just not a good time, but you don't have to be sorry, please. It was nice of you to call."

"Kathy."

"Don't worry. It's not your fault. Everything will be fine. It'll all be fine. Trust me."

I hate everything about this fucked-up family. I wish I'd never heard of these assholes.

"Thanks, Kathy," I say sweetly.

"Oh, of course. Nice of you to call. Goodbye."

I wish that bastard never washed up on my beach.

33

I'M RUNNING THROUGH my options, but I don't have too many, and none of them seem very good. Am I supposed to ask one of the moms? They can work miracles with many subjects, but I don't think they have a lot of expertise in this field. Drew's one of those limousine liberal types, so he can't do much good. I think Gandle and I should keep some distance for a little while. And Carson has made it pretty clear that he's not looking to help. Now, Grady would know plenty about this sort of thing, but I wouldn't want to use a chip with him on this. I do know someone who could help, except that he'll be such a prick about it I don't really want to ask.

Back in the dark ages, sometimes I used to go shooting with Frank. And he would bring this collection of pistols, shotguns, and assault rifles, a private arsenal that could spoil a Texan. He once told me that after one of the school shootings, he ran out and bought an AR-I5, in case they decided to ban them. "Why you looking at me like that?" he'd asked.

But what other choice do I have? I need to protect my family.

So tonight, I give Frank a try, and just like I figured, he can't help himself. I call him up, and when I ask him for a little bit of advice, he goes quiet for a long time. I wait for him to respond but he doesn't, and I know he's still there—I can hear him breathing into the phone—and just when it's almost more than I can stand, he starts giggling like a schoolgirl.

"Oh man," he says. "This is awesome."

"I'm serious."

"Can I come with you?" he asks, teasing.

"No."

He's coughing.

"Please? I'll give you a million dollars."

He sounds plastered. He probably is.

"I said no."

"We could bring the boys."

"That's not funny."

I'm not bringing the boys to buy a shotgun.

"Why don't you just borrow one of mine?" he asks, as if I'm looking for a shorter board.

"I need my own."

And I need to get it fast.

"This a big step," he says. "I'm proud of you. This is gonna be fucking awesome."

34

THE LOCAL PUBLIC library is the backbone of any community in America. Most other municipal services are unimportant. I dropped Luke off at school this morning and came here to clear my head. I'm sitting in the periodicals section with my fellow refugees, going through the morning headlines. We try not to look at each other.

I have all the ingredients of a true believer. Guys like me have as much raw material as you could ever need to build a zealot or a radical or something much worse. But I would like to avoid winding up in that place where I find myself sending angry letters to the editor, airing my insights and grievances on social media, or charging the barricades alongside my misguided comrades only to find out far too late that yes, once again, we were the schmucks who had been led astray. A lot of stuff I see online pisses me off. But I like keeping on top of what's going on in the world. So I do my best. I don't get into politics, if possible, and I stay far away from Twitter—anything I can do to avoid all those guilty clicks, that tasty noise designed to get me riled up. When all else fails I walk around the block.

But sometimes it pays to read the news, to check the tape. Sometimes you get lucky.

PROSECUTORS INVESTIGATE UNION CHIEF'S DEALINGS WITH INVESTMENT FIRMS

Federal prosecutors have opened an investigation into the financial dealings of Kevin Reilly, the powerful president of the New York City Police Officers Union.

The United States Attorney's Office in Manhattan is investigating whether Mr. Reilly, the union leader of the country's largest police department, may have accepted illegal payments from investment firms while head of the union for nearly a dozen years, according to a copy of the subpoena served to the union that was reviewed by the *Wall Street Journal*.

In the subpoena, prosecutors demanded the union turn over a lengthy list of financial accounts and documents to federal investigators. They have also requested information on significant cash deposits made into the personal account of Mr. Reilly, as well as information related to several business trips Mr. Reilly made to Las Vegas, Nevada, and St. Barthélemy over a multiyear period between 2011 and 2015.

Prosecutors appear to be investigating so-called pay to play allegations, whereby Mr. Reilly received personal compensation in both cash and travel expenses from financial institutions in exchange for allocations of union pension investments to be managed by these firms.

The subpoena also requested records regarding the union's financial interactions with a large group of institutions. The list includes hedge funds such as Sedona Capital, Avon Research, North Park Funds, Gardiner Capital, Katahdin Partners, Milford Advisors, Nevis Funds, Stronghold Investments, and Campden Hill Research. It also includes private equity firms such as

GDR Investments, Cameron Advisors, Coopers Investments, Gloucester Capital, Hadrian Advisors, Spring Lake Capital, Southbrook Partners, and Acadia Capital, among several other financial institutions.

"This is a preliminary information request, and we have no further comment at this time," read a statement released last night from Gardiner Capital. Tom Foles, a representative for GDR, declined to comment.

I'll bet you declined to comment, Tom! How's that feel, buddy?

Funny how that happens. Funny how Tom has so much to say when they can plan a murder in some small town, but when the US attorney comes knocking unexpectedly—he shuts up quick. They were bribing their investors. Bribing the decision makers with cash and trips to Vegas and St. Bart's, for chrissakes!

I almost missed their name in the article, skimming it so fast, but I spotted them, right there, front page, below the fold. How much more do I need? Fair-haired boys, just a few steps away from the golden fleece, don't tend to leave serious firms, yet somehow that's what Townsend wanted. It doesn't add up. Unless he was cooperating with the feds. Who knows whether he had a sudden attack of conscience or if the cops had something on him? But we know he wanted out of there. That's a motive. That's a reason. And playing for a lot of money is another reason—a shitload of money an even better one. Avoiding some jail time at the back end is an added kicker. All at this mysterious firm where partners have a tragic habit of checking out early. So many accidents.

I'm really looking forward to this part.

I pick up Luke after school and we head to the box.

I fly through today's workout, feeling light on my feet, moving through each station like a machine. At the end, I don't collapse in a broken heap or lie on the floor, staring up at the ceiling. I'm still upright. Huffing and puffing, but still standing. I wonder if Gandle notices. She's the one who wants to make detective.

As people filter out, I skip over to my bag for my phone, then present the article to her. This time I'm giving out instructions.

"You need to read this," I tell her.

And she does. She takes a few minutes, but she stands there, scrolling through it, squinting her eyes. When she finishes, she stares out across the endless depths of the box. She looks up at me.

"When did this come out?" she asks.

"This morning."

She considers without expression and returns to my phone, taking another few minutes to read it again.

"What do you think?" I ask her.

She bites at a blister. "Now don't get your hopes up too much."

But that's not a *Pete, forget about the autopsy* or *you don't want to do this* or *you're a stay-at-home dad and you suck.* No, this sounds a lot different from all that stuff, and the way she's looking at me feels even better. She gives me the phone back and takes a sip of her protein shake.

"Kind of a coincidence here, huh?" I prod her. She actually *nods.*

"I'm thinking I should bring this to the sheriff. Now slow down, take it easy, but I think he should see this. We should check this out."

She's smiling now, too, and she winks at me. A wink's worth a year of her punches to my solar plexus, and she might know that.

"I gotta get going," she says. Shifting gears from her postsession calm, she stuffs clothes into her bag and starts walking with purpose, no stop and chat with Liz at the front desk. But she can't miss a quick trip inside the rumpus room, to ruffle Luke's hair, a little kiss on top of his angelic head that doesn't distract him from pushing a dump truck over a train set, growling sound effects. He doesn't even acknowledge her as she stops at the door.

"Maybe your dad's not so silly," she says, before turning to walk out.

Now when my son gets older, I'll explain all of this to him, and I won't forget this part, because it's true. Whenever you get a guy who has been striking out a lot—and it doesn't matter if they're called or he swung out and missed—that guy knows when he makes some good contact. And it always feels pretty good.

But some other parts of this story could get tricky. I'm still figuring out how to explain this to him or anyone else, and it's easy for people to get the wrong idea about this sort of business. I don't think my thing with Gandle is sexual. I'm not kidding, I really don't. But it does feel like there is something that I may need to work out at some point. I never said I wasn't looking for her attention or approval—that much seems clear.

Luke picks his head up for a moment. He looks over his shoulder at me and smiles.

Let's hope I get this thing under control though, right, buddy? Because something's going on. I just haven't figured it out yet.

35

Some calls I'm not afraid to make. I've been waiting almost twenty years for this one. I noticed he hasn't called me, of course, because he just can't handle that I finally sniffed something out, miles ahead of him. This one feels good.

"Big boy!" he cackles. "I had a feeling you might be calling me."

"Drew, how goes it? You read the article?"

"I did, sweat pea."

"And?"

"Interesting," he says. But nothing else.

"So. Looks like you got one wrong, huh?"

"Slow down, bud. Slow down."

Slow down? Try checkmate, Drew. This is my victory lap, you can put away your cigar.

"What do you mean slow down?" I ask, picking up momentum.

"Remember how we used to talk about overreacting to recent news?"

No way. Not this shit. I'm not a first-year analyst anymore. I'm not taking any of his quizzes, best case earning a grinning silence, worst case public humiliation.

"Are you kidding me with this?"

"No, I'm not," he says. "There's an article out. Topic you're pretty hot on. You're trying to connect the dots, but I'm just saying…"

"A bunch of bullshit," I help him out. He can't admit he whiffed, so now he's spinning crap. You don't make it far admitting when you're wrong—I just figured Drew was past all that.

"Do you remember we talked about biases?" he asks.

I'm not doing a behavioral finance lecture. And I'm in no mood for any ancient sayings, *if it's in the news, it's in the price,* from a business with a thousand ancient sayings, each one more useless and annoying than the last.

"Did you read the article?" I ask him.

"Did *you* read the article? There's a lot we don't know yet."

"They were bribing their customers!" I don't really care if my voice is rising. "They were flying them out to Vegas and all that other crap."

"They're one of thirty firms mentioned there."

"Thirty crooked firms."

"Bud. The article says they're one of thirty firms, thirty *reputable* firms, by the way, who—"

"Who says they're reputable?" I snap. Why is Drew doing this? What's happened to him? Mr. Tells-it-like-it-is. The math here isn't hard to do. They're a bunch of crooks, screwing people, with a serious amount of money involved, and they got caught.

"I do. I say they're reputable. Look, I know most of these guys, a lot of them anyway. Some of them are pricks. Some of them are tough customers. But most of them are decent people. And I'm a long way, a *long* way, from believing that thirty of the smartest, biggest firms—"

"Thirty of the biggest crooks," I correct him.

"Buddy, look. You're heated on this one. I think you're a little clouded here, seeing red. And by the way, just so you know, I'm invested with some of these guys."

Well, that wasn't so hard. It explains things. This business poisons the soul.

"That makes sense," I tell him. "That's convenient."

"Go easy, bud." He laughs as he searches for the next pinch of Skoal. I can hear the nice-size chew, situated between cheek and gum. This is the guy lecturing me right now about what's rational.

"You've gotten rich off these guys and you think I have a bias?"

"Jesus Christ, sweat pea, I haven't gotten *rich* off these guys. It's been pretty mediocre. *Really* mediocre, actually. Maybe if I knew anything about venture capital, I'd say something different, but I don't, and that's been the place to be for a while, much to my chagrin. But I took a risk like a grown-ass man, and it didn't work out. It is what it is. Poor me. Boo-hoo."

I worked for this guy for almost twenty years. Loyally. He always had a habit of speaking in parables, but now, for him to talk down to me like this, like I'm a child.

"Then why invest with them?"

"Good question, buddy. Good question," he says, laughing in a way that sounds as if it were anything but. There's that familiar sound of tobacco and saliva hitting a cup.

"Try this out," he says. "Everybody's got to figure out what to do with their money. That is, if they have any. You only have so many options. I look at this stuff same as anyone else. The sad part I don't like to admit is that I did the math, and I figured that the sum of these guys wouldn't beat a simple index. Probably worse. But here's the thing no one tells you about ETFs and index funds. They're no fun. They're boring. So, I have some money, *some of my money*, with a few guys I knew from banging heads back in the old days. They pick up my calls. And if I'm in New York or Boston we grab lunch, maybe get a few ideas, to feel like I'm still in the game. Keeps me involved with planet Earth. You ever have trouble filling your days, bud?"

This was my mentor.

"I guess I just wouldn't understand," I tell him, knowing that Drew belongs to a group of men who can say "it is what it is" about any topic and then feel this simple statement absolves them of all responsibility until the end of days. *That is, if they have any.* For him to say that to me! *Some of my money.* He's lucky to have it and won't admit he invested with a bunch of thieves.

"Yeah, you do," he says. "Take David out in Chicago. I've known the guy for thirty years—our kids played together, for chrissakes. You're telling me he's slipping people cash under the table? For what? Ten million bucks from a pension fund? The guy's a billionaire. I don't see it."

"That's exactly the kind of thing David would do," I tell him because I do know David, I used to cover him—he's a sociopath and a freak.

"It doesn't make any sense. You don't risk your firm and your reputation for a few more shekels. These guys aren't *stupid.*"

"You and I disagree," I tell this lottery winner. This prick from a privileged era.

"Look, this whole thing of yours…"

"What whole thing?"

"Just take it easy for a sec, bud."

Could be worse. He didn't say *don't get all emotional on me.* Or hysterical.

"Do me a favor," he tells me. "You still there? Just sleep on what I said. I know, I know, I'm not gonna say any more. Just think about it for a bit. Sleep on it, okay?"

"Sure." I have a feeling that I'll think about this conversation for a lot longer than tonight.

"Say, bud, did you ever…?" he begins to ask, but his voice trails off.

"Did I ever what?" I snap, building up my courage to ask something else.

"Nothing. Hang in there. I'll talk to you. Take care. I'll see you around."

"Hey, Drew?" I pause for a second, to steady myself. "One last question."

"What's up?"

"You said, *some of these guys*...?" My old boss doesn't respond, and the silence is awful. He's making me ask him. "Do you have money with GDR?"

"Hang in there, bud," he says.

Kids always remember the first time their father truly disappoints them. It never feels good. And like a sad child learning the high price of adulthood, I hang up on him, thinking, *If that's what it takes? If that's what you're asking? If that's what it costs? Then no. I never want to grow up.*

36

It's a thin crowd at the Bull tonight. Outside, the rain comes down in sheets and scares away all but the most committed patrons. Luke and I sit alone at the bar. Warm and dry. He nibbles at a toasty mac 'n' cheese and nurses his sippy cup while his dad has a steaming bowl of clam chowder. They have a fire going. Noel perches on a stool behind the taps, swiping through his phone, probably one of the four or five newspapers he reads every day. I keep smiling and looking over at Luke, feeling grateful and satisfied to have paid our dues in this kind of place.

The roar of the gale fills the room and I look behind us to see a new customer closing the tavern door. He stomps his feet on the doormat. A wiry figure stands in the entryway, clothed in a rain slicker and rubber boots. Water's still pouring down from his hood and ball cap. He has a thin raggedy beard covering a face scarred by the sun that makes him look much older than he probably is.

The man sets a course toward us, and although there are plenty of open booths around, he sits downs a few stools over from us at the bar, a comfortable creature in his natural habitat. The scent of stale cigarettes follows him. He orders beer and whiskey and starts drinking them quickly.

"How you guys doing?" he asks after a while.

"Fine," I tell him. I have my arm around Luke and I hold him closer to me now. Noel's on his feet, paying the man some attention. The guy wipes his mouth with the back of his hand and considers his next option. I try not to look at him, and soon of course, I'm staring.

"Have you two met before?" Noel asks. I wish he hadn't. Neither of us responds.

"Pete, this is John," says Noel. "John, this is Pete, the fella I was telling you about."

I'm not sure what that means, and I don't think John knows either, but he doesn't look worried about it.

"Can I get another round?" he asks.

I'd prefer it if Noel didn't tell people around town that I'm looking into what happened to Townsend. He fixes John another pint of beer and a small glass of whiskey. John takes his drinks and stares off into space.

"Good you lads get a chance to meet," says Noel cheerfully. "John, this is the fella who was asking about your man." He can't help himself.

"Asking about what?" John says distractedly.

"It's nothing," I tell him. Noel frowns at this. I lift Luke out of his seat onto my lap, thinking we might get the check and catch an early bedtime tonight.

"No, no—it's all right," Noel says. "John was the one who found him."

The fisherman. The fisherman who dragged Townsend out of the water.

"Wait," I say. "You're the one who found him?"

Noel nods, pleased with his work. John seems less enthusiastic.

"Damn," I offer. He doesn't disagree. But I collect myself enough to let inspiration strike and I ask him, "Do you feel like another beer?"

Noel smiles like a proud parent.

We talk for a while. John's lived out here forever. He's worked a lot of different jobs. *Did you ever want to live somewhere else? Who doesn't?* But he loves the place, and though it's changed—*everything's changed*—it's still home, even if he hates a lot of the new people. He was married himself once. And he has a son.

"Do you mind if I ask you about when you found the guy?" I say when the timing feels right. He peers down at Luke. "Don't worry about him, it's cool," I insist.

John shoots a glance at Noel for approval, and I'm not sure why, but Noel assures him that everything's fine.

"Sure," John says with a shrug.

"Can you tell me about what happened that morning?" I ask.

"I got down to the beach about five a.m. I'd been having some luck at one of the sandbars. Low tide was six thirty. I was out there a few hours before I packed up. Then I was driving along the beach for a bit when I saw something getting tumbled about a hundred yards down the shore."

"Was he floating?"

He sighs again, looks at Luke and shakes his head.

"This *thing*," he says. "This *log* was getting rolled on the sand in the tide. I gunned it over there and ran into the water. I dragged the log up onto the beach, thought about trying to do, um...to do CPR on this log...but the way it looked...it was ice cold."

"How did it look? I mean, could you tell what kind of injury he had? What might have happened?"

He takes a drink and holds up his hands in protest. "I don't know. But it didn't look good."

"Then what?"

"I called 911. The cops showed up pretty fast. Because they need to clean up *logs* in the ocean. And I sat around for a few hours. Gave them my statement. That was it."

"Did you talk to the sheriff?"

"No."

"Did you talk to his deputy? Stocky woman?"

"Nope."

"Which cops did you talk to?"

"I don't remember the guy's name."

"Maybe it was Marine Patrol. Maybe that's a jurisdictional thing."

He doesn't have a view on this, though, and I don't know anything about it, either.

"What happened next?"

"That was it. I was ready to get out of there. So then I went home and had some beer."

"Gotcha."

"I mean, nobody knew who the thing *was* and I didn't, either. So, they sent me home. Then I read about it in the papers a few days later. Saw the picture. It was pretty weird."

"I'll bet."

"You saw his picture?" asks Luke.

John closes his eyes for a second, and when he opens them he stares at his beer.

"Yeah," he tells Luke, then glares over at me.

"Do you want another round?" I ask him.

"No, man. I don't." He looks pretty tired. He lets out a deep sigh. "Yeah, it was weird, when I saw the picture in the paper. Turns out I had just seen him."

"*Wait.* You knew Townsend?"

"No, but I'd seen him around."

"When?"

"I don't remember. That week. Maybe a few days earlier."

Brooke said he drove out late Wednesday night. He went missing Thursday.

"Where?"

"Just around. You know how it goes."

"Where did you see him?"

"At a bar."

"Which one?"

"I don't know."

"Did he come around here?" I ask Noel suspiciously, who gives a quick shake of his head. He's been listening very closely.

John shrugs. It feels like he knows but for some reason doesn't want to tell me. Why wouldn't he want to say—is he scared? Or embarrassed about something? He's embarrassed to tell me which bar...

"Was it Lucky's?" I ask him.

He nods at this and gives his glass a close inspection. Why the hell would Townsend be at Lucky's?

"Are you sure it was him?"

He may not respond to the question, but he doesn't look uncertain about the answer.

"What night was it?"

"Hey, man, I don't know what this is all about."

"What night was it?"

"It was Wednesday or Thursday," he says. "I think it was Thursday. I'm pretty sure."

37

THIS AFTERNOON LUKE starts screaming and doesn't stop. Not two minutes into my warmup at the box, his wailing drifts into the main room. Aunt Liz and I have an unspoken agreement that she can stop him from leaving the premises or hurting himself, but she won't handle soiled diapers or inconsolable grief. The working arrangement of any uncle or aunt.

I scurry off the gym floor into the rumpus room and try to comfort Luke, but he wants no part of it. So I carry him outside for more discussion. It's embarrassing. You can have kids around these sorts of places, if they behave and they handle their business. Most people can't help but find them adorable—it can work. Until it doesn't. And then you're filled with shame, the sudden recognition that you've asked for special treatment, that others don't come to gyms or bars or libraries to hear temper tantrums, much the opposite. You start to doubt your whole strategy toward a lot of things. You see a future that must now include a lot more of your time spent around the house.

But I manage to calm him down and he agrees to come back inside and play nice. By the time I get him settled I've missed the warmup and stretching, and barely manage to grab a kettlebell and medicine ball before the main event kicks off.

There's some new monster in class today. He's a younger guy, maybe thirty, not that tall, but he looks as if he were raised in this place. He's wearing some camo board shorts and a fire department T-shirt that's having difficulty with his arms and shoulders. Full head of hair. During the workout, the guy just chews through each station and never stops until he finishes his last rep before any of the other mutants, then lies spent, a heaving sweat angel on the floor.

I chip away at the session. The kettlebell, the pull-ups I can't really do, the rower I'm usually best on. When I finish my fifth round, I need to sit on the floor for a while and think about things, and I don't feel good.

Gandle strolls across the room. It seems like she knows the new guy because she's walking over to him. They must know each other well, because she plants a pretty good one on him. Jesus. Maybe a little open mouth in there for a second—this is no peck on the cheek. Then for good goddamn measure, as she turns around to walk away, he grabs a decent handful of her ass. She spins back to push him playfully in the chest. She looks pretty happy.

I really don't feel good, at all.

But I make it over to the playroom, giving Aunt Liz a short wave on my way past the front desk. I unfold the stroller and begin packing up our stuff. This doesn't feel like a day to sit around and chat after class.

Gandle walks into the playroom. It looks like she managed to separate herself from the new guy and found some clothes. She put on a T-shirt with sweatpants and now she's here to fawn over her favorite member of the box. She seems pretty comfortable. And why not? Why should she feel embarrassed? She hasn't done anything wrong.

"What's going on?" she asks.

"Nothing."

"We're still waiting to hear back, before you ask. This kind of thing, lot of bigwigs involved, it gets political, so we're still waiting."

"Sounds great," I tell her. That's all very fascinating. That's all really good stuff.

"How about you? Anything new?"

"Nope. Same story."

Why should I bother? She puts up with me because we go to the same gym. I'm just some dude with a cute kid and that's it—what the hell else could I be? If I was too stupid to figure that one out before, I think I just got the message pretty clear.

"All right," she says. "I'll see you later, I guess."

"Yup. See you later."

For a moment after she leaves, it's just me in the rumpus room with Luke and my self-pity for company. But at some point, I realize I need to stop being such a drama queen and I skip out to the parking lot after her.

Her cruiser's not in the lot. Maybe she already fled the scene?

But then I see her sitting in the driver's seat of a nice-looking truck. She's wearing one of those mesh hats that have made a comeback recently. There's a dog in the back, a German shepherd—I didn't know about him, either. The youngblood rides shotgun, and Gandle doesn't look miserable sitting next to him. I guess he's not just a pretty face, also quite the comedian—he must have told a real knee-slapper.

Gandle starts the engine and begins to pull out of her spot. No more fondling each other or playing kissy face or anything, but the night's still young. The dog sits alone back there, panting on the flatbed, tall and regal, his tongue hanging out of his mouth. There they go. Probably off to fix some fences.

So, she found a nice young stud, with half my body fat, twice my dead-lift, and probably a bigger dick. Nothing was ever going to happen between us, but it's nice to feel wanted. Hopefully those two muscle-bound first responders go home and enjoy his big hose after many a long shift. Good for them. She doesn't owe me anything and I don't need to prove anything to her, either. It's good I know that now. Good, good.

Now I don't have to go out and do something stupid.

38

I FEEL LIKE a bag of dicks, Frank texts me, today.

Hey, got a question for you, I write back.

Hammered last night, he says.

I regret nothing, he adds. I'm not weak.

Did you ever see Townsend around Lucky's? I ask.

What am I going to do, just sit around? Am I supposed to just listen to what Gandle told me and wait like a schmuck until she hears back about the union angle, trusting her whole "proper channels" routine? Not happening. Lately, I've become a little more skeptical about what Gandle tells me. Besides, fortune favors the bold. God hates a coward, Detective.

If I can prove Townsend was at Lucky's the Thursday night he went missing, this whole thing becomes very straightforward. Hard for him to drown just before sunset if he was throwing them back with John and the regulars here that Thursday night. But since no one will trust John's recollection, and I'm not sure I can, either—even though when sobered up, he seems like a decent fellow—I need to find someone to corroborate his story. That means I need to go back to the front lines.

R u serious? Frank asks, like somehow, I knew he would.

Yeah. Did you ever see him?

No don't think that was his scene. Not his kind of crowd.

Frank makes a fair point. The thought has bothered me since John's confession at the Old Bull.

Heard he was there the other night, I write.

I'm lying around in my own filth.

Nice

What r you up to?

Do you know if Manny's working tonight?

I hate you, he says.

Is Manny on or not?

Yeah should be

Thx

I feel like shit today, he says.

Every town in America has two kinds of bars. There's one where an Irish bartender pulls taps, the summer folks stand in line to hear the bands, they have a room big enough for the college kids to make out on the dance floor, and on weeknights they host trivia. You can go there to watch a few games, if you find a stool, they serve fried food, and you can bring your kid to eat there if the spirit moves you. Then you have the other kind of bar. The kind like Lucky's.

A few miles off the highway, down an empty side road, Lucky's Bar and Grill sits alone on a clearing in the woods overlooking a pond. The building's not much more than a modest red barn and a few barred windows covered by neon beer signs to welcome visitors. It would be easy to pass by it without stopping, or even speed up, as many do. This isn't a place to bring a kid. But if you want to lay a bet, purchase a substance, get in a fight, or worse, then you've come to the right spot. Over the years, Lucky's has sent a good deal of business Gandle's and the sheriff's way.

I can't understand why Townsend would come to a joint like this. I know the reasons why *I* did. Sometimes you just want to take yourself to pieces in a dark corner, hidden away from the watchful eyes of the civilized world. But for a guy like Townsend? Most of his life was a journey dedicated to keeping a great distance from Lucky's, or anywhere like it, or any place in the country where he could imagine bumping into one of their customers. Pulling up and parking alongside the few cars in the dirt lot out front, I still can't imagine how Robert Townsend ended up here that night.

Manny stands guarding the door and looks happy to see me. He's an entrepreneurial sort, always looking for potential customers. We hug it out, like the good old days.

"Pete, how's it, bro?" he asks.

"Living the dream, Manny."

"Haven't seen you around in a long time. Miss you, bro."

"Me, too. Frank keeping you busy, staying out of trouble?"

"Same old. What's up?"

"Actually, I had a question for you."

"What do you need?"

"Did you hear about that guy they found washed up on the beach a few weeks ago?"

"Yeah," says Manny, but he looks disappointed with the question. "I heard." Maybe he was hoping for *What's the line on the Jets game? Got anything on you?* That kind of stuff.

"You ever seen him around here?"

"No."

"You sure?" I pull out my phone for a decent picture. "This guy right there. Did you ever see him around?"

He looks annoyed, glancing at my hand and shaking his head.

"Nah. Never seen him."

"Here or anywhere else?"

"I don't know the guy, yeah? Never saw him on the water, Pete. I heard what happened. Like everybody else. Bad luck. But I didn't know him."

Something about his answer feels off to me, but I know better than to ask a guy this size again.

"Thanks. Thanks man. Who's working the bar tonight?"

"Jared."

"I don't remember Jared."

"He's one of the new guys. He's a dick."

"Does he work Thursday nights?"

"No. Thursday's Colin. Why?"

"Just wondering."

I don't remember Colin, either. Those were dark days.

"You're not going in there asking around on this guy, are you?" He sighs. "That what you up to, bro?"

"So what if I am?"

His colossal shoulders slump, and he shakes his head.

"Pete, good to see you, yeah? But think, long time since you been here. Maybe some guys in there don't like you asking questions about a dead guy. Know what I mean, bro?"

"I heard he was in here the other night."

"That's not what I mean, bro."

"I'll see you in a bit," I tell him, whacking his tree trunk of an arm. I step through the door.

The scene inside is grim. That familiar red glow barely lights the room. The place feels like a deserted outpost long abandoned except for these few last survivors, still fighting some brutal civil war. Huddled around their tables, they commiserate over atrocities suffered by their families, stoking their hatred and plotting their terrible revenge. A corner booth houses a group of what can only be meth addicts. They look emaciated, filthy, faces all sunken cheekbones, sipping on glasses of soda through straws. Two older men, gaunt figures, long beards, perhaps John's contemporaries, sit alone at the far end of the bar, hunched over the serious business of drinking themselves to death. No women, but one or two might stumble in later, and then heaven help them. Not much changes around here.

The two most approachable sorts are perched at a round table in the center of the room. The handful of other customers look like they've been put through a wood chipper, but these two almost seem like a couple of normal guys about my age, just watching the game, seeking a little protection from the outside world while they can. I ask them if I can sit down.

The bigger one wears a dirty hooded sweatshirt and a camo hat, and he sports a thick red beard. He shrugs a confused yes. His smaller friend, in a weathered long-sleeve work shirt, ignores my introduction, never taking his eyes off the game on the TV screen behind me.

"You guys want another round?" I ask, settling in.

The smaller guy still doesn't answer, too absorbed by the game, but his redheaded friend looks at his bottle.

"I'm good," he says, without much joy.

This used to be easier. Maybe I only bought drinks deeper in the night, when people were more open-minded to strange offers. Behind me, the skinny bartender wipes down the bar with a towel. Over by the door, Manny has stepped inside for a bit and perches on his stool, watching. He shoots me a nod, and I return it. But now it seems he's had enough because he stands up, walks back past our table, and announces, for any who may care to know, "I'm gonna take a shit."

When a massive Polynesian man wanders over to the bathroom, squats down on the toilet, and forces out a monstrous dump, that must be quite a thing. Quite a thing. But I return to the business at hand. The redheaded guy is looking at me.

"What's up? I'm Pete," I say extending my hand. He shakes it, but his catatonic companion still doesn't respond. It must be the fourth quarter. A real barn burner.

"You come around Lucky's a decent amount?" I start.

"Some," Redbeard admits.

"Mind if I ask you something?"

He shrugs and scratches a fuzzy cheek.

"I was wondering if you'd ever seen a guy here."

"A guy?" he says, raising his eyebrows.

"Yeah."

"Why?"

I pull out my phone in response and show him a photo of Townsend's smiling mug. The redhead peers down at the picture and takes a sip of his beer. He looks back at me and furrows his brow.

"Are you a cop or something?" he asks.

"No."

"You're not any kind of cop?"

"No."

"Then why you asking?"

"Because I need to know if he was here. It's important."

His friend's still transfixed by the TV, his mouth hanging open. He doesn't look unhappy.

"No," the ginger man says. "Never seen him."

"You sure? Can you look again?"

He glances back at my phone. He brings his bottle up and finishes it.

"Don't know him," he says.

"Do you surf at all?" I ask him. He closes his eyes and rubs his face.

"No," he says. His friend just stares behind me, and still seems contented. He could be a real shredder on the waves, seen Townsend a dozen times, he may even speak English, but no one will ever know. It's a shame. Big Red and I sit around, looking at each other for a bit.

"The guy was a surfer," I explain, and when he doesn't respond for a while, just considers the empty bottle in front him, I add, "That's why I was asking." He seems no more fascinated by this.

"I need a cigarette," he says after some reflection. "You want one?"

His silent partner looks down from the game at me now. But I'm not sitting here alone with Chatty Cathy.

"Sure," I say, glad he asked. "Thanks."

"Let's go," says Red, getting to his feet. The little dude watches me now as I stand up and follow the big guy out the door. A quick cigarette—maybe the guy's friendlier without his downer buddy at his elbow—this doesn't have to be so hard. The two of us step out into the night.

"What the hell does Manny want?" he asks.

I look back over my shoulder to see the front door close behind me and I turn back just in time for Red to punch me in the face.

His fist lands flat against my cheek. Lucky it wasn't my chin or worse, but this doesn't feel too good, and my legs almost buckle, though I stay on my feet, and he's winding up, reloading with that right hand again, but I just manage to grab a piece of his throwing arm and shirt.

And now a collision. We crash into each other like two sumo wrestlers, perverted and crazed. Pawing at each other. I have a good grip on him with my left hand and get his right arm pinned against his side with my arm wrapped around his back, grabbing his shirt and some of his fucking hoodie. But I only have a bit of his other elbow, and he's swinging away at the back of my head—he doesn't have much leverage and it's his off-hand—but he's still swinging. We spin around the pavement, locked in a tender embrace like two drunk lovers taking a lost whirl on the dance floor. But he pivots and he's under me now, and I'm backpedaling, picking up speed, and it's my back that slams into the door first. I'm lucky to keep my wind. Now, pinned against the door, he leans into me—he's strong as hell, Jesus, what does *this* guy fucking deadlift?—still got that right arm tied up, but his left keeps swiping at me. This doesn't feel good and it's not getting any better. I can't hold him up forever, he's too strong. I need to put him on the ground. Put him on the ground somehow and pound the shit out of him or tie him up and wait for Manny to get the hell out here from wherever the fuck he is? *Breathe. Breathe.* Don't forget to breathe, or you won't hold him. Just keep him wrapped up, choke him out with his stupid-ass hoodie if you have to—but now the fucker bores the top of his head under my chin, driving up past my face and I'm trying to push him off me, his beard scraping my cheek. What the hell does he want? A make-out session, bang a little face in the parking lot? His breath on my neck, grunting. What the fuck's he doing? No. No no no no no...

Oh god it hurts!!! Oh, Jesus!!! Not the ear! Not the ear! Not my fucking ear!!!!

I'm screaming. Screaming fucking agony as those teeth gnaw into my cartilage and when I grab his hair and pull him off me, part of my ear goes with him, spraying blood down his chin, but now that right hand's free and he's swinging with some purpose and catching me good, this one's got some spirit and this is bad and getting worse because I can't keep my feet—the ground doesn't rush up to meet me, I'm falling hard, going down—now my back's on the pavement, a hand held up in front of me as if I were shielding my eyes from the sun but I can barely see the punches let alone block that fist and it keeps hammering down, landing hard on my face, and now he grabs my wrists, pinning my arm under his weight and he rears back and oh *shit*—we got another headbanger—he snaps that skull into my eye, it sounds like the crack of a bat, and the back of my head hits the pavement and that's about it.

That's about it for me.

39

MANNY WAKES ME up. Nice of him.

Laid out on the ground, looking up at the stars, cold cement on the back of my head. I glance down at my feet but nothing's working, my hands are raised slightly in surrender, but I'm not sure why. A tuft of the guy's crimson hair is stuck under my fingernail. Peering down disturbed something in my head, something quite awful. I close my eyes, just to lie here for a moment, let these rough seas pass. There's not a lot I can do. A hateful judge pounds his gavel in my head, but the court will not come to order—*please have mercy, Your Honor*—but still, they won't quiet down, so he keeps clubbing that block with his mallet, shouting threats of contempt. A deep breath makes it all so much worse. I open my eyes again, but I can barely see out of my left one. My ear screams at me from somewhere.

"You okay, bro?" asks Manny.

You tell me. How's it look?

I turn my head, slowly. I can't sit up like this, so I roll over onto my side, no small effort. From here I can get one arm under me and hoist myself to rest on my elbow.

"You all right, bro?" he asks again.

"No," I tell him, and I'm not. I've been a lot better.

The swaying deck of the street steadies slowly as the ocean begins to calm. I taste a sticky salt in my mouth and my tongue searches my teeth, checking for loose residents.

"Let me see that, bro," says Manny, peering down at my face, concerned. "Get you some ice. Be right back."

I'm not going anywhere fast—my equilibrium's a little off, no rush, bro. He jogs inside and soon returns with a bag of crushed ice and a towel that looks like it's gotten some good use.

"Put this on your ear. Put the ice on your face. Your eye."

"Thanks, Manny." His mammoth paw pats my shoulder.

"You'll be all right. That guy's gone. He's outta here. Don't worry. You're okay."

I sit on the ground, elbows on my knees, considering my next steps. But I'm begging, now, please make the pounding stop, dear god, this violence, we know that yes, surely, I've sinned, but this fucking headache, good Christ, my poor head.

"Hang on just a sec," I tell the consoling giant. "I might need a minute here, okay?"

And I do. But after some time, I stand up. Manny nods at me when I make it to my feet.

"Maybe you should get that ear looked at. That eye, too?"

I press the ice to my eyebrow in agreement, thinking *yes*, a professional should see to this.

"Hey, one thing, though?" he asks and cocks his massive head to the side.

How can I help you Manny? What would you like me to do?

"If we don't call anyone, that's better for me." He shrugs. "I don't need that, you know?"

"I can drive. I'm good."

"Thank you. Sweet as, bro. Good, good."

I climb into my car. Manny's back soon with another bag of ice, a plastic cup of water, and another towel that looks cleaner than the first. He hands them to me through my window and shakes his head sadly.

Why the long face, Manny?

"I'm sorry," he says. "I tried to...I tried to warn you, bro. Sorry, eh?"

"I know, Manny. I know. But hey.... I might need just another minute, if that's cool?"

"No worries, bro. No worries, yeah? You're good."

Driving to the hospital, that's about twenty minutes away. I choose a CD for the road, my hands clammy and shaking, but I've done this before, and when you drive yourself to the emergency room because of your own idiocy, all of us get to decide what music to play. I use Springsteen in such times, but the choice is personal and important and one that each of us has to make for ourselves. There's a certain dignity in not calling an ambulance and finding your own transport in moments of crisis, but much less— a great deal less—in getting pinned to the ground and beaten senseless. Holding the ice to my face, I wrap the cleanest towel around me in a head-band, trying to stop the bleeding from whatever's left of my ear. A terrible thing, to glance up at the rearview. Look at this one-eyed monster, blood-shot, pale and sweating, breathing heavy, sweet Jesus—*eyes on the road! right of the yellow line!* A high-speed wreck or head-on collision—there's no dignity in those, either.

Now comes time for reflection and second-guessing. And oh, this post-game will wear into the wee hours, the Twitter commentary merciless, with so many experts weighing in with opinions made worse by the fact that I probably won't disagree with the meanest jabs. It's not a good feeling. All these years, every time I piss someone off enough to get punched in the face, I end up grabbing at the guy like some goddamn sex offender, trying to tie up his best hand, often the one he just hit me with. I can't seem to think of a better move, and it always ends with me getting my ass kicked. Maybe I should just start swinging for my life? These critics, those bastards, they're right. I never really learned how to fight.

Even if I'm not sure I can afford tuition, I still wonder how many classes you need to graduate. How many fights does it take to become a decent scrapper? Maybe just a few more? I'll have to find a different dojo. Maybe if I had gone to that damn boxing gym, or the jiujitsu class, but we may never know. What I see in the rearview doesn't look pretty. Under my crooked bandanna, the swelling's already starting, and sweat's pouring off my face—just a few more? A bloodshot cyclops stares back in the mirror.

I don't know how many more of *these* I've got in me.

You do all kinds of thinking on these sorts of drives. I pull into the hospital and cruise past the emergency room entrance, find a space in the parking lot, and turn off the engine. I sit in the quiet for a moment. Ever since I had a kid and took up these stupid sports, I've dreaded sending a certain sort of text. But no choice now, the day has come and she needs to know. I just hope she's still up.

Dema? R u free to sit tomorrow? It's important. 7am start? Lmk tonight? Asap?

I'll just tell my wife, trying to get on the water early looks epic, need a little help from Dema in the a.m. I'll think of something. And if that doesn't work then I'm in real trouble.

I steal a last look in the mirror. Surveying the scene, the victim's body shows bruising, discoloration, blunt-force trauma, bite marks, clear signs of a struggle. But I tell myself, before walking up to check in at the ER—I should probably stop smiling.

The last time I woke up in a hospital were those magical days and nights when Luke was born. I slept on the pullout they roll in for you, the tiny contraption built for hobbits and elves, always that one bar hitting the small of your back every night. In recognition of her recent efforts, my wife had earned the better bed in the room. I envied her. But then the skin against skin, holding that tiny creature against my chest? I miss that cot.

Waking up in agony after a few hours of wretched sleep, it hurts to read through my phone. Until Gandle walks into my room and sits down in a chair next to me. I don't want her seeing me like this. She doesn't look happy.

"I might need a day or two off from the gym," I tell her.

"That's not funny," she says.

"I'm all right. It's okay. I can take it."

"That's not what I meant."

"It's not that bad. I'll be back. I have something new, something good." And a headache that would kill a weaker man.

"Good? Pete, the good news here is they say your orbital socket's not broken, and your retina is still attached. But the doctor said those were close, and that's just way too close for me. But you do have a serious concussion. Your ear. And your *face*. Pete, if this isn't that bad, I don't want to see any worse."

"We can finish this."

"No. This needs to stop. It's my fault. And believe me, I'm sorry."

"But we have too much evidence. I heard a new piece—"

"We don't have any evidence," she says unhelpfully. "We have nothing at all. Nothing's coming back on that subpoena from these firms. I don't think GDR's a real target of that article you showed me. There's just nothing here, Pete. You had a bunch of questions and you tried to run them to ground. You really tried and all that you've done—I won't forget it. But it's over."

"How can you say that?"

"Because I give a shit about you, Pete. You and your family. Now the sheriff's going to talk with you in a day or two and—"

"You're not listening to me." She *never* listens to me. "I heard something the other night. Townsend was in Lucky's that Thursday."

"Stop," she snaps. What's her fucking problem? Has *she* had a rough night?

"Did you hear what I just said? He was at Lucky's! That means this was no accident! John the fisherman saw him, that's why I went there—"

"He went in the water Friday morning," she says flatly. "We know that." What the hell is she talking about?

"He went in Friday morning, Pete," she says again. "We have his cell phone location. He left his house at five a.m. He drove to the beach, something went wrong out there, he drowned, and he got pretty banged up. We thought he went in Thursday afternoon at first, we released that to the paper, but we checked—"

"What do you mean at first? What are you talking about?" I may need a nurse.

"Coroner thinks he'd been in the water about thirty-six hours when the body was found. But they can't be precise—it's a six-hour window, give or take. Thirty-six hours would put him in the water at midnight, maybe one a.m. His wife told us that she'd just talked to him Thursday, at around four o'clock. Said he was going surfing. So that's what we thought, and that's what we told the press. According to Verizon—we were wrong."

"I don't understand."

"When you told me at the gym that you saw him down at the beach on Thursday, I checked it out and called Verizon—they had his location. His cell was never off. He was home Thursday night just after dinnertime and he drove down to the beach Friday morning. But there's no reason to make that public."

"You could have said something." No reason?

"I couldn't. And I'm sorry. By the time you came to the station and talked to us about seeing Townsend, the bad surfing conditions? You just confirmed everything we'd already found out."

I need a minute with all this. My poor head. *The coroner said thirty-six hours.* What was Friday morning? Friday's the day after Thursday. It's a school day. Oh, my *fuck-ing* head.

"How could you not tell me?" I don't understand. I need some time to think.

"I'm sorry," she says. She keeps saying sorry all the time like *I* do! "But you're not a cop. You're not a cop and I need this job. I need this one to work out. I couldn't risk it."

"On someone like me?"

It's been a long fucking night.

"I didn't say that. You're a good guy. I mean that."

Jesus, she's pretty vicious.

"But we're just better off as friends?"

"We *are* friends," she says hatefully. "But this whole thing was a mistake. I'm sorry. Listen to me. You need to let this go. But I am your friend, and I'm around if you need me."

When I walk in from the hospital Luke bounds over to the door, thrilled to see me. But then he looks up at my face, sucking his thumb, and he's not smiling anymore.

"*Wait!*" he cries, holding a palm out. He turns and runs away from me. I ignore his command and shuffle toward the living room, where I collapse on the couch.

"*Wait!*" I hear him yell again. Now comes a terrible screeching sound that won't stop. I sit up to see him dragging a chair from the dinner table across the room into the kitchen—his progress slow and probably scratching up the floor, but tonight I'll let this go. Tell Mommy it's my fault, buddy. Just put it on my tab.

He drags the chair in front of the refrigerator. He climbs on top of the chair and stands, looking at his options. Reaching up above the fridge, he struggles with the freezer door, hanging off it—I'm ready to leap into action, this looks a little precarious. The freezer door opens, he keeps his balance, mercifully, and reaches a hand inside, selecting a bag of peas. He closes the door, climbs down from the chair, runs over to present me with the frozen bag, and points at my face.

"*Ice it!*" he cries, jabbing a finger at me. I follow his instructions. Then I grab him up with my other arm and hold him close to me, breathing him in.

Over his shoulder, I can see Lauren standing in the doorway watching us, her hands on her hips. She doesn't share in the moment. She just shakes her head and walks out of the room, leaving the two of us alone.

There are many occasions when a husband will feel grateful that he married a smart woman, but when he needs to spin a semiplausible tapestry of utter bullshit to avoid a high-stakes argument, that isn't one of them.

By the time she gets Luke down for the night, I'm already laid out on top of the covers, barely awake but without the energy to stand and turn off the light. Lauren tiptoes inside the room, but she stops to stand by the foot of the bed, studying her patient.

"Are you sure you're all right?" she asks.

"It's not that bad. Really. I'm fine."

From the look on her face, it doesn't seem like she agrees.

"You're fine?"

"I'm good. Really."

She hesitates and considers this for a moment. Like she's trying to figure out the right thing to say, which makes two of us. The text I sent her from the hospital this morning wasn't heavy on specifics. She might be wondering why I didn't answer my phone or respond to any of her messages. Not to mention, if she called the hospital for more information and heard about my overnight stay, my story starts to get a bit tricky. And if it goes anywhere near a barfight at Lucky's, I'll wish I never got up from that pavement.

"I tried to call," I say, lamely.

She sits down on the bed and inspects my injuries more closely. If she feels sympathetic or concerned or something else right now, it's very hard for me to tell.

"What happened?" she asks.

"The board hit me in the face."

"Jesus."

"I don't know how I did it. I feel pretty stupid."

"What about your ear?"

"The fin. I got finned."

She winces at this. Whether it's in response to the injury or my explanation, I don't know.

"It looks worse than it is," I tell her.

This earns me a pretty deep sigh but doesn't seem to warrant any other response. Then she comes and lies down next to me. She rests her head against my chest and soon I can hear her crying a little bit. All I can do is hold her, trying to think of something better to say, but nothing jumps out at me. I feel terrible. When she stops crying, we lie here together, listening to the sound of her breathing. My heart is pounding—I have to wonder if she can hear it, and if she can, that probably doesn't help.

"I'm worried," she says. "I'm really worried about you."

Her voice does not sound angry. She sounds sad, maybe even a little scared.

"I'm sorry. I'm sorry for everything. I'm sorry about all this."

She turns her head and looks up at me. Her eyes seem pensive at first, but they soften, and when she hugs me closer, I hug her back, and we hold each other for a while. I didn't expect it to go this way. I'm sort of stumped. So, we just lie there together for some time, staring at the wallpaper.

And then something funny happens. She starts to rub my stomach, her nails tracing circles around my belly, but then they stop and change direction, and then she gets a little more creative, her fingers start asking some questions. I didn't see this coming. And I don't think it will work, so I try to sit up, but she sort of, gently, pushes my chest back down, laying my head against the pillow.

"It's okay," she says.

I'm a little nervous. All right, I'll admit it, I'm scared shitless.

"It's okay—come here," she says, fumbling around, getting rid of some unnecessary items. "Look at you," she adds. "There he is."

And much to my surprise, she's right. Because we haven't done this in a long time, and she really hasn't done *that* for a while. This whole thing is really going a lot better than I expected, and with some good timing, she sits up on me and says *come here*. She kisses me and I understand what she's saying—in fact, I'm really with the whole program now, very into it, I'm fine with everything, I'm very okay, it's a terrific idea, my wife is a brilliant, sophisticated woman, very wise and it really is okay, lovely even. And it's all over pretty quick.

"I'm sorry," I tell her again, and she kisses me.

"It's okay," she says, laughing. "I've *missed* you," she whispers to me, giggling. "It's really nice to have you back."

Lauren snores beside me, but I can't sleep with so much on my mind. At some point, I creep into the bathroom in the dark where, like a considerate husband, I close the door behind me softly, and only then do I turn on the dimmed lights. Just so I can stand there in my boxers, staring at the grotesque in the mirror, and try to work some of this stuff out. I got my ass kicked. It happens. Okay. So what? I'm still here. Still standing, right? So, yeah, it sucks. Am I standing here or not?

The bandage on my ear looks rusted. Little drops of blood have dripped through the soaked gauze and dried in a scarlet trickle down my neck. It takes me a moment, as always, but I get there in the end. Christ. In all the excitement, I must have popped some stiches. That happens, too, I guess.

One more thing to think about.

40

INSTEAD OF BREAKFAST at home this morning, I bring Luke to the diner and treat him to a plate of Russ's famous pancakes. There's a lot of stuff I need to process after the last few days, and this booth seems like a decent place to get a grip on things while tucking into some sausage and home fries. I just need to clear my head for a few hours. Except that the guy who walks through the front door and heads toward our table won't help any of that.

"You're in a better mood than I expected," the sheriff admits with no hint of a smile.

"I guess I'm doing all right," I say. "Can't complain." Just a little regeneration through violence, Sheriff. No matter what they tell you, don't believe them—women love the rough stuff, they dig bruises and scars—they can't help themselves, it's genetic. I don't know if I can keep getting the shit kicked out of me *every* time I want to get laid, but at this point, I'm open-minded. We'll see.

"Your face doesn't look so good," he says, stepping past Luke's high chair to sit down in our booth. The diner's pretty slow this time of year. There are plenty of open tables.

"Stuff happens," I tell the guy, who could have sat somewhere else.

"Yeah, with some people, it sure does."

"What's up?"

"You want to tell me about it?"

He does look concerned.

"I fell down some stairs. Got bitten by a dog."

I smile and wink at Luke, who nods.

"Hey, Pete. If he's done with his pancakes, would you mind if just you and I talked for a minute? I'm sure Annie would love to get her hands on him."

Luke pours a cup of water on his short stack for some reason. And so, I unstrap him from his high chair and bring him over to Annie behind the cash register. The sheriff watches them play peek-a-boo together, for a moment. But when he turns back to me, his smile vanishes.

"Do you read a lot?" the sheriff asks.

"I guess so," I say shrugging.

"I'm a big reader myself."

"Good way to pass the time."

"I like a lot of World War Two stuff." His fingers drum the table.

"Sure. Churchill's the best."

"I was just thinking about something I read once. Did you ever hear about some of those parents who lost a child during the war?"

"Maybe. I'm not sure what you mean."

Luke huddles over the counter next to Annie, armed with a new set of crayons.

"Well," says the sheriff. "There were stories of these parents in the Midwest whose sons were killed over in Europe. And some of them just couldn't deal with it—couldn't handle that kind of a loss. Some of the mothers refused to believe what had happened. You never heard about this? So, they would go on making the kid's bed every morning, do his laundry, tell neighbors how much they were looking forward to their son coming home. Some of them kept that up for years."

"No. I hadn't read that."

"Sometimes we can't face what's right in front of us if it's too painful, too hard. So we tell ourselves a story, instead. You know what I mean?"

I'm not sure how to respond to that.

"Pete, this whole thing has to stop. I've tried, I've really tried, and I think I've been a little more than fair with you. But looking at you now—I wonder if maybe I haven't done you any favors."

"I'm really not looking into anything. You've got nothing to worry about."

The sheriff doesn't look convinced. He lets out a long sigh.

"Did I make a mistake that day on the road?" he asks.

"No. No. Listen to me. I told you that's over. I'm never going back to anything like that. Ever."

"Can you let this thing go?"

"Did you ever talk to Carson Townsend?"

He slams his fist on the table hard enough to make the silverware jump. Annie glances over at us. The sheriff looks like he's ready to kill somebody. He holds his fist clenched in the air for a second, then points his finger at me.

"That's the second time," he says pounding the table again. "Why, goddammit? *Why?*"

The whole place is watching us now.

"Wait a minute," he says, his face contorting terribly. "You did. You did, didn't you?"

His mouth hangs open, and he scans around the diner for a moment before glaring back at me, wild-eyed. He looks *horrified*.

"That's it, isn't it?" he says. "Jesus Christ. You don't know, do you? You don't know anything because you're not from around here. That's why. You didn't understand when I warned you before—because you're just some idiot. Jesus! That's what this whole thing is about. Oh, Christ Pete, what have you done?" The question catches in his throat.

"What are you talking about?"

"What is *wrong* with you?" he asks, now standing up from his seat to leave.

"Wait. What is this?"

"Look at me," he barks down at me. "Look at me right now. You never speak to that man. You never mention that family name again. Ever. If I hear you poke around this thing ever again, so help me God, Pete, don't test me on that, damn you. You stay away from that man."

"I don't understand. What's this about?"

But the good sheriff is in no mood. He lumbers out of the diner without saying goodbye to anyone, not even Luke or Annie. At the doorway he turns back one last time to look at me.

He doesn't like what he sees.

Outside in the parking lot I have Luke buckled into his car seat. But I sit behind the wheel with the engine off. I'm a little rattled and I need to settle down before I do any driving.

But I'm sinking now, so I need some information here, quick. The last time we spoke wasn't the most pleasant, but at a time like this, I don't have a deep bullpen of people who can help me out. After our last pissing contest, I pray Drew's old armadillo skin hasn't weathered and that he'll still take my call, because I bet he's done some digging on something—he can't help himself, he can never resist. He told me as much. *I'll ask around*, he said. Right now, I'm hoping he did.

El Jeffe, I text Drew.

He comes back to me about ten minutes later and I let out a sigh of relief that he hasn't boxed me for my petulance last week.

Sweatpea! he says. Nothing sticks to this man. He can summon a short memory as he wishes, like flushing a toilet or flicking a switch. I envy him this, as my brain, of course, has grown constipated, bloated by minor slights and petty grudges.

Do you have a second? I ask.

Not now bud, I'm at Lindsay's tennis game not supposed to be texting even, he says.

Call you after, we'll kiss and make up, he says.

Look forward to getting my filthy little hands on you, he adds for good measure.

I had question for you, I text him.

Shocker

Did you ever hear anything about Carson Townsend?

Whatever rally he's watching feels like a long one—ad out or a tie break, perhaps. That or his super computer's still churning. But he's typing back to me now.

Give me 10 minutes?

Sounds like he heard something. I picture Drew extricating himself from his seat at the country club after the end of a set, apologizing all over the place to his wife, who shakes her head in silent fury as he ducks out for one more fire drill. This must be pretty bad if he's willing to risk that kind of reaction.

Are you someplace you can talk? he asks.

This really doesn't sound good.

"How you doing, buddy boy?" Drew asks without malice. The man really does have chain mail armor for skin—he could care less about our last dustup.

"What do you know about Carson Townsend?" I ask.

"I heard some stuff. It's not pretty."

"And?"

I wish he could get to the point. It isn't like him to tiptoe around.

"Well, it's a strange one."

I'll need him to be a little more specific.

"What have you heard?"

"He had some sort of breakdown," he says. "A mental problem of some kind. Had to leave his firm, had to leave the business."

He had to leave the business. He said he ran a family office! Was that all just *nonsense*? I grab my face in my hand, rubbing my forehead, and I feel like my lungs don't work. A breakdown!

"I don't know the exact *diagnosis*," says Drew, seeming to linger over that last word. "But people think it's some sort of paranoia, a form of schizo-phrenia, maybe." I thought he was just some eccentric billionaire, some inbred WASP. "But anyway, he deteriorated and became difficult to deal with. Obsessive. Manic. Full of conspiracy theories. It's pretty fucked-up," he adds finally.

Thinking back to that day he lit into me, the panic in his voice—this is worse than anything I could have imagined.

"What sort of conspiracy theories?" I ask, feeling sick. Remembering that conversation I had with Drew, when he asked me again if I'd gone to see Townsend. And I lied to him. The sort of fib Drew probably sniffed out before it left my mouth.

"Do you want to get into all this?" he asks gently. He's stepping on egg-shells with me all of a sudden, and I'm not sure why.

"What sort of conspiracy theories?" My voice is a little too loud. I'm picturing the look in Townsend's eyes as he sat there staring at me, that miserable day. Would I have ever really looked into GDR if not for that moment? I feel dizzy. What a disaster.

"He thought everyone was out to get him. That people were trying to kill him. The firm. Clients. Competitors. He said they were watching him."

Sounds familiar. Carson's speech that day—*What if they find you first?* Good Christ.

"What else?" I ask him. I can't help but wonder if Drew, who never believed the GDR angle, might have figured out my secret source, the one who put me on their trail. And if he didn't, then the way I'm talking right now will lead him down that path in a minute. I'd like to avoid any sunlight on that humiliating angle if I can. But I need to hear this.

"He couldn't really function," Drew says. "People tried to help him. But nothing worked. He and his family agreed he should move out to their place in the country, out by you guys, where I guess he has some care."

Some care. Oh, please no. Please tell me I'm wrong. I feel sick to my stomach, knowing the answer before the rotten words even cough out of my mouth.

"Is he—" I ask Drew. "Is he married? Did he ever get married?"

"Carson? No. Not that I heard of."

Oh, no. Kathy. The way she stood there, with her hand on his back. Oh God, I feel sick. She's his nurse, not his wife.

"I heard he can barely leave the house," says Drew. "It's scary stuff."

Well, that's one version of a family office. Maybe they let him manage the remote or the thermostat. He's probably up there right now, playing with a fucking train set! *Think of the poor bastard trapped in that pretty asylum, sitting there in his study all by his lonesome and probably squirming in terror at every little sound in the house.*

Go easy on the guy, buddy. There's no need to pick on the dude, getting all sanctimonious and smug. Don't you see that's the direction you're headed? Haven't you noticed how you sometimes talk to yourself? Sure, you'll probably wind up in a much smaller place and you won't have as much help, but don't sweat the small stuff, Pete, you're pretty much on the same track.

Don't you remember those times back in the city? When you didn't have a job, and you wouldn't leave the apartment for days, and sometimes you could barely get out of bed? I know you try not to think about it too much. But how long did that last, bud? It must have started before Luke was born, before you could help out, because that gave you a little purpose, pulled you out of the worst of it, right? Could it have been before Lauren got pregnant, even? Don't you remember how she'd come home from the office, and you'd still be right there, in the same spot? The years are starting to add up here, buddy. Jesus, how long were you sitting on that couch?

Why don't you ever talk about any of this, huh? You never shut up about everything else. There's no reason to feel embarrassed, right? Isn't that what Lauren always says? People always use that line, don't they? But whenever they tell you how no one should be ashamed of this sort of thing, haven't you always wanted to scream *Well maybe this is exactly the kind of thing I should be ashamed of? Why shouldn't I? I mean, why the hell not?*

What's got you so spooked, sweat pea? Did you think all that stuff was behind you? And that if you go back there, you'll go back to the way you used to feel? It's bad enough already that pretty soon at school, they'll start going around, asking all the little kiddies what daddy does for a living, and when they get to Luke—what's he going to say? How's he going to feel? You've thought about that, right? Do you worry that someday, years from now, he'll have to tell a professional type about coming home to see his father, sitting there hiding his watery eyes, some useless candy-ass who'd been there all day because he didn't even have the strength to get up off the couch? Do you worry you'll *infect* him, Pete? Did you poison your savior? This sort of thing's in the blood—isn't that right?

I forget that it's my turn to say something.

"Anyway," says Drew winding up, breaking the silence. "I figured—a guy like that? He could be hard to get ahold of."

"Yeah," I mutter. "That makes sense."

"I'm sorry."

Drew's sorry. That's not good. Because if he's sorry, then he might know what I've done, that I've based this whole thing on the sad delusions of some lunatic. Maybe he's connected the dots.

Why so sorry, boss? Because a guy like Carson might not take his brother's death very well? Or that I'm so lost and desperate I couldn't tell there was something wrong with the guy? You bummed that you wondered about this but didn't tell me and now you've figured it out? It's never easy on the oracle, seeing the inevitable. If it makes you feel any better, my man, I really don't think you should blame yourself.

What a waste. How pathetic. What a joke. Now what? Just don't break down and lose it in front of your old boss. Jesus. Take a deep breath.

"Pete?" Drew says to me.

Well, we can close the book on this—no need to wonder anymore if he's figured it out. I should've known. All this time. So many years of *sweat pea, bud, buddy boy, tough guy, dumbass, dipshit, my man, my bright young man*—a hundred nicknames. But he's never called me Pete, until now.

"What's up?" I ask. Thinking, boy I must really have him worried. Thinking, *Jesus, what a fucking mess.*

"Why don't you come up here one of these days?" he asks. "You and the little guy drive up, we'll get some food, a few drinks, a cigar. What the hell? Sally would love to see you. Okay, shit, *I'd* love to see you—it's been a while. No tasty waves up here, but we'll play some golf or whatever you want. Or you could leave Luke with Lauren, and you drive up here, whatever. But we'll catch up, we'll talk. How's that sound?"

"I'll have to check my calendar. But one of these days, sure."

I'm breathing pretty heavily and I don't know if he can hear me. Rough country here.

"That's right, bud," he says. "Sure. Good. You do that. And, Pete? You call me anytime. Whenever. You call me anytime you need me. You got that, bud?"

"Sounds good. No sweat."

"Sure. Of course. You get back to me. And, Pete, listen to me now—you hang in there. Hang in there, all right, buddy?"

"Will do. Thanks, man, talk to you later," I say, hanging up.

It's a long time and a tough one, sitting here, collecting myself until I feel together enough to drive. I don't pound the dashboard or sob or throw my head back and scream in anguish. I'm a husband and a father now, I suffer quietly *like a grown-ass man*. I will keep this misery to myself and work it out. Finally, my son, still strapped in his car seat, breaks the silence. He's furious with our lack of progress—no one wants to feel stuck—but like all of us, he wears himself ragged, wailing but hearing no response, and so after a while, he passes out.

I listen to him snoring back there. Thinking about some of the arguments we'll have in the years ahead. That check's in the mail, without a doubt. Those times when kids won't listen and refuse to understand as they march, confident and stubborn, racing onward toward the glory of their noble deaths. When they invest their entire identity and ego so deep in a cause until there's no way out. I've seen this sort of thing before. Quite closely, in fact. But what can you do? What can anyone *do*? You beg, plead, get tired, try different tactics, you get frustrated, maybe you're even disappointed sometimes. And it's rough.

But you always have their back.

Some point later, this merciless day ends. I'm lying in bed tonight when my wife crawls in beside me, mischief on her mind. She's playful, maybe trying to get us into a healthy rhythm again, like the good old days. But she's picked a tough night.

"I think I hear him," I tell her, sitting up.

"Are you sure?" she says. "Just give it a minute. Come here. He'll cry it out."

But I stumble out of bed toward my son's room with no response, no explanation, nothing—I'm pretty much tapped out. It's too bad, we almost had a good thing going there for a little while. But not tonight, hon. I'm sorry. Very sorry. Tonight, I'm headed for that couch.

41

"WHAT'D YOU SAY to the guy?" Frank asks. We're eating at the Bull tonight with Luke perched alongside us at the bar.

I wave the question away, pointing toward my son. There are things I'd rather not discuss in front of him, and it pisses me off that I have to explain stuff like this to Frank sometimes, but at least he nods his head, understanding. I already gave him the play-by-play of the fateful evening, and I don't need to relive it again.

"The Jets covered the spread," says Frank unhelpfully, ordering another round.

"We missed a good one today," I grumble, trying to change the subject. "We drove down to check it out. But I can't with the ear."

Luke nods in agreement. He points at my head, adding, *"With the ear!"* for good measure.

"We got on it this morning," Frank says. What the hell does *we* mean?

"Who was out there?"

"Just me and Kevin."

"Do I know Kevin?" I ask as calmly as I can manage.

"I'm not sure. Drives a Tundra. Curly hair? He's from around here."

"Is he any good?"

"Yeah, not bad." Which means the guy's a professional.

Thanks, man. Thanks for the look this morning. Thanks for everything.

"Could you watch Luke?" I ask him. "I'm going for a leak."

I can hardly piss straight I'm so preoccupied. Since when does Kevin get invited? Why do the Kevins of life always seem to show up during weeks like this one? What the hell is that all about? Sometimes, in certain bathrooms, it just seems like things keep getting worse.

But I make my way back to the bar, sit down next to Luke, and sneak in for a quick snuggle.

"Is this boys' night out?" a voice asks. "This looks like trouble right here."

The three of us look over our shoulders to see Brooke's friend Nia standing behind us, clearly amused by the scene. We swivel around in our stools to greet her—we can talk to Noel whenever we like, but women like Nia don't grow on trees, and they don't tend to darken the door of this place, not in the off-season, and even if creatures like this were roaming these lands, they wouldn't walk over to our motley crew, say hello, and seem happy to see us.

"Hey! What's up?" I ask as she comes in for a hug, and oh I needed this, I've had a rough fucking week—but why's she pulling back in terror? Don't be ashamed, Nia, we haven't done anything wrong.

"Jesus," she says. "Are you all right?" She means my face. And my ear. Noel nods grimly, acknowledging, and Frank looks tickled by this.

"Oh, it's nothing. That's nothing. I'm fine. So, what are you up to?"

"I needed to get out of the house," she says, collecting herself, trying not to stare at my damage. "And I heard the food's decent here."

"How's Brooke doing?" I ask.

"I think she's finally getting some sleep. Which is good. She's starting to get out more, too. Who's this little guy?" Yes, yes, look at *him*. I'm not something you'd need to see, right at the moment.

"This is Luke. Say hello. Can you say hello, buddy? It's all right. He's playing shy. And this—" I begin, but the Judas, the ungrateful shit bastard, has turned back to the bar. "This is Frank."

"Nia," she says as he reaches back to shake her hand.

She puts in a to-go order and stays with us for a drink. I try asking about her work and how she wound up with such a cool job—did she start out in TV? But she seems more interested in talking to Frank, who, maybe just to annoy me or show off, now comes across as aloof and unimpressed. I can't tell if this approach intrigues her. But he calls it a night early. And so, when her food's finally ready, Nia starts to pack up and say goodbye for the evening.

"Hope you feel better," she says.

"I'm fine. It looks worse than it is."

When she walks out, Luke and I watch her go, and I get this feeling that I have a great kid, but I'm not very interesting and even a little hard to look at, right now. Tonight, even Noel seems busy with customers, although the place isn't that packed, and why not, why shouldn't he be? I don't even drink anymore. I look at my watch and wonder why I'm still here at a bar with my son. Isn't it getting very late, and shouldn't I get him home to bed? Maybe Frank's getting on the water early with his new buddy tomorrow. Either way, I'm not needed here.

I'm not needed anywhere, really.

42

I HATE THIS playground. I usually go to the one behind the high school, but the evil bastard ruined that place for me. So, we've come here to the big leagues, instead. On a Saturday like this it bursts with explosive little children of all ages, and each seems more caffeinated then the next. Sure, it's the "nicest" playground, but that means on any given weekend with decent weather, every parent within a ten-minute drive funnels their kiddies to the same spot. This time of year, you get fewer takers for the beach. So, we wind up with a few dozen toddlers, their minders, three jungle gyms, a swing set, and a sand pit to manage. Luke loves rolling in this artificial beach, showering himself with germs.

I'd like to take him home, but he's having a moment. "Five minutes," he cries. I'm such a pushover. I coddle him too much, and he manipulates me well for a small child. He only has to shoot me his impish grin and I'm lost. I know that at some point in the future, indulging him like this will cost me dearly somehow.

He finally relents and walks over, demanding *Carry me! Carry me!* No stroller for His Highness. I snatch him up, sitting him on one arm, and pushing his empty stroller with my other hand.

"Don't suck your thumb," I tell him. "Please, buddy? It's all sandy, I don't want that in your mouth. It's dirty. Please, buddy? All dirty."

"All dirty," he agrees.

"No, not your other thumb. Please, buddy. You could get sick. We need to wash your hands."

I have ulterior motives, of course. While Luke was rolling around in the petri dish over there, Daddy has been holding in a titanic pee-pee. So, we walk over to the public restroom about fifty yards away. Inside, the men's room smells of chemicals and urine, but it looks reasonably clean. For a public park, at least.

"You first," I say, grabbing his hips and hoisting him up to the sink. "Come here. Put your hands under the tap. Nice and clean. Clean, clean, clean."

"Clean, Clean, Clean," he agrees, before demanding to work the controls. "I want to! Soap. Soap. Clean." He pounds the soap dispenser, then tests the limits of the water pressure.

"That's enough," I say and let him down from the sink. "Stand here, don't touch anything. Don't touch anything. Daddy's going pee-pee. See? Pee-pee."

I know this part fascinates him as he stands next to me, expecting something incredible, and as always, I hope this won't cause permanent damage. Once finished with my business, I try to lead by example.

"Okay. Stay there. Daddy washes his hands, too. Soap. Clean. Clean. There. Now, let's go. Don't go anywhere, okay?"

I dry my hands and fetch the stroller from the corner. No more carrying today, Daddy's back hurts, time to strap him in now, no more games.

Of course, she's texting me. Why wouldn't she? What are the chances it's something really important?

Where r u? she starts.

R u still at the playground?

What time will you be home?

Has he eaten lunch yet?

If he does eat lunch make sure to wash his hands because the play-ground is full of germs and he'll get sick.

My phone is dying.

If you call and I don't pick up.

Got it, I text her, which I hope covers everything.

My little partner has scampered off. The seasoned inmate always knows when the warden gets distracted. Grabbing the stroller I head outside after the escapee, but I can't see him.

"Hey, buddy!" I call out.

He loves this game. I try the right side of the building, creeping along the wall like a melodramatic burglar and turn the corner to jump at him suddenly, but he's not there. Very sneaky. So, I walk to the other corner of the building, past the women's room, and poke my head around the side. He's not back there, either.

"Where did Luke go? Where could he be?" I sing out as I have a hundred times before. This little dance is almost our family sport, although we proba-bly shouldn't play it in public. And it seems like I'm losing this latest contest.

It's actually not my favorite pastime. These brief moments of pivoting around a room, head on a swivel, hoping for that shock of recognition, there are things I'd rather be doing. I should really get an eye on him.

He's not in the open field behind the toilets. Looking back now toward the playground, of course, there are a thousand little tykes running, spin-ning, screaming, chasing each other, but Luke's not among them. He's here somewhere, obviously.

"Hey, Luke!" I give a good shout, not angry, but with a little bass in my voice.

Sometimes he likes playing with the stroller, but where is the damn thing? About five yards behind me, right where I left it, but with no stow-away on board. A less reasonable guy could start getting a little concerned.

This kind of aggravation is what I'm talking about. She sends me these fucking pointless texts all day every day and I have to respond to this crap and it's just annoying. What a waste of my time. These goddamn texts! If she were here now, she'd be freaking out. Driving me nuts.

Sometimes he likes to watch the pickup basketball. It's usually easy to spot him on the sidelines—he's a good deal shorter than many of the players, and they don't suck their thumbs. The court's jumping today with the regulars, five on five, shirts and skins. But he's not over there, either.

This isn't good. He could be anywhere. What if he's scared out of his wits?

He must have run back to the playground. So, I sprint over now, screw the stroller. But it's just a sea of children and nannies. I check the slides, he could be hanging on inside the plastic swirly one, but he's not there or on the swings, either. Seven girls in the sand pit. *He's here somewhere, no need to panic, don't panic, you'll see him any second.* This isn't funny. This isn't good.

I need one of the moms. One of the moms could help me out. Those women solve everything, I'll just go to confessional, beg forgiveness. They'll know what to do. A dozen or so women stand huddled around a group of parked strollers, but I don't know any of them.

"Have you seen a little, um, a little boy with brown hair?" I ask.

"*Qué?*" a woman says, looking confused.

"Dónde…" I begin, but my language fizzles out. I don't know what the hell to do, sorry, I don't know what the hell to say, this is bad, really bad. I need to get my shit together.

The guys playing hoops. They would have seen something. I'm sprinting now. How can I be so stupid? I have one job, one *fucking* job! Just him and that's it. How could this happen? *How could you let this happen?*

"Hey! Hey!" I'm yelling at the guy bringing the ball up the court. He walks slowly, eyes up, confident, dribbling like a casual expert. His defender crouches, backpedaling in front of him.

"Hey, buddy!" I shout to the point guard. "Hey, fellas! Hold up a sec."

"What up, man?" the ball handler says, slowing his steps but not stopping. His teammates jostling under the basket stop shoving each other and throw angry looks in my direction.

"Have you seen a little kid?" I ask them.

The guard picks up his dribble, holding the ball to his hip. What's his problem?

"A little white kid?" I ask.

The ten guys on the court stand still, looking at me with confused faces. One dude under the rim shrugs his high shoulders. Why are they staring at me like this? Do they just see some crazy old fuck—

I feel sick, sick to my stomach. It's not possible. But an image is scarred in my mind now, so I can only stammer the question.

"Have you seen a big guy my age around here? A big white guy? With a little kid?"

Some sick fuck!

"A guy with a little kid!" I scream. "Have you seen anyone?"

But the defender shakes his head at me. Then he turns his eyes back to the point guard.

"All right, hey, ball in. Check. Let's go," he says to his opponent and now they start playing again.

No one's by the toilets. The field's empty. Every grown man, they're on the court, every other adult—they're just nannies. Wouldn't I have seen him?

I'm sorry, buddy. Please, if you just, if you turn up, I'm sorry. It's my fault. I'm sorry.

Directionless now, I'm stumbling, spinning, more and more frantic. What was he wearing? Where the hell could he be?

"Are you okay?" a woman's voice asks.

No, I'm not okay. Some bastard took my kid and I'm not okay.

"I can't find a little boy," I tell the woman. Is she a nanny or mother? I've got no clue.

"What does he look like?" she asks. "It's all right. We'll find him."

"It's not all right. He was just here. He's got brown hair. He's barely three. He had a blue shirt on. A blue sweatshirt. He could be anywhere."

"Where did you last see him?"

"We were in the men's room. Right over there, but then he just wasn't there. He's not at the playground. I don't know what to do. He never does this. It's never happened before."

"Could he have made it to the parking lot?" she asks.

The guy's car. Or a van.

"Have you seen a big guy with a little kid?" I ask her.

She shakes her head, bewildered.

"Let's check the bathroom again," she says.

We scurry toward the red brick of the restroom. She's looking back over her shoulder, checking for her own child every few paces. But I'm running ahead now. Into the men's room, he's not here, no feet in the stalls. I told her that! I told this stupid fucking woman.

"Hey! Sir!" she yells.

I scramble outside toward the sound of her voice.

"Sir!" she yells again. The shouting is coming from behind the building. Please, buddy, I'm sorry.

Well, he looks happy. He stands there, smiling at me, sucking his thumb, quite pleased. I snatch him up. He's laughing now, and I turn to the woman.

"Thank you! I don't know what to say. Thank you. I can't even begin to thank you."

"De nada," she says. Walking away now, she waves at us, smiling as she heads back to the playground, her face saying *happens to the best of us, we've all been there, I understand.*

He's still giggling. But nothing's funny. So I plop his little ass down and I have him by both shoulders now. You don't shake him, you never shake a kid, but I'm right up on him now. I squat down and I get in his face, and

I get in his face like I never have because he needs to hear this, no fucking around, and I have to hold him. He wants to be somewhere else but he's not going anywhere and maybe I'm louder than I'd like, but he needs to hear this.

"NEVER. YOU NEVER EVER DO THAT! YOU HEAR ME? DO YOU HEAR ME? NOT FUNNY. IT'S NOT FUNNY. YOU NEVER DO THAT. WE DON'T PLAY HIDE-AND-SEEK HERE. YOU DON'T SCARE DADDY. YOU COULD GET HURT. DADDY COULDN'T FIND YOU. WHAT IF DADDY COULDN'T FIND YOU? WHAT WOULD YOU DO? YOU'D BE SCARED! YOU'D BE SCARED. YOU COULD GET HURT! DO YOU UNDERSTAND? LOOK AT ME. LOOK AT ME. YOU NEVER DO THAT AGAIN. TELL ME YOU HEAR ME. SAY IT. YOU HEAR ME?"

"Yeah."

He's not laughing anymore. My face can't help anything.

"I'm sorry, Daddy," he moans between wails.

But that's it. Because if I was bad the other day, panting like a wuss, forget it, I'm gasping now and I might break down and sob. I hug him and hold him close and he's *really* not laughing anymore, so I whisper, "I'm sorry, buddy. I love you. You scared me. I don't like to do that. I don't like to yell at you. I want to keep you safe. You can't do that. I'm sorry. You just scared me. I love you."

I sit there holding him and look back to the playground. It's still chaos. The world doesn't wait on us. This is my fault, I caused all of it. I'm responsible for everything.

"I'm sorry, buddy," I tell him. "Let's go home. Daddy's sorry for everything."

No more of this. That's enough. This has to stop.

43

I CALLED DREW last week and asked if he somehow could reach out to GDR and tell them that I was very sorry to piss them off and more importantly that they would never, ever hear from me again. He told me this wasn't necessary. That no one was trying to hurt my kid. But when I told him that I didn't know what else to do that might make me feel better, he said that he'd take care of it. Then he told me not to worry about any of this stuff and that I should take it easy for a little while. And that I should trust him. I tried to thank him, and he said to hang in there and get some sleep. So that's what I've been doing.

This has been a rough stretch. I thought I had seen the darkest depths over these past couple years, but the last few days make my previous dives seem like dips in the shallow end. I'm pretty down.

I don't feel interested or good about anything. Most topics seem useless and unworthy of further discussion. The future appears pointless and bleak. I know how they say you can somehow train yourself to get in a more positive mind-set, but right now I just can't think of anything to look forward to, at all. This will probably get a lot worse.

I went to the gym yesterday but didn't finish the workout. At the end of the class, I was barely breathing hard I'd dogged it so bad. Halfway through the session I began to wonder, What was the point of all this huffing and puffing and agony? I'm surprised the question hadn't occurred to me sooner, and this morning didn't bring me any closer to the answer. I left the box carrying Luke without speaking to Gandle, who didn't say anything to me, either, and I don't blame her. Nobody asked what happened to my face. Why would they give a shit?

There are no waves of any kind. I checked the websites but decided against driving down to the beach and looking at the ocean, hoping for inspiration or chatting with strangers doing the same thing. I've learned that's not a good use of time.

In other news, for inexplicable reasons, my wife seems to be around the house a decent amount recently. She's been watching the little guy. Which means I have absolutely nothing to do. I am completely alone. Lauren claims that she's worried about me, that I seem bummed out about something, that I *don't seem like myself lately*, which I find pretty funny, and that I should *really think about talking to someone*, which I don't find funny at all and won't do. When she asks me that kind of thing, sometimes I wonder if she's just trying to piss me off.

But ever since I found out that stuff about Carson, really, I just feel ashamed and afraid, more than anything else. I'm hearing voices in my head, and they don't sound good. They keep telling me how I've wasted my life, to take one example, just as a for instance. They're saying that I had plenty of chances, more than most people get, but I pissed them away and those doors will never open again. And if given my druthers about the whole thing, I'd prefer it if no one else notices—I'd rather nobody see me in this kind of state. I don't want to talk to anybody, either—I got a good taste of that catching up with Drew the other day. No. Let's keep this between us girls, if we can.

I can't really remember a time when I felt this bad. I was cross-eyed for most of the dark ages, but it's not the same thing. Sometimes, when we still lived in the city, I would get pretty low.

Like that day I came home and found a man in my apartment. That wasn't great. Luke and I had been out for a walk in the neighborhood one afternoon. I used to plop the little guy in a BabyBjörn, slip the straps around my shoulders, and the two of us would hit the streets.

I don't tend to draw much attention and wasn't used to this. But with my son strapped to my chest, all kinds of people, beautiful women in a hurry, angry drunks, old ladies, guys working construction, they would often stop midsentence, crane their necks for a better look at this magical creature, and smile at me. I guess it was like being a celebrity or a woman with an incredible chest. And sometimes on our trips, when Luke would pass out, his head drooping and bobbing, people passing by seemed so happy that I had to stop and look at our reflection in a store window. I'd watch him hanging out there, sound asleep.

But that day I came back to the apartment and walked into Luke's room so I could unpack him on his changing table. And there was a guy in there, on the floor on his hands and knees. He wore jeans with work boots and a tool belt. A tall cardboard box leaned against the far wall and he had all the parts from inside laid out on the carpet around him.

"Señor," he said happily to me and Luke. "Hola. Hola."

I nodded back at him, tried forcing a smile, and then I walked out of the room. I needed to get the hell out of there. There weren't many places to go, though, the apartment wasn't huge, and Luke needed to sleep. So I went back into the other bedroom and sat down on my bed, thinking it over. After a while, I unbuckled Luke and laid him out on the bedspread, checked his diaper, then rolled him onto a pad, and I took out the spare diaper and road wipes and a tiny tube of A&D from the carrier pocket so that I wouldn't have to go back to the other room. After I changed him, I put the stuff you don't keep in a doggie bag, tied it off, picked him up, and walked over to drop the bag in the basket in our bathroom. I went and sat in the chair in the corner and held Luke, still thinking it through.

I had been out of work for a while, almost two years by then, and it was hard to believe. But I didn't have a job, and my wife was paying another guy to build my son's new crib.

I was still sitting there in the bedroom a few hours later when I heard Lauren turn the front doorknob. She was back at work then, done with maternity leave. She was talking on her cell phone when she walked in.

"No," she was saying to someone. "No. That doesn't make sense. So we're gonna need a better answer on that."

Her shoes were very loud as she walked inside the apartment, and she didn't stop pacing around the room.

"Did he sleep?" she asked me, looking in the mirror.

"Yeah," I told her.

The phone was still in her ear and she kept checking herself out.

"Hey, Lauren."

I'm not sure if she heard me.

"Could I talk to you about something?" I asked.

"Did you see my text?"

She leaned over to take off her shoes and started rubbing her foot.

"Can I talk to you?" I asked her again.

"Well, he owes me a phone call. I'll take care of it," she told someone, but I think she was talking to me when she said "Did you see my text?"

She's a multitasker.

"Can you put the phone down for a second?"

She glanced at me, closed her eyes, and turned away again, shaking her head.

"I'm sorry," she said, and she wasn't talking to me. "I'm sorry. Could I get you to hold for one sec? Just give me one minute."

She pressed the phone to her shoulder and sighed.

"Yeah?" she asked me.

"Did you hire a guy to put together the crib?"

"Yeah," she said again.

"I'm not trying to be a jerk. I'm just saying this kind of stuff, it's important, okay? It's important to me."

I thought we had talked about this.

"Pete. I just can't. I have too much to do. I just can't deal with this."

I didn't say anything, but the look on my face probably did. She rolled her eyes and she sighed.

"I'm sorry," she told someone on the phone. "No, no. It's nothing. I'm sorry about that. No. No problem. I'll take care of it."

I don't miss that apartment. I don't miss the city. I was glad when we left.

But I can't stay in the house all the time like my old friend Carson. There is only one place on Earth left for someone like me and—good news!—the library's open. Although today it doesn't take too much time among the stacks to make an unfortunate discovery. Reading is hard. It takes so much effort and concentration! Reading is a huge pain in the ass. What a headache. I'm not sure why I ever logged so many hours here with papers and books, it's stupid. It's fucking primitive. I really hoped it would never come to this, but I'm out of alternatives. I've never wanted my wife to come home in the middle of a weekday and find me lying on the couch binge-watching some series. It's not even raining today. But I've come to the end of something. I need to go somewhere dark and just sit, breathe, and stare at a television for a while with my hand down my pants.

Just one decadent day. No more self-improvement shit. I might even buy some ice cream and fried chicken to give myself twenty-four hours of the most degrading kind of sloth, really embrace my own depravity. Except my fucking wife is around. Think of all that judgment. The image of me reclining with a drumstick and Häagen-Dazs, watching my third episode of a British TV show could very well end any passion in my marriage. But I need a day to regroup.

I can't figure out why more people don't get the joke. There's nothing to watch on all these streaming services—I don't understand all the fuss. After you've seen two or three top picks, what do you have left? These stand-up shows don't seem too special to me anymore. Most of the new series are dog shit. It's almost as if they're pumping them out as fast as they can with no thought to the quality, like it's some sort of arms race. No. The best menu of movies and TV on planet Earth resides in the DVD section of the library. It's glorious. They don't just have an incredible selection, it's also well organized—alphabetical. Totally ingenious. No more scrolling through a website, breathing out of my mouth. Or idiot suggestions based on my viewing history. I haven't felt this good all day. They should burn every book in this place. Standing here I cannot understand why I torture myself, decoding all those stupid goddamn paragraphs! All those pointless sentences of various lengths and the different words they use, amounting to what? Yippee. Yahoo. And if the foreign language stuff wasn't so good, I'd say chuck all the international films with subtitles—dub them into extinction. Reading has no place on days like today.

"Do you have any good picks?" a woman behind me asks. "I need some recommendations."

That voice sounds familiar.

"Oh hey, nice to see you."

"Hi, Pete," says Brooke Townsend. "How have you been?"

Women who look like this do not come to public libraries very often. They sit on their boards as charitable acts. They don't *use* them, not on weekdays, anyway.

"I'm great, thanks," I tell her. My stitches will come out soon.

"I hate to ask," she says. "Are you all right?" Jesus, was I hyperventilating in the fiction section? What kind of guy makes a grieving widow concerned about him and his mental state? But she means my face.

"Oh yeah. I had a brutal wipeout surfing. Pretty big day out there. But I went anyway."

She doesn't look impressed with my tales of daring, and I realize this was the wrong story to tell a woman whose husband drowned surfing. But she wasn't supposed to be in this place of quiet, that's why I came here. I shouldn't speak to other people in this sort of mood.

"Oh, by the way," she says, changing the subject. "I heard you ran into Nia the other night."

"It was fun to see her." Even better if I wasn't rudderless, dysfunctional, and totally alone.

"Yeah, she said something about that." A quick smile from Brooke. "I didn't realize you were friends with Frank."

"Oh, sure," I say, smiling, proud and stupid. I'm buddies with the local legend.

"How do you know him?" Women are always interested in Frank. Go figure.

"Well, from our kids' school. And we surf together."

She nods and smiles at this and I'm not sure why.

But hang on a second! What the hell am I hearing? Why did *she* ask me that?

"Sorry, wait a minute," I tell her. "How do *you* know Frank?"

"What do you mean?" She frowns, confused.

It's a basic question, and I want an answer. That's what I mean, Brooke.

"How do you know Frank?" I ask her again. There is no trace of warmth in my voice.

And this wide-eyed woman shrugs at the obvious, the simple truth, and one that I'm the last to know about, I guess.

"Frank's our caretaker," she explains.

Frank works for the Townsends. Frank works for the Townsends but never felt the need to mention it to me. Not once, this whole time.

Brooke's looking at me again, concerned.

"Pete?"

"Yeah."

"I think I must be distracting you."

I feel like I missed something.

"No, no. Not at all. I'm sorry—I think I just tuned out what you said."

"That's all right," she says, smiling. "Do you have any DVD recommendations?"

"Yeah."

"Anything in particular?"

"I don't know. I mean, I guess it depends."

Felix, eavesdropping in the comics section, shakes his head and throws up his hands. He's a lonely and frustrated man. He's also very jealous. But right now, even he could do better than this.

Brooke laughs and tries again. "What kind of stuff have you gotten into lately?"

Frank works for the Townsends.

"Pete?" she says, snapping me out of it.

"You know something, Brooke? Lately, I'm into some pretty weird shit."

She has another good laugh at this. I manage to get my feet under me a little and we chat for a bit longer. With so many questions to ask, I have to keep my composure. Like, *How long has he been working for you?* And *How well do you know him?* That sort of thing. Turns out "a while" and "pretty well." Considering all the things that need considering, I think I stay pretty calm. And before Brooke leaves, I manage to give her an incredible DVD recommendation, something I'm better at than anyone else in the world.

But I don't ask her why Frank never mentioned any of this to his buddy. I can think of plenty of reasons why he didn't say anything about knowing Townsend ever since his body washed up on the beach, but right at the moment, only one of them makes any sense to me.

I sit and chew on this for a while. Most of the time, when I need to make a tough decision, I tend to procrastinate. But today for some reason it doesn't take me that long to come up with a solution, so when I realize what has to happen and what I need to do next, I don't drag my feet. I hop in the car and call from the road.

"Pistol Pete," says Walker when he answers.

"Hey, Grady. How are you?"

"Same shit, different day. How about you?"

"Good, thanks. Living the dream."

"Making any progress?"

"You said if I got jammed up on this thing, I could call you."

"Uh-huh. I remember."

"I hate to ask but I need a little help on something."

"Well, give me the needle," he says. "I'm listening."

"I need Anthony to look into somebody for me."

44

I DON'T TEND to lie awake in my bed and stare at the ceiling. I prefer to screw my eyes shut and gnaw at myself, grinding my teeth. Since I ran into Brooke, these past few nights, I haven't gotten much sleep. What rolls out of bed this morning is a pitiful specimen. Look at this rotten assembly of pieces, swollen eyes, tongue starting to fester, the hairline a tragedy that no one should ever see, and standing up—oh yes, just what we needed, there goes the Achilles—after all that we've been through, these crooked rat bastards turn up strung tight as a racket from the tops of my calves to the soles of my feet. But there's no time to wallow. No use thinking one more second about what that scumbag Frank's been up to—I need to stretch out some of these kinks. Luke's wailing from somewhere, and it feels like he's been screaming for a while. I shuffle into his room and pick the king up out of his crib and let him roam the castle halls. I fix him a bowl of cereal and grab a sexy cold can of Diet Coke for Daddy. Nothing else in the cupboard but quick temper or anxiety. I've run myself ragged sitting around waiting. Now I'm coiled as a rattler, mean as a co-op board, and ready to snap like a twig.

I'm clearing Luke's bowl, ready for the next evolution, all frayed nerves and twitches, when the call I've been waiting for comes through.

"Check your email," Anthony says.

"What am I looking at here?"

"Something you need to sign and scan back to me if you want to hear anything more."

"What is this?"

"A nondisclosure agreement."

"You're asking me to sign an NDA?"

"I'm not asking shit," he explains nicely. "I'm telling you. You need to sign that thing or that's the end of this conversation."

"It's about a thousand pages," I tell him.

"Take your time."

"It feels like the type of thing I should have a lawyer look at."

"Yeah, probably."

"My printer's broken."

"Go figure."

"I need to get back to you on this."

"Sure. But don't come back with the wrong answer. Without those signatures, don't even bother."

He was all right, meeting in person the first time, even if he did scan me for a wire, but at least he wanted to keep the lawyers out of it. But he's a little more salty today.

"Good talking to you," I tell him.

"That's the way it is."

He found something. That's the only thing this could mean. And whatever he found made him want to cover his ass before talking to me. Of course, that's part of the sales pitch. You have to sign something that only an idiot would agree to, which probably means I lose the right to sue them until after the world ends, but anytime for any reason if they feel the urge—Grady can still come after me. He could have just ignored me and never called back. Or made something up. But if he's spooked enough to make this kind of demand, then he's telling me he has something that I want to see.

I find Luke and round him up.

"Are we going to the beach?" he asks.

"We've got to stop at Staples first, buddy. I need to send a fax."

As soon as I scan the signature pages and push send on my email, I give Anthony a call right from the store, but it goes to voice mail. I hit him up again, standing there next to the printer, holding my breath and trying to keep Luke away from the scissors. But he doesn't pick up, so we wait. I pace the aisles, pushing Luke in his stroller, tapping my feet. And by the time he screens my third call, we need to make a trip to the store's men's room, which doesn't get a lot of use from most retail customers and is not very clean. We both have to go. But I'm so amped up I can barely manage to stand on one foot and use my sneaker to lift up the seat.

Luke still has to get to school. So I herd him into the car and drive over, pulling into the lot a few minutes early, and watch all the moms come in soon after us. When the procession starts, I walk him over to the front door. Before the steps, I lean down to Luke and give him a good squeeze. But I don't dawdle—I'm a little distracted. It's not a day to stand outside and chat. I'm walking past the line of moms holding kids by the hand when my phone buzzes.

"What's up, Anthony? Thanks for coming back to me."

"Are you somewhere you can talk?"

"One second," I tell him, glancing around. There are no moms within earshot, but I step into my car and slam the door behind me. "Go ahead."

"Sorry about all that unpleasantness earlier. Just part of the job."

"No worries. You feel better now?"

"Always better when you can talk a little more freely," he says, which is very nice to hear.

"So, what do you have for me?"

"I figure you probably guessed that we did a quick background check on you before Grady called you back. Not that we don't trust the opinions of investment bankers, but we still have to keep them honest."

"It crossed my mind," I admit.

"You were a pretty simple case. Your approach was a little weird. I didn't like it and I told Grady to ignore you—but I guess he's never been a stick-ler for rules. Sometimes, I think what he has against that firm clouds his judgment. You know what I mean? But either way, we didn't find any red flags, nothing that would present a problem. And then Grady took a shine to you."

"Glad to hear it."

"Yeah. You two got along famously. And when I met you—you seemed pretty solid."

I can't get a read on him. He played bad cop this morning but now he's got what he wanted. I figured he might start by asking about Townsend and how Frank relates to that mess, but it seems like he could care less.

"Where you going with this?" I ask.

"That brings us to your *friend*," he says slowly.

When I asked Grady for help, I gave him a name and nothing else. I never said we were buddies. Anthony wants me to know he hasn't missed anything.

"Now your friend Frank," he says again. "This guy isn't a simple case. This guy raises a ton of red flags. This guy is a problem."

"What kind of problem?"

"Desperate," he says. "The desperate kind. We've got a guy who'll prob-ably file for bankruptcy before the month is out. He's a bunch of payments late on his mortgage, and it's the second mortgage on his house. Maxed out his credit cards and everything else he can find. When he does file, that will make it the second time he goes into personal bankruptcy, and the second home he loses to foreclosure. He's had a spotty employment history, but that's just the start of it."

"Jesus," I mumble, thinking back on all those domestic scenes I witnessed at his place.

"We think he's a degenerate gambler. The wife has a steady income, but it doesn't seem to be enough. He burns through their cash, and he's had to get a little creative to stay afloat."

"What does 'creative' mean?" I knew about the bets, but this is bad and getting a lot worse.

"The guy's an endless trail of raising money for long shots and bullshit schemes. He's a defendant in several real estate and investment fraud suits. The list of plaintiffs includes former classmates, partners, and one brother-in-law. The guy was ripping off his own friends and family. Now he's got nowhere to go. No one left."

He was born in this town, but in all the time I've known the guy—how many people has he introduced me to? Manny, maybe? But the moms and Noel and so many decent human beings for some reason, they all seem to hate his guts. That's why he walks around town like a ghost, why he hides out around the lowlifes at Lucky's—and when he's not there? What does he do? He hangs out with me.

"Are you still there?" he asks.

"Yeah."

"We think he's got a problem with the sauce. He's got a DWI, a D and D—that's drunk and disorderly, destruction of property. An assault arrest in there, too."

I knew Frank liked to get after it, but I never heard about the assault charge, and now phrases like *a hangman's break* and the image of a body tumbling around in the white water run through my head.

"That doesn't sound good," I manage to admit.

"He's not someone you'd want to do business with," he says, with something in his tone I don't appreciate.

"If you're trying to say that when I approached Grady, I was somehow working with—"

"I'm not trying to say shit. I'm giving you the information you wanted. Information *you called and asked for*, by the way. Which, for reasons beyond my understanding and repeated advice, somehow my client felt he owed you. So, that's done. You got what you wanted. But there're a few other things you need to hear. You still listening?"

"Yeah."

"First off. Don't try to contact Grady Walker again. All right? Don't do it. Very simple. Understood?"

What's he telling me? I'm friends with a shady character, which means I'm guilty by association? That doesn't make sense.

"If I was trying to get cute, why would I call Grady and ask you to look into—"

"Stop," he says. "It doesn't matter. This is nothing personal, all right? I'm not enjoying this, and believe me, Grady's not happy about it, either."

"It's bullshit!" I bark at him, feeling as bitter as any other loser who learns he's been played for a sucker, again. The degenerate who screams at the dealer, curses the table, and wonders if anybody in this lousy casino can at least bring him a drink?

"Are you done?" he asks.

"Probably not," I grumble.

"Well, can you listen to one goddamn thing and remember it?" he asks.

"Sure."

"This friend of yours," he says. "This guy, Frank?"

What else don't I know about this friend of mine? The best friend I've made since I moved to this shitty town?

"Look," he says, and now his voice becomes the desperate lawyer pleading with his client before he takes the witness stand. "Be real careful with this guy. Okay?"

"Okay."

"Real fucking careful. 'Cause with a guy like this? You hearing me?"

"Yup."

"Keep him in front of you. All right?"

"I got it," I tell him.

Before he hangs up, Anthony sounds just as sincere when he says, "Good luck, man."

45

I'M BACK AT the scene of an unpleasant evening. If you ever get jumped and beaten unconscious, most people will say that afterward, you should steer clear of the place where it happened for as long as you can. But I need to break with conventional wisdom if I want to find some real answers. Which means everything tonight has to go according to plan.

The last time I walked in here asking too many questions, I wound up in the ER and lost part of my ear. Tonight, parking across the road right out front, I'm not even going inside. But still, I think to myself, looking over at the terrible place, all the belligerence happened right outside the front door of this shithole.

I'm not proud of this one, at all. Sometimes I wonder if there's a part of me that's always asking for it. Because if this goes wrong, really wrong, then I'm going to face some tough questions, and if I get roughed up again at this same damn spot, I won't have many good explanations. But I need to know. I need this, I need it so bad I can hardly think about anything else. Which is a problem. If you let yourself get desperate, you start taking dumb risks. Like I said, I'm not proud of this one.

I take the stroller out of the trunk first. I push it around to the side of the car, stopping to wave at Manny standing guard outside the front. The big guy waves back at us and scratches his head. I unstrap Luke, plop him in his stroller, and clip him in.

"Where are we going, Daddy?" he asks.

I tickle his stomach explaining, "I need to talk with an old friend."

When I told myself that if I ever did make it back here again that I would never come on my own without help, this wasn't the sort of backup I had in mind. This needs to work. No matter how sinister Manny's secrets, he couldn't do something in front of my son—he might sort me out later, and that won't be pretty, but not with Luke right here at my feet. No one would do that, right? I don't think so, I can't believe that anyone would, but pretty soon here, we'll find out. I push the stroller across the road and we walk up to the monster guarding the front door.

"How's it, bro?" asks Manny, who looks pleased to see us, anyway.

"Living the dream, Manny," I tell him, and we hug it out.

"You look better. Sorry about the other night, yeah?"

"Don't worry about it." What's a concussion between friends? We're good, bro.

"Who's this little guy?"

"This is Luke."

"How's it, bro?" the mastodon asks, grinning down at him. He extends a hand not much smaller than Luke, who shakes his tiny head at this stranger who could grind his bones to make his bread. "How's it, Little Man? You here for a drink? You a tough guy, eh? Tough guy, bro? Ready to start trouble with me, eh?" So far, the giant doesn't seem immune to my son's powers, and I don't think I'd want to meet the guy who was.

"Hey, Manny. Something I been meaning to tell you."

"Oh yeah?" he asks, still playing patty-cake with my son. "What's that? What's he got to tell me, Little Man? What's going on, little bro?"

"A cop came by to see me in the hospital."

You notice when a bear turns his head and looks your way. And this grizzly doesn't smile as he towers over me, staring down in silence. I think Manny's done with patty-cake for the night.

"This cop that I know," I tell him. "She came by the ER the other night."

He doesn't seem happy to hear this.

"That's nice," he says. "How do you know this cop? You got a lot of cop friends?"

"No, just this one. I met her at my gym. Do you know the box in town? Have you ever been?"

Manny looks at me, unimpressed.

"Anyways," I tell him. "We're sort of friends, and I guess the hospital called the station, and she came by."

"That's sweet. Real sweet, bro. She sounds like a good friend."

"Well, I just thought you should know, because she came by asking me a bunch of questions."

Manny's eyes widen at this.

"Oh, yeah?" he says. "What kinds of questions? What kind of stuff you tell her?"

"I didn't tell her anything. She knew everything already. She asked me what I was doing at Lucky's. She knew that's where it happened. She asked me if I knew the guy who did this to me. I didn't. Told her I couldn't recognize him if I tried."

"What else she say, bro?"

"She asked if I knew that Townsend was at Lucky's that Thursday night."

"He wasn't around here," Manny growls, growing angrier.

"Well, that's what I told her. But she said they know that he was. She said they already knew that." If Manny was born in this country, no doubt coaches would have spotted him early and groomed him to tear quarterbacks limb from limb on Sundays this time of year. But he wasn't. So, he works the door here at Lucky's in addition to his less savory side hustles. He looks pretty steamed now, nostrils flaring.

"Cops lie," he says. "She's lying. Don't you know that, bro?"

"Right, you can't trust them." Unless you're a rich kid, I could add, but I don't.

"Then what? What else she ask you?"

If somehow you can catch the giant cyclops sleeping, you need to stick him in his eye. And then you get the hell out of there while you still have the chance.

"The cameras," I tell Manny. And now his massive chest starts to heave, swelling up like a bubble. "She asked me if Lucky's had any security cameras the way they do at the Bull. I told her I didn't know, but I didn't think so."

A good poker face was never one of Manny's great strengths. His eyes drift away from me to my son and then he stares out at the road. He's thinking, of course, that Lucky's does have security cameras, because without them the employees would rob the place blind, so the owners run it like a police state. Maybe he's even thinking about getting rid of some of those recordings in the near future. But how it might look suspicious to anyone asking, if he did.

"Anyways. I just thought you should know."

"Well," he says, trying to sound confident, "that don't mean nothing to me, bro. Dude never came in here, so that's just cops messing around, like I said."

"Right."

You've got nothing to worry about, Manny.

"That it?" he asks, shooting me a suspicious glance.

"Yeah. That's all she said. I'm sorry about this. I just thought you should know, in case any cops came by asking questions."

Manny looks around like he's waiting for a bus.

"Well, good," I add. "I'm sorry I didn't come by sooner."

"Nah," he insists, inspecting his boots. "No worries, bro. No need. You coming in for a beer now?"

"I got the little guy. Can't really bring him around bars, so we better be getting home."

He nods in agreement but says nothing else.

"Good seeing you, big man."

Manny doesn't respond. He spreads his arms out wide and never takes his eyes off me. I look up at him, and my windpipe slams shut and cuts off my breath. Manny wants another hug. I can't help thinking about the last time I got a little too cozy with another guy around this place—it didn't work out very well. That beard against my cheek, his breath on my neck, then pinned to ground, that fist pounding my face, like getting caught in the gears of some awful machine.

I step forward to him. Drawing closer for our parting embrace, I feel his arms wrap around my back, holding me to him, squeezing me with terrible force, when—at last—he relents and frees me to step backward. I'm more than a little relieved. Smiling innocently at Manny, I offer a nod goodbye.

Now I back up the stroller and turn to roll Luke away from the scary stranger. Looking both ways before crossing the road, a casual walk back to the car, I lift Luke out of his vehicle, get him into mine, and buckle him snug in his car seat. I fold the empty stroller, like a veteran, throw it in the trunk, slam the door closed, walk back around, and get into the driver's seat. I glance out the window at Lucky's to see Manny across the road, hands jammed in his pockets, except now he's walking toward us. Fast. Something's on his mind. He's not looking at anything else but me. And whatever he has to say, maybe it's better if I don't hear it in person.

I start the car. But now Manny picks up his pace—for a guy his size, he's light on his feet. I could throw it in drive and peel out right now, before he gets to me. But that sends a message, and not a good one. I lock the doors, delicately, subtle as I can. And buckle up. Manny's crossing the road, he's almost on us. I look in the rearview, no cars on the street coming behind us. Last chance. Do I wanna be here for this? Or fuck it, get out of here and go?

"What's up?" I ask, rolling down my window. He rests an arm on my roof in response, and peers down at me. We look each other over for a while.

"What's up?" I ask again. What'd you forget? He stares at me.

The gearshift and the gas pedal are calling my name and right now, they sound pretty good.

"Don't come around here anymore," he says, finally.

"What do you mean?"

"Don't come back here."

"I didn't tell her anything, Manny," I start to say, but he's not looking for a speech.

"I'll do you a favor. Let me help you out here, bro. Don't come back. Not for a few beers, not by yourself, not with your little bodyguard here. Not with..." He's about to say Frank, but he stops himself.

"I didn't tell her anything." My tone's dejected.

"Just bad luck, eh? Coincidence your cop friend stopping by, yeah? Just an accident, huh? Like you had here the other night? Some tough luck on you, huh, bro?"

Yeah, I'm a little accident-prone, Manny.

"Your face looks bad," he says. "You caught a few good ones the other night, yeah? But could have been a lot worse, you know what I mean, bro?" He cocks his head.

I nod at him. Yeah, I get the picture. But he doesn't look satisfied.

"Okay. I got you. I hear you, Manny."

"One more thing. You and me? We're done. We're done, bro. I tried to help you the other night. But you don't listen. Well, you listen now, yeah? Don't come around here again."

Manny's had his say. He stuffs his fists back in his pockets, turns away, and lumbers back toward the bar, crossing the street. I watch him go, sitting here, trying to catch my breath. But when he reaches Lucky's entrance, he looks back toward us, and before I can stop him, Luke waves goodbye to the giant from his car seat. Manny glares at us from the doorstep, eyes hidden beneath his hood. He shakes his head at us one final time before turning to shuffle back inside, returning to his stool and the half-lit world he guards, the post he never leaves.

I think that went pretty well. It could have gone a lot worse. We've got a long way to go, but it was a start.

Still parked here on the side of the road, I'm trying to slow things down and collect myself, but my engine's revved pretty high. Threatening a man who could kill you with his bare hands and eat whatever's left tends to raise your heart rate a bit. It gets you going. And if you do it with your favorite thing in the world sucking his thumb at your feet, that can add a jolt to the occasion as well. And there's still plenty of things that can go wrong with my plan.

It's getting dark now—the light goes fast this time of year. Sitting here in the car, looking at the last of a crimson sunset over the cornfields, smelling the sea breeze, hearing the crickets starting up as another day in our corner of the world comes to an end, I reach my arm back and get a handful of Luke's hair, fingers soft on his scalp. Thinking how I might pull this off, that this whole thing might even work. But still. This next part could get a little rough.

"Pretty isn't it, buddy?" I ask him. *"You see the pretty sunset?"*

I might as well take a second to enjoy this. Stay here in this moment.

Besides, at this point, it's too late to have second thoughts. Because I started something, back there, and now that this thing is in motion, I can't make it stop. In for a penny, in for a pound, and all that. No, I started something and how it all ends, I don't know, but I set this thing rolling, it's picking up speed, so I can't do much now but stay the hell out of the way and watch where it goes.

46

THIS WOULD HAVE been a lot easier if we could have just gone to the beach.

I tried more than once. I texted him a few times to see if he wanted to grab a session. He ignored my messages last night. Then this morning he responded with a simple *can't*. The surf looked all right today, which means he really did have a job to do, or he lied and just went with his new buddy Kevin. Or maybe some version of both. But either way, this could have been a lot cleaner if we did our patented on-off coparent arrangement—I could have handled this while he was out on the water, but I'm running out of time, and I don't have any other choice.

Parking in Frank's driveway, I step out of the car but leave Luke strapped in his seat. I walk up the lawn to his front porch, stand there collecting myself, give a quick look around, then, taking a good firm grip on the screen door, I yank it sideways with some violence until I begin to feel the rusty hinges fall off the rotten wood. I hold the frame steady, so it doesn't clatter. I walk back to the car to unbuckle Luke just before he starts to cry, but I assure him over and over, "I didn't forget you, buddy. I didn't forget you." I open the front door, poke my head in and call out *hello?* But hearing no response I walk inside anyway. I carry Luke into the den, where we find poor Stacy blinking sleep from her eyes on the couch. Jake sits riveted in front of the TV.

"Oh god." She yawns. "What time is it? Hey guys, come in, come in."

"I didn't mean to wake you. Do you want us to get out of here?"

"No, no, you didn't," she claims. "Don't be silly."

Luke slides in next to his friend, and the two of them stare spellbound at the screen.

"Hey, Stace? I'm sorry to tell you. But I think something's wrong with that screen door. It doesn't look good."

Stacy pulls a pillow over her head and groans into it. When she takes it away from her face, she looks like she might cry.

"Could you tell Mr. Wonderful?" she asks "When you see him, could you tell him to come in here for a minute? At his convenience? If that works with his schedule?"

"I'm sure it's no big thing," I mumble, slipping out of the room.

I walk through the garage and step out the side door to the backyard. I can see Frank's shed framed against the cloudless sky under a bright, low moon flanked by pine trees, their sinking limbs draped over the roof like elbows perched on a shoulder, or arms hanging loose around a neck. A light from inside glows through the lone window. The scream of whatever tool he's using and the soft volume of angry music spills out from behind the door over the lawn. I keep walking toward the shed. This would have been a lot easier at the beach.

Frank's inside but doesn't notice me come in. He wears a dirty blue T-shirt and a white dust mask over half his face, and his hands and forearms are covered in tiny debris. A shortboard lies out on his sawhorse at some uncertain stage of creation. He leans over the board with his planer, rubbing the belt down the nearest edge. His phone rests on a bench behind him, shouting a song from his playlist, and between the scraping and the music, he doesn't hear me open the door and step inside.

"How's it going?" I ask.

He looks up from his work at me, not pleased by the interruption. But he stops the sander, stands up straight, and half smiles. He shrugs by way of response, lays the tool atop the board, and grabs a small towel for his hands. The infamous cooler rests by the bench, and he selects a new can.

"Think tomorrow could be decent?" I ask him.

"That's what they're saying."

"Yeah, should be good."

He sits down on his bench, elbows on his knees, looking at his project. I'm trying to breathe normally. But I need to get this done.

"Did you see those pictures I sent you?" I ask him.

He doesn't seem interested.

"Did you see my email?"

"No," he admits.

"Check it out," I prod him. "You need to see this."

"Yeah, I will in a sec."

He doesn't. But as I stand here, not speaking, he gets tired of me staring. When he reaches down to the bench for his phone, I lean over his shoulder, looking on like an excited little schoolboy.

"What do you think?" I ask, nudging him.

"Take it easy," he says. He unlocks his phone, pulling up his Gmail to see the message I just sent him. He clicks on the first link to photos of a side-by-side picture of the DeWalt and the next-best drill driver for the DIY entrepreneur.

"Yeah, I've seen these before," he grumbles.

"Which one would you go with?" I ask him. Thinking *1184. 1184. 1184.*

"I thought you were obsessed with the DeWalt? You won't shut up about the thing."

"Yeah, but when I walked into True Value, I panicked." *1184. 1184. 1184. His birthday maybe? Someone's birthday? Not important. Just think November 84. Thanksgiving 84. November eighty-four—think Olympics in Los Angeles, Jordan playing on the US Team just out of Chapel Hill, think Thanksgiving 84.*

"It really doesn't matter," he says.

It matters to me. All of this matters a great deal to me, Frank. He lays the phone by his side on the bench and I wait for him to stand up, step back to his project. Just as he opens his beer and begins to take his first sip, I slip the knife in.

"Oh, before I forget. Stace said to tell you she needs to talk to you."

Frank winces at this.

"Awesome," he says, rubbing his temples. "That's just awesome. Did she say why or anything?"

"I don't know. She said some stuff about how something was broken and had to get fixed. But she kind of seemed like she was a little bit chafed."

The news pains him as much as I'd hoped. He closes his eyes and shakes his head.

"Fuck," he says. He stands up and storms out of the shed, bringing his beer with him.

I watch him pace to his house—he might look back this way—but he doesn't, and not until he opens the back door to his home do I sprint to the table, grab his phone, and punch in his password November 1984. 1184. And Christ, it's not working! I glance at the door. Can't turn off the goddamn music. Slow down, try this again, 1184—his phone unlocks, it's open, thank God, and I'm pulling up his texts now, almost knowing already what I'm about to see. The first one's from some guy named LARRY: Call me. need to talk asap. But sure enough, the second name on his list is Manny. What does the big fella have to say?

Your boy knows something. U got a problem. Hes asking questions

And then no response. No response from my friend. Manny sent the message last night at 7:15 p.m. Not too long after our chat outside of Lucky's. I read it again and again and still the same thing, but there it is, and when you find it, like you knew you would—then what else do you need? I still have his phone in my hands, thinking, What else? What else should I try to find? And how much time do I have?

I glance out the shed, looking down the grass to the house and see the back door opening—that didn't take long, shit! I rush back to the bench and lay his cell down—is this where he left it? Best guess, no time to think it over, and now I whip out my own phone and bury my nose in the screen. Frank stomps through the door into the shed, grumbling to himself, "already fucking asleep," and heads for his cooler, grabbing a can and slumping down on his bench. He sits there with his forearms resting on his legs and studies the board for a moment. He holds the beer in both hands, but he doesn't open it. He just sits there, still as a statue. Something on that board has his attention. He turns his head slowly toward me, and when he looks up, our eyes meet.

And now he knows. He knows I figured this out. And maybe that's not such a good thing, the way he's looking at me now.

"Did the boys go down? Is Jake already out?" I ask him. He doesn't respond. He just sits there on the bench, coiled and ready to spring.

"Is Luke asleep?" I ask.

Frank nods and then slowly, as if some thought just escaped him, turns his back to me and bends down, reaching to open his toolbox. He begins to inspect the contents inside it. I glance around the shed at the tools hanging from thick nails in the wall—a sledgehammer, a shovel, a spade, heavy sheers—and now I can see over his shoulder that Frank has found something that looks like a ball-peen hammer, rusted head, wooden handle. He cocks it in his hand and studies the head, feeling the weight, as if he were picking out a new one at the store. You don't use a hammer to shape surfboards. But he drops the ball-peen back into the box where it lands with a good clank. I need to get out of this shed.

Franks stands up and puts on his mask. He turns the music off on his cell phone and slips it into his pocket. Picking up the sander, he steps over to the shortboard at the saw table.

"I'm going to check on the boys," I tell him. He nods again, without looking at me. I backpedal to the exit, keeping my eyes on him, and slip out of the shed. Outside, my footsteps are quick on the grass. I'm half expecting to look over my shoulder and see that hammer arching toward my temple. Just a few more steps to the back door and then inside to find Luke.

"Hey, Pete!" Frank calls behind me. I turn around to find him. He's standing there in the doorway of the shed, a dark figure silhouetted by the light behind him, face covered in shadows. We look at each other for a moment. He raises an arm and waves me over, like calling a child in for dinner.

"C'mere, man," he says.

I don't move an inch.

"Come over here for a minute," he says again.

His hands are empty, but that shed has every weapon he could ever need. He might have a few on him right now.

"Come on, man. I don't want to have to shout," he calls like an impatient parent. Don't make me have to ask you again.

I walk toward him. He leans against the doorframe, and now he stuffs his hands in his pockets, so I slow down to a stop, some distance from him, but still a long way from a safe one.

"We need to talk," he says. I nod at this but can find no better response, thinking to myself *watch his hands, watch his hands, he's a quick little bastard.*

"Yeah, the two of us, we need to talk," he says again.

"All right, what's up?"

"No, not like this. Not here, man. Why don't you go back inside and grab Luke." I hate the sound of my son's name coming out of his mouth. He sighs. "Yeah, go get Luke home and get him to bed."

"Sounds good."

"Right, and then—why don't you shoot me a text." His eyes turn cold at this.

"Yeah, I'll do that."

"Good. Then we'll meet up."

"Where?"

"Where else?" he says, throwing up his hands. "Where do you think?" But he glances around at the night, without answering his own question. Then, as if satisfied that everything seems in the right place, he turns casually and steps back inside, into his sanctuary.

I dart in through the back door, race into the living room, and snatch Luke up in my arms but manage to wake Stace. She's woozy and blinking as she calls out after us, "Good night, guys, thanks for stopping by." I offer a thumbs-up and okay with one hand, not wanting to disturb Luke slumped on my shoulder. We sneak out through the front hall. The screen door, well busted, almost comes off in my hand, but I catch its fall and scurry down the front steps, manage to get Luke in his car seat, hop inside, pull onto the street, and glance in my rearview. I just need to get Luke home safe. Maybe I could even call Gandle from the road? I don't know. But not until I make a few turns and still see the road empty behind me do I manage to take a few deep breaths.

Home now, I carry Luke sleeping in my arms, stepping lightly up the porch, feeling him breathe on my shoulder. I lock the door behind us. I scurry into his room and stand there with him next to his crib, but don't put him down just yet. We hold each other, rocking gently, the way we do. Then I whisper to him as he snores against me.

"I've got to go now, buddy. And you need to sleep. I love you, buddy. I've loved you from the moment you came into this world. You're the best thing that ever happened to me. But I have to go do something now. I'm sorry. I need to do this. But either way this goes, you remember—I love you, buddy. You got that? You hear me? You're my man."

Lauren's asleep in our bedroom. It's never a good idea to wake her up, so I creep to the front hall closet and forage as quietly as I can. Reaching to the top shelf, I push away the debris that camouflages my hiding space—the candles, the spare blackout lamps, the stocking stuffers—until my hand finds the barrel through its case. I pull down the Remington and lay it on the floor. Then I grab a white bucket from up there that doesn't see much use but holds a few boxes of buckshot cartridges and stuff one of them in my jacket. And what else? Am I showing up for this sit-down with a shotgun on my lap? Carrying it ready for the O.K. Corral? I doubt it. What else could I use if I had to? The box cutter. The old metal handle is rusted, but the blade still works, and the weight feels good in my hand. I pat down my pockets, taking inventory, and slip out the front door into the night.

My phone vibrates with a text. Frank couldn't wait for my call, he's coming on strong.

The River. Let's go, it says.

Sounds like he has something to get off his chest.

47

I CREEP ALONG the dirt road, bouncing over potholes, easing the wheel to veer around the deepest ones, if I can. The route is battered but not windy—it's a straight shot down to the beach. There are no houses back here, nothing out the car windows but a wall of reeds floating past in the darkness and the empty road ahead. The grass-topped dunes appear carved out against the ocean beyond, that black surface covered in scars tonight, twitching, reflecting in the moonlight, reaching out to the horizon where the world ends.

As I get closer to the beach, I realize something I should have thought of before I drove halfway down here, so I slow to a crawl but don't stop. I strain my eyes, but I can't see Frank's truck anywhere. No sign of Frank, either. Checking in the rearview, there's nothing but dust kicked up from my bumper, lit up like red smoke from my taillights, and out the side windows, still nothing but darkness. The road is narrow. Turning around won't be easy if I have to do it in a hurry, not until the end, where the dirt meets the sand in a half-ditch that's still a brown lake, even days after the rain.

A few car lengths before the filthy moat, I roll to a stop and shut off the engine. And I turn off my lights. My rearview's still empty, but the console's still glowing. I figure wherever Frank is right now, he can see me a lot better than I can see him. I reach back to grab the Remington and lean it upright in the passenger seat next to me. It occurs to me in a way it previously hasn't that Frank owns a few firearms himself, his constitutional right. I want to get out of the car, and I begin to steel myself to open the door when a text comes. A message from Frank.

You don't need the shotgun, it says.

I drop the phone and grip the steering wheel. I peer through the windshield, scanning everywhere around me, but still nothing. Where the hell is he? Wherever the bastard is right now, he can see me pretty well. The moment my car turned off the blacktop, he could probably watch my approach—I should have come up with a better strategy.

But if he wanted to do something stupid, he could have done it already. Why give me a warning? Just to rattle me, maybe. I finger the box cutter in my pocket. I look at the swamp in front of me. I could just turn the key, push the pedal, and jam the wheel around to tear ass out of here, away from this stupid place. Let the sheriff and Gandle handle the sneaky bastard. It's still an option. I could have just texted Gandle the second I got out of that shed. I'm not sure why I didn't. So now I lay the Remington in the backseat, open the car door, and step out into the night.

Standing in the road, all I see is a thick forest of reeds and fescue. But no trace of him, yet. Nothing but the wind at my back, the ocean ahead, and the sound of my breath in my ears. I walk forward, slowly toward the ditch, the foul water lit up by the bright sky. I still can't see Frank. I creep around to the edge of the moat, rocks under my sneakers. Feel my shoes hit the sand and keep moving forward. Up ahead, through the path to the ocean, I can see a faint glow coming from somewhere. I walk toward it. Coming up between the dunes, the faint light grows brighter until I find its source around the bend. Down the beach, Frank sits on the back of his truck, watching a fire he built in a hole he dug out of the sand.

I walk over to him slowly, stopping to stand a few feet upwind of the fire pit, facing the smoke and the water behind it. He doesn't look up. I don't say anything, either, and the silence that follows is long enough that I almost wonder if he saw me show up. I glance around. On a Friday in August, you might see a few other bonfires or trucks in the distance. But this time of year, it's just the two of us out here tonight.

Frank seems distracted. He studies the fire, as if the sparks rising up into the sky are something worthwhile, a project that requires great care and attention. Back there in that shed, if I had said the wrong thing or taken the slightest misstep, he would have come at me with an axe. But right now, I'm not sure he'd notice. Frank looks weary, used up. He doesn't look like a man hoping to start a fight. Maybe he wants to get this over with. Maybe he meant what he said when he told me, *we need to talk.* If I could convince myself of this, it would help to get my weight off my heels and let me find a little more moxie.

"Did you really bring your kid with you to Lucky's?" Frank asks, blinking wide-eyed at the flames.

"It was an aggressive call," I admit. He nods at this.

"Yeah. That was some move. And then the shit with my phone—that was cute."

"Nice out here," I tell him. "A little cold, but it's nice." He rubs his forehead with the heel of his palm.

"You got Manny real worked up," he says. "Which most people try not to do," he adds, more of an observation than a threat. "Most people try not to piss him off."

"That's a nice fire," I tell him after a while. It doesn't seem like Frank is planning on trying to kill me tonight, but if he thinks I'm too frightened, he could change his mind. "Is that kiln-dried?" I ask, inspecting the logs like a strange uncle. "That's good wood."

"You are one stupid son of a bitch," he says, sounding more exhausted than angry. "A stubborn bastard, too."

Frank has always been a bit of a bully, and you never beg and plead with those types, you can't ever let them see you're scared—they enjoy it too much. I need to let him know I've got all night. I'll stand out here with him until that fire burns to ashes and he drinks every beer in his truck and then I'll drive with him to the package store to buy another case. We could grab a fresh cord of wood on the way if he wants, but we'll still turn around and come right back to this spot and start the whole thing over again. *I'll stand right here until you tell me what I want to know.* He needs to believe that, otherwise this will be a long night. We stare at each other over the flames for a while.

"All that stuff with Manny?" he asks. "Was that just spin? About the cops?"

"Is that why you wanted to come down here? That's all you meant when you said we needed to talk?"

I'm not acting like a hard-ass just to try something whacky and fun. I don't have as much information to trade as I'd like, so I need to ration what I do have, and manage my short stack. Then there's the other thing. He doesn't *know* what I don't know. He can *think* whatever he likes, and he can stare across the table all night, but he can't see my chips. And he needs to know what I have pretty bad, that much I *am* sure about. Any color I could give him about what the cops think—he's desperate for any scrap—would really help him out. Frank should have told me he knew Townsend all these years. That wasn't very nice.

But he doesn't steam with anger the way I might have expected. I've never seen him this tired. Frank has run for too long with some of his working parts rusted or worn out and now he's starting to break down. He may need to tell me the truth just to keep from cracking up.

"Do you want a beer?" he asks. "You sure? You're wired pretty tight."

I don't even shake my head. Just standing here, waiting him out, I can't help but think of our first date at the playground, when he gave me the silent treatment. The memory helps me keep my mouth shut.

Frank sighs like a breeching whale. He rubs his face in his hands. And now he starts, of course he does, he can't sit around all night.

"If we're really doing this," he says. "Let's get two things straight, all right?"

"Sure." *I'm not an unreasonable man. Whatever's easiest. How can I help out?*

"First," he says. "It's a onetime deal. Tonight only. We get through this shit, then it's over, no more questions, no hard feelings."

"That works."

He looks at his feet for a moment. But then, for no good reason that I can see, he starts to laugh, a snort at first, that turns into a giggle, then becomes a deep belly laugh, and now he's really howling. It's unsettling.

"What's the second thing?" I ask him. He stops his chuckling and collects himself.

"This whole thing," he says, and points a finger at me. "You remember, it was your idea. Right? Just remember. You wanted to hear this."

One day a long time ago, Frank and I were sitting on this same beach, and he asked me if I had ever gone broke. I thought the question over for a minute—the topic seemed complicated to me, at the time. It still does. I could have told him that I'd had some rough years. That I had "blown myself up" at least once. Seen some serious drawdowns in my capital, friendships, self-respect, and reputation, and could have added that some of these assets were more precious and harder to replenish than others. Any honest answer would involve some qualifiers, most of which I didn't want to discuss with him or anyone else and still don't. My own background, or my parents, for instance. I was also pretty sure, and still am, that once we started down certain topics, my wife's name and her income would soon come up. *Who needs that?* It also occurred to me that Frank wasn't asking just for yucks. Before long, I turned to him, and settled on a simple *no.* I still think it was the best answer I could have given him. Frank had a different one. He has visited rock bottom more than once.

"Why does anyone ever do anything?" he asks now, standing up to throw another log onto the burning pile. Frank is not a romantic.

"I'm tapped out again," he says after a while. "Busted. The house, the bills, the kid. And yeah, okay, the bookies at Lucky's, the poker, the online stuff. Whatever I get my hands on, it goes pretty quick. I win a few times, but then I just can't ever quit. You get up for a few days, claw back to breakeven. Who the hell wants to break even? What's worse than that?"

I can think of a few things, but you don't interrupt a confession.

"I needed something," he admits. "This time, I'd really fucked up. I'd flushed everything. I was borrowing just to pay the interest on all this stuff—it never ends. I would have lost the house. Couldn't go through that again. Just nowhere to borrow another cent."

Why didn't you ask me? I wonder to myself.

"So, I went to this dude I knew," he says, pacing slowly by the fire. "Dude I worked for. Knew him for a long time. Dude with more money than he'd ever need, or his family could ever spend in their lifetimes. I went to him and asked for help. I ask for a lower number—you never start with the real number. I asked for something, to help my family out. That's what I told him. *I need to help my family.* Do you know what he said?"

I look at him with a shred of sympathy but can't offer too much else.

"Yeah, you guessed it," he says with venom. "He turned me down. Dude with a house on the ocean couldn't spare a dime. Not for someone like me. He just couldn't swing it. *I'm sorry Frank,* he said. *I don't do that sort of stuff. Sorry I can't be of more help.*"

The response seems to have left an impression on Frank. He remembers it very well.

"I stewed on that a little," he says. "Thought it over for a while. I started thinking how I could motivate the guy to help out his fellow man, the common man, right? Because I knew something about this dude's private life. I've worked for him for a long time, and sometimes I see him with this woman, always just the two of them, coming and going at odd hours. It wasn't hard to figure out what they were doing—I've got a key to his house. This guy's a real piece of work. So, I scheduled a little sit-down with him at Lucky's. It was a Thursday night a few weeks ago. Figured we'd do it in a spot where he wouldn't get too emotional. Talk about it over a beer like two adults. Anyways, I made him an offer—help me out and I won't tell Brooke about his thing on the side. I told the dude, *Look, I'm not asking much for my services, and this way, your nice wife never has to know you've been sticking yourself in some strange.* He's got plenty of money, so that's an easy one, right? You know what the guy said?"

I'm starting to get the picture.

"He didn't react well. Told me where to go. I figured I'd give him a little time to cool off and think about it. Then the fucker left me to pick up the tab."

Frank opens another can and spits in the sand at the recollection.

"I didn't see it going down the way it did," he says. "Didn't think my night would end wrapping his ass up in a tarp and putting him in the back of this truck." He sounds exhausted. Defeated. There's something horrible in his face as he looks at me and tries to explain.

"The paddle out was interesting. I took a longboard from his garage, twelve-footer, a big, thick bastard, this thing could float some real weight. And he was a lanky fucker, heavy as hell, but I got him out of the truck, hanging off my shoulders, and carried him down to the water. It reminded me of lifeguard training stuff from summers when I was a kid—did you ever do that? No? Not your thing? Well, I dropped him facedown on the board, folded his arms underneath him, pushed the board into the white water, and then I laid down a little toward the back, on top of him. Then I started digging. It was like paddling one of those big rescue boards in with a passenger. Except I was heading out, not coming back in. You know what I mean? Why you looking at me like that?"

"Why didn't you just chuck him in the water and get the hell out of there?" I ask him. He doesn't acknowledge the point.

"There were a lot of moving parts," he explains, jumping back up to the flatbed. I can't tell if he's kidding.

"I had a lot of shit to do before sunrise," he says, in the tone of a busy parent. "I needed to get his truck and his cell phone to Hammy's beach by six a.m. Otherwise, none of this stuff would hold up. I had to get him in the water and I didn't want to be carrying him around Hammy's when it started to get light out. That wouldn't be good. But I didn't even want him *found* that morning, if I could help it. And it was already pretty late by the time I got him into his wet suit, that wasn't easy, took a lot longer than I thought, but I got him in the back of my truck. And then I took a look at the boards in his quiver and picked out a few to borrow. He had a big standup needle. Must have been almost two a.m. when I got in the water at Hammy's. We got lucky with the moon, but I had to giddy up. So, I paddled his ass out there, took a couple waves on the chin getting through the break, almost lost the fucker, but I made it out, made it out past the break. Caught my wind for a bit and then kept digging farther from shore. I paddled for a while. We were a long way out there. And when I'd had enough, I rolled him over the side and watched the current take him down the coast. Then I headed back in. That part was easy, the wind was behind me, I was really moving. I made it back to the break and caught one almost all the way into shore. I ditched the board in the water, as if the poor guy snapped his leash. I never heard who found it, or if they did. But if you saw a nice twelve-footer at low tide one Friday morning, would you call it in?"

Frank looks less and less disturbed. He shrugs at me. And I can't help but wonder if some part of him isn't *proud* of this last bit. If maybe Frank isn't self-aware enough to admit why he didn't just throw Townsend in the ocean, and maybe he paddled the guy a mile offshore into a face full of wind chop under the moonlight just to prove something. He did it to see if he *could*. Because it was *heavy*. It was gnarly. It was rough. It was *interesting*, dude. The kind of shit tough guys need to think up and do. Maybe the hardest thing for Frank with this stuff is *talking* about it and trying not to grin. I don't know. But there's some of that, at least.

"So," Frank says now that he's built some momentum. "I drove my truck back to Townsend's and put his stand-up back in the garage where I found it. Snatched up his wallet and cell phone, his flip-flops, a T-shirt, a jacket, and some jeans. Waited around until five thirty to leave his house with all the stuff in the backseat. I used kitchen gloves for the wheel, I'm sure I left plenty of my carpet, traces of whatever stuff in the front seat, but I drive it all the time to keep up the battery, that's why they pay me the big bucks. Right? No big deal. So, I drove his truck to Hammy's and that's where we left it."

I try to stop him but can't find my wind, the air's trapped in my chest. He keeps using that word. At first, I thought he was talking about Townsend. But if he slipped up it doesn't seem to bother him. Frank's mood is improving as he unburdens himself, and it's not just the beer.

"What do you mean *we*?" I ask him. Frank stares at me, curious. Not puzzled. More like he's found something to hold his attention. He's not happy, but he doesn't seem worried, either.

"You mean you really don't know anything?" he asks, wide-eyed.

I'm missing something. And I feel a terror build up inside me, like I can't find the leak, and the water keeps rising. This is a bad time to get caught out wrong-footed. Frank's shaking his head, now. This isn't good.

"Pete," he says sadly. "You really need to talk to your wife more, man."

48

I'M A LITTLE confused, here. I'm scrambling to find an explanation, waiting for that shock of recognition, but nothing shakes out. I'm not Drew, I can't settle down, I can't see through the noise, and now I'm left with the feeling that I've missed something important. The dread building now to panic with the final horror of learning what it seems I was the last to discover. When Frank begins to explain, he's not telling me something I suspected. I don't know the words before he says them. None of that stuff. I don't have a clue.

Still, he walks me through it, helping me out like any good buddy would. The story of another strange evening by the water, but not as pretty and calm as this one. There was no moon shimmering off the ocean, no bonfire. Outside it was windy. Patches of rain rolled in. It was a dreary fucking night.

"I didn't stay at Lucky's long," Frank says. "After Townsend left, I went home and I wasn't doing much, the usual shit, just sitting around and playing with myself for a while. But a few hours later I got a phone call, and it's Lauren. I figured it wasn't a coincidence she was calling, and I didn't want to deal with that mess, right? So, I didn't pick up. But my phone kept ringing. And I started thinking. I didn't have a great feeling about it. So, I texted her."

"What'd you say?"

I feel a little bit cloudy.

"I said, *What's up?* But she didn't text back. She called me again, and finally I picked up. She says, *I'm at Townsend's place. You need to get over here now. We need to talk.*"

"What night was that? What was that, a Thursday?"

"Yeah," he says. "Yeah, it was."

"She has her night class on Thursday."

Frank says nothing to that.

I'm not proud of this, but at first, I don't understand why my wife would be calling Frank from Townsend's house—it takes me a little while. Mondays is her Moms' Group, right? Then Thursdays she has night class. Why was Lauren over at Townsend's? But then it starts making more sense, and I think I get the picture now. Frank never spells it out—he lets me do the math. And I can't think of that many good reasons why she'd be over at his place the same night Frank tried to blackmail Townsend for stepping out on his wife. This is one of those things that I missed.

"Anyways," says Frank. "I hopped in my truck. And by the time I get over there, the place is a real mess. I walk in the door, and right there in the front hall, Townsend's laid out on the floor. Lauren's kneeling over his body. It wasn't good."

I picture her on that black tile next to him. Weeping over a man who isn't her husband.

"What the hell happened?" I ask.

Frank looks wide-eyed at the fire and shakes his head.

"I guess they got into some kind of scrap," he says.

Some kind of *argument*?

"What do you mean? What did she say to you?"

"She starts bitching at *me*," he says. "Yeah. She goes apeshit."

I frown at this. Frank nods and wades in.

"She's hollering at me, *You did this. This is all your fault. You did this.* She keeps saying—*You did this.* She went nuts. Batshit. And then later, when she calmed down a little bit, she called it an accident. Over and over, she kept saying, *it was all just an accident.*"

"What are you talking about? What the hell happened?"

"I don't know everything, but I guess Townsend called her after he met me at Lucky's and told her to come over to his place. He doesn't tell her anything's wrong. But anyways, they sit down next to the fireplace, or whatever they do, and then he gives her the bad news that it's over between the two of them. My name came up, I guess, he called me all sorts of bad stuff. But the point is, he tells her how now he has this problem, and they can't keep fooling around. Whatever he said, she didn't take it too well. They get into an argument. If she went ballistic at me, who knows how pissed she was at *him*? But I guess it got physical. I don't know if he fought back—she didn't have any bruises or anything, her eyes were swollen up from crying, maybe she surprised him somehow, I don't know—but she caught him good upside his head with a stoker, and I guess he went over that railing upstairs. He goes over the railing and he must have landed wrong—I'm not sure how, but the dude didn't land the *right way*, that much I know. But he falls, he lands on that tile floor, and that's it for his neck. And that's it for Townsend."

I'm back to that image of Lauren kneeling in the hallway, only this time she's pleading with an unresponsive Townsend, begging him to say something, move a muscle if he can hear her, screaming at him to *wake up*. However long that lasted I hope he wasn't awake for any part of it. What if only his eyes were left moving inside a helpless body—who knows how they might have turned to look at her in those final moments? Or if he could speak to her what he might have said? I hope he was out, for Lauren's sake as much as his. I wonder how long she knelt there with him before she decided to call Frank. I feel a little sick.

"I didn't have a lot of time to think," Frank says, watching me uneasily. "It all happened pretty quick. She said she needed my help. She said she needed my help to clean this up. She said we could fix this—there wasn't much time—but with my help, she said we could. It was just an accident, she said. That I could help her out. Or if I wasn't up for it then I might as well call the cops, right then. So, I had to make a decision. It wasn't an easy one. But I made it."

"You sure did."

"You think I should have called the cops? You think that would have been better?"

I'm not going to answer this one. Not for Frank and sure as hell not tonight.

"So, then what?"

"Well, then we got to work," he says. "We scrubbed the floors, bagged up what he was wearing and found some new clothes and shoes for the trip, and the cell phone we'd need for the second trip back at 5:30 a.m. We put him on a tarp and carried him into the garage. That's where we got the wet suit on him, that was a bitch. But we got him suited up and into my truck and we drove it out to the beach. After I got him on the water we went back to Townsend's, cleaned up whatever else we could, and a few hours later we drove his car with his phone and his clothes out just like it was some dawn patrol session at Hammy's. That cell had to stay in his house until sunup, just in case the cops ever thought to check."

In my old job we used to have an expression called the *Wall Street Journal Test*. The basic premise was that whenever you wondered if something felt inappropriate, you should ask yourself how you would feel if the next day you, your boss, your friends and family, you all had to read about it in the morning paper. If you could answer that question, it could save you a trip to a compliance officer. Or a visit to HR. I don't think this whole thing would pass the *Wall Street Journal Test*. I really wouldn't want to read that headline. WIFE OF STAY-AT-HOME-LOSER-DAD BANGS FINANCIER AND KILLS HIM IN ARGUMENT. Sources say Pete was too stupid or depressed to notice her betrayal.

And really, where the hell was I while she was out carpooling with my friend at five in the morning? Zonked out on the couch next to Luke, probably. When you hardly ever sleep in the same bed as your wife, it's easier to miss these kinds of things. Jesus. What a mess.

"That night she was over there with him," Frank says, interrupting my train of thought. "Whatever went down—she really lost her shit. What do you think set her off like that?"

I look over at him. Is he fucking with me? My wife was humping some guy he blackmailed *and never told me*. Thanks, buddy. You want to hear me say that?

"No mystery," I tell him, not enjoying this. "You threatened him, he thinks it over and decides to break up with her. Figures it's going to come out one way or another. Maybe he tells Brooke first, beats you to the punch. Maybe he thought breaking it off was all for the best, that the whole thing had run its course. He's had other women on the side. So, he invites her over to break it off—blames it on you, of course, but it was fun while it lasted. Something like that."

"You think that's what did it? Pulling the plug on them fooling around?"

"What am I missing?" I ask. Frank's looking out at the swells rolling in over the water. What more does he want?

"She was in love?" I say. "Is that what you want to hear? She loved him. She wanted a different life with a different guy. A bigger life. Maybe he promised her a bunch of stuff I couldn't. But then, when you pushed him, he thought it over and he cracked, but he didn't break the way she wanted.

He wanted to end their thing, and it sounds like she didn't take the news too well. My wife has a temper. What am I missing?"

I need to sit down, but I don't want to get any closer to him. Frank nods to himself.

"Yeah," he says. "That sounds about right."

I could use a little bit of a time-out. But I have to gather myself, because if this show is one night only, I can't sneak out early with the other pikers. I need to stay for the final act.

"Since we're having this heart-to-heart," I tell Frank, "let me ask you something. When you went by his house that night, you find Townsend's neck broken in an accident. My wife says, *get over here. I need your help.* Why go? Why help her? Why would you help her make it look like a drowning? Why would you risk all that?"

Were you bored? I could ask. Overcome with guilt about blackmailing Townsend? Did you worry about hurting my feelings? None of those sound right.

Frank reaches behind him and grabs a few logs, then hops off the truck and throws them into the fire. They go up quick with the coals this hot. He looks at the flames for a while.

"Did she offer to help *you?*" I ask. "Let me guess. She said she'd take care of everything, right? You got a few problems, some money issues, a 'little cash-flow thing,' and she knew that. Why else would you pull that stuff with Townsend? So, when she called you, she says it's your lucky night. Think pretty quick, she needs an answer, but if you help her out, she'll make all your worries go away. She'll take care of everything. Right?"

Standing by the fire, he crunches his empty can and sails it onto the flatbed.

"Sounds like you got everything figured out," he says.

————

She might have been swinging at someone other than Townsend. Maybe, in that moment, it wasn't the sharp rejection, or the coldness of his calculated decision, or the sudden end of her fantasy life stoking her fury, but just the thought of her marriage—her mediocre *is this all there is?* type of marriage to her profoundly uninteresting husband, a grown-ass man, who spends his nights in a hoodie and ski hat, looking for answers. Staring into this bonfire on an autumn beach, I imagine her slowly realizing she was going back to *all that*. No wonder she was pissed.

"I still don't understand," I say aloud, but more to myself. I knew she was unhappy, but still, the betrayal, the cheating, and all the rest of it? "I just didn't see this coming."

Frank shakes his head. He could look a *little* more sympathetic—but he doesn't.

"How're things at home?" he asks. "You guys getting along? Does she show you a lot of attention? You two fooling around much? She ever seem a little cold to you?"

We're both very busy and tired. To an outsider she could seem distant.

"She's a little prickly," I say. "I thought it was just a typical couple with a baby kind of deal. The usual stress."

Then again, after I stopped working, there were times when I wasn't in the best mood. Lying around in the same sweatshirt most days, shaving and showering when the mood struck, and at the lows hoping to get selected for jury service. The years of Sundays. Feeling like I couldn't get out of bed. Women notice that sort of thing.

"Sure, the usual," says Frank. After a pause, he wonders, "Did she start paying more attention to how she looks?"

Only every gym class on the East Coast since we moved here. Along with every diet ever invented. Plus, a whole new wardrobe.

"Yeah," I admit. "A little bit. But don't they all do that type of stuff? Is that supposed to mean she was messing around on me?"

"Did she ever accuse you of messing around on her?"

More than once. I thought she smelled Frank's philandering on me—the scent of associated guilt. Back when I was drinking too much, out late too many nights. But when your wife accuses you of such things, you find yourself pleading, even apologizing for things you haven't done—it sure throws you off the scent.

"I can't really remember," I say. He pokes a stick in the sand to tell me he understands.

"How about all those Girls' Nights? She does a lot of that kind of shit. You and Luke are real regulars at the Bull, no dinners at home with Mommy? You ever ask her where she's going? All those Moms' Group meetings. You ever listen to who's with her? Do you even know whose house they're at?"

I don't know much about Moms' Groups. I'm not invited to such events. All I need to know is when I'm on duty. I can't pick up on other details. Who has the bandwidth for all of that?

Still, I'm picking up on a pattern here.

"Those goddamn night classes," I tell him. What working mother wouldn't want to add a course load to her schedule? Still trying to convince him that I'm getting the joke I add, "The laundry."

He wouldn't know this one.

"Of all the chores around the house," I explain. "What's the one thing she insists on doing?"

Not Luke's, of course. Not those piles of tiny onesies and pajamas and socks, but she insists on doing hers. Think of all those nasty stains and smells I might discover.

"What else?" I ask. C'mon. What else?

"You ever feel like she's keeping good tabs on you?"

I close my eyes and groan.

All those texts. Where r u? What time will u be home? Where r u? Where r u?

Needing to know my whereabouts. Always. Constantly. With great urgency. Why would she do that?

And then the waiting. All those endless nights around the house, passing the hours just waiting for her to come home when she said she would. The insane excuses, the train delays, the traffic, the acts of God, always leaving me staring cockeyed at my watch.

"What else?"

"You sure you want to keep doing this?"

"What else?"

"You could have lived anywhere," says Frank. "Why this town? Why the sudden move? For the easy commute? Real estate looked cheap around here?"

I think that's about enough.

"OK," I tell him. "Just no way for me to know, I guess."

49

WHEN YOU HAVE kids, sometimes days and nights blend together. You look at a calendar and wonder how the year vanished. But tonight, I think I'll remember. This one will stand out.

"Have you two been talking?" I ask him. "Since that lost night, that tragic accident. You two keeping in touch here and there?"

Nice to imagine your friend conspiring with your wife. All these weeks, the two of them sharing information about how much I knew and what I'd found. A happy thought for any husband.

"What do you think?" he asks unhelpfully.

I think I deserve an answer.

"What does she know?" I ask. "About me? About how close I got to this thing?"

"She knows."

"And tonight, our fireside chat—does she know about this?"

"She knows everything."

"You tell my wife everything? Is that how it works?"

He laughs. He *snorts*. Looking exasperated with me. Sorry to bother you with all these silly questions, Frank. I don't mean to piss you off. Now he shakes his head again.

"You're not the only one sneaking around like a ninja looking at other people's cell phones," he says. "Maybe every wife does it, but Lauren sure checks yours. She keeps good tabs on you."

God help me, that explains a lot.

How often can I even *find* my phone? All those times she helped me search for it. *It's in the couch, Pete.* Swearing to myself I checked there earlier. Christ.

Of course she looks at my cell. She's known every move I've made these past few weeks, always a step ahead of me. Every call. Every email or text. That means she and Frank know about Grady, even Anthony.

I look around the empty beach for a moment. Just the two of us down here.

"Why are you telling me all this?" I ask him.

Frank's eyes narrow, as if he's listening to a petulant child.

"You're wondering about me?" he asks. "Why have *you* been so obsessed with this whole thing? Do you know the aggravation you've been giving me, stirring this shit up? When I tried to help Lauren out, the last thing, the last *goddamn* thing I expected was for you to go all Nancy Drew on this stuff. Why did you need to poke around so much—who the hell was Townsend to you anyway? You and your goddamn secret project, Ranger Rick 'Murder Investigation'! Jesus. What the hell is wrong with you, by the way?"

He points a finger at me and spits. I look away from him, shaking my head.

"You've already got Manny set to explode, snooping around his bar, and you're begging some chick cop, some fat-ass gal pal of yours from that stupid gym you can't shut up about, you're begging her to reopen the case! You think I've got this thing locked down airtight? All those calls from Lauren to me that night? Who knows if you dig up something I haven't thought of. What are you trying to do, send me and Lauren to the fun house—is that what you want? You need to stop making noise on this, you crazy shit! Get another fucking hobby."

Frank keeps on ranting, and I can't ignore him. He asks some good questions.

"We all tell you this whole time that you're nuts. The cops want nothing to do with it. We tried every move in the book, but you just keep coming and coming. Why didn't you back off? Don't you think that's a little sick?"

I don't have a great answer for him. It's complicated. I wanted to get involved in something. I was only trying to help. I don't know, it's hard to explain.

"You kept going on and on," says Frank, almost babbling now. "Flapping your ball washer about the conditions, the waves and the wind. Saying Townsend wouldn't go out in that. Like you're an expert! Like you know one damn thing about surfing—you dumbass kook sonofabitch!"

I feel like doing something stupid. I could take a run at him and see what happens. Maybe I can yank him off the truck and then just pound the shit out of him. He called me a kook! Of course, my last scuffle earned me a trip to the ER. And even *if* I come out on top of this bout, that would be the end of this conversation—I won't learn anything else. So, I might just have to tough this one out.

"Look," says Frank. "The guy who was banging your wife is dead and the cops think it was an accident. You might want to be happy about that."

"I'm not really that psyched."

"What the hell do you want? You want to go talk to the cops? Then what? Maybe they give you a merit badge. A pat on the back? For what? So the cops can show up at your house and take Lauren away in handcuffs? You want to see me in prison? Why? What for? So you can tell everybody how you cleaned up the streets? It happened. Jesus, nobody wanted this. We're not master criminals. It was—"

"Just an accident?" He glares at me, but I'm not backing down. He knew about the affair and never bothered to tell me. Must have slipped his mind. "Just a fluke?" I ask, cocking my head at him, and now he stares down at his feet.

Neither of us says anything else for a while. We both try to ignore each other. Looking out at the horizon, in the moonlight, I can see a boat in the distance. On a different kind of evening, I could imagine most of the crew in their bunks sound asleep, except for the one duty-bound sailor who drew the night watch, a guy enjoying a few predawn hours alone with his thoughts, but tonight, this doesn't do much for me.

"Whose idea was it?" I ask.

"What? With the body?" He says it so innocently.

"Yeah, the ocean. The wet suit. The whole thing."

"C'mon, you know the answer to that one already. She's a smart woman. Who do you think?"

I stand here in the sand next to the fire and rub the side of my damaged face.

Yes, she is, I think to myself. She's a smart woman. And I'm not as quick. Which means there're a few more questions I need to ask.

"You said you tried every move in the book to get me to drop this," I tell Frank.

"Yeah. I guess I did."

"What sort of moves did you try?"

Frank throws another log on the fire that looks well seasoned, but it's hard to tell in the dark.

"It's kind of a long story," he says.

"Are you trying to get cute?"

"No. Take it easy."

Some sick bastard threatened my family. So, if he tells me to chill out right now, I'm going to use the box cutter on him and throw whatever's left in the fire.

"That whole thing really started the night Carson called you," he says. "When she trashed your kitchen? She was freaked. She thought you could fuck up everything and— What's wrong?"

"Nothing. Keep going."

I think of Luke sitting in the kitchen among the wreckage, shouting his innocence while Lauren sobbed into her hands. And I sent the poor little scapegoat to bed with no TV or dessert. She's a cold one.

"Anyways," he says, "when you went to meet with his crazy-ass brother, she was pretty spooked."

"That's when you sent that scumbag in the Range Rover to follow me around?"

"No. She had someone tailing you even before that. Back when she found out you were talking to the cops."

"Oh, yeah? And who'd she hear that from, huh? I never told her." I stare, accusingly.

"Dude, you brought a three-year-old with you down to the police station."

My partner went and ratted me out to his momma. I can picture the two of them. Luke talking about a field trip down to the precinct where Daddy told a story to the cops. Lauren always wants details, but sometimes Luke's light on specifics—she must have hammered him. *What kind of story? There was a man. Down at the beach!* That wouldn't have been fun. But she's too scared to ask me anything, and I won't quit bugging her about Townsend and GDR.

"That must have made her a little uncomfortable," I tell him.

No wonder she wanted someone to keep an eye on me.

"Well," he says, "turns out she was right to be worried. You kept running around on this thing. She's just getting more and more freaked, and so pretty soon she tries to think of some ways to slow you down—maybe even get you to stop. That's when she had me feed you that bullshit about some scary dude looking for you. Shake you up a little. And by the way, the guy she really hired to follow you? He drives a Corolla."

It takes me a minute to think through how that story had me looking over my shoulder, and looking out for the wrong car while I was at it. But if that seems clever, it still doesn't make sense to me.

"Why would you do that?" I ask. "I mean, you two had been telling me everything was an accident, that it was all in my head. Why would you turn around and say the boogeyman's coming after me?"

"Yeah, well, we tried that. We tried to lie low for a while. But how'd that work out? You just wouldn't quit. You went to the funeral. You're talking to the brother. She figured we had to try something else."

The black Range Rover was a nice touch. He keeps saying she, but that idea smells like Frank. He hates them worse than I do.

"What about my cell phone and my laptop?" I ask. "You know anything about that?"

"Little bit."

"Like what?"

He raises his eyebrows and rubs the back of his neck.

"I grabbed them out of your car that day while you were out on the water. She figured you would run, tell that bitch at the gym. I gave the stuff to Lauren, and that night, she sneaks them back in the house, somewhere you can find them. And we keep the calls and texts coming in, so you'd know where to look."

"Why? So that I look like an asshole to the cops? So I'd start to think I was going crazy?"

"Pretty much."

So, these two chuckleheads were having some laughs playing their tricks. That still leaves a Neanderthal who threatened my kid.

"What about the guy at the playground?"

"You just kept upping the ante," he says. "You went to see Brooke. You're talking to that dude Walker—the one with a bug up his ass about Townsend, right? You bought a gun—that was good. And then her guy says you're driving like an asshole, pulling U-turns on the highway and shit. Something had to give."

"So, you figured you should send him to have a chat with me? And that would smooth things over?"

"Do you really think that I did most of the thinking? That I wore the pants on any of this? You don't believe that."

"Where'd she even find that guy?" I wonder aloud.

Frank looks a little guilty.

"He's my old bookie," he says.

"Perfect."

"She asked me for someone."

"He's a sweetheart."

"Yeah, he's a pretty sick dude."

A lot of this stuff is pretty sick, Frank. Still, it was only tough talk, just a bunch of noise. Sticks and stones and all that. At least no one got hurt, right?

The wood hisses on the fire and something is tickling what's left of my ear. I've got another question to ask him.

"What about that night at Lucky's?"

"I'm sorry," he says. "That wasn't my call."

Maybe I do need to talk to my wife more. Better than getting my face pounded in again by some cannibal and spending another night in the ER. But Frank's sorry, at least.

"You had nothing to do with it, huh?"

"I had to tell her you were going," he says. "I didn't think anyone in that place would even talk to you, but she said if the cops found out Townsend was there that night—then we're finished. We're fucked. So, she said we need to take care of this. And she had Manny set it up. Manny knew some guy who owes him a favor, so when you show up, he has him there waiting for you. And things got out of hand."

Yeah, that night was a long way from playing games with my phone. Somewhere along the way my wife lost her perspective on things.

"She had Manny on speed-dial—is that it? They're old buddies?" I ask.

Something about Frank's *it wasn't me* routine is starting to annoy me. As if he had no part in this immaculate conception.

"I told him what she wanted him to do," he says. "But it was her money. Sure as hell wasn't mine. You think I'm the one driving the bus? You think she was looking for any of my input?"

There is a ring of truth to this. I can't see Lauren having a lot of patience with Frank. You have to think there was some finger-pointing going on between the two of them.

"You're just the messenger in all this, right?"

"What do you want me to say? You know her. When she has her mind set on something, she doesn't mess around. I'm sorry, okay? I never thought it would go down like that."

"How'd you think it would go?"

"You think I tell Manny what to do? You think I'm all that? You think Manny wants people coming around asking questions? Just come on by and ask about anything, whenever you're in the mood? You think he wants that kind of rep? You think most of his regulars do?"

I'd guess no, if I had to. I knew about some of the shady stuff that went down in that place, the drugs and the girls, but maybe it was worse than I thought. I don't think I'm going back there anytime soon. But I'm getting a little tired of all my guessing.

When you come to the end of something that really matters to you, where you risked it all on one bet that would change everything in your life, sometimes when you finish this thing, you get there and it's over and somehow you've won, but that's when you start to think, okay, so what? Who gives a shit? None of this means anything. Sometimes that feeling doesn't go away, either.

Frank seems introspective, himself. Standing around the fire in silence for a few minutes, he isn't really drinking anymore. I've never seen him look this old.

"Don't you want to know?" he asks.

This seems like an odd question, under the circumstances. I think I've shown a little more than mild interest in things tonight.

"Know what?" I say.

"If it was me, I'd want to know."

How much more of this can I take?

I tell him, "Spit it out, for chrissakes."

"How long this was going on?"

What's the difference? Look where it ended.

"Yeah, I guess so. Maybe. I don't know. What are you saying?"

"You think she met him out here?"

Where? At the gym? She doesn't really go out to bars or restaurants. We're not very social. When you have kids, you just try to get some sleep when you can. Does it matter?

"I have no fucking idea," I tell him.

"You think she met him when you guys were still living in the city?"

That might make more sense. But who knows? What's the difference?

"Maybe. Why?"

"Think about it," says Frank.

She was pretty specific with the place she had in mind. We could have lived anywhere, but we never even looked anyplace else.

"You mean that's why we moved out here?" I ask. "She followed him?"

"Maybe she did. But that's not what I meant."

Through work. You meet a thousand people through work. That's where accidents happen. All sorts of inappropriate behavior. A client, maybe?

"Then what do you mean?" I ask.

"If it was me, I'd want to know how long. I'd want to know that."

I'm missing something. Like always. What's he talking about? Frank looks worse right now than he has all night. He looks *devastated*.

"I'm saying they've been together since I started working for that guy," he tells me. "That was a long time ago. Do you get that?"

"So what? Where you going with this?"

He doesn't respond. For a guy who likes getting right to the point, Frank's taking some time with what he's got to say, and it's wearing on him. His eyes are empty.

"Is he yours?" Frank asks me. "Luke, I mean. Don't you want to know if you're his father?"

I don't buckle or stagger or drop to my knees. But I heard what he said and I'm out on my feet. And now there's something wrong inside my chest. I don't know what they call this, but it goes stabbing down into my stomach—it hacks away and carves me open. This is pretty ugly stuff, and now there's trouble further south.

For a long time, neither of us says anything, so I stand there, watching the fire and not much else. Frank doesn't want to look at me, either. And when I turn toward him, I say this, so he'll hear me.

"Don't ever ask me that again."

Sometime later, I need to take a seat, so I hop onto the back of Frank's truck and join him, studying the flames and jumping sparks. We sit together, in the quiet, for a long time. I have more questions but don't feel up to asking any of them at the moment. So, we perch side by side for a while—we both have a lot to think about. Frank keeps the fire burning, but it gets chilly out here this time of year, and I've had a rough night. If this fight had any decent ref, he'd have stopped this thing by now.

But then I start feeling sick again and I have some trouble with my breathing. When it passes, I settle down, and now I think it's time for me to go.

Frank says he wants to stick around for a bit.

"Put out the fire?" I ask. He rubs his neck.

"I don't really feel like going home." He groans. "You know what I mean?"

I shoot him a glance and shake my head. He has nothing else to add. And it's very late.

I push myself off the truck, landing in the sand, and wipe my hands on my sweatshirt, taking in this scene at the beach for a bit. The wind has dropped, and you can hear a good nine or ten seconds between the breaking waves. And for some reason—I can't explain why we do such things in certain moments—I look over at him.

"What do you think about tomorrow?" I ask.

"Looks doable."

"Could be good."

"Yeah. We should get on the water."

"With the boys," I suggest.

He nods, smiling at this.

I turn to go. Walking toward the road, I make my way slowly in the sand. But he calls out to me, *hang on a sec, just one more thing.* I look back, and he waves me over. At this point, what's the difference? I walk over to the truck and stand looking at him sitting there, his legs hanging off the tailgate. He's wincing.

"What's up?" I ask him.

He looks around the beach, then over his shoulder, and now leans forward, squinting down at me.

"Did you break my screen door?" he asks.

"Yeah, I did."

He bites his lip, and nods again.

"That's fucked-up," he says.

50

Driving away from the beach, I soon find myself going about sixty-five on a back road before I decide to pull over and regroup. Starting the car again, I continue at a less frantic speed, but the slower pace only makes me more pissed. I grip the steering wheel, not because I feel like choking her or wringing her neck. No. I want to see the look in her eyes as I hold her head in my hands and push my thumbs through her face, forcing my fingers into her skull and squeezing until I feel something break. I want to hear a snap, crackle, and pop.

How the hell could she do this to me? All these years we've had together, the things the two of us have been through, and this whole goddamn time she was running around on me? Oh, and isn't she cute? Think about all those nights I kept getting rejected, the times I kept hearing the *honey I'm too tired, please, Pete, I'm exhausted*—yeah, no kidding, she's worn out from screwing some other dude. All these years, she never shows me one ounce of warmth or affection—or even a little kindness—and the whole time I sat there telling myself that I couldn't really blame her, since she was stuck with a guy like me—like it was all *my* fault! She's pretty clever. Think about why she moved us out here, for chrissakes! You figured she needed to get away from her cramped apartment with some good-for-nothing husband who got laid off a couple years ago and never leaves the couch. No. She just wanted to be closer to that scumbag! A guy who happens to be married himself—Jesus, it gets even worse, he was married to a perfectly decent, lovely woman, who's beautiful, but did either of those lovebirds give a damn about destroying another marriage? No, of course not! Does she think I've never been tempted, that no women ever flirted with me since I walked down the aisle? That I don't have fantasies like everyone else? But see, the thing is—I deal with it. I take a cold shower or look at my taxes— whatever it takes. And then how does it end? She kills the guy! Then she tries some sinister cover-up, some creepy-ass shit—that I guess was her idea all along.

Meanwhile, what have I been up to? Every night those two were waist-deep in each other—where was I? Sitting around changing diapers, washing dishes, looking the world over for a stuffed animal, waiting for our little angel to fall asleep. And what about Luke? How could she bring this anywhere *near* him? What is she, stupid? I can't have someone like that around my kid. How can I know he's safe? What if she gets caught some- how, popped redhanded with this thing, what would that do to him? Did she really think no one would ever find out? And what the hell could she do next?

Did she think she could just use me as some cheap sitter every night while she's out banging some asshole up the street? I'll have to ask her when I get home. Does she think she can do this to me? That I'd let her get away with it? That I'm just gonna sit here and take it? This woman, I mean, she's got another thing coming. Maybe I'll snatch her ass out of bed, and we can straighten this out.

I don't want to sound oversensitive, but I'm upset about this.

My cell phone buzzes in the center console next to me. Probably a new text, must be from Frank—boggles the mind to think what else he feels he needs to share with me. It seems like I got a pretty full download already, a full night's worth, at least. Something that can't wait until morning. You figure that can't be good. So I turn it over for a look.

Hey, she says.

I check my rearview. The last thing I need is a trip to the station, so I'm slowing down, signaling, and again I pull over to the side of the road. I need a moment with this. What the fuck is she up to? Maybe she even knows where I am right now. *Hey?* What the hell does that even *mean?* She knew I was out here with Frank, and she wanted to open with *Hey?* But she's writing something again. Here it comes.

We need milk and toilet paper. children's motrin.

There she goes! The fucking woman can't help herself. It never stops.

I look around and check the rearview. The road's empty.

But now I break into a smile and soon I'm laughing at this. I can't stop. I'm sitting here on the side of the road, giggling like a fool.

That's not bad. Not bad at all. She gets major style points for this, at least. She always had a sense of humor. But now she's writing again.

The ultra-strong. Not the ultra-soft.

Pulling onto the blacktop again, heading for the twenty-four-hour CVS, I still have a smile on my face. I can't respond, of course, not even an *ok*—I hope this really pisses her off.

At the end of the day, I still need to show her who's boss.

Walking in the front door, I may have cooled down from the worst of it, but I still need a little time to myself. Best to head for Luke's room, first. Cautious as a burglar, I ease open his door, creep over to his crib, and stand there, watching my son. Luke sleeps with his cheek against the mattress, trusted monkey at his hip, arms on either side of his head, and his thumb in his mouth, his tiny chest lifting then sinking in gentle cadence with his snoring.

I'm a little emotional right now. I have a lot on my mind. This thing tonight has fouled up most of my life and left few parts undamaged. But my son looks no different. Not to me, anyway. No, he sleeps well, safe and sound. And why shouldn't he?

Tiptoeing back into our bedroom, I head for the bathroom, where I turn on the main light, leave the door open, relieve myself, flush the toilet, wash my hands, and afterward come nowhere close to putting down the seat. I know she hears this, gritting her teeth! The room is dark, she lies in bed, but I can tell by the sound of her breathing that she hasn't fallen asleep. I start getting out of these clothes. My boots have tracked sand through the house and my belt buckle sounds like a cannon hitting the floor, where it will remain all night until morning, inside of my jeans. I get into bed. I lie down beside her, my hands resting behind my head atop the lone pillow she hasn't stolen from me, even though she has seven good ones herself. I stare at the ceiling. There's a lot of things I have to tell her and many questions I need to ask, and she will have to answer them and be honest when she does. She rolls over, and I can feel her looking at me. But I stare at the ceiling some more.

"Let's talk about this in the morning," I tell her. "I need to get some sleep."

51

LAST NIGHT I drove by the Bull and found a good parking spot in the back. I sat there in the dark car for a minute or two, looking into the lit windows, and I could see guys standing around inside holding glasses of beer to their chests. They were shooting pool and laughing while Noel grinned behind the taps, listening to a story. They had a fire going. I pulled out of the lot and drove home. I've had a rough couple weeks. Since my chat with Frank on the beach, whenever I'm outside in public, I get this feeling that people all around me—fellow pedestrians, other drivers, police officers, even the moms at school—they all giggle as I pass them, snickering, like they know something, enjoying the joke it seems I was the last to hear. It's been a dark stretch.

I mean, what kind of moves do I have here?

I could go turn her in now, then have a long talk with the sheriff and Gandle about accidents and decisions made under great duress. Let's say they believe me, they reopen the case, and they can even *prove* it and ultimately convict her—then what does that do? My son loses his mother. They send Mommy upstate, and we drive up for supervised family hours or maybe the occasional conjugal visit. Neither option interests me. Imagine the three of us sitting at a table in a crowded prison visiting room, my wife wearing her orange jumpsuit and chain-smoking cigarettes (her hair a mess), surrounded by other convicts with their families, maybe passing her contraband that she will smuggle back via uncomfortable methods. That doesn't sound great.

It also assumes if the case gets reopened that I wouldn't be a prime suspect. The humiliated cuckold. Who doesn't have a good alibi, as Gandle memorably pointed out. And the way Frank and Lauren have been acting, I wonder if they have some fail-safe, a final trick up their sleeve.

Or I could file for divorce. How would that go for me? An unemployed man with no significant assets. What reason could I offer to her friendly lawyer and the kindly judge. Irreconcilable betrayal? I think not. If I found a job, any fucking job anywhere out here, any kind of seat—still, what's my best-case scenario with Luke, three nights a week? What kind of life is that? Plus, in this case, we're not talking about your standard adversary in the typical vindictive end to a marriage. This woman has proven it's unwise to make her angry. Divorces are always cruel, destructive affairs, and my wife has shown a real appetite for both. She could raise the stakes, threaten to take everything—she could ask for full custody.

It gets worse. That night down on the beach, when Frank asked me if Luke was my son, I can remember thinking that for a guy with few parenting instincts, that was pretty clever of him to bring up. It was also pretty harsh. But I wonder now if that question wasn't planted by someone who wanted to make sure I got the message loud and clear. Just to get me thinking. And although I pray she would never do this to me, she still holds the last card if she gets cornered and desperate. The nuclear option. The same one that women have held over us for a thousand years. I can hardly stand thinking about it, but she could demand we take one of those tests. And I have my limits—there are some things I couldn't bear, and I just don't have the stones for that. No fucking way. I need to protect him, no matter what it takes.

She might not even need to ask my permission. Maybe she even already has something. All the genetic fingerprints the labs would need are left on one of my goddamn toothpicks or a Q-tip. Who knows? She's turned my house into a crime scene. She's made me the frantic accomplice, desperately destroying all the evidence before he hears the sirens come. Trying to clean everything up. Just like always. I've caught myself washing glasses, emptying my trash cans, and scrubbing down the toilet with the focus of those first few faithful days of New Year's resolutions, only to later come out of the trance and find I'm staring at my toothbrush, searching for answers.

But somehow, I need to move forward, even if there are times when I feel like quitting and giving up. Sometimes I think it's all a big joke. Just one, long, stupid fucking joke that takes you a while to get. So maybe I need to keep a sense of humor about the whole thing, because when you can't do that anymore, then you're in real trouble. Maybe I just need to learn to take a joke.

I mean sure, my wife killed a guy, this guy that she was fucking. But who am I to judge her? Look, if you want to talk about a woman who could really do some damage, you should have met my mother.

We all tell ourselves stories to make it through the day. Some of us need to tell our stories to other people, and some folks like to keep this stuff to themselves. Either way, we all have them. But sometimes we learn that our stories were just fantasies. Worse than nonsense—they were frauds we bought off a swindler. When we realize that we were duped, we feel ashamed, and we never thank the messenger. But once we lose our stories, then we don't know what to believe, and the questions never stop. I've found the betrayed are often left with very little, almost nothing but their questions.

That's what she wanted, of course. She had Frank give me a message, to get me thinking and second-guess myself to death. She wanted to steal what I treasure, to rob me of what matters, and she did, she made off with some items of real value, and even if I could get them back, I'd still torture myself with doubts. I can remember a few old stories that used to seem important. Ones like, I have a wife and I know who she is. We always wanted to raise a family together. Although we have our silly differences and I bitch about her a lot, we still love each other very much. But I've lost these versions—they were taken from me, gone forever now, and I miss them already.

But I have done some thinking. And I've learned to recognize the difference between a tale you tell yourself and the truth you know. There are certain choices you get to make on your own without all the experts and commentators and everybody else. But you need to decide what you're all about. And I've made my decision. Which means there won't be any long discussions or endless meetings or debates or polls required, I won't ask the group or bring it to committee, and we will not put this to a vote. Some things you know. So, I will state the simple facts.

I am his father. And he is my son. That's it. That's done. I know that now. That is all I know and there will never be another version. That is the truth. And that is not a story.

52

LUKE WANTS TO help me bring in some firewood. These past few weeks have been rough. I've tried to keep busy. Needing a new project, I started cleaning things in the house with so much vigor and attention that I've scrubbed items I never knew existed. I'd like to feel more useful. But today, a damp November afternoon just before Thanksgiving, Luke asks to join my latest venture. He stands behind me on the grass in front of the woodpile, jumping up on his toes in excitement and giving out instructions. He demands that I pick up the wet logs that weigh down the green tarp covering the pile, that I must pull back the tarp itself so Luke can select only the finest wood for our chimneys—no, no, *that one* he cries, yes, yes, yes, that's good—and he cheers as I drop them into the canvas log carrier. Although even single logs are too heavy for him—they also have splinters, which don't mix with small children—he insists on helping bring the bag inside, squeezing his tiny fingers around the handle next to mine. We can only proceed as fast as his pace will allow us, and carrying a heavy load through the garage—that gets worse up the stairs and means the going is slow. But we make several round-trips, each of them filled with giggling and complaining and magic and that terrible worry that this time won't last forever and whenever it ends, I pray he treats me better than I treated my father when I was a young man. Plus, I get to enjoy this moment more, knowing I will get a few hours of freedom afterward.

Lauren has become more available to help out around the house recently, as the night classes, Moms' Groups, and client dinners have all stopped with no explanation. We don't discuss this phenomenon. We don't discuss anything. We speak little more than necessary. In this way, not much in our relationship has changed.

Tonight, after I put Luke down, I stare into my fridge, trying to find something worth eating. Behind me I can hear Lauren's footsteps. Heavier than Luke's naughty steps whenever he escapes at this hour. They're getting closer. She stops in the doorway.

"We should talk," she tells me.

I close the fridge and turn around to look at her. She hasn't said that kind of thing for a while.

"Now?" I ask.

She nods at this.

We make our way over to sit down at the kitchen table. We look at each other for a while. She's exhausted, wearing dark circles under her eyes and a sweatshirt. She leans in with a tired smile, her chin in one hand. She drums her fingers on the table.

"Please don't eat all his food."

"I won't," I tell her.

"He needs it for lunch tomorrow."

"There's more chicken in the fridge," I say, chewing a mouthful. "I'll go to the farm stand in the morning. Get some more avocados."

"Sure."

Sometimes my wife has a way of saying *sure* that can mean a lot of different things.

"You said that you wanted to talk," I tell her.

"Yes, but I don't want to talk if you're already getting angry."

"Who's angry?"

She drums the table but lets the matter go. She looks over at me for a long time, as if weighing an important decision.

"We need to talk," she says again.

And although I have thought of little else these past weeks, even found myself rehearsing what I need to say, tonight Lauren doesn't mean, of course, that she wants to hear me speak. Those aren't the kind of talks she likes to have. She has something to tell me.

"I need to tell you something." I might be shrugging, but I can only wonder where this will lead. The range of topics she might want to discuss seems very broad, and thinking through the list makes me a little uneasy. This doesn't sound like the beginning of a confession, though. She's looking at me very strangely.

"Okay." When she doesn't respond, we sit here, sizing each other up for a little bit. This doesn't feel like a casual matter.

"I have some news," she says. She keeps looking at me funny. She seems embarrassed and happy and afraid all at once.

"You have some news." But saying the words aloud, I realize I've heard her use this phrase before.

She nods her head. I'm thinking about what she said and how she's looking at me.

"Really?" I ask.

She nods again. She breaks into a smile, but then corrects herself. I guess we're both a little confused.

"You're serious?"

"I'm serious," she says, biting her lip to stifle a nervous laugh.

"Are you sure?"

"Pretty sure."

Then she does have news and it is serious.

"You're pregnant."

"Yes," she says, looking somewhere between terrified and excited. She watches me, interested to see how I might react to this latest news. I'm curious about that myself.

I close my mouth, since it's hanging open, and I think I'll keep it shut, since I'd probably stammer if I tried to speak. Besides, in certain moments, a guy can say things he will later come to regret and this, right now, this is one of those times.

I have some questions. Like *How?* And *When?* And *Whose?* Basically, the usual shit guys tend to keep to themselves, in other words. I have all the standard questions, and a couple others. But now's not the time to start telling my wife what I'm thinking. She's still studying me, worried.

"That's incredible," I decide to tell her.

"It's wonderful."

I remember that night I came home from the hospital and our tumble together afterward. That time I popped my stitches.

"Come here," I tell her.

She doesn't move.

I stand up slowly out of my chair, and she watches me carefully. As I hold my arms out and step toward her, she only looks more frightened.

But I hug her to me and hold her close. Not too tight. And when she wraps her arms around my back, I wince—her hands feel cold and lifeless.

We stand here on the kitchen tile, rocking together as I rub her back. But my mind is already someplace else. Thinking back to the fire down at the beach and something Frank asked me that I couldn't figure out.

What do you think set her off like that? She really lost her shit.

I picture that lost Thursday night. That fateful evening over at Townsend's. Lauren goes over there all excited for another romantic visit sitting by the fireplace. Only she finds Townsend in a terrible mood, their conversation growing more and more disappointing until he explains that whatever they had going has to stop. Maybe when she got pregnant that first time, all those years ago, maybe she didn't know who the father was. She might never have told him about it—I don't know, and I'll never find out. But that night by the fireplace, when he tried to leave her again, maybe this time she begged him to stay. Maybe she told him about the baby. But she didn't like his reaction. If the man she loved had abandoned her, when she was with child? And for the second time? Nah, she wouldn't like that at all. I'd bet most women wouldn't.

Some version of that, anyways.

Or maybe not?

We had those postfight sympathy fucks. Of course, those could have been premeditated moments of passion. Maybe Lauren knew she was pregnant and needed to cover her tracks. I don't know. I hope not.

"That's incredible," I say again.

"I know," she whispers in my ear. "I'm just so happy."

I pull back from our embrace to look into her eyes. She's smiling at me now.

"Yeah," I tell her. "I almost can't believe it."

She keeps on smiling, and I sit down.

"Wow," she adds.

I nod in agreement, and now we sit in silence together for some time. I mull it all over, thinking through things for a while, but then at some point, very much to my surprise, I have this sense of calm. What Lauren's thinking about I have no idea, but she cannot stand this quiet. I don't feel like helping her out tonight, though.

"So?" she says looking at me. She lingers on the word, expecting some response. Lacing my fingers together, I stretch my arms above my head and stare over to the window.

"Are you all right?" she asks finally, with a hint of concern in her tone.

I don't answer her.

"Say something." She's always giving me instructions. But tonight, there's a tremble in her voice.

Maybe she worries about what I might do. That I could hurt her somehow. If I'll kick the shit out of her, for instance. The thought of this does not disturb me.

Then again, maybe she just wants to know if I'll leave or stick around.

"Pete?" she asks.

But that's enough. I have things to do. I think we've talked this out. And you never get to the stuff that really matters, if you're distracted all the time.

I pull out my phone and start flipping through it. We have a lot going on this week. The playdates, the lessons, school—there's plenty on the calendar. Tomorrow looks sunny, if a little cold, and the wind's side shore but not too bad, with low tide at noon, and they're saying three-to-four-foot swells.

"What are you doing?" she asks.

"Nothing," I explain.

"Pete? Can you look at me? Can you talk to me at least?"

It just never ends. She keeps on asking.

53

Most visitors don't fall in love with beach towns between the months of December and March. You don't get much snow that will stick, and it can seem like you only see a gray ocean with barren trees lining the roads. When some people say the winters are hard out here, they don't mean the weather, they mean something else. Most of the restaurants and the shops in town close for these months, and the streets are empty. You get less traffic, but with so few visitors, it sometimes feels like walking through a huge stadium long after the big game has ended. Some parts become desolate. You wouldn't think you could ever miss any of the summer crowds, but anyone can get lonely this time of year, and many do.

But a package arrives today that I've been waiting for. I'm not new at this anymore, so I planned ahead. I didn't bother asking my wife's permission. I knew we'd need this, so I ordered it without discussion. Which was satisfying. But even better, Luke can help me put this one together. And since the item will end up going in his room, I think it's best if he supervises the creation, because when it comes to sleeping arrangements, children don't like surprises.

"What is that?" Luke asks, pointing at the tall, thin cardboard box. I slit the tape along the top with an X-Acto knife, which I then retract and store at a decent elevation.

"It's a crib," I say, and I watch his eyes begin to widen. He considers this for a moment. We both do. He sucks his thumb. It's a lot to take in.

"Hold on to this, buddy," I tell him. You can't throw out the instructions. "We need these, too. Keep track of these."

He takes the pack of bolts, pins, nuts, and the tiny Allen wrench in his hands and begins to study them. He's very pleased. And why not? I am, too. This doesn't happen every day. It's exciting.

So, we get to work. I pull out the front and back rails, the posts, a stabilizer bar, the top rail, and the mattress support, and I begin to assemble them. You don't tighten the bolts until the end, that's a rookie mistake, just enough that it holds. Luke looks on, as if he's watching some crazed Mennonite outcast hammering away in a field, in spite of the rain, this rogue maniac carpenter hell-bent on raising this barn on his own, so he shouts at the storm and he curses his god as the lightning draws near. He furrows his brow at this. The new arrival will be an adjustment for him.

Now I feel a familiar presence standing in the doorway, peeking in to check on us. We don't stop working, and she doesn't say anything. She studies the scene, bug-eyed and cautious for a moment, until she turns and slips off down the hall.

It feels like I'm sleeping in Luke's room again tonight.

Lauren has started showing signs that the strain is more than she can bear. Her temper is short and violent, she has sudden outbursts, fits of rage before withdrawing, sullen and silent, for long stretches of time. More than usual, even. It's only been a month since I heard about the baby, but she seems even more concerned with my whereabouts than she did back when she was sneaking around on me. *Where are you going? What time will you be back? Why are you looking at me like that? Are you mad?* Those sorts of things. That's the trouble with all these wicked deeds. You never give anyone else the benefit of the doubt.

In fairness to her, I've been a little distant myself, lately.

But I'm not scared for the next part. I'm almost looking forward to this. The nights without sleep won't be pretty, but that will get better. My swaddle is fearsome—I can take on all comers. And the bottles and the burping, the skin against skin, and those walks with the BabyBjörn? When he's wrapped up like a little burrito against your chest but he's still light enough that your back doesn't hurt? All the stuff you don't want to miss.

Luke catches me staring.

"What's wrong?" he asks.

He won't stay this age forever.

"What's wrong?" he asks again.

"Nothing," I tell him.

"What's wrong?"

"Nothing. Nothing's wrong, buddy. Everything's good."

ACKNOWLEDGMENTS

This book would simply not exist, let alone have been finished or published without the superlative efforts of Jenny Belle. I owe an enormous debt of gratitude to Jenny for editing several drafts, letting me join her weekly workshops, and basically keeping me sane throughout the whole process. Any writer on the planet would be fortunate to work with someone half as good as Jenny.

Thank you to Donna Brodie, who runs the Writers Room, an invaluable resource for me while working on this manuscript. I am exceptionally grateful to fellow workshop members Barbara Miller, Meryl Branch-McTiernan, Nicola Harrison, Steve Reynolds, Rob Wolf, Mario Gabriele, Joanie Leinwoll, Barbara Gaines, Marilyn Simon Rothstein, Andy Delaney, Kristina Libby, Maria Pramaggiore, Kathryn Kellinger, and also Allan Ishac for making it happen in the first place.

Thank you to my terrific agent, Emma Parry at Janklow & Nesbit, not only for taking a chance on me and working through several revisions, which seriously improved the book, but also for her marketing wizardry. Not to mention her knowledge of *Withnail & I.* I am an extremely lucky guy on many fronts. I also need to thank Ali Lake at Janklow for her significant contributions to this story.

A huge thank-you to my editor, Rachael Kelly, at Grand Central for her tireless efforts with this manuscript and willingness to work with me. Rachael stepped in, made an immediate impact, and has been relentlessly helpful while working with an author who is a huge pain in the ass. I am very fortunate that she did. And it would be unforgivable not to mention how grateful I will always be to Wes Miller for his support of this book and willingness to take a risk on an unknown entity. I owe an enormous thank-you to the terrific Sarah Congdon for her cover design. The only tricky part about Sarah's work was that the different options she gave us were all really cool. On the tough decisions front, a huge thank-you to my copy editor, Shelly Perron, and production editor, Jeff Holt, for their thoughtful eyes, gracious delivery, and delicate touch. All mistakes are mine and not theirs.

Matt Woolsey, Andre Appignanni, Clay Ezell, James Millard, Matt Edgerton, Blake Mather, Craig Campbell, Jen Fritz (Ben too), THE SUGHRUES, Keenan Mayo, and Mack Ewing read drafts of this manuscript, or offered advice and spiritual guidance, and were a hell of a lot of fun to be around when they did.

I am extremely grateful for the efforts of Jason Richman at UTA and Maialie Fitzpatrick, as well as Checka Propper and Shelby Leshine of DEK productions and, of course, Nicole Yorkin and Dawn Prestwich.

I would also like to thank Carolyn Waters and the staff at the New York Society Library, which was a godsend for me and many others during the Covid lockdowns. I am grateful to the Jefferson Market, New York Public, the Bobst, and the Hampton libraries as well.

Mom and Dave, thank you for never being anything but supportive of me on this strange adventure. Probably better if we follow up on this offline.

Matty and James, you two are the best thing that ever happened to me. But you're way too young to be reading this and should probably be in bed. Remember, this is a work of fiction! This isn't a memoir! I made it all up!

Jacqueline, thank you for putting up with me. Anyone whose spouse tries to write a book and starts talking to themselves all the time will probably need a few glasses of wine, but you deserve some kind of award for this one. Thank you for everything.

ABOUT THE AUTHOR

Sam Garonzik graduated from Duke University and worked in finance before he began writing fiction. He lives in New York with his wife and two children. *A Rough Way to Go* is his first novel.